THE STABBING IN THE STABLES

Simon Brett worked as a producer in radio and television before taking up writing full time. As well as the Mrs Pargeter novels and the Charles Paris detective series, he is the author of the radio and television series *After Henry*, the radio series *No Commitments* and *Smelling of Roses* and the bestselling *How to Be a Little Sod*. His novel *A Shock to the System* was filmed starring Michael Caine.

Married with three grown-up children, Simon lives in an Agatha Christie-style village on the South Downs.

The Stabbing in the Stables is the seventh novel in the Fethering Mysteries series. Simon Brett's most recent novel, *Death Under the Dryer*, is out now in Macmillan hardback.

Also by Simon Brett

A Shock to the System   Dead Romantic   Singled Out

The Fethering Mysteries
The Body on the Beach   Death on the Downs
The Torso in the Town   Murder in the Museum
The Hanging in the Hotel   The Witness at the Wedding
Death Under the Dryer

Mrs Pargeter novels
A Nice Class of Corpse   Mrs, Presumed Dead
Mrs Pargeter's Package   Mrs Pargeter's Pound of Flesh
Mrs Pargeter's Plot   Mrs Pargeter's Point of Honour

Charles Paris novels
Cast, In Order of Disappearance   So Much Blood
Star Trap   An Amateur Corpse   A Comedian Dies
The Dead Side of Mike   Situation Tragedy
Murder Unprompted   Murder in the Title
Not Dead, Only Resting   Dead Giveaway
What Bloody Man Is That?   A Series of Murders
Corporate Bodies   A Reconstructed Corpse
Sicken and So Die   Dead Room Farce

Short stories
A Box of Tricks   Crime Writers and Other Animals

SIMON BRETT

THE STABBING IN THE STABLES

A FETHERING MYSTERY

PAN BOOKS

First published 2006 by Macmillan

First published in paperback 2007 by Pan Books
an imprint of Pan Macmillan Ltd
Pan Macmillan, 20 New Wharf Road, London N1 9RR
Basingstoke and Oxford
Associated companies throughout the world
www.panmacmillan.com

ISBN 978-0-330-42697-8

and to buy them. You will also find features, author interviews and
news of any author events, and you can sign up for e-newsletters
so that you're always first to hear about our new releases.

To the Equestrian Trio of

Sandie, Sophie and Coco

Chapter One

'A horse?' Carole Seddon echoed with distaste. 'You're planning to heal a horse?'

'Well, to have a go,' said Jude.

'But I don't see how it can possibly work. Horses don't have human understanding. A horse won't know it's being healed, so how can it be healed?'

Jude chuckled, and her bird's nest of blonde hair rippled before resettling around her plump face. 'What you're saying, Carole, is that because a horse doesn't know it's being healed, it's not going to fall for the idea that it *is* being healed – as a human being might. You're saying horses aren't that gullible.'

'Well . . .'

'Yes, you are.'

'Maybe.'

'I know you don't believe in healing.'

Carole tried to find some form of denial, but all she could come up with was, 'Let's say I don't understand it.'

'I don't understand it either. I just know that it sometimes works.'

'Yes, but not with animals.'

'There are many authenticated reports of animals' ailments having been cured by healing.'

'Huh!' That was Carole Seddon's customary response to the world of alternative therapy, and to many other things that challenged the security of her sensible life.

They were sitting in a part of that security, the kitchen of her house High Tor in the West Sussex seaside village of Fethering. The tidiness of the room, the gleaming surfaces, the neatly aligned pots and pans, the rack of spice jars whose labels had been dragooned into facing the front, all conspired to cancel out the cosiness that the Aga should have imparted. In front of the stove, Carole's Labrador Gulliver, satisfied by his late-afternoon walk on Fethering Beach, snuffled in a contented dream of saving the world from killer seaweed.

'So whose horse is it?'

'Woman called Sonia Dalrymple.'

'Do I know her?'

'No. She's a client.' Jude always used that word to describe the people who took advantage of her occasional healing and balancing services. 'Patient' never sounded right to her.

'Oh.' Carole managed to fill the monosyllable with exactly the same ration of scepticism that she had put into the 'Huh'. Her attitude to Jude's 'clients' was that they were slightly flaky people with insufficient self-control – and probably more money than sense. Carole's view was that when you were genuinely ill, you went to your GP, and when you weren't genuinely ill, you put up and shut up.

Carole Seddon suffered from the innate puritanism of a middle-class southerner in her fifties, a system of values that had been dinned into her by timid parents in the post-war austerity of her upbringing. She was suspicious of the foreign, the unknown and, most of all, anything with the slightest whiff of mysticism. She hated herself for her hidebound world view, but it was too much part of her personality to yield to major change.

That personality was, she liked to think, reflected in her appearance. Her grey hair was cut sensibly short, and her pale blue eyes were assisted by sensible rimless glasses. Bright colours and patterns were eschewed, and the only part of her wardrobe aspiring beyond Marks & Spencer was a well-kept, though now ageing, Burberry raincoat.

But over the previous few years chinks had appeared in the carapace of correctness with which Carole Seddon had deliberately surrounded herself. As she grew further away from the trauma of divorce from her husband David, as she became more reconciled to her unwarrantably early retirement from the Home Office, she had not exactly mellowed – indeed, the idea of 'mellowing' would have been anathema to her – but she had entertained the possibility that there might exist valid attitudes other than those with which she had been brought up. This process had been partly assisted by a rapprochement with her son Stephen, engineered by Gaby, the girl to whom he was now married.

But the greatest change in Carole Seddon had been effected by the serendipitous arrival of Jude in Woodside Cottage next door. Carole would never have admitted it, because she was not an advocate of any kind of sentimentality, but her friendship with Jude was the most potent agent in the recent thawing of her character's permafrost.

The attraction between the two women was unlikely. In spite of the fact that Carole wanted to organize every moment of the future to within an inch of its life while Jude was comfortably content to let events come to her, their relationship survived remarkably well. And the detail that from time to time that relationship had incorporated murder investigations was regarded by both women as an inestimable bonus.

'So for what imagined ills does this Sonia come to you?' Carole continued sniffily.

Jude smiled an easy smile. 'There is such a thing as client confidentiality.'

'Yes, I suppose there is' – the temptation to add – '. . . in your kind of world,' proved irresistible. 'And it's her horse?'

'As I said. He's called Chieftain.'

'She must be rich.' There were certain triggers within Carole that resulted in this knee-jerk reaction, and all of them came from her childhood when her parents had made sacrifices to put her through private education. Anyone who had a horse must be rich; equally

4

anyone who had a boat. The same went for anyone who went skiing – and certainly anyone who went waterskiing. The fact that all these indulgences had now become widely available to the general public did not change Carole's views. In the ineluctable way of prejudices, they stuck.

'As a matter of fact, Sonia is quite well heeled.'

'I thought so,' said Carole, prejudice vindicated.

'But that's not important.'

Oh no, of course not. Owns a horse, and can afford to splash out on alternative therapies, but the money's not important. Carole kept such reactions to herself.

Jude's grin suggested she had read the thoughts without their being voiced. She sat at the kitchen table, swathed in her customary layers of fabric – more of them at this time of year to fend off the February chill. Jude didn't always wear the same clothes, but they always gave the same impression. She dressed in a profusion of floaty shirts, skirts and scarves, which never seemed to define where one garment ended and the other started. The outline around her plump body was always imprecise, but it generated a feeling of comfort – and, to men, an undoubted sexual allure. People were always at their ease around Jude – something that could never be said of Carole.

'Anyway, what's wrong with the horse?'

'Chieftain's lame. Trouble with his knee.'

'Do horses have knees?'

'Of course they do. Their legs are hinged in the middle, you know.'

'Yes, I know they are, Jude. But "knee" sounds a

rather prosaic word for a horse. I thought they were all "fetlocks" and "withers" and . . .' Carole's repertoire of equine anatomy ran out.

'I can assure you they have knees, as well as fetlocks and withers.'

'Ah.' She still needed something with which to come back at Jude. 'I thought, if horses were ill, they were taken to vets.'

'And if a horse is taken to the vet, and the vet can't find anything wrong . . .?'

'Oh, I see. Then their owners resort to alternative remedies.' Carole couldn't stop herself from adding, 'Just like gullible humans.'

Jude grinned again. In anyone else, such a grin would have been infuriating, with her, somehow it wasn't. 'Except, you've already established that horses can't be gullible.'

'No. Well, maybe not,' Carole conceded. 'Anyway, when you came in, some time ago, you asked if I could do you a favour. So far as I can recollect, you haven't yet said what that favour is.'

'No, I haven't.'

'What is it then?'

'I wondered if you'd mind giving me a lift to the stables, so that I can have a look at Chieftain.'

Carole's first reaction was to refuse. It was late afternoon, nearly time for a television chat show to which she was becoming secretly addicted. But her puritan instinct told her that wasn't really an excuse and, if she used it as such, she'd have to admit to Jude that she actually watched the thing. So she said yes, she'd love to give her friend a lift to the stables.

As they drove along in Carole's sensible, recently vacuumed Renault, Jude provided a skimpy background to their destination. Long Bamber Stables were on the Fedborough road, maybe a mile up the River Fether from Fethering. They advertised regularly in the *Fethering Observer*, offering DIY full/part livery, an indoor school, hacking, riding lessons and other services.

Though Jude had not been there before, she had heard from Sonia Dalrymple that the stables were owned by a married couple, Walter and Lucinda Fleet. In riding circles, Walter Fleet had apparently once been known as a promising eventer (whatever that might be, Carole inevitably interpolated) whose career had been cut short by a serious fall from a horse. Jude had also got the impression that Lucinda Fleet was not Sonia Dalrymple's favourite person.

But that was all she knew. Except for the fact that Sonia had agreed to meet her outside the stables at six that Tuesday evening.

'And how would you have got here if I hadn't given you a lift?'

'I knew you would give me a lift.'

Carole saw Jude's teasing smile, illuminated by the headlights of an oncoming car, and seethed quietly.

The parking at Long Bamber Stables was some way from the main gates, and when she switched off the engine, Carole insisted on staying in the Renault. She'd even brought a book with her – and there was always a torch in the glove compartment, because she had a paranoid fear of running down the car's battery.

Jude didn't argue, although she knew Carole's decision to stay arose from her unwillingness to meet Sonia Dalrymple, someone new, someone who believed in alternative therapy, someone who was rich enough to own a horse. Saying she wouldn't be more than half an hour, Jude walked across the tarmac to the stable gates. She checked the large watch, fixed by a broad ribbon to her wrist. Three minutes to six.

The buildings appeared to make up a timber-clad square, no doubt with loose boxes lining the inside and paddocks behind. There was no roof over the yard onto which the gates opened, though somewhere inside there must be a covered indoor school and storage barns. A little way away from the stables stood a modest red-brick house, presumably the home of Walter and Lucinda Fleet. Although she couldn't see it, Jude could hear the swishing flow of the River Fether which ran alongside the site.

To her surprise, there was no light over the gates, nor could she see any evidence of lights inside the yard. There was no sign of Sonia Dalrymple either.

It was cold. Jude waited for a few minutes, stamping her feet to maintain circulation but no other vehicle appeared to join the Renault in the car park.

A thin February moon cast a watery light over the scene. Jude could see that the double gates were closed, and she looked in vain for a bell-push or knocker. Apart from the underscoring of the river, the only sounds were distant rustlings and clompings, presumably from the horses within.

Jude checked her watch again. Nearly quarter past six. Though she didn't know Sonia Dalrymple that well, her client had always been punctual for her appointments at Woodside Cottage.

Surely Sonia had said to meet *outside* the stables. She must have been held up somewhere. Sonia had twin teenage daughters, so no doubt she'd been delayed by some crisis in ferrying them somewhere. Or maybe Jude had got it wrong, and the arrangement had been to meet *inside* the stables, near Chieftain's box. Worth trying. If the gates were locked, Jude would know she hadn't got it wrong.

Just as she had the thought, there was a sudden outburst of neighing and heavy-footed stamping from the horses within. Something had disturbed them. More likely, someone had disturbed them. Sonia Dalrymple must be inside the yard. Odd that she hadn't put any lights on, though. If the stables were locked, Jude would hammer on the gates to attract attention.

But when she turned the heavy metal ring, they readily gave inward, letting out a grudging creak of timber. Jude pushed through into the hay- and dung-scented yard, where near-silence had reasserted itself. As she did so, from the far side of the square courtyard she heard the sharp impact of wood on wood. A gate closing?

Jude moved into the centre of the square where the moonlight was strongest. She'd been right about the loose boxes, forming the walls of the yard. Unseen horses shifted uneasily. One whinnied, troubled by the presence of an intruder. There was no sign of human life.

On the other hand, there was a sign of human death.

In the middle of the courtyard lay the body of a man. The pale moonlight glistened on the blood that had only recently ceased to flow from his face, throat and chest.

Chapter Two

Jude's plump body moved with surprising speed back across the tarmac to the Renault. Carole took a moment or two to interpret her friend's excited gabble, but once she understood was quickly out of the car. With her torch.

Its beam did not improve the look of the body. The man had been the object of a frenzied assault. A trail of bright blood spots suggested he had been backing away from his attacker. Deep gashes on his hands showed he had tried to protect himself, until he had tripped over backwards or collapsed from his injuries.

The horses in the stalls shifted nervously, some snorting with unease at this new invasion of their domain.

Carole looked back along the trail of blood. A few feet beyond where the broken line stopped – or in fact where the spillage had started – the door to a wooden two-storey building hung open. A solid door, not divided in the middle like those on the loose boxes. Hinged metal bars and heavy padlocks hung from rings on the frame. From inside there was a slight glow from a hidden light source.

'What's that, Jude?'

'I've no idea. First time I've been here. Saddle room, tack room maybe . . .? Mind you, the blood spots suggest that the victim and his attacker came out from there and—'

'It's not our place to make that kind of conjecture,' said Carole, suddenly all sniffy. 'We should ring the police. You've got your mobile, haven't you?'

'Yes.' Jude reached reluctantly into the pocket of her coat. 'I wouldn't mind having a quick look around before we—'

Carole's Home Office background would not allow the sentence to be finished. 'This is a crime scene. It would be deeply irresponsible for us to disturb anything.'

'Just a quick look?' Jude wheedled.

'No.' A hand was held out for the mobile. 'If you won't do it, then I will.'

After a short hesitation, Jude said, 'I think we should tell the Fleets first.'

'What?'

'The people who own the place. They must live in the house next door. They should know what's happened on their premises before the police arrive.'

Carole wavered just long enough for Jude to say, 'I'll tell them,' and set off towards the gates.

'Do you want the torch?'

'No, I can see. Besides, I don't want to leave you alone in the dark with the body.'

'We must call the police as soon as the Fleets have been informed,' Carole called after her friend's retreating outline. 'We must be very careful we don't tamper with a crime scene.'

She stood still for a moment, then let the torch beam explore the space around her. Not onto the body – she had seen quite enough of that for its image to haunt her dreams for months to come.

Most of the loose-box top-halves were open, but the moving ray of light did not reveal any of their inmates. The horses lurked in the recesses of their stalls, snuffling and stamping their continuing disquiet.

A complete circuit of the yard revealed double gates at the far end, offering access to the paddocks beyond, and other gates leading to barns, tack rooms and the indoor school. The torch beam ended up once again fixed on the open door. Carole felt a sudden, overwhelming temptation.

She shouldn't do it. Everything she had ever learnt during her extensive dealings with the police told her she should touch nothing, explore nothing. Jude's footprints and her own might already have destroyed important evidence. To investigate further would be the height of irresponsibility. Her duty as a citizen dictated she should stay stock still where she was until the police arrived. Or, perhaps even better, go back to the Renault and wait there.

On the other hand . . . how were the police to know she wasn't just another incompetent, invisible woman in late-middle age? In most recent dealings she'd had with them, that's how she had been treated. There could be any number of reasons why an incompetent, invisible woman in late-middle age might go through that open door. She might be looking for bandages, cloth, something to staunch the wounds of the victim, unaware that her ministrations would come too late. She might be looking inside the wooden building for someone to help. She might go there to hide from the homicidal maniac who had just committed one crime and was about to commit another. She might . . .

Almost involuntarily, Carole felt her footsteps following the torch beam towards the open door.

The lack of lights in the Fleets' house was a discouraging omen, and repeated ringing of the bell confirmed that no one was at home.

For a second, Jude contemplated ringing the police from their doorstep, but quickly decided not to. Maybe, after all, Carole could be persuaded into a little preliminary private investigation before the call was made?

But the walk back from house to stables was interrupted by the beam of high headlights turning into the car park. Jude stopped, thinking the Fleets might have returned, but quickly recognized the black Range Rover as it drew up beside her and the driver-side window was lowered.

'Jude – so sorry. Have you been waiting hours? I got horribly delayed.'

Even though flushed and flustered, Sonia Dalrymple's face was still beautiful. She was a tall, leggy blonde in her early forties, with a fabulous figure toned by riding and a metabolism that helped her never put on an ounce. Her voice had the upper-class ease of someone who had never doubted her own position in society. No one meeting her would ever be able to associate such a goddess with the deep insecurities which had brought her to Jude in search of healing.

'No, don't worry, there's no problem.' As her client doused the headlights and got out of the car, Jude realized how inappropriate, in the circumstances, her words were.

Sonia Dalrymple was wearing cowboy boots and the kind of designer jeans which had been so gentrified as to lose any connection with their origins as working clothes. She had a white roll-neck sweater under a blue and white striped body-warmer. The blonde hair was scrunched back into an untidy ponytail.

'I'm really terribly sorry. Come on, let's see how old Chieftain—'

'Sonia, something's happened.'

'What?'

'I was just trying to tell the Fleets . . . at least I assume they live in that house.'

'Yes, they do.'

'There's no one in. There's . . . Sonia, there's been an accident in the stables.'

The woman's face paled. 'Oh, God. Is Chieftain all right?'

'Yes. All the horses are fine.'

Sonia's reaction of relief seemed excessive to Jude, but then she wasn't a horse owner.

'No, I'm afraid it's a human being who's suffered the . . . accident.'

15

'Who?' The anxiety was at least as great as it had been for Chieftain.

'No idea. It's a man.'

'What's happened to him?'

'He's dead.'

'Oh! But . . . how?'

'It looks very much as if he's been stabbed to death.'

'You mean murder?'

Jude nodded grimly. 'Come and have a look.'

Inside the stables Carole stood exactly where Jude had left her, torch modestly pointing downwards. Sonia was hastily introduced, and Carole moved the torch beam to spotlight the dead man.

'Oh, my God!' A deep sob shuddered through Sonia's body.

'You recognize him?' asked Jude.

'Yes. This is – or was – Walter Fleet.'

Chapter Three

Once summoned, the police were quick to arrive. Soon the car park of Long Bamber Stables seemed to be full of white vehicles and whirling blue lights.

Having quickly explained their presence at the stables, Carole, Jude and Sonia were politely hustled away from the central courtyard and asked to wait until someone had time to talk to them further. When Carole complained of the cold, they were offered the shelter of a large white police van.

Just as they were getting in, they saw a battered Land Rover swing into the car park. It stopped suddenly; the engine was left running and the headlights blazing, as a woman jumped out. She looked at first sight like a smaller version of Sonia Dalrymple. Similarly though more scruffily dressed, she was ten years older. Her beauty was in decline, and the blondeness of her hair had been assisted.

'Oh God,' she snarled at the policemen who'd turned to greet her. 'Don't say the Ripper's struck again!'

*

'So,' said Ted Crisp, 'she was worried one of the horses had been attacked, not a human being?'

'Exactly.'

'Apparently there have been a series of cases recently,' Jude amplified. 'All over West Sussex. Horses being mutilated. By someone the local papers have taken to calling the Horse Ripper. She thought one of the ones in Long Bamber Stables had been attacked, and that's why all the police were there.'

'And – sorry – I'm losing track a bit here . . . which woman was this?'

'Lucinda Fleet.'

'Right. So then she discovered it wasn't one of her horses who was the victim – it was her husband?'

'Yes. Walter Fleet.'

'Ah, right.'

'You sound like you know him, Ted.'

'Wouldn't say "know". He used to come in here from time to time, that's all. So old Walter's copped it, has he?'

'Afraid he has.'

They had been surprised how early it still was when they got back to Fethering. The events they had witnessed and their questioning by police detectives seemed to have taken a lot longer than they really had. As is often the case after experiencing a shock, Carole and Jude were amazed to find that the rest of the world continued to turn as if nothing had happened. It was only half past eight when the Renault drew up outside High Tor, and the decision was quickly made that they needed a drink at the Crown and Anchor.

Once inside, as the first large Chilean Chardonnay began to warm them, the decision to order a meal was also a quick one. Ted Crisp, the landlord, said – atypically effusive – that the steak and ale pie was 'to die for', so they'd both gone for that. After the cold and the atrocity they had witnessed, the fug of the pub interior was very welcoming. So was Ted: large of bulk, scruffy of hair and beard, even scruffier of fleece, sweatshirt and jeans.

'How did she react then – this Lucinda – when she found out her husband was dead?'

'She managed to control herself very well,' replied Carole, with appropriate respect for such restraint.

'Hm,' Jude ruminated. 'I think her reaction was more one of relief. She'd been really worried that one of the horses had been injured. When she found out it was just her husband murdered, she didn't seem so bothered.'

'People react differently to that kind of shock,' said Carole tartly.

'Yes, sure. Just the impression I got.'

'Do you know anything about this Lucinda or her husband or the state of her marriage or—?'

'Ted, we met her for the first time an hour ago. The circumstances in which we met her husband were not conducive to confidences. We know nothing about either of them – or the state of their marriage.'

'All right, Carole. I didn't know that.'

'Sorry.' She smiled to reinforce the apology. Ted smiled back. For a second their eyes connected. Carole still found it strange to think there had once – however briefly – been a physical relationship between them.

'But maybe you know something,' Carole went on, 'if Walter Fleet was a Crown and Anchor regular?'

'No. He didn't come here very often. Anyway, last thing men go to a pub for is to talk about their wives and marriages. They come here to get away from all that.'

'Yes. So all we do know about the Fleets,' said Jude, 'is what I've heard from Sonia. Which doesn't amount to very much. She implied that she didn't particularly care for Lucinda Fleet. She also hinted that the marriage wasn't a very happy one. That's all we've got.'

'But we can find out more.' Carole's pale blue eyes glowed with eagerness. 'You'll still be seeing Sonia, won't you?'

'Oh, sure.' Jude looked at her friend with an expression that was half teasing. 'But why should we want to find out more?'

'Well, it was a murder; we were on the scene. Natural curiosity dictates that we want to know who killed Walter Fleet.'

'But surely' – Jude maintained her bantering tone – 'that's up to the police to find out?'

'Yes,' Carole conceded, 'but we're bound to be interested, aren't we?'

'No doubt about it.' Ted Crisp chuckled. 'You two are *bound* to be interested. So tell me, Carole – who do you think did it?'

'We have no information. We can't possibly answer questions like that at this point.'

'And it is entirely possible,' Jude contributed innocently, 'that the police will solve the crime. Indeed, that they have already solved the crime. Most murders are pretty straightforward.'

'I agree. Usually the police have to look no further than the person who claims to have discovered the body. Which in this case was you.'

'Yes, Carole.'

'Alternatively, they look to the victim's live-in partner, who is quite frequently standing there with the blood-stained murder weapon still in his or her hand.'

'Though not in this case. Lucinda Fleet arrived after the murder had been committed.'

'But we don't know where she'd come from, do we? She might have been present when the murder was committed – actually committing it – and then she might have run across the fields to where her Land Rover was parked and—'

'Possible, I suppose. Mind you, the same could be true for Sonia Dalrymple—'

'What do you mean?'

'I mean that I don't know where she'd been before she came to the stables. I assumed she'd been held up doing something for her kids, but now I think about it, they're at boarding school, and she did seem to be pretty flustered, even before she saw the body.'

'Then Sonia's a potential murderer too.'

Ted Crisp scratched his beard. 'It must be difficult going through life, being as suspicious of everyone as you are.'

'I can assure you,' Carole replied, 'it's quite easy.'

He chuckled. 'But to be honest, at the moment, you really know nothing, do you?'

'No,' Jude agreed.

'That doesn't stop us having theories, though.'

'All right. So what is your current theory, given the virtually complete lack of information from which you are working?'

'Well,' Carole said, we know Lucinda Fleet was worried her stables had been visited by a horse mutilator . . .'

'Yes.'

'Say that was true. A horse mutilator – this Horse Ripper – had got into the stables. He was about to do his dirty work when Walter Fleet surprised him. The Horse Ripper killed Walter so he couldn't identify him to the police?'

'Well . . .'

'It's not much of a theory,' said Jude.

'It's the only one we've got,' Carole snapped.

The arrival of their 'to die for' steak and ale pies at that moment curtailed further discussion of the crime.

Chapter Four

The murder of Walter Fleet was duly reported on national and local news, and made the front page of the *Fethering Observer*. But there was no announcement of an arrest and, as ever, beyond bland statements at press conferences, the police gave away little of their thinking or their progress in the investigation. Which, for Carole and Jude, was extremely frustrating.

The one new piece of information that did emerge in a television bulletin was the nature of the murder weapon, which had been discovered at the crime scene. (Carole and Jude had not spotted it, because it had been lying up against the corpse.) The stabbing and slashing at Walter Fleet's front had, it was announced, been done with a bot knife. Helpfully, for people with little equestrian knowledge – like Carole and Jude – the inspector holding the press conference showed a photograph and explained what a bot knife was.

Among the many medical complaints suffered by horses is infestation by botflies, a condition sometimes known as the bots – or even botts with two tees. A bot knife is used to scrape the eggs of the parasite out of a horse's hair. In the illustration shown on the television, viewers saw a black-handled knife with a curved serrated end, which looked more suited for slicing grapefruit than committing murder.

But clearly it was an object that could be found around any stable yard, a fact which suggested to Carole and Jude that the stabbing of Walter Fleet was a spur of the moment rather than a premeditated action. The unsuitability of the bot knife as a means of killing someone served only to support that theory.

From Sonia Dalrymple, Jude found out more about botflies and their treatment, data which she gleefully passed on to Carole. The adult botfly looks not unlike a bee, and favours laying its small yellowish eggs in the thick hair on a horse's chest or behind its front legs. The presence of the eggs irritates the host, who tries to remove them by biting and licking the infested area, but these actions have the opposite effect of encouraging growth inside the eggs. They also give an opportunity for the tiny maggots to get transferred into the horse's mouth and thence into its digestive tract. Here the maggots feed away, taking essential nutrients from the host and sometimes even creating a total blockage which can cause the animal to starve. When they are full grown, the maggots are excreted in the horse's faeces, and in the comfort of the warm dung hatch out into adult botflies. And so the cycle continues.

Carole found all this was rather more information than she required.

But she was very keen on the idea of Jude staying in touch with Sonia Dalrymple. The owner of Chieftain was their one legitimate link to Long Bamber Stables and, on the assumption that the police didn't instantly solve the case and make an arrest, she could be of great value to the two inquisitive women.

The stables did constitute a rather unusual crime scene. In most cases, after a murder the police seal off the relevant area, move all the people out and strictly control who is allowed back in. Horses present a different problem. There is a limit to the time they can be kept locked up in their stalls, but nothing is likelier to destroy a crime scene than having a large number of horses trampling over it. As a result, the police had to work fast on their forensic investigations. Then, before the normal business of the stables could continue, owners were encouraged, if possible, to find alternative short-term accommodation for their horses. In Sonia Dalrymple's case, this was not a problem. Her substantial home, Unwins, had its own stabling, which had accommodated Chieftain and her children's pony Conker for some years. The departure of Sonia's twin daughters to boarding school and the increasing amount of travel undertaken by her and her husband Nicky had led them to put the horses into Long Bamber Stables. Returning them to their home stabling until the police investigations were complete was the obvious solution. And also meant that Jude's visit of potential healing to Chieftain could be easily rescheduled.

She arranged to go to the Dalrymples' house at three thirty on Friday afternoon and that morning invited Carole to Woodside Cottage for a cup of coffee.

'Can I give you a lift to Sonia's?'

'Bless you, but it's no distance. I can walk. I need the exercise.'

Carole's tightening mouth showed her disappointment. She didn't want to be excluded from any part of the potential investigation. Jude could feel her unease, and also sensed there was something else troubling her neighbour. There was a secret Carole wanted to confide. Knowing better than to prompt her, Jude waited for the revelation to be made naturally.

'There's something I have to tell you.'

'Oh, yes?'

'It concerns Walter Fleet's murder.'

'Mm?'

'Well . . .'

Jude looked evenly at her friend, a smile playing round the edges of her lips.

'You know, after you'd found the body . . .'

Jude nodded.

'. . . you went off to the Fleets' house . . .'

Another nod.

'. . . and I stayed by the body . . .'

'Yes. Because, as you had pointed out to me, it would have been very irresponsible for either of us to do any investigation of the crime scene.'

'Mm.' There was a long, awkward silence. 'Well, I'm afraid I did.'

'Did what?'

'A little investigation of the crime scene.'

'Oh, Carole, brilliant!'

'I know I shouldn't have done but—'

'Never mind that. What did you find out? Did you go into the tack room or whatever it was?'

Carole nodded, her shame now giving way to excitement. 'Yes. And I reckon it was a tack room. Full of bridles and halters and bits of leather and rope and stuff. But there was a second level too. Not quite a second floor, but one half of the space was boarded over, and there was a wooden ladder leading up to it.'

'Did you go up the ladder?'

This time the nod was defiantly proud. 'There was a little lamp switched on. A sleeping bag, a few other oddments. It looked as though someone had been camping out up there.'

'Any sign that whoever it was had been there recently?'

'The sleeping bag was half-unzipped and crumpled. Looked as if someone had just leapt out of it.'

'I suppose you didn't feel as to whether it was still warm?'

'As a matter of fact I did, Jude. Hard to tell, though. The night was cold, any warmth would have dissipated pretty quickly.'

'Hm . . . I wonder who'd been up there . . .'

'Unlikely to have been Walter Fleet, given the fact that his house was right next door.'

'Unless he was up there on guard.'

'How do you mean?'

'Well, going back to the Horse Ripper theory . . .'

'Oh, I see what you mean. The Fleets were worried about someone breaking into the stables at night, so Walter might be up there, keeping watch for intruders?'

'It's a possibility.'

'Yes. But it was quarter past six in the evening when you found his body. He wouldn't have been in his sleeping bag at that time of night.'

'True. So the more likely scenario is that someone else was upstairs in the tack room. Walter surprised them. An argument and a fight ensued. and he got killed by this . . . person . . . whoever it was?'

'Mm.'

'Hell having no information, isn't it, Carole?'

'Yes. If only we had one fact – like the time the murder took place.'

'Well, I think it was only moments before I found the body.'

'Why, because the blood was still flowing?'

'I don't think it was still flowing, but it certainly hadn't started to congeal. And blood would clot pretty quickly with the weather as cold as it was. Also, there had been a sudden commotion from the horses. Something had disturbed them only moments before I went into the stables. In fact, it was the noise that made me go in. I thought Sonia must be inside.'

'So maybe the murderer . . .?'

'And I've just remembered another thing . . .' Jude's brown eyes focused intently as she tried to recapture the scene. 'Just as I entered the stables, I heard a clattering, like a gate shutting. I think, if I'd gone in a few seconds earlier, I would actually have seen the murderer!'

Chapter Five

When Jude had described Sonia Dalrymple as 'quite well heeled', she had been guilty of understatement. Her client was extremely well heeled. Unwins, where the Dalrymples lived, was what West Sussex estate agents would describe as 'an equestrian estate' off the Fedborough road some half mile nearer Fethering than Long Bamber Stables were. But Jude didn't have to go on the main roads for her visit; 'the pretty way', along the towpath of the River Fether, would get her there in a brisk twenty minutes.

Her refusal of Carole's offer of a lift had been only partly for health reasons. Jude's deep understanding of the human body left her in no doubt as to the importance of exercise. She ate sensibly and walked whenever she had the opportunity. This regime didn't seem to have any effect on her bulk, which had been quietly expanding since her early forties, but it made her feel good in herself.

Apart from that, though, Jude didn't really want Carole with her for this visit. Sonia Dalrymple, for all her confident exterior, was a highly sensitive, even shy woman. And, though Carole would probably have intended just to drop Jude at the gates, there was a danger she might be asked to wait – or decide, out of her natural curiosity, that she wanted to wait. Carole's presence on the premises would undoubtedly have put Sonia on her guard and destroyed the confidential mood in which Jude hoped to find her.

The February air was sharp on Jude's cheeks. The tidal Fether, swollen by recent rains, churned in full spate ominously close to the towpath. On the horizon the South Downs undulated, green mounds giving way to ever mistier grey. A startled pheasant flew up from the grass by Jude's side, creaking like an old football rattle. The landscape's harsh winter beauty con-tributed to a sense within Jude of well-being – and also of excitement.

Sonia Dalrymple's husband Nicky worked for an international bank. His actual role there was never defined; all Fethering gossip knew was that, whatever he did, he was paid an enormous amount of money for doing it. Unwins was only one of the family's three residences: there was also a mansion flat overlooking the Thames in London, and a villa in Barbados.

Their Fethering house had been built in the early nineteenth century as a farmhouse. Over the years, as with so many farms in the area, the land had been sold off for development, but some ten acres, now con-verted to gardens and paddocks, had been retained. The Dalrymples had renovated and designer-decorated the house so completely as to erase any vestiges of its humble agricultural origins. The same transformation had been wrought on the outbuildings. A barn had been converted into luxury guest flats, the old cowshed into a state-of-the-art stable yard.

Sonia's Range Rover was parked on the gravel outside the front door. Open garages revealed a couple of random Mercedes. And Sonia herself, as ever, maintained the image of casual wealth. Above tight black trousers and black buckled shoes, she wore an off-white Aran sweater, which on her contrived to look like a designer garment.

She offered the option of coffee before they went to see Chieftain, and Jude accepted. The more opportunity they had to talk, the better. Sonia was her only link to Long Bamber Stables and the death of Walter Fleet.

'How're you feeling?' asked Jude, when she was settled at the breakfast bar of a kitchen which had stepped straight out of a lifestyle magazine. The question was posed casually, but both women understood its importance.

Sonia Dalrymple, however, was not about to go into 'client' mode. Jude was there to see to the horse. 'I'm fine, thank you.'

'Is Nicky around at the moment?'

'He's in Frankfurt on business. Left early this morning'.

'And the girls are well? Presumably they've heard about what happened at the stables?'

'Yes, I rang the school that night. Rather they heard it from me than on the television news.'

Jude looked round the kitchen. There was evidence of the twins everywhere, childish drawings of horses

31

laminated and preserved from their first school days, photographs of them in riding hats, cartoon-character fridge magnets, proud clusters of fading rosettes. Maybe all that was wrong with Sonia Dalrymple was common or garden empty nest syndrome. Since their birth, she'd devoted all her time and attention to the girls' needs. Suddenly they were away at boarding school and her role had been taken away from her. Add to that a frequently absent husband and the awareness the forties bring of beauty's finite nature, and it was no wonder that, in spite of all her material comforts, Sonia should feel out of sorts. But Jude suspected there might be some other, more deep-rooted explanation.

This, however, was not the time for psychological probing. Keep the conversation light. 'You must be relieved to have got your horses out of Long Bamber.'

'Yes. They're both much more relaxed now they're here. Horses are very sensitive, you know. They could tell there was something wrong, and they didn't like the police clumping round the place.'

'Any idea how long it's going to be closed?'

'I asked Lucinda. The sooner they re-open the better, so far as she's concerned.'

'But presumably she needs some time to adjust to her husband's death.'

'I think getting back to work is going to be her best therapy. She's losing money, apart from anything else. She can't charge owners if their horses aren't there. And then she can't do any riding lessons or anything like that.'

'No. When you talked about Lucinda earlier . . .'

32

'Hm?'

'You know – before Walter's death – you implied that theirs wasn't the happiest of marriages.'

Sonia looked flustered and busied herself with the coffee machine. 'Oh, did I? I can't remember.'

'I remember. You did.'

'Well, it doesn't do to speak ill of the dead . . .'

'No, but everyone's going to. I'm afraid, when a murder happens, the people involved become public property.'

'I agree. But that's not something I would wish to encourage.' Sonia sounded almost prissily righteous. Jude wondered whether such righteousness was a convenient excuse to keep away from the subject. When they'd last spoken about the Fleets, Sonia had shown no such inhibition. 'I think,' she continued piously, 'that gossiping about her and Walter can only make Lucinda's situation worse.'

'Maybe. Though I wonder how bad her situation actually is.'

'Jude, what on earth do you mean? Her husband's just been murdered. Isn't that enough to make any wife feel pretty devastated?'

'She just didn't seem to *be* devastated when she first heard the news. Almost relieved, I thought.'

'She was in shock. She didn't know what she was saying.'

'She seemed much more worried about the idea of one of the horses having been injured.'

'Well, that *is* horrible. There have been some very nasty incidents recently. This ghastly Horse Ripper.

The thought of someone doing that to Chieftain or Conker . . .' Sonia Dalrymple's slender frame shuddered '. . . it just doesn't bear thinking of.'

'Why do people attack horses?' asked Jude gently. The question had been exercising her mind recently, and she had been doing some research into the matter.

'God knows. They must be sick. And, actually thinking about it, Chieftain would probably not be in any danger. But Conker . . .'

'Sorry? What do you mean?'

'Conker's a mare. These people always seem to go for mares. Particularly pregnant mares. They slash them round –' She blenched '– round the genital area. It's so cruel. A horse'd never hurt anyone – well, only in exceptional circumstances.' Another shudder. 'No, it's horrible.'

Sonia handed across a cup of coffee with a finality that suggested the cue for a change of subject. But Jude was not so easily deflected. 'So Lucinda and Walter weren't love's young dream, then?'

'I'm not saying that. Obviously there were tensions. There are tensions in every marriage.' The wistfulness with which this was said might have led to some revelation about the Dalrymples' own marriage, but Sonia visibly restrained herself. Maybe giving away the Fleets' secrets was preferable to giving away her own.

'Look, Jude, Lucinda reckons life has dealt her a pretty rotten hand, and in many ways you can see her point. Just before they got married, she and Walter were the golden couple. They were both eventers. He was reckoned to be a shoo-in for the British team at the next Olympics, and she wasn't far behind his standard. They were both very good-looking and became media darlings, photographs in the tabloids, the lot. Walter was set fair to clean up – sponsorship, media appearances, the after-dinner circuit – it all looked very promising.

'And then, just before they were due to have this big society wedding, he had this really bad fall at Burghley. It was the worst kind – his horse reared and fell on him: fractured ribs, pelvis, both legs, God knows what else. He was lucky to survive. Took more than a year for the surgeons to put him back together. At the time there was quite a lot of publicity – lots of cameras at their wedding when it did finally happen. Oh, and a charity fund was set up for him, whip-rounds in equestrian circles, he even appeared in a wheelchair on the BBC's *Sports Review of the Year*, saying what a good recovery he was making and how positive he felt about the future, but . . . people forget, and the money raised didn't last for long . . . his earning potential was massively diminished.

'Anyway, rumour had it that Lucinda didn't take well to this change in their circumstances. You can't blame her. It would take a very exceptional woman to handle that situation without complaint and . . .'

Sonia paused, wondering whether she had gone too far, so Jude tentatively prompted, 'And Lucinda Fleet isn't a very exceptional woman?'

'She . . . well, I don't think the role of carer came naturally to her. She's quite selfish and certainly used to be very ambitious. Walter's long hospitalization put a damper on her own eventing career, and by the time he was fit again, they couldn't afford to continue. All the money they'd got they put into buying Long Bamber Stables. From being a jet-set golden couple, they ended up mucking-out, dealing with stroppy owners and giving spoilt little brats riding lessons. I got the impression Lucinda blamed Walter for that.'

'How did you get that impression?'

'Not very difficult. She kept blaming him in public. Not just for that, but for everything else, as far as I can tell. I don't really know why I felt coy about telling you all this. You'd hear it from anyone who had met them. The Fleets are one of those couples who are constantly sniping at each other, very publicly failing to get on. Being with them socially was like sitting next to someone with an open wound.'

Sonia shook her head with distaste at the image, but, after her initial reticence, she seemed relieved to have got all that off her chest.

'So I suppose,' Jude suggested, 'if the marriage was that bad, then Lucinda Fleet definitely had a motive to kill her husband?'

'But why now? If she was going to do it, why didn't she do it ages ago? They'd stayed together for over fifteen years.'

'The final straw? None of our backs are immune to the final straw.'

'Suppose not. Just seems unlikely to me, though.'

'Well, maybe—'

They were interrupted by a ring at the doorbell. Sonia went to answer and she returned with a girl of about thirteen or fourteen, thin-faced and spotty, still uneasy with the new conformation of her body. Her top teeth were transected by a metal brace, and a ginger streak had been inexpertly dyed into the front of her wispy brown hair. She wore a puffa jacket a couple of sizes too small for her, grubby jeans and smart ankle-length riding boots. A battered riding hat hung by the strap from her hand.

'Jude, this is Imogen.'

The girl said a quiet hello, without making eye contact.

'Imogen's been riding Conker – that's the girls' pony – while they're away at school. You know, to see she gets some exercise.'

'Mrs Fleet up at Long Bamber said you'd brought him back here. She said you might not want me to ride him here, but I knew you would. You don't mind, do you, Mrs Dalrymple?' There was a desperate plea in the girl's voice.

Sonia contemplated turning down the request, but decided against it. 'Not a problem, Imogen, she could do with stretching her legs. But just in the nearest paddock, no further. I'll close the gates to the others.'

'Yes, that's fine. Thank you very much, Mrs Dalrymple.'

Sonia looked at her watch. 'Shouldn't you be at school, Imogen?'

'No,' the girl replied quickly. 'We finish early on Fridays.'

'Ah.' For a moment Sonia looked as if she might

question this, but didn't. 'So have you been home already?'

'Just to change.'

'Was anyone there? Your mother, or your father?'

'No. Mum's gone off to work, and Dad – I don't know where Dad is. He'll be back later to get my supper.'

There was a defiance in the girl's tone and Jude was aware of some subtext between Sonia and Imogen in what was said. But what that subtext was she had no idea.

'Jude's come to look at Chieftain – see if she can sort out the old boy's lameness.'

'Oh, right.'

'Actually, Jude, you may as well come out with us now. And, Imogen, that hat doesn't look very safe. Maybe you should borrow one of the girls'.'

They collected Conker's saddle and tack from a utility room off the kitchen. 'We used to leave this stuff in the stables, but there've been so many break-ins locally, that, what with a decent saddle costing over a thousand pounds . . .'

After the warmth of the kitchen, the outside air stung their faces, as Sonia led them through a garden gate to the stable yard. She had put on a weather-beaten Barbour, which, on her, contrived to look like a designer original. 'You saddle her up, Imogen, while I close the gates, then wait till I've checked everything before you mount her.'

'I've done it lots of times, Mrs Dalrymple. You don't need to check anything.'

'I will check, though, thank you.'

The firmness in Sonia's voice cast the girl down, but her mood was swiftly changed by the sound of a cheerful whinnying from the stables. The three women had just come into the horses' eyeline, and they were accorded an appropriate welcome.

'See, she recognizes me,' Imogen shouted gleefully, and rushed off. 'It's all right, Conker. It's all right, lovely girl. Immy's here to look after you . . .'

Jude grinned at Sonia's raised eyebrow. 'Little girls and horses, eh?'

'Yes.'

'So much easier to deal with than boys.'

'At this stage, certainly.' A shadow crossed Sonia's face. 'Mind you, things change. I'll just go and do the gates.'

'I can help. You do that one, I'll do the one over here.'

They reassembled outside the stables. Chieftain, tall and black, intrigued by the activity, leant curiously over the door of his stall and let out a few breathy snorts. Conker, a solid brown and white pony, was saddled up ready to ride, and Imogen, standing holding her reins, could not disguise her impatience to be off. She was wearing her own battered headgear and, although one of the twins' hats was once again offered, was determined not to change.

Sonia checked the tension of the saddle girths, and passed them as fine.

'I told you they would be, Mrs Dalrymple.'

'I still needed to be sure. If you had a fall, it'd be my responsibility.'

Chastened by the slight asperity in these words, Imogen said, 'Yes, of course, Mrs Dalrymple. May I get up?'

'Sure.' Sonia held the pony's reins, while Imogen, with practised ease, swung herself up into the saddle. 'Just in this paddock?' she asked wistfully, eyeing the neat course of jumps that were set out in the field beyond.

'Just in this one for today.' As the girl and pony trotted meekly off, Sonia's eyes followed them. 'Poor kid.'

'Poor? Why?'

'Parents are going through a very sticky divorce, and focusing all her energies on Conker seems to be Immy's way of coping. She's actually been very helpful, you know, constantly up at Long Bamber, mucking-out for her, all that stuff. But the trouble is, of course, that Conker's not her pony, and when Alice and Laura come back for the Easter holidays – Well, they squabble enough about getting fair shares on Conker with just the two of them. I see ructions ahead.'

'So maybe you should start to restrict Imogen's access to the pony?'

'Yes, I should, but I have to tread carefully. That girl's in a highly emotional state at the moment. She's very fragile.'

Jude looked across at the paddock. Imogen and Conker seemed to be one creature, cantering around without a care in the world. But if riding the pony represented the only peace in the girl's fraught teenage life; Jude understood Sonia's problem.

'Anyway, enough of that. Will you have a look at Chieftain? See if your magic healing hands can do anything for the poor old boy?'

Chapter Six

Sonia Dalrymple led Chieftain out of his stall, and Jude was impressed by the sheer size of the beast. 'He'll be more relaxed outside. He's still a bit nervous being back here, and he might not like a stranger invading his space.'

'He might lash out at me, you mean?'

'It's possible. He hasn't got a vicious nature, but most horses are wary of people they don't know.'

Jude chuckled. 'Just like my friend Carole.'

'I sometimes think it's a pretty sensible attitude to life – can save disappointment later.' Again Jude detected some buried hurt in Sonia's words, as if she spoke from unhappy experience.

The block in which they stood had been carefully and expensively converted. By comparison, Long Bamber Stables looked shabby. Two stalls faced each other across a paved central area. On the far wall metal rungs were fixed, leading up to a closed trapdoor.

'Plenty of storage space you've got here.'

'Yes. That was designed as a hayloft, but we've never really used it. We never bought hay in very large bulk, so it was simpler to keep it down here. And now the girls have gone . . .'

Sonia kept reverting to that. As though to break her mood, she turned to stroke Chieftain.

'He's big, isn't he?' Jude said.

'Sixteen hands. When Nicky bought him, he had some idea about hunting with him, but . . . well, Nicky hasn't got the time and anyway, this bloody government's put paid to hunting.'

'Does Nicky ride him at all?'

'Yes, he does sometimes.' The question seemed to make Sonia uncomfortable. 'But he's so rarely home for any length of time.'

'And he couldn't ride him at the moment, anyway, with the horse lame.'

'No,' Sonia agreed, as if that ended the conversation.

'Is Chieftain a stallion?'

'Gelding. Makes them a bit more manageable. Though you do have your petulant moods from time to time, don't you, you beautiful boy?'

Chieftain seemed to understand the endearment, and nuzzled into his mistress's blonde hair. Sonia found a piece of carrot in the pocket of her Barbour and slipped it up into his mouth. He crunched it appreciatively and reached down towards the source for more.

'No, that's it, Chieftain. That's it for the time being.'

Jude stepped cautiously towards the huge horse. 'OK. So where's the lameness?'

'Front left. Knee might be slightly swollen, it's hard to tell.'

'Will he be all right if I just touch him?'

'Better if I introduce you to him first. Give him this.' Sonia slipped another piece of carrot into Jude's hand. 'He'll be your friend for life then. Chieftain, Chieftain, who's my big boy?' Again the horse responded to the affection in her tone and nuzzled against her. 'This is Jude. I want you to meet Jude. Hold your hand out – not the one with the carrot in.'

Tentatively, Jude did as she was told. Chieftain appeared not to have noticed the gesture. 'Can he see it there? Horses have a big blind spot, don't they?'

'He knows it's there. Just wait.'

She kept her hand out, and slowly the gelding lowered his massive head to sniff at it. The warm breath made Jude feel as if she was under a hand-dryer, and she was aware of the proximity of the huge teeth. But all that touched her were a couple of whiskers that tickled along the skin of her hand.

'He's getting used to the idea of you. This is Jude – yes, isn't it, boy? All right, offer him the carrot.' Jude slowly advanced her other hand. 'Keep it flat.'

For a moment Chieftain was uncertain. Then, with one sudden quick movement, he dropped his head and daintily abstracted the treat. So close, the crunching sounded disproportionately loud.

'He'll be all right with you now, Jude.'

'So you'll hold him – if I just touch his knee?'

'Yes. Very gently, though, because if it's giving him pain . . .'

'I'll be gentle.'

Jude could feel the horse tense as she touched the

injured leg above the knee. Through his coat, she could feel the enormous coiled-up strength within. Softly, almost caressing, she moved her hand lower, down the straight ridge of bone until she began to feel the angularity of the knee. Chieftain stamped and skittered uneasily. She was getting near to the trouble.

Sonia Dalrymple brought her head close to the horse's, and murmured soft words of comfort to him. He was partially reassured, but the tension within his huge frame tightened a few more notches.

So slowly that the movement could not be seen, Jude let her hand slide down over the irregularities of the knee. 'This is where the trouble is, all right. It feels like it's on fire.'

'Actually burning hot? So it's infected?'

'Possibly. But it's not that kind of heat. It's a heat I can sense rather than feel . . . from where the focus of the pain is.'

'But can you heal it?'

Jude grinned ruefully. 'I can try. I'm afraid any healer who guarantees to cure a problem is a healer I wouldn't trust.'

'Well, please do your best. Chieftain hates not being able to gallop around, don't you, boy?'

The horse let out a long shuddering breath of assent.

'All right,' said Jude, slowly bringing her other hand down till the two encircled the injured joint. 'Let's see what we can do.'

*

Carole was feeling restless. *The Times* crossword, her daily anti-Alzheimer's exercise, was proving particularly intractable. She had a feeling they'd got a new compiler, and his mind – she felt sure it was a he with an illogical masculine mind – didn't work the same way as hers did. Or the same way generations of other *Times* crossword compilers had trained hers to work.

She knew, though, that the unyielding crossword was a symptom rather than a cause of her malaise. Partly she was frustrated by the knowledge that Jude was over at Sonia Dalrymple's house, possibly getting vital inside information about the background to Walter Fleet's murder.

But Carole had another, more enduring, anxiety. It had been a long time since she'd heard from her son and daughter-in-law. September and Stephen and Gaby's magical Fedborough wedding now seemed a long while ago. At the time, Carole had felt a rapprochement with the younger Seddons, even – in spite of the presence of her ex-husband David – a sense of family. And that had been maintained by frequent phone calls after their honeymoon and a surprisingly jolly visit to Fethering at Christmas. But through January and into February communication had become much less spontaneous and frequent. Carole, who, in spite of her forthright exterior, was always ready to put herself in the wrong, wondered what she had done.

Stephen, she knew, was always busy, doing whatever it was he did. Their increasing closeness had not brought with it a greater understanding of his work; still all Carole knew was that it involved money and computers. Gaby too had a demanding job as a theatrical agent. No doubt they were just preoccupied with the frenetic lifestyle of a successful newly-married couple about London. No reason why they should think much about their parents' generation.

But this likely explanation did not allay Carole's unease. There was another detail that troubled her. Stephen and Gaby were still living in his house in Fulham. At one stage – indeed when she was first introduced to Gaby – they had been down in West Sussex house-hunting, with a view to moving out of London. Such plans were still being discussed in the run-up to Christmas, but since then – no mention.

Carole could not hide her disappointment from herself. Though, if ever the subject had come up in company, she had treated their potential move rather as an inconvenience, huffing about being quite all right on her own and not wanting her privacy invaded, she had secretly welcomed the idea. And she was surprised by how much the prospect of its not happening upset her.

She had contemplated taking the initiative and ringing them, even getting to the point more than once of lifting the receiver, but she didn't want to appear needy. The last thing a newly-married woman wanted was an intrusive mother-in-law.

But the lack of information still rankled. Jude's absence that afternoon made her feel even more unsettled, so Carole decided she had to do something. If she had inadvertently offended her son and daughter-in-law, then it was time to build bridges or mend fences or some other metaphor of that kind.

She had both Stephen and Gaby's work numbers, but she rang their house. Better just to leave a message; then they could ring her back at their convenience. Mind you, of course, if they didn't ring her back, then she'd feel even worse. That'd certainly be making a statement that they didn't want to have anything more to do with her.

But the thought came too late, the phone was already ringing and – to her surprise – it was answered. By Gaby.

'Oh, sorry. I wasn't expecting anyone to be there.'

'Carole. It's good to hear you.' But Gaby's words sounded automatic. There was no energy. The natural bubbliness of her personality seemed to have gone flat.

'I just thought it had been a while since we . . .'

'Yes.'

'So you're both all right, are you?'

'Fine, yes. Stephen's very busy at work.'

'So what else is new?'

'Exactly.'

'And you?'

'Yes, fine.'

'I meant work, because surely today's a working day?'

'Yes, I'm having a day off. Few things I've got to catch up with round the house.'

'But you're OK?'

'Absolutely fine, yes.' But the listlessness with

which the words were said was at odds with their meaning.

'Well . . . I was thinking it would be nice for us to get together again soon.'

'Yes, yes, it would.' But there was no pursuit of the idea, no suggestions, no consultation of diaries.

'Fine, Gaby. Well, I'll give you a call again when . . . Maybe an evening . . . Talk when Stephen's there.'

'That might be better. He has so many more demands on his time than I do, I don't dare make arrangements without consulting him.' As an excuse, it was perfectly acceptable, but Carole still sensed an unwillingness in Gaby to fix a meeting.

'Right. Well, I'll call soon then. And,' she went on haltingly, 'do give Stephen my love.' Such words of effusiveness did not come naturally to her.

'Yes, of course I will.'

'Well, good to talk to you, Gaby.'

'And you.'

'And look forward to meeting up soon.'

'Mm.'

'Goodbye then.'

'Bye.'

As she switched off the phone, Carole wished she hadn't made the call. Her paranoia had only increased. Before she had spoken to Gaby, she could still nurture the fantasy that everything was all right, but now she'd heard the lack of enthusiasm in her daughter-in-law's voice, that was no longer possible.

What on earth could be wrong? Feeling lousy and taking a day off work could be a sign of early pregnancy, but if that were the case, surely Gaby would have told her? And she wouldn't have sounded so doomy. That was the really distressing thing about the call – that the normally ebullient Gaby had sounded so down, so positively depressed.

Oh dear. Please God there wasn't something going wrong in the marriage. Guilt for the effect her own break-up with David had had on Stephen swelled within her.

She had another look at the *Times* crossword. The clues might as well have been written in a foreign language.

Chapter Seven

It wasn't working. Jude couldn't identify what was wrong, but she knew it wasn't working.

She could feel the warmth from Chieftain's knee, which felt almost as though it were burning between her hands. But she was imparting no answering warmth to the horse.

Healing doesn't always work, Jude knew that, but on this occasion she felt it was her fault. Her concentration was straying. While she should have been channelling all her energy into the injured knee, she was distracted by other thoughts. She was aware of the unidentified pain within the woman standing at her side. She was aware of the confusion within the apparently carefree child cantering round the paddock on Conker. Usually she managed to shut her mind to such extraneous concerns, but that afternoon she couldn't.

Maybe if she was alone with Chieftain, in his stall perhaps, with no distractions? But would he tolerate that? Would he feel sufficiently at ease without the familiar presence of his owner?

Jude released her hold on Chieftain and straightened up.

'Done the job?' asked Sonia eagerly.

A rueful shake of the head. 'Doesn't feel like it, I'm afraid.'

'But there is something wrong with the knee? That's where the trouble is?'

'Oh yes, I can feel that.'

'Well, what are you going to do about him?' In Sonia's voice there was both disappointment at the failure and the peremptory tone of someone who has always expected good service.

'All I can do is try again another day. I'm sorry. I'm wrong today. I can't clear my head sufficiently to get a proper focus. Maybe I'm the wrong person, anyway. You should have gone to someone who specializes in horses in the first place.'

'Ah.' Sonia didn't pick up the suggestion, or explain why she hadn't consulted an expert. 'Oh, well . . .' She shrugged. 'I'll put him back in his stall. You won't like that, will you, boy? Whenever I bring him out, he thinks we're going for a ride. Gets very disappointed when nothing happens.'

Chieftain expressed his disappointment with a bit of half-hearted rearing and some disgruntled whinnying, but, bowing to the strength of his mistress's personality, allowed himself to be shut back into his loose box.

'Come on, Imogen,' Sonia called out as she locked the bottom half of Chieftain's door. 'That's enough.'

'Oh, can't I stay out a bit longer?'

'No. It's getting dark. Now, I can trust you to put Conker back safely, can't I?'

'Yes, of course, Mrs Dalrymple.' Imogen walked back towards them. Girl and pony looked equally dispirited by the curtailment of their fun. The dark clouds of the real world seemed to gather over Imogen's head.

And the dark clouds of the encroaching night lowered over the three women.

'You remember where the saddle and tack go, don't you?'

'Of course, Mrs Dalrymple.'

'Make sure it's all neat. And, before you leave her, check Conker's got plenty of water – and that her haynet's full.'

'Yes, Mrs Dalrymple.'

'Then come through to the kitchen. I'll have some tea ready.'

'Thank you, Mrs Dalrymple.'

In the kitchen Sonia produced a very tasty-looking fruit cake, and Jude had no inhibitions about taking a slice.

'Shop-bought, I'm afraid. My cake-making skills are not up to much.'

'I don't think anybody's are these days. Nobody's got the time.'

'Oh, I've got the time,' said Sonia rather bleakly. Then quickly she recovered herself. 'I keep buying cakes – it's mad. Keep thinking the twins are going to come thundering in from school as hungry as horses, and . . . well . . .'

'A time of adjustment,' Jude suggested.

'Yes. Just that.'

But this wasn't the moment to probe deeper into Sonia's unhappiness. In a strange way, it would almost have felt unprofessional. The woman was a client, but this afternoon's meeting was not being conducted on that basis. Jude moved the conversation on.

'Are Imogen's parents actually divorced yet?'

'No, they're in the process. That awful stage where they haven't quite got their accommodation sorted. They're both round the house at different times, trying to avoid each other. And then occasionally they do meet and there's yet another row. Or at least,' she added hastily, 'that's what Imogen's told me.'

'Can't be much fun for her.'

'No, and she spends most of the time with her mother, which can't help.'

'Oh?'

'Hilary Potton is a Grade A cow. Very self-absorbed and neurotic. I don't think Immy gets much support from her – poor girl has to use most of her energy propping up a hysterical mother.'

'And what about the father?'

'Don't know a lot about him. Think he's called Alec, but . . .'

'Is he fond of Imogen?'

'Oh yes. Well, I assume he is. Fathers usually are fond of their daughters, aren't they? Not to say besotted.'

'Is that how Nicky is with your girls?'

The question seemed to take Sonia by surprise. 'Yes,' she replied formally. 'He's very fond of them.'

'But, going back to the Pottons' divorce . . .'

'I don't know much about it, really. Just that it's proving very difficult for everyone involved. And, of course, they'll both suffer financially. I mean, before the marriage broke up, there was talk of them buying a pony for Imogen – you know, she'd had riding lessons at Long Bamber, she was very keen – but no chance of that now. Alec – Alec Potton works as a salesman of some kind – fitted kitchens, I think – so they never had much. And with the divorce happening, there's certainly no spare cash. Which is another reason why I feel I shouldn't make a fuss about Immy riding Conker – in spite of the way I know Alice and Laura will react and . . .' Sonia Dalrymple shook her perfectly coiffed blonde hair in exasperation. 'God, everything's so bloody complicated.'

'Yes, but surely—'

Jude was silenced by Sonia putting a finger to her lips and nodding towards the door from the utility room, where Imogen was just entering.

'Conker all settled, is she?'

'Yes, Mrs Dalrymple. She wanted me to stay.'

'Well, you must come and ride her another day.'

'Can I come tomorrow?'

Sonia looked flustered. If she wanted to wean Imogen off riding Conker before her daughters' term finished, the task wouldn't be an easy one. 'I'm not quite sure what I'm doing tomorrow, Imogen.'

'You don't have to be here. It's Saturday. I'm off school. And I know where everything is.'

Jude observed the set-to with amusement. Imogen Potton was a very strong-willed young woman, but Sonia Dalrymple's experience with her daughters had taught her how to stand up to strong-willed young women.

'No, I'm sorry. I'm afraid I can't allow you to ride Conker when I'm not here.'

'But, Mrs Dalrymple, you let me when she was up at Long Bamber.'

'That's different. There are people up there keeping an eye on things. Mr and Mrs Fleet – well, Mrs Fleet now. And her helpers, and other riders. It's totally different here.'

'Oh, I—'

'Imogen, I'm sorry. You have to obey me on this. You are not to ride Conker unless I am here. If you had a fall, I'd be responsible.'

The words were said with finality, but as Jude had expected, Imogen wasn't going to be silenced that easily.

'But I won't have a fall. Conker knows me, she behaves when she's with me, Mrs Dalrymple.'

'Imogen, I don't want to have to say this again. You are not to ride Conker unless I am here. Apart from anything else, you couldn't get her saddle and tack if the house was closed.'

'But I could borrow some—'

'No. I am telling you you are not to ride her unless I am here! And if I find out you have been disobeying me on that, I will stop you riding her altogether. Is that clear?'

'Yes, Mrs Dalrymple,' the girl mumbled.

For a moment there was a silence. But Jude was unsurprised when Imogen came back again. 'So, can I ring you tomorrow lunchtime, see if it's all right?'

Sonia looked flustered. 'Well, er . . . I'm not sure exactly where I'll be at lunchtime tomorrow. Maybe it'd be better if you left it for a couple of days.'

'I'll ring you lunchtime tomorrow,' said Imogen firmly, and with satisfaction. She reckoned she'd won the round. Then, remembering her manners, she added, 'And thank you very much for letting me ride Conker today.'

'My pleasure. Now, as you see, Jude and I are having some tea and cake. Shall I get you a cup?'

'No, thank you. I'd better get home.'

'But you can't go home on your own.'

'It's fine. I walked here. I'm only in Fethering. It's not far.'

'When you walked here, it wasn't pitch dark.'

'But, Mrs Dalrymple—'

'No.' Sonia sighed. 'I'll give you a lift. Just let me finish my cup of tea.'

'I don't want to be any trouble.'

'Tell you what,' Jude interposed. 'I'm walking back to Fethering. I'll see you home, Imogen.'

The girl didn't look enthusiastic, but Sonia leapt on the idea with relief. 'Yes, that's a very good solution.'

'Where do you actually live, Imogen?' asked Jude.

'River Road,' came the sulky reply.

'Perfect. It's on my way. I live in the High Street.'

'Well, Imogen, now that's settled, will you have a cup of tea?'

'No, thank you, Mrs Dalrymple. I really should be getting back. Mum worries.'

'She'd worry more if she thought you were walking round on your own in the dark.'

'She wouldn't care.'

'Oh, I'm sure she would.'

Jude decided it was time to halt the development of another disagreement. Draining her tea and picking up her coat, she announced that she was ready to leave. 'Have a look at Chieftain in the morning. Try walking him around a bit. Though I'm afraid you're unlikely to find much improvement.'

'I'll live in hope. Now what do I owe you?'

Jude raised a hand to banish the idea. 'You can pay me if he gets better. If not, don't worry.'

'Paying by results? Is that how most healers work?'

'It's how I work.'

'All right. If you insist.'

'I do. Anyway, many thanks for the tea, and good to see you.'

'Yes. And I'll give you a call about . . .' In the presence of Imogen, Sonia Dalrymple was embarrassed about her client status with Jude and didn't want to discuss the details of her next appointment.

'Yes, fine,' said Jude, understanding immediately. 'Well, Imogen, shall we be on our way?'

*

The television chat show that Carole wouldn't admit to anyone she watched was beginning to exercise quite a strong hold over her. Though the idea appalled her, she was conscious of beginning to schedule her day around the programme. Oh dear, she was becoming old and set in her ways. Part of the afternoon elderly target market for all those stairlifts, annuities and walk-in baths they kept advertising in the commercial breaks.

Carole felt little guilt about her secret vice. She enjoyed the programme and there was nothing wrong with that . . . so long as nobody ever found out she was actually watching it.

But even her favourite chat show could not completely eradicate from her mind the unease planted there by her non-conversation with her daughter-in-law. Stephen and Gaby hadn't yet been married six months – surely things hadn't soured that quickly?

Maybe Carole would have to ring Stephen and question him about the situation. It wasn't a prospect she relished.

Her programme came to an end, and Carole stayed to watch the news. That was an indulgence she could always justify. It was important, as one got older, to keep abreast of current affairs. That night's offerings weren't very edifying – more people killed in pointless international wars and intractable civil ones, a minor royal committing yet another gaffe, the government setting up another target destined never to be attained. The mixture as before.

It wasn't until the local news came on that there was an item to surprise her. And the surprise wasn't a pleasant one. The previous night two mares had been slashed at with knives at a stable yard in West Sussex. The incident had taken place west of Horsham, some way away from Fedborough and Long Bamber Stables, but the news was still unsettling.

Jude had an exceptional knack of getting people to talk to her. Even the most buttoned-up individuals usually succumbed after a few minutes to the easiness of her company. But she made very little headway with Imogen Potton.

As they walked back along the Fether through the gathering dusk, overtures about school, tastes in music and television, even her beloved Conker, were cut short by curt monosyllables. The girl kept just the right side of rudeness, but she left no doubt that she'd rather be on her own. Her instinct was to run off and leave Jude; only the fear of her behaviour being reported to Sonia Dalrymple and ending her riding rights prevented her from doing so.

Imogen had started by trailing behind her minder, swinging her battered riding hat at her side, but, soon realizing that this formation opened up too much danger of Jude looking back and making eye contact, she now marched resolutely ahead.

'Will there be someone at home when you get there?'

The girl couldn't refuse to answer such a direct question. 'I think my dad'll be there. Mum works late on a Friday.'

'What does your mother do?'

'She serves at Allinstore.' Fethering's only – and highly inefficient – supermarket. 'Money's been tight since they started the divorce proceedings. Mum thinks the work is very definitely beneath her.' Imogen seemed to derive some satisfaction from her mother's discomfiture.

'So what time will she be back?'

But the brief window of communication was closing. All Jude got was a terse 'Later.'

'Well, look, if you have any problems, or you're left on your own too long this evening, give me a call.' Jude stopped for a moment and scribbled down her mobile number. The girl hadn't waited for her and Jude had to hurry to catch up and hand it across. Silently Imogen shoved the scrap of paper into the pocket of her puffa jacket, but not in the manner of someone who was ever going to use it.

Jude tried again. Surely the murder of Walter Fleet would get some reaction from the girl.

'Horrible, that business up at Long Bamber, wasn't it?' Silence. 'You know, the reason why Conker and Chieftain have been moved back to the Dalrymples.'

'I *do* know what you're talking about,' said Imogen pityingly.

'It must have been a shock for you,' Jude persevered. 'I mean, because you spent so much time up at the stables.'

'I didn't spend much time there.'

'But I thought you looked after Conker, helped with the mucking-out . . .?'

'Not very often.'

This seemed a direct contradiction to what Sonia Dalrymple had said, but Jude didn't question it.

'And you must have known Walter Fleet quite well.'

'Not that well. He was just an old guy who was around, that's all.'

Old? Early forties. Jude wondered how old Imogen thought she was. 'But he and his wife ran the place. You must have had quite a bit to do with him and—'

'I didn't know him well,' the girl said firmly, and to emphasize the ending of the conversation, ran a few steps ahead. 'We're nearly there.'

The River Road destination to which Imogen led the way was a substantial family house, probably with four or five bedrooms. Though Sonia Dalrymple had dismissed Alec Potton's earning potential, and it was as nothing compared to her husband's, he must have been doing pretty well to buy a property like that in Fethering. But the house was showing signs of neglect: the exterior paintwork was blistered and flaking; the front garden had grown shaggy. Its lack of maintenance seemed all too straightforward a symbol for the dividing family within. The blank stare of the unlit windows with undrawn curtains was distinctly unwelcoming.

'It's all right. You can leave me here,' said Imogen when they reached the garden gate.

'No, I'll see you in, check there's someone there.'

'I am fourteen, you know. I am capable of being in the house on my own. In fact, I spend most of my time in the house on my own. It's not a problem.'

'Do you have any brothers and sisters?'

'No.'

'Well, let's just see if there's anyone in.'

'For heaven's sake, I can be left alone! You sound just like my mum, not letting me be on my own for a single minute. Either she's got to be there, or she's got to fix up for Dad to be there or . . .'

Imogen let out one of those exasperated sighs that only teenage girls can do properly, and stomped off up the garden path, reaching for her house key. She opened the front door, turning to bar entrance to Jude. Her unwanted escort was being given a very definite message to leave.

'So, is there someone in?'

'Yes, of course there is. Da-ad!'

But the only answer to her long call was an echo in the empty house. Imogen looked taken aback, then let out another louder wail, which again produced no response.

'He said he'd be here. He promised to be here.' But resignation quickly overcame disappointment. 'Don't worry, I'll be all right. You can go.'

'But couldn't you give your father a call on your mobile to—'

'If he's not here, he's doing something else,' said Imogen sharply. 'Work probably. He's on the road some-where. I can't disturb him when he's working.'

'But surely he's . . .'

Jude's words trailed away at the sound of a car drawing up behind her and Imogen's eyes brightening with recognition.

'He's here. You can go.' Even the pretence of politeness in her words had now slipped away.

Jude turned to see a tall man emerging from a rather grubby BMW. 'Sorry, Immy love, got delayed.'

Alec Potton was in his early forties, louchely stylish in a shapeless corduroy suit. In spite of his receding hair, he was an attractive man, and the warmth of his handshake to Jude after she had been grudgingly introduced showed that he was well aware of his attractiveness. Over the years of being what could only be described as fanciable, she knew all too well the subtext of extra hand pressure and extended contact by which men expressed sexual interest. The instant thought came into her mind that perhaps Alec Potton's relish for other women was the cause of the divorce currently in progress.

'Can't thank you enough for looking after Immy,' he enthused. Closer to, Jude could see that his good looks were marred by nervous anxiety. He was a man under stress. And a lot of the stress seemed to be related to his daughter. He looked at her with something approaching fear, as though afraid she might crumble to dust at any moment.

'It was no problem. Virtually on my way back.'

'Anyway, thank you – Jude – was that the name?'

'That's right – Jude.'

'Well, thank you for holding the fort. I'm back in time to get my daughter some supper. What do you fancy, Immy? What have we got in the house?'

'The usual boring rubbish.'

'Oh. Well, maybe I'd better take you down the Crown and Anchor, hadn't I?'

'Mum said we should stop eating out all the time. We've got to economize.' It was said piously, but with an edge of humour. Imogen relished the idea of a meal out with her father.

'Ah . . .' Alec began soberly, 'if Mum said that . . .' He was silent, before continuing wickedly, 'All the more reason to have supper at the Crown and Anchor.'

Putting his arm around his daughter's shoulders, he led her towards the car. As he did so, he looked closely at the jumper she was wearing under her puffa jacket. 'Is that mine?' She nodded. 'You cheeky cow.'

Though she hadn't yet seen Imogen with her mother, Jude felt pretty sure she knew which side the girl was taking in the divorce contest. The eyes with which she looked at her father were full of adoration.

'Hello. Stephen?'

'Who is this?'

'It's your mother.'

'Oh, look, I'm sorry. I'm right in the middle of something. Can I call you back?'

'Yes. Yes, of course.'

And that was that.

Chapter Eight

'You said they were going to have supper at the Crown and Anchor. Maybe we should do the same?'

Jude was amazed. The suggestion was a most unlikely one, considering who it came from. Carole was always reticent, even shy. The idea of her volunteering to manufacture an encounter with Alec Potton and his daughter was totally out of character.

'I think that might look a bit obvious, don't you? I mean, given that I've only just met him, and that I'm not Imogen's favourite person.'

'Yes, I suppose it might.' But Carole was desperate to find out more about the circumstances of Walter Fleet's death. A murder investigation was the only thing that promised to take her mind off the subject of Stephen's marriage. 'I'm just so intrigued by it all.'

'Me too. Mind you, no doubt we'll soon hear that the police have made an arrest and the case is solved.'

'Well, we haven't heard it yet, have we?'

'No.'

'Oh, but there was something. On the news.' And Carole related what she had heard about the Horse

Ripper's activities near Horsham. 'It's such a horrible crime. Why do people do it, Jude?'

'I don't know. I'm quite interested in it, though.'

'What a disgusting thing to be interested in.'

'Maybe. But human behaviour fascinates me: what brings people to do the things they do, and particularly the appalling things. I've been making a note of the dates of these local horse mutilations, and collecting the newspaper cuttings. I must get the *Fethering Observer* – it's sure to report this latest one.'

'But why are you doing it?'

'I'm just getting data together, trying to see if any pattern emerges.'

'What kind of pattern?'

'I don't know. Responses to the lunar cycle, international events, anything that might make sense of the senseless.'

'But horses . . . Horses never do anyone any harm. Why on earth do these people do it?'

'There are as many theories as there are psychologists. Some researches have suggested there's a link to paedophilia. Personally, I find that quite convincing.'

Carole shuddered. 'There are some disgusting people about, aren't there?'

'Oh yes.' But Jude was always going to take a less rigid view of such matters. 'There are also a lot of people about who suffer enormously from instincts which the world finds unacceptable and over which they themselves have very little control.'

'What – are you making excuses for paedophilia?'

'I'm not making excuses for it. I'm just saying it

must be very difficult to go through life with feelings which the entire world despises.'

'Huh.' Although Carole was a *Times* reader, there was, at bottom, a lot of *Daily Mail* in her. But she was still hungry for the displacement activity of investigation. 'Isn't there anyone else we know who's got something to do with the Long Bamber Stables set-up? Don't we have any other contacts?'

'Don't think we do, I'm afraid. We could ask Ted Crisp. A lot of people come and go through the Crown and Anchor. He might have heard something.'

'Yes.'

'Or, of course, we do know where we can find Imogen's mother.'

'Oh, really? How do we know that?'

'Sorry, I forgot to tell you. Imogen told me that her mother works at the checkout at Allinstore.'

Carole's knee-jerk reaction was characteristically snobbish. 'Really? I thought, from what you'd said, that they were a nice middle-class family.'

'Divorce has unfortunate effects even on nice middle-class families. I gather Imogen's mother is doing it for the money.'

'But it's an extremely public way of earning money. I mean, everyone in Fethering sees you sitting at a checkout. It's very humiliating.'

Jude thought about this. From what she'd heard of Hilary Potton, she wouldn't be surprised if she'd sought out that kind of humiliation; a public martyrdom to show all of Fethering the straits to which her husband's behaviour had reduced her. She shared the thought with Carole. 'Anyway,' she concluded, 'Mrs Potton, so far as we know, has only the most tenuous of links to Walter Fleet. I mean, her daughter rides at Long Bamber, but that's about it.'

'Maybe, Jude, but tenuous links are all we seem to have at the moment.' Carole rose and picked up her handbag. 'Anyway, as it happens, there are a few things I need from Allinstore. I'm going straight down there.'

The building must have been converted from something else; it couldn't have been designed as a supermarket, unless by an architect who was either incompetent or had a wicked sense of humour. The large pillars which supported the roof seemed to have been placed where they would cause maximum obstruction to the smooth flow of shoppers. Some vindictive expert in space management had elected to put the tills directly behind two of them, so that most people seemed destined to make their purchases sideways.

An equally dead hand was in charge of the supermarket's stock. Shelves were either overloaded with the things nobody ever wanted, or empty of the products everyone required. Carole Seddon used Allinstore infrequently. Her major shopping was done in one weekly foray to Sainsbury's. She only resorted to the local supermarket when she had run out of something. And, given the strict way in which she organized her life, she very rarely did run out of anything. Jude, among whose priorities housekeeping took a much lower rank, was a more regular visitor to Allinstore.

Still, there are certain rules of domestic life. You can never have too many tins of chopped tomatoes on your shelves. And an extra pack of kitchen rolls never goes amiss. More importantly, these were both products which could be little harmed by the supermarket's erratic buying policy.

Carole put a four-pack of each into her basket and then, in a fit of wild spontaneity, added a bottle of fizzy spring water. It wasn't a brand she had heard of, but it was commensurately cheap.

Identifying Hilary Potton was not too challenging a task. Only two of the tills were manned, and there was no way the spotty teenager with variegated hair and a nose stud had given birth to Imogen. So, even though the girl's queue was shorter, Carole deliberately took her basket to the other one. Once there, the polite middle-class tones she heard as totals were announced left her in no doubt that she was on the right track.

Hilary Potton was strong-featured with thick, carefully shaped eyebrows and black hair cut fashionably short, the kind of woman to whom the words 'striking' and 'handsome' rather than 'beautiful' would be applied. The blue Allinstore tabard didn't do her any favours, but in a suit or well-cut leisurewear she would have looked very good.

There was only one customer in front of her when Carole, angling herself awkwardly around a pillar, had a little moment of panic. What was she going to say to this woman? What possible advance in her tenuous murder investigation did she hope she was going to achieve? Jude should have come; she'd be much better at creating a conversational bond. Why on earth had Carole decided to come to Allinstore in the first place?

Of course it didn't matter. If she made her purchases without a word being exchanged, nobody would think anything odd. That was why people went into supermarkets. On the other hand, she wouldn't have any trophy of information to take back in triumph to Jude. And Carole's hypersensitive nature was beginning to think that Jude was already having the lion's share of this investigation.

The other customer had left. Carole placed her basket in the bay designed for it and said fatuously, 'Just essentials.'

'Ah, but those are the very things that are essential,' Hilary Potton responded.

This was promising. Not only a response, but one with an element of levity in it. Must build on this start.

'Mind you, I can never find all the essentials I need in here.'

The words came out stilted, and Carole regretted them as soon as they were spoken. Criticizing the supermarket was probably not the best way of engaging in conversation with one of its employees.

Serendipitously, however, she had managed to say exactly the right thing. 'Tell me about it,' said Hilary Potton, raising her eyes to heaven as she scanned Carole's purchases. 'I'm afraid I hardly ever shop here – can never find the stuff I want.'

'No, I'd got the impression Allinstore wasn't the greatest supermarket on the planet.'

'That is an understatement.'

'And what are they like as employers?'

A shrug. 'Probably no worse than most. Anyway, beggars can't be choosers.'

'Oh?'

But the prompt was not needed. 'Hard to find part-time work round here. You know, that'll fit in with the demands of a teenage daughter.'

'Yes, I'm sure it must be.'

'Still, if your husband walks out on you, what choice do you have?'

There was an impatient shuffling sound from someone lurking behind the pillar. Further extension of the conversation was impossible. Carole was told the total for her purchases and paid the exact money.

But she didn't think the exercise had been wasted. If nothing else, it had confirmed Jude's conjecture about Hilary Potton setting herself up as a public martyr. The readiness with which she had started denigrating her husband had been striking. And Carole felt sure there was a lot more where that came from.

When she relayed the information she had obtained to Jude back in Woodside Cottage, it did seem pretty meagre. Basically what it came down to was that Hilary and Alec Potton were going through a very sticky divorce, and there was no love lost between them. Which everyone in Fethering already knew.

But Jude was characteristically positive about the contribution to their investigation. 'Though whether we should dignify what we're doing with the name of "investigation" is a moot point.'

'Well, there's been a murder – no question about that.'

'No. And we were the first people on the scene, so we definitely do have an involvement. But we have no information of real relevance. We haven't even got any suspects.'

'Jude, are you suggesting we should give up our non-existent investigation?'

'Of course I'm not, you idiot.'

The thought, before she'd met Jude, of anyone calling Carole Seddon an 'idiot' without losing her goodwill for ever, was an unlikely one. Now she found the use of the word rather comforting. Yes, it was possible for a personality even as frozen as Carole's to thaw.

'No, we'll press on in the face of total ignorance, until we find out who killed Walter Fleet.'

'Unless, of course, the police get there first.'

'Phooey. No chance. It would take away the fun if they did, though, wouldn't it?' Before Carole had time to respond, Jude went on, 'Now look, I was about to knock up a prawn salad. You will stay and have some, won't you?'

'Well . . .' Carole's first instinct was to say no. When she came to think of it, her first instinct in response to any invitation was to say no. But Jude had lit a fire whose light flickered pleasingly onto the chaos of her sitting room, and the second glass of Chilean

Chardonnay was slipping down a treat. The offer was certainly more appealing than the remains of a fish pie sitting in the fridge at High Tor. And Carole had already done Gulliver's evening routine of feeding and a trip out to the rough ground behind the house to do his business. Besides, sitting at home, she knew she'd worry about the fact that Stephen hadn't rung her back, or feel that she should ring her ex-husband David to find out if he knew anything about the state of their son's marriage.

'If it's no trouble, Jude . . .'

'Of course not. I'm going to do it for myself, so . . . Help yourself to more wine. I won't be long.'

After her friend had disappeared to the kitchen, Carole looked around the room, and tried to work out how there could be comfort in such confusion. Jude's approach to interior design reflected her wardrobe. Everywhere firm outlines were softened by swathes of drapery. What logic dictated must be sofas and armchairs became vague shapes under accumulations of throws, rugs and cushions. Even the horizontal lines of mantelpiece, tables and shelves were rendered irregular by the bizarre collection of objects which were placed on, or depended from them.

Such untidiness went against Carole's every instinct, but she couldn't deny the room was a relaxing environment to inhabit. Whatever she was sitting on seemed to cosset and blur the angularities of her body. From the kitchen, the reassuring mumble of Radio 4 could be half heard. Carole leant forward to the bottle on the table in front of her, and topped up her glass.

'We spoke too soon.'

Jude was standing in the kitchen doorway.

'What?'

'We were guilty of underestimating the police.'

'What are you talking about?'

'Just heard it on the news. The police have taken a forty-seven-year-old man in for questioning in connection with the murder of Walter Fleet.'

Carole found herself fumbling with her key when she let herself in to High Tor. She had had more wine than she normally allowed herself. But then she and Jude had had a rather frustrating evening. Though they'd listened to later bulletins, and watched the television news – including the local version – nothing more had been announced about the police's advance in the murder investigation. A forty-seven-year-old man. That remained the sum total of the facts revealed.

Not for the first time, Carole resented the omniscience of the police. They had all the information at their fingertips, which did make it very difficult for ordinary members of the public with a healthy interest in murder to compete.

The red light on the answering machine was flicking, and immediately her anxieties about Stephen and Gaby returned. Not that she was expecting to find out much from his message – he would just say that he was returning her call – but the reminder of his existence was sufficient to press her panic button.

But the message wasn't from Stephen. And Carole

didn't even have time to worry that he hadn't called her back. Because the person who had called was much more intriguing.

'Hello. My name's Lucinda Fleet – you know, from Long Bamber Stables. I was trying to contact your friend Jude, but I don't know her surname so I couldn't get her through the phonebook. Actually, I'd like to contact you too, Mrs Seddon, because you were there that night when . . . Anyway, I'd be most grateful if you could call me back. I'd really like to talk to both of you.'

Well now, that's convenient, thought Carole.

Chapter Nine

'The point is that Donal would never have killed Walter.'

'Sorry, we're not up to speed on this. Who's Donal?' asked Jude.

'He's the one who the police have taken in for questioning. Surely you know Donal? Everyone round here who's ever had anything to do with horses knows Donal.'

'I'm afraid I've never had anything to do with horses.' Carole didn't mean it to sound sniffy, but that was how it came across. Story of her life, really.

It was lunchtime the following day, and they were in the Crown and Anchor. Lucinda Fleet had been keen for them to meet as soon as possible.

Saturdays were normally the busiest days at Long Bamber Stables but, with the police still conducting their investigations, there was nothing Lucinda could usefully do – just tot up the amount of money she was losing while the stables were out of commission.

'Donal,' Lucinda explained, 'is always around Long Bamber Stables. He's always around anywhere where there are horses.'

'You mean he works for you?'

'No, Jude. Not officially, anyway. I might give him the odd tenner for helping out, but he's not on the pay-roll.'

'So what does he do?'

'He's an ex-jockey. Really does know what makes horses tick. If you've got a stallion with a bad attitude, Donal's your man to sort it out. You've got a mare who's having trouble foaling, same thing. I recommend him to any of my owners who've got problems the vet can't sort out. Donal seems genuinely able to communicate with horses.'

'So, what, is he some kind of healer?' Carole couldn't say the final word without an infusion of scepticism.

'I don't know about that, but he can sometimes work wonders. Mind you, great though his communication skills with horses, he's not so hot when it comes to humans.'

'Oh?'

'I'm afraid, Jude, that Donal has rather a propensity for getting into fights. He's got a drink problem, and every drink he takes seems to shorten his temper a bit more. He's been inside a good few times because of the fighting.'

'And that's why the police have taken him in?' asked Carole.

'Presumably. A violent death, and the first person they look for is someone with a track-record for violence. A prison record suits them even better.'

'You said you know he's not guilty. How do you

know?' asked Jude. 'Have you got proof that he wasn't at the stables at the relevant time?'

'No, I don't. He could have been there, for all I know. But Donal's not capable of murder.'

'Did he and your husband get along?' asked Carole.

'No, they didn't actually. Walter thought Donal was a thieving layabout – which he was sometimes – and Walter didn't want him hanging around Long Bamber. I didn't mind, because sometimes he was very useful to me. That was another issue on which my husband and I did not see eye to eye. Walter was always an intolerant bigot.'

No inhibitions about speaking ill of the dead then. Lucinda Fleet was maintaining the detachment she'd shown when first informed of her husband's death.

'You used the word "thieving",' said Carole. 'Was that just colourful language or do you mean Donal actually was – is a thief?'

'Oh, he's a thief all right. I have to have eyes in the back of my head when he's around the stables. But that's part of the deal with him. If you want to take advantage of his knowledge of horses, then you have to reconcile yourself to losing a bit of small change, or tack, or anything else you've left lying around.'

'His knowledge of horses must be pretty excep-tion-al.' Carole sniffed.

'It is. That's the point.'

There was an asperity in Lucinda's tone which suggested Carole was rubbing her up the wrong way. Jude intervened to defuse the situation.

'Anyway, why did you want to talk to us? We don't

even know Donal, so we can't be much help providing an alibi for him or anything of that kind.'

'No, but you were the first there at the scene of – at the scene of the crime. You might have seen something that proves the police should be looking for someone else.'

'Don't imagine they didn't ask us about that,' said Carole. 'Those detectives gave us both quite a grilling.'

'Yes, but if there was just something . . .'

'The only detail I remember,' said Jude, 'and I told the police this, so it's nothing new – is that when I went in through the stable doors that night, I'm pretty sure I heard the noise of a gate or door closing the other side of the yard.'

'The murderer making his getaway?' asked Lucinda eagerly.

'Possibly. Maybe even probably.'

'But you didn't see anyone?'

'No, just heard the noise.'

'So that doesn't help Donal at all.'

'"Fraid not.'

'Where does Donal live?' asked Carole suddenly.

'Here, there, everywhere. Someone who knows as much about the local horse population as Donal can always find an empty loose box or outbuilding some-where to doss down in. So I suppose he's officially "of no fixed abode". Which is of course another reason for the police to arrest him.'

'I only ask because that night at the stables' – Carole had gone too far to cover up her professional lapse now – 'I went into what I believe you call the tack room?'

'The big one?'

'Yes.'

'That's my tack room, where I keep all the tack that belongs to the stables. Every owner has their own tack room too, but theirs are much smaller.'

'Well, I went in there, you know, having seen the body – looking for someone to help – and I saw that there was a kind of bed made up there, with a sleeping bag.'

'Yes, that sometimes gets used. If a horse is ill or foaling, some of the owners insist on staying on the premises. It's not used very often.'

'I got the impression, the night I was there, that it had been used quite recently.'

'No,' said Lucinda firmly. 'I'd know if someone was sleeping there.'

'So Donal never slept there?'

'Good God, no. I put up with a lot from him, but there's no way I'd let him doss down in my stables. Other people's stables, maybe. Well, I know he squats in other people's stables. Not mine.'

'Ah. Right.'

The conversation was temporarily becalmed. Lucinda Fleet still reminded Jude of a smaller, more mature version of Sonia Dalrymple. But close to, the differences between the two women were more cruelly marked. Lucinda looked older than she had in the police spotlights at Long Bamber Stables. Probably late forties. Her face, which must once have been as pretty as Sonia's, was scored with tiny lines and weathered by a lifetime of working out of doors. Though she took care of the nails, her hands were cracked and reddened. Even so, all the hard manual work – and presumably the riding – had left her with an enviably trim figure.

Beneath the woman's no-nonsense exterior, Jude could sense a deeply hidden thread of pain. Not the pain of her recent bereavement, but something longer-lived and more profound. Maybe one day Jude would find out its source.

Carole jump-started the conversation again. 'Just another thing about this Donal . . .'

'Yes?'

'You describe him as a kind of vagrant, who's always hanging around places where there are horses.'

'If you like.'

'Well, isn't that exactly the sort of person the police suspect was responsible for all these knife attacks on horses?'

'No!' Lucinda was suddenly animated and furious. 'Donal would never do anything like that! He might hurt a human being – he's done that often enough in his cups – but there's no way he'd ever do harm to a horse. Donal loves horses.'

Jude came in smoothly to ease the slight atmosphere following this exchange. 'Could I get you another fizzy water, Lucinda?'

'No, thanks.'

'Or . . . we were thinking of having lunch here. I don't know if you . . .'

'No. I never have lunch.' She looked at her watch, a man's one on a battered leather strap. (Maybe Walter's? Maybe her one gesture of mourning for her dead husband?) 'I must get back to the stables. Always too much to do.'

'Incidentally,' asked Jude, 'about the stables, Lucinda.'

'Hm?'

'What are your plans?'

'What do you mean?'

'For Long Bamber Stables. I mean, now Walter's dead?'

Lucinda looked at Jude curiously. 'Well, keep the business going. I have no other visible means of support. Walter's death doesn't really make much difference to that.'

'Oh?'

'Walter was only ever front of house. Schmoozing up to the owners – particularly the women. He never did any of the actual hard work.'

'Was that because his injuries prevented him from doing any?'

Lucinda Fleet let out a snort of derisive laughter. 'It was very variable – what Walter's injuries did and didn't allow him to do.'

'Ah.'

'No, he was fundamentally lazy. Loved life back when he was the golden boy of eventing, and people fell over themselves to do things for him. When he lost that status, he still expected people to fall over themselves to do things for him. Only the trouble was, by then he wasn't surrounded by "people". Just me. Which meant that I ended up doing everything. I know it doesn't do to say such things, but it's a huge relief to me that Walter's dead.'

That was pretty unambiguous. The two neighbours exchanged a look. Carole reckoned they were both thinking exactly the same thing: Lucinda Fleet was as tough as the old boots she was wearing. But that wasn't what Jude was thinking.

'Do you think there's something going on with her and Donal?'

'Who – Lucinda?'

'Yes, obviously, Jude.'

'Why should there be?'

'Well, she made no secret of the fact that her marriage was unhappy, so maybe she sought – I don't know what the word is – solace perhaps?'

'Sex.'

'All right. Outside the marriage? Maybe that was a reason why she liked having Donal around so much, and why Walter loathed him?'

'I think you've been reading too much *News of the World*, Carole.'

'I have *never* read the *News of the World.*'

'I know you haven't. Just a joke. But you do seem to be developing rather a prurient mind. Isn't it possible that Lucinda just found Donal useful to help out with the horses – like she said?'

'Well, yes, it's possible,' Carole conceded, 'but there

has been a murder here. High emotions are involved. If Donal was Lucinda's lover, he might well have wanted Walter out of the way. And the police must have had some stronger reason to arrest him, you know, beyond the fact that he's a vagrant who hangs round horses.'

'They haven't arrested him. They've only taken him in for questioning.' Jude found it odd saying lines like that. Usually, it was Carole, with her Home Office background, who was hot on details of police procedure.

But her friend was too excited to bother about such things. 'I think it's very likely that Donal did kill Walter Fleet.'

'Which Donal are we talking about here? The ex-jockey?'

They hadn't heard the approach of Ted Crisp to their alcove, bearing the steak and Guinness pies they'd both ordered.

'Yes,' said Jude. 'Why – do you know him?'

'Certainly.' Ted scratched his beard. 'He holds something of a record here, actually.'

'What's that?'

'He is the only person I have ever banned from the Crown and Anchor. There have been people who I've warned, but generally speaking the natives of Fethering are a biddable, docile lot. Donal's the only one who's ever started a fight in here.'

'Who did he have a fight with? Was the other man one of your regulars?'

'The other man used to come in occasionally. Won't be doing that so much now, though.'

'Oh?'

'Because he's dead. He was that Walter Fleet – you know, the one who got stabbed up at Long Bamber.'

'And Donal picked a fight with him? In here?' asked Carole.

'That's right. Six months ago, maybe a bit longer. Hot summer evening, I remember that.'

'Do you know what the fight was about?'

'Hard to tell. Donal was so drunk, he was hardly intelligible. And Walter wasn't in a much better state either. They had this big slanging match, and then Donal went for Walter.'

'If they had a slanging match,' said Jude, 'you must have heard something.'

'It was all pretty indistinct. But I do remember Donal shouting something like, "You're not worthy of her! She's beautiful and you don't deserve her!"'

Chapter Ten

In spite of what Lucinda had said in his defence, Donal – who must have a surname, though neither Carole nor Jude knew it – was looking the most likely candidate for the killer of Walter Fleet. And that impression was confirmed when Jude heard from Sonia Dalrymple that the horses were being allowed to return to Long Bamber Stables. That news definitely implied the police's investigations were at an end. They had got their man.

Carole and Jude were disappointed by this conclusion, but they couldn't really argue with it. Starved of information as they were, they knew any alternative theories they produced about the crime would be nothing more than conjecture. They weren't privy to the facts at any level, whereas the police seemed to have more than enough facts at their fingertips to secure a conviction.

So, without a murder mystery to worry away at, they would both have to return to their normal lives. For Jude that would not be too much hardship – back to the routine of Woodside Cottage, her clients, her occasional mysterious visits to London. (The mystery of these visits was really only in Carole's mind. Jude had a wide circle of friends, many of whom her neighbour was destined never to meet. She also had lovers, though there were more of these in Carole's imagination than reality. Jude didn't deliberately hide the details of her London relationships, but Carole was always too genteel to enquire directly about them. So the aura of mystery intensified – a situation which, in fact, suited Jude very well.)

For Carole, however, the return to normal life would not be so easy. The murder had offered a welcome distraction from thoughts of Stephen and Gaby's marriage. Her son still hadn't rung back. She couldn't put off making a phone call to David much longer.

The day after their meeting with Lucinda Fleet, she steeled herself to do the deed. Sunday, he was sure to be in. In his little flat in Swiss Cottage. The flat she had never seen and never intended to see. How did retired civil servants like David Seddon spend their time in little flats in Swiss Cottage? That was a question towards which she did not allow her mind to stray.

She had to look his number up. It was the only number she ever had to look up. Every other one she remembered. A psychologist would have had a field day with that.

'Hello.'

'David, it's Carole.'

'Ah. Erm . . . hello.'

He didn't sound either surprised to hear her, or particularly moved by the fact that she'd rung him. It

was impossible for her to know what he was thinking –
as indeed it had been right through their marriage.

'How are you?'

'Not so bad. You, Carole?'

'Mustn't grumble.'

Neither of them contemplated volunteering more
about their lives than this. In the run-up to Stephen and
Gaby's wedding, David had tried to make some kind of
rapprochement towards his ex-wife. Now he seemed to
have given up the unequal struggle. Carole preferred it
that way.

'I was just wondering, David, whether you'd heard
anything of Stephen and Gaby recently . . .?'

'Erm . . . not very recently.' Apparently it was the
first time he'd thought about them for a while. 'No, I
suppose I haven't, not . . . erm . . . very recently.'

Carole had forgotten how much his little habit of
hesitation grated on her. 'So you haven't seen them?'

'Not since . . . well, not since Christmas, now I
come to think of it.'

How could he not have thought of it for so long?
How did David actually spend his retirement? What
thoughts did actually go through his head?

'No, I haven't either. I spoke to Gaby a few days ago,
but . . . I just wondered if you had any news of them.'

'No, I haven't. But I'm . . . erm . . . sure they'll be in
touch. When they've . . . erm . . . when they've got
something to say.'

Yes. So that was it. As she put the phone down,
Carole wished bitterly that she hadn't made the call.
Hearing David's voice had only upset her more, and

brought back to her mind Stephen's inheritance of bad relationships.

'Jude, it's Sonia.'

'Hello. Everything all right?'

'Well, yes.'

Tuesday had come round again. Walter Fleet had been dead for nearly a week. There had been no word of funeral plans, and there wouldn't be any for a while. Police forensic investigations had not finished; they had yet to release the body.

'You sound a bit uptight, Sonia.'

'No, no, I'm fine.' But the tension in her voice contradicted her words. 'I just, um . . . I just wondered whether you would come and have another look at Chieftain.'

'I'm happy to, but I didn't do him much good last time.'

'No, but you were distracted. With Imogen around and everything. I really do think it'd be worth you having another go.'

'OK. If that's what you want.'

'When could you come up here?'

'I thought the horse had gone back to Long Bamber.'

'Yes, most of them have. But Chieftain and Conker are still here.'

'Right. I could come when you like, really . . .'

'This afternoon?'

After the call had ended, Jude had the very firm

impression that Sonia Dalrymple wanted to see her about something. And it wasn't Chieftain.

As she walked up from the towpath towards the house, Jude surmised that she was not the only visitor that afternoon. A BMW, built on the lines of an ocean liner, stood on the gravel, and its appearance was quickly explained. As soon as she had opened the door to Jude's ring, Sonia whispered, 'Nicky's here. He's come back unexpectedly early from Frankfurt. He mustn't know you've come to see Chieftain.'

'Oh?'

'I'm afraid he'd be rather sceptical about the idea of *healing* a horse.'

'Just like my neighbour Carole. Well, look, don't worry. I'll just—'

'Good afternoon. I don't think we've met.'

The man who stepped out of the sitting room behind Sonia moved in an aura of charm. Nicky Dalrymple was tall, dark-haired and almost unfeasibly handsome. His welcoming smile was formed by perfect teeth and, though his life seemed to be spent shuttling from one international hotel to another, he clearly spent plenty of time in those hotel's gyms. The polo shirt, casual jacket and chinos he wore looked like a catalogue illustration. He and Sonia did make a dazzlingly attractive couple, entirely in keeping with their luxurious home and fleet of expensive cars.

'Hello, I'm Jude.' She could see the panic as Sonia searched for an alternative explanation for her arrival.

'Nicky Dalrymple.' His handshake was predictably firm and strong.

'I just popped by to talk to Sonia about a charity event I'm setting up, but I can easily call another time.' Jude had never had a problem with lying when the necessity arose.

'Nonsense. Come on in. We were just having some tea. Be easy enough to find another cup, won't it, Sonia?'

'Yes, of course, Nicky.'

While she scuttled off to the kitchen, he led Jude into the sitting room. She had not been in this part of the house on her previous visit, but again the image was straight from the pages of an interior-design magazine. The furthest wall was all glass, with a vista to a terrace, the garden – remarkably neat and sculpted for February – the paddocks, and then up towards the comforting contours of the South Downs.

Nicky Dalrymple gestured Jude towards one of the plethora of sofas.

'I gather from Sonia that you're just back from Frankfurt.'

'Yes. A meeting didn't last as long as it was scheduled, thank God, so I was able to get an earlier flight. Always love getting back here, but . . . I'm afraid what I do is very time-hungry.'

'I can imagine. Banking, isn't it?'

'In the broadest sense, yes.'

'Well, that's a subject about which I cannot claim to know anything – and please don't feel that you need to explain it to me.'

That prompted another of his perfect smiles. 'Very well, I won't. And what do you do . . . Jude – was that right?'

'Yes.' Having been tipped off about Nicky Dalrymple's views on complementary medicine, she contented herself with, 'Oh, I'm retired.'

Fortunately he didn't have the opportunity to follow this up with questions about her past career, because Sonia came in at that moment with the required cup and saucer.

Jude commented on the beauty of the view, and some conversation ensued about the advantages of living in the Fethering area. Nicky asserted that, as soon as he got home, he felt he was shedding an accumulation of stress, like a snake discarding an old skin.

Though getting home may have had that effect on him, Jude didn't get the impression it worked the same magic for Sonia. In the presence of her husband she seemed positively on edge, trying to anticipate his reaction to anything that was said, desperate perhaps to please. Jude received a new insight into the condition of Sonia's marriage, and perhaps a clue to the reason why she had sought help in alternative therapy.

'I gather from Sonia that all Fethering is talking about the murder up at Long Bamber Stables.'

'Yes. Didn't you know Walter Fleet?'

'No. Sonia does all the horsey stuff. I'm afraid I don't have time. When we bought Chieftain I had this idea of riding him out with the hunt, but – God, life takes over, doesn't it?' There was no doubt that Nicky Dalrymple knew how to ride. He carried an air of omnicompetence: a man who'd played all the right sports at all the right schools, and probably been captain of most of them. 'Anyway, now the government's banned hunting, that all becomes a bit academic. Perhaps we should think about getting rid of Chieftain.'

'Oh, we can't do that,' said Sonia, shocked.

'I didn't say we would, darling. I said we'd have to think about it.' But when he did think about it, if he decided that the horse should go, Jude knew no amount of argument would change his mind.

'Maybe the girls' pony's becoming surplus to requirements too.' Nicky continued. 'What's he called?'

'She. She's called Conker,' Sonia replied, with a weary intonation which suggested her husband made a point of not remembering the name. 'And we couldn't possibly get rid of her. Alice and Laura would kill us.'

'Who knows? A bit of time at boarding school's going to change their priorities. Entirely possible that they'll come back for the Easter holidays without a thought of horses in their head. They'll probably have moved on to boy bands, or possibly' – he shuddered – 'even real boys.'

'They don't meet any real boys at that school.'

'Don't you believe it. If they're anything like I was at boarding school, they'll somehow manage to arrange encounters with the opposite sex.' He laughed a man-of-the-world laugh.

'Well,' said Sonia firmly, 'we'll wait until we find out the girls' views about Conker before we even think of getting rid of her.'

Interesting, Jude thought, how much stronger

Sonia's defence had been when her daughters' concerns were at risk rather than her own. Chieftain was her horse, but she'd let him go if Nicky insisted. There was no way, though, that she'd let the twins be steam-rollered. Jude was also getting the impression that Alice and Laura had inherited their father's strong will, in fact that they were quite possibly right little madams. Sonia's role in the family was that of making concessions to everyone.

Jude was also interested to note that Nicky Dalrymple was behaving as if the conversation was a kind of performance, including her in their domestic life. His ordered family circumstances were almost being paraded in front of her.

'Anyway, about this murder,' he went on, 'I gather from Sonia that the police have arrested someone?'

'Technically only taken someone in for questioning,' said Jude. 'Some kind of itinerant horse expert called Donal.'

Nicky raised his eyebrows in the direction of his wife. 'You didn't tell me you knew the suspect's name, darling.'

'I didn't know it.'

Jude suspected that Sonia was lying.

'He's not that Donal who came round once to look at the girls' pony . . . erm . . .?'

'Conker.'

'Yes. Was it him?'

'I don't know.' Sonia was flustered, and she looked to Jude for help. 'Do you know anything more about this Donal?'

'Just that he knows about horses. He's helped out Lucinda Fleet from time to time up at Long Bamber Stables. Bit of a reputation for being light-fingered – and for starting fights when he's in his cups.'

'Got to be the same fellow.' Nicky Dalrymple grimaced with distaste. 'Scruffy little herbert, whose Irish charm I have to say didn't go far with me.'

'But he did cure Conker of that coughing.'

'How do you know the pony wouldn't have got better on its own?'

'Well, I can't prove that, Nicky, but—'

'I think that Donal was full of blarney and Jameson's. I told him so at the time. Just a bloody snake-oil salesman, getting money out of gullible housewives for his so-called healing. Do you believe in all that mumbo-jumbo, Jude?'

She could feel focused pleading from Sonia's eyes, and replied sedately, 'One does hear remarkable instances of alternative therapies working.'

'Huh! Mind you, there's usually another explanation for whatever's happened. A lot of injuries and illnesses just clear up under their own steam.'

Nicky Dalrymple was clearly not used to being contradicted. In other circumstances Jude would have happily introduced him to the concept, but for his wife's sake she knew this wasn't the moment. 'Well, thank you so much for the tea. I'd really better be off.'

'But you haven't talked about your charity thing to Sonia yet.'

For a moment Jude was thrown, having forgotten

the lie she had told. Then hastily she said, 'We can do that another time.'

'No, tell me what the charity is. We always try to do our bit, don't we, Sonia? We're personally major contributors to the ILPH.'

'I'm sorry, I don't know what that is.'

Sonia supplied the information. It stood for the International League for the Protection of Horses.

'So what is the charity you're working for?' Nicky Dalrymple insisted.

'Erm . . . well . . . It's the NSPCC.' The only one she could think of on the spur of the moment, but a perfectly admirable charity. And it did help humans rather than animals, which Jude – unlike most residents of West Sussex – always thought was the greater priority.

'Let me give you a contribution then.' And Nicky Dalrymple's cheque book came out of the pocket of his jacket. 'Now, who should I make it payable to?'

Jude looked across at Sonia, who made an imperceptible shrug. If Jude's lie was going to bring benefit to some suffering children, then what harm was done? It wasn't as if Nicky couldn't afford it.

'Just to the NSPCC then, please.'

Nicky filled in the cheque, pulled it out of the book and handed it across with a flourish. 'But don't you want to talk about the details of the event . . . because I've got some papers I should be going through – so if you want to be on your own?'

'No, really. I'd better be on my way.' Jude had an instinct that, even if he were not in the same room, her husband's presence in the house might inhibit Sonia from saying what she really wanted to.

'Well, I'll say goodbye then. Pleasure to meet you, Jude. Jude . . . what? I don't know your surname.'

'Everyone just calls me Jude.'

Nicky stayed in the sitting room, and Sonia closed the door against the potential draught as she led the way to the front door.

'What did you want to see me about?' Jude whispered.

'I just wondered if you'd heard anything from the police, you know, about what evidence they have against Donal?'

'No more than anyone else has. What I've heard on the news bulletins.'

Sonia looked disappointed, but not surprised at being disappointed. 'You haven't any idea what he's said to them?'

'How could I? I'm afraid it's only in crime fiction that the police share all the latest developments on a case with nosey local spinsters.'

She'd said it as a joke, but Sonia didn't smile. Instead, she whispered, 'But if you do hear anything about what Donal's said, you will let me know, won't you, Jude?'

Odd. Two women, thought Jude as she walked along the towpath towards Fethering, both deeply concerned about a vagrant Irishman. For the same reason? Or for different reasons? More importantly, for what reason?

The weather had suddenly turned very cold. After

a few mild days that had held the promise of spring, winter had reasserted its icy grip. The waters of the Fether, rushing fast past the towpath, looked icily uninviting, and the leaden sea beyond held no element of welcome. Jude's hand, nestling for warmth into the pocket of her fleece, encountered something unexpected, and closed around Nicky Dalrymple's cheque. She looked at it. A hundred pounds for the NSPCC. Oh well, it's an ill wind. Who was it who said lying was a bad thing?

Chapter Eleven

The Seaview Café on Fethering Beach was, surprisingly, open all year round. In the summer, the tall windows at the front were concertina-ed back and the concrete floor was so covered with sand it seemed like a continuation of the beach. The café was open from eight in the morning till eight at night. Then the space was loud with the shrieks of children, and the blue-overalled women behind the counter were kept busy all day supplying pots of tea, fizzy drinks, hamburgers, chips, crisps and ice creams.

In the winter everything was different. All the windows were shut, and the place steamed up like a huge terrarium. Wind wheezed through ventilation grilles and the odd cracked pane. Opening hours were eleven to five, and the average age of the winter population trebled that of the summer. The occasional child whose route from school passed the beach might drop in for a Coke and a bag of crisps but, generally speaking, the customers were well past seventy, and usually sitting on their own. The women behind the counter had plenty of time to peruse their *Sun*s and *Daily Mail*s, and among the clientele pots of tea were made to last a very long time.

Carole Seddon usually avoided the place. In the summer it was too noisy, in the winter too dispiriting. But that Wednesday afternoon she'd had no choice. She'd got delayed shopping and, as a result, started late for Gulliver's afternoon walk. Because of her rush, she had omitted to have a pee when she got back to High Tor and on the beach, feeling the sudden drop in temperature, found herself desperate to relieve herself. The toilets on the front were locked against vandals throughout the winter, so the Seaview Café was her only option. Also, dogs were allowed in there.

Carole was by nature a law-abiding soul, and she could no more have gone into the café to use its facilities without making a purchase than she could have dismembered someone with a chainsaw. So, with mounting discomfort, she ordered a pot of tea at the counter and waited while it was prepared. She then took the tray with obsessive concentration across to a table and tied Gulliver's lead to a convenient radiator pipe before rushing off to the ladies.

When Carole returned, considerably relieved, she noticed a woman she vaguely recognized, zipped up into an anorak and sitting at an adjacent table. Whether she had been there earlier, Carole couldn't say – taking in the other customers had not been her primary priority – but the laying-out of the woman's tea things and the half-eaten doughnut suggested she had.

'Looked like you were in rather a hurry. It's the cold weather.'

The woman's smile identified her to Carole, and allayed any resentment she might have felt about public discussion of her bladder. It was Hilary Potton, who clearly didn't think Carole remembered their previous encounter. 'We talked in Allinstore. I was on the till.'

'I recognized you.'

'I do four to eight every weekday except Wednesday, with a late night on Friday. This is my day off.'

'Not a very nice one. Freezing out there, isn't it?'

'Certainly is. Handsome-looking dog. Labrador?'

'Mm. Called Gulliver. Extremely good-natured, but not very bright.'

'Oh, they're good family dogs. We had one . . . in happier times.' Hilary sighed rather dramatically. She indicated the plastic seat opposite her. 'If you'd like to join me . . .?'

It went against Carole's every instinct to start fraternizing with people she didn't know, but this was different. She had been trying to find out more about Hilary Potton, she had made the initial contact, and now she was being offered a second opportunity on a plate. 'Well, if you don't mind . . .' she said, moving her tray across to the other table.

'I'm just here waiting for my daughter. She's at the house with her father. Things are easier at the moment if we don't meet.'

'Yes, I gathered from what you said at Allinstore that all was not well.'

Hilary Potton snorted at the inadequacy of this description. 'All not well? What we're actually talking

102

about here is a state of total war. I'm afraid my husband and I just do not communicate. I've tried to build bridges, but he's tried even harder to destroy them. Are you married?'

'I'm not wearing a wedding ring.'

'Doesn't mean anything these days.'

'All right. I'm not married. I'm divorced.' Carole still had difficulty in saying the words.

'So will I be soon – thank God!'

'Oh yes,' said Carole, casually probing. 'You implied when we spoke in Allinstore that all wasn't well with your marriage.'

'You have a gift for understatement. I'm sorry, I don't know your name.'

They quickly established their identities and addresses. Carole was cautious not to reveal that she already knew Hilary's details. She thought further prompting might be needed to get back to the subject of the Pottons' failing marriage, but it proved unnecessary.

'So was your story the same as mine? Husband couldn't keep his hand out of other women's knickers?'

'No. No.' David may have had many shortcomings, but that wasn't one of them.

'Well, in my case, Alec – that's my husband – so far as I can gather, he'd been at it with various women virtually from the moment we got married. And I, trusting little domestic idiot that I was, never suspected a thing. He's always travelled a lot – he's a salesman – so I believed all his stories about having to work late, having to stay over for conferences, and all the time . . .' She seethed like a kettle boiling dry. 'Let me tell you, it's going to be a long time before I ever trust a man again. I think most women would be a darned sight better off without a man in their lives.'

'I agree.' Carole nodded towards Gulliver, trying to lighten the atmosphere. 'Dogs are much more reliable.'

'What really humiliates me is the sense that everyone else probably knew about it. All the fine folks of Fethering sniggering at me behind their hands and saying, "Oh, Hilary's such a meek little fool. She hasn't a clue what's going on."'

'They always say the wife's the last one to know.'

'That's not much comfort!' This outburst prompted a ripple of geriatric interest in the Seaview Café. In a lower voice, Hilary Potton apologized, 'Sorry. As you may have observed, it still rather gets to me.'

The geriatrics returned to contemplating their cooling and dwindling cups of tea.

'I'm not surprised, Hilary. If it's any use – and I know "time is a great healer" is a peculiarly unhelpful comment – but things do get better eventually.'

'Thanks for the "eventually" – that's really cheered me up!'

'Sorry.'

'No, Carole. I do appreciate it. I'm sorry, at the moment I'm still just so . . . blindingly angry.'

'Maybe part of that never does go away.' Carole thought of the way David's voice, his constant 'erms' could drive her into unreasoning fury.

'It's the selfishness of it that really gets to me. The money, apart from anything else. I mean, I've supported Alec all the way in his career. When I first knew him, he worked in a shop. Then I backed his decision to get a marketing training and become a salesman, which meant, goodbye, regular salary and hello, commission. And I've stood by him when times were hard, been prepared to tighten my belt a bit, put Imogen through the state school system, dig into my own savings for her orthodontic work, forgo family holidays, that kind of thing. And now I discover that all the time Alec was spending our money – our money! – on squiring various tarts out for meals and booking them into hotels for sleazy sexual encounters. Ooh, it makes me so furious!'

Carole managed to interject a 'Yes', but that was all she was allowed.

'And the effect it's had on Imogen – that's our daughter – well, I just daren't begin to imagine the harm he's done her by his selfish and appalling behaviour. I mean, she's at a very difficult stage of any girl's life and Alec's just adding to the pressure. This is the time when she should be forming her own ideas about the adult world, about how relationships work. What kind of an example is she getting from her father?

'And she's feeling our change of economic circumstances. Imogen's absolutely mad about horses, and we were getting near the point of buying her her own pony – but now, oh no, we haven't got any money for that kind of luxury. We haven't got any money for anything. We've still only got the one car and Alec has first call on that because he has to use it for his work. So that's extremely inconvenient. And now I'm reduced to the indignity of sitting like a dumb teenager behind the till at Allinstore, simply to pay the grocery bills.'

Hilary Potton had to stop, simply to regain her breath, so Carole managed to ask, 'And is Imogen as angry with her father as you are?'

'Huh! No. Isn't that bloody typical? In a show of classic adolescent perverseness, she's actually taking Alec's side. She blames me for some reason. Well, I know what the reason is. It's because I'm there all the time. I'm the one who does all the day-to-day looking after her. I'm the one who sees she gets fed, that her washing gets done. I'm the one who tidies up after her and has to listen to her whingeing about everything all the time. And Alec – as he always has done – just swans in every now and then and buys her affection with treats. Even now – even when our financial circumstances are so dire – he keeps taking her out for meals. And, of course, because she hardly ever sees him, Imogen worships the ground he walks on. Ooh,' she seethed, 'until the last eight months I hadn't realized just how much of a disadvantage it is to be born a woman. We think we've all got liberated, we keep being told we have equal opportunities, but when it comes to the crunch, everything is skewed in favour of men. And we're so powerless to do anything about it. You hear these stories of spurned wives cutting up their husband's suits or spilling all their vintage wines or smashing up their BMWs, and until recently I've thought, "Oh, for heaven's sake, how petty!" Recent events have changed my mind, though. I'd do anything I could to get revenge on that bastard Alec.'

Carole's wish to find out more about Hilary Potton was certainly being fulfilled. In spades. But she reflected that, to unleash such an outburst on a virtual stranger, the woman must have very few close friends. Or maybe her fury against her husband was just so strong that anyone unwary enough to come within range was liable to get caught in the crossfire.

'You say your daughter's interested in horses . . .'

'What?' Hilary Potton had to be dragged out of her dreams of vengeance. 'Oh, yes.'

'I was just thinking . . . Because there was that dreadful business up at Long Bamber Stables. I hope she had nothing to do with that set-up, because it would just be another trauma for the poor girl.'

'That certainly hasn't helped. She's still in a pretty bad state; she seemed to go into total shock when she first heard about it. You see, Long Bamber's the stables where Imogen's had all her riding lessons. She spends quite a lot of time up there, mucking-out and what have you. So, yes, she's heard all the gory details about Walter Fleet's death.'

'But – poor child – she wasn't round there at the time of the murder, was she?'

'No, thank goodness.' Hilary Potton looked affronted at the suggestion. 'Safely at home with me, I'm glad to say.'

'Good. And I'm sorry, this sounds very prurient, but since everyone in Fethering is discussing the murder, does Imogen have a theory about what happened? Has she said anything to you about—?'

'Shall we go then?'

They'd been too absorbed to hear her approach, but suddenly a girl who Carole assumed must be Imogen was standing beside them. She was wearing school uniform. Perversely, in spite of the cold, she had her fur-trimmed anorak hooked on a finger over her shoulder. A dyed ginger lock flopped over her spotty forehead. Her expression and body language matched perfectly: both bespoke sulky teenage resentment. Whether or not she'd heard the end of their conversation was impossible to know.

'Yes, Imogen. This is Carole Seddon.'

The girl nodded curtly and gestured towards the door. She was damned if she was going to show any interest in her mother's friends. She was damned if she was going to show interest in anything to do with her mother. She hadn't wanted to come to meet her in the Seaview Café, and was not about to start disguising her feelings on the subject.

Experience had taught Hilary Potton that trying to get politeness out of her daughter in this mood was a losing battle, so, with a hurried farewell and vague intentions to phone Carole and meet up again, she followed Imogen out of the Seaview Café.

Leaving Carole frustrated about her last, unanswered question, and pondering guiltily the effects of marriage breakdown on the children involved.

*

On that evening's Radio 4 six o'clock news it was announced that the police had released the man they had been questioning about the death of Walter Fleet. Without charge.

Chapter Twelve

'So you didn't get the impression that Hilary Potton was a murderer?'

'No, why should she be?'

'Just that anyone who had any involvement with Long Bamber Stables should be on our list.'

'Well, no, I don't think she is a murderer. Though I think she's a potential murderer.'

'Aren't we all, in the right circumstances?'

'Speak for yourself,' said Carole tartly. 'Mind you, the "right circumstances" for Hilary Potton would have to be very specific ones. There is only one situation in which she would murder someone.'

'Ah?'

'. . . and that's if the victim were her husband. Then I think she'd be capable of any atrocity.'

'But Walter Fleet was not her husband.'

'No. I don't even know whether she'd ever met him . . . though I assume she would have done. You know, dropping Imogen at the stables or picking her up.'

'Hm.' Jude sipped at her Sauvignon blanc in the High Tor kitchen on Wednesday evening. Maybe she was beginning to widen the cracks in Carole's gentility, she thought mischievously. Even a year ago, Carole would have insisted on their taking their drinks through to the sitting room. Hanging round kitchens drinking used to be total anathema to her – but she was changing.

'I was really surprised to hear that this Donal character has been released,' Carole mused. 'I'd been very definitely coming round to the view that he'd done it.'

'Well, it's good news, isn't it?'

'In what way?'

Jude grinned triumphantly. 'If he didn't kill Walter Fleet, then somebody else did. And we're still in with a chance of finding out who.'

'I'm afraid I'm going to have to cancel my appointment.'

'No problem. Lots of other things I can do Friday afternoon. Do you want to fix another date, Sonia?'

'Erm . . . no. Not at the moment. I'm sorry, everything's a bit all over the place. I'm rather stressed.'

'I thought that was why you were coming to see me,' said Jude.

'Yes.' There was a silence from the other end of the phone. 'The fact is . . . er . . . if we could leave it for a little while?'

'As I say, no problem.'

'Good.'

'And how about Chieftain?'

'Oh, he and Conker have gone back to Long Bamber.'

'No, I meant you are temporarily suspending your treatment with me. I wondered if the same went for Chieftain. Or has his lameness got better?'

'No, it hasn't. Yes, actually I would be grateful if you could have another go at him, Jude.'

'Of course. I still feel a bit frustrated by my failure last time. So, when could you make it?'

'Erm, well . . .' Sonia Dalrymple sounded uncharacteristically flustered. 'As I say, things are a bit . . .'

'Are you all right, Sonia?'

'Yes, absolutely fine.' The response was too quick to be genuine. 'Look, tell you what, Jude, because my movements are a bit unpredictable over the next week, would you mind going to try your powers on Chieftain on your own?'

'I don't mind, but what about him? He's not going to take very kindly to a relative stranger coming into his stall and fondling his knee, is he?'

'No, but Lucinda or Walter – that is, Lucinda or one of her grooms will hold him and keep him quiet while you do your stuff. He'll be fine with them.'

'OK, I'll have a go.'

'I'll give you Lucinda's number. And I'll give her a call first to say you'll be in touch. Then you can fix a time that's mutually convenient.'

'I'll do that. By the way, I assume you've heard that the police have released Donal without charge?'

'I did hear that, yes.' There was quite definitely a note of relief in her voice.

'By the way, it was a pleasure to meet Nicky the other day.' Though Jude wasn't quite sure 'pleasure' was the right word.

'He was pleased to meet you too.'

'And do please thank him on my behalf.'

'What for?'

'His donation to the NSPCC. It was a very generous cheque.'

'Oh, that's typical of Nicky – ever the master of the grand gesture.' For the first time, Jude almost heard a hint of criticism.

'Is he still with you?'

'No, he flew off to Singapore yesterday morning.'

And once again, there was unmistakable relief in the way the words were said.

Jude hadn't been back to Long Bamber Stables since the night of Walter Fleet's murder, and that Thursday morning the premises looked a lot less forbidding than on her previous visit. The weather had brightened and, though the February cold still scoured her face, the thin sun promised that, one day, there would be a spring.

She had come on her own, walking along the towpath, past Unwins, the mile or so to the stables. She hadn't told Carole about her visit. This was not with a view to excluding her friend from any part of their investigation – though she knew that, if Carole ever found out, that was the way she would see it. But Jude needed the minimum number of people around her when she was on a mission of healing. Her previous lack of success with Chieftain rankled – not because she allowed herself any vainglory about her healing skills, but because the failure felt like unfinished business. And, besides, the horse was still suffering.

Following the instructions Lucinda Fleet had given her on the phone, Jude let herself in by the main gates, and closed them behind her. In daylight she could get a much better view of the stable yard. What struck her most was how dilapidated all the structures were. On her previous visit, the moon and police spotlights had flattered the buildings. Now she could not be unaware of the ancient cracked weatherboarding, the rusting corrugated iron and missing tiles on the various roofs.

A couple of the stable doors were fully open. Their usual occupants, tethered to posts in the yard, puffed out steamy breath and clattered their hooves disconsolately on the stone surface while their stalls were mucked out. Jude could hear the scrape of thick-bristled brooms and spades from inside. She moved towards the nearest stall and found herself facing Lucinda Fleet, who was sweeping water out into the gutter round the edge of the yard.

'Ah, good morning. Can you wait till I finish this? Have to get up as much water as possible this time of year, otherwise it freezes. If you're cold, wait in the tack room over there. I won't be long.'

Given such an adventitious offer, Jude gratefully took it up, and walked across to the tack room. The interior was lit only by the light that came through the open door and a cracked, discoloured window. On the far wall were rows of saddles on metal supports.

Halters and bridles hung from pegs. Just inside the door, under the window was a high bench, whose surface was covered with horse impedimenta, some of which – like curry combs and riding crops – Jude could identify, but others had functions she could not begin to guess.

What was odd about the space was how clean everything was. From the description Carole had given of her torchlit visit to the tack room, Jude had expected everything to be blurred by a thick patina of dusk, and it took her a moment to realize that the new tidiness must have been the police's doing. Of course, the whole area was a crime scene. Every item within the tack room must have been examined for fingerprints or other clues. Some had probably been taken away for testing in forensic laboratories. And what remained had been neatly returned to its place, to await the accumulation of further layers of dust.

One item of equine equipment that wasn't on the bench was a bot knife. The pictures in the papers and on television news ensured Jude would have recognized one if it had been there. Its absence was hardly surprising. Though they might inspect and return most of the room's contents, the police were never going simply to clean and replace a murder weapon. But Jude thought it was a fair guess that the bot knife had been on the bench the night Walter Fleet died.

She looked at the ladder leading to the upper level. It didn't face the front door; it was at right angles to it. Screwing up her eyes with the effort of imagination, she tried to visualize the scene. Carole had said the little upstairs light had been on. Walter Fleet, maybe doing a security check around the yard, had seen the glow of that light through the tack-room window. He had opened the door, maybe seen the intruder, challenged him . . . And then?

After a quick look out across the yard to see that Lucinda was still involved in her mucking out, Jude crossed to the ladder and climbed up. The angle was very steep, not easy to ascend or descend in a hurry. She peered into the space at the top. Sufficient daylight penetrated up there for her to see that all evidence of anyone having slept there had been removed. The boards were bare, again swept unnaturally clean.

No surprise, really. The information available to the forensic police from a sleeping bag and other bedding must be invaluable. Maybe they had even found some DNA trace from Donal. Although Lucinda had denied he ever slept up there, from what she'd heard of the man, Jude reckoned he was quite capable of creeping in after dark when he needed a bed. Maybe evidence that he had been there was what had prompted the police to take him in for questioning.

As she lowered herself heavily down the ladder, Jude again tried to visualize what had happened: Walter Fleet standing in the doorway. No light except for the diluted moon and what spilled down from upstairs. If the intruder was up there, Walter might just about have been able to see him. Or her. Or to hear him. Or her. Whether or not the intruder had plans to commit burglary or some other crime, he or she was still a trespasser and had no right to be there.

Some kind of conversational altercation must presumably have taken place. Jude thought it unlikely that Walter had actually climbed up the ladder before finding his murderer. Made more sense that the murderer had come down to his level, with a view to escape. But Walter was barring the doorway. So the murderer must have picked up the bot knife from the bench and attacked the man who stood in the way of his freedom. Walter would have staggered back from the first onslaught, which would tie in with where the blood spots in the yard had started. The murderer continued, slashing away at his victim in a frenzy, until Walter Fleet fell backwards, dead. And then the murderer had rushed away from the scene through the wooden gate at the far side of the stable yard. Only moments before Jude had entered through the main gates.

That was the bit that was so frustrating. To think she'd been literally seconds away from seeing the perpetrator of Walter Fleet's murder.

Chapter Thirteen

'You look thoughtful.' Jude hadn't noticed Lucinda's approach, until she stood in the doorway.

'Yes, I'm sorry. A bit distracted. I'm afraid it's because . . .' She let the words trickle away. Probably not the right moment to raise the matter.

Lucinda Fleet had no such inhibitions. 'You're thinking about the night Walter died.'

'Well, I—'

'Don't feel embarrassed about it. That's all anyone who comes here thinks about. And for you – since you found the body – it must be impossible for you not to think about what happened.'

'I can't deny it. But how are you coping?'

Lucinda shrugged. 'I'm coping, getting on with what has to be done here. As you probably know – since everyone in West Sussex seems to know – our marriage was not the happiest since records began. Once I've got over the trauma, I think I'll be quite relieved. Oh, and once the funeral's happened. Hopefully that'll kind of put a lid on things.'

'When is the funeral?'

'I wish I knew. The police haven't released Walter's body yet.'

'That must be awful for you.'

'Not the best fun I've ever had, no. God, what it'd be like for someone who actually loved their dead spouse, I can't imagine.'

'So the police are still doing forensic tests on . . . on the body, are they?'

'I assume so. I'm afraid I'm not the first person with whom they share information.'

Join the club, thought Jude. 'But presumably there's no doubt about how he was killed?'

'What on earth do you mean? You saw his body – slashed to pieces with that bot knife.'

'Yes, but sometimes a murderer might have killed someone by another method, and then slashed the body to disguise how he'd really died.'

Lucinda Fleet cocked a wry eyebrow at Jude. 'Big reader of crime fiction, are you?'

'Sorry. Just an idea. It's inevitable, when something like that happens, everyone comes up with pet theories about it. A lot of local gossip.'

Lucinda raised her eyes to heaven. 'Tell me about it. Well, congratulations on coming up with a theory I haven't heard before – and I've heard a good few of them. No, the bot knife is definitely what killed him. The police questioned me quite a bit about Walter's health, physical state, what have you. And left me in no doubt that it was the attack with the bot knife – wielded by some unknown assailant – that did for him.'

'Right,' said Jude thoughtfully. 'And I don't suppose you have any idea who that assailant might have been?'

The shoulders under Lucinda Fleet's faded body-warmer were raised in a nonchalant shrug. 'Not a clue. I would assume some vagrant who was dossing down in here—'

'But not Donal?'

'No, very definitely not Donal. And thank God the police have realized that too. You heard they released him?'

'Yes. So, you were saying?'

'Yes, well, I assume this vagrant – probably a drug addict hoping to find something here worth stealing – anyway, Walter must have disturbed him and – I don't know. Whoever it was, though, he may have done me a favour. Soon maybe I'll be able to reclaim what's left of my life.'

'Once you get the funeral out of the way.'

'Yes. That, as I said, will be a great relief to me. Not least because it is the last time I will ever have to see any of Walter's ghastly relatives.'

'You don't have any children, do you?'

'No.' Lucinda might have been about to say more on the subject, but decided against it.

'And – this is sheer nosiness, Lucinda, but since you know everyone in the area's coming up with their own theories about Walter's death . . .'

'Yes?' she asked patiently.

'Was Walter well heeled? Did he leave a lot of money?'

Lucinda Fleet let out a harsh laugh, and gestured

around the yard. 'What do you think? Neither of us had any secret stash of cash, I'm afraid. Everything we had we put into this place – which, as you can see, is in fairly desperate need of maintenance. And would have had that maintenance years ago, if we'd had any money to do it with.'

'Yes. I understand.'

'Anyway, perhaps we should go and have a look at Chieftain.'

The two horses who'd been tethered during the mucking out were now safely back in their stalls. Lucinda led the way across to a half-open loose box, over which a neat brass plate proclaimed the name 'Chieftain'. Hearing their approach, the owner came forward and poked his head out to see what was going on.

'You know a lot about horses, don't you?'

'If I don't now, I never will.'

'And what's your view on healers working with horses? Are you in the sceptical camp?'

'Certainly not. I've seen it work too often to be sceptical. No, I've come across quite a few horse healers in my time, and they can certainly do the business.' Lucinda slid across the outside bolt of the loose box. 'Come on, Chieftain boy. You come out and let Jude make you better.'

As soon as she addressed the horse, Lucinda Fleet was transformed. The brusque, even harsh, exterior she presented to her fellow humans was replaced by a sudden empathy, not a sentimental approach as to a pet, but a deep and strong understanding of how horses ticked.

Chieftain, clattering out into the yard, was clearly used to Lucinda's hand on his halter, but he eyed Jude warily, as if he recognized her but couldn't place where they'd met. She was once again struck by the enormous bulk of the horse, and the amount of potential for damage in that strong sleek body.

Lucinda led the gelding across to the rail where the other two horses had been tethered, but she kept hold of his halter. 'Stroke his nose, Jude. Give him a moment to get used to you.'

She did as she was told. Chieftain sniffed around her hand in an exploratory manner, then nuzzled his large nose towards her ear. This was not a gesture of affection; he was still assessing her. After a moment, he moved his head away, either satisfied that she was harmless, or simply bored with her.

'See if he minds you touching his leg.'

Jude did as Lucinda suggested. Very gently, as she had done before, she put first one hand on his upper thigh, then the other. Chieftain showed no signs of objecting, so she moved her hands slowly down until she could feel the warmth from his knee glowing under them.

'Right, if we can just keep very quiet and still, I'll see if I can "work my magic" on him.' Perhaps in an unconscious homage to Donal, she said the phrase with a trace of an Irish accent.

'Lucinda! We've come to ride! Could you get the horses ready!'

Chapter Fourteen

The would-be patrician voice came from a short stocky red-faced man, dressed in Barbour, jodhpurs and knee-length riding boots, all of which appeared to have come straight from the shop without any detours to collect mud or wrinkles. The costume of the tall, magenta-haired woman beside him matched his exactly and was equally untouched by real life. She was a good twenty-five years younger than him, and looked expensive.

With a look that contrived to say a lot about her opinion of the new arrivals, Lucinda whispered to Jude, 'Sorry, need to sort these out. Victor and Yolanta Brewis they're called. Just moved into the area. He's a property developer and she's – well, I'm not sure I can think of a nice word. I'll tether Chieftain to the rail.'

'Can I keep working on his knee?'

'If he doesn't mind. But if he gets at all restive, please stop. I don't think I'm insured for you getting kicked in the head.'

Jude tried to channel her energy into the injured knee, but it was hopeless. Not that Chieftain behaved badly – he was as docile as a rocking horse – but she couldn't focus on the job in hand. All she could hear was the loud conversation from the other side of the yard.

'Come on, Lucinda, chop, chop,' urged the man. 'I left a message earlier with one of the girls, asked for the horses to be ready when we arrived. I haven't got time to hang about, you know.'

'Nor have I,' said Yolanta, in heavily accented Eastern European English. 'I have an appointment with my personal stylist in Brighton at two o'clock.'

'I'm sorry,' said Lucinda, busying herself with collecting saddles and bridles from the tack room.

'Didn't you get my message?'

'No, I didn't, actually.'

'That's bloody bad. I spoke to a girl who said she'd pass it on. She deserves a good dressing-down. Where are your girls?'

'They only come in for a couple of hours in the morning. They've gone.'

'Well, make sure you find out who it was who took the message and give her a good dressing-down when you next see her.'

Lucinda Fleet didn't answer, but led the couple across towards two adjacent stalls. Over them, carved wooden plaques advertised the names 'Tiger' and 'Snow Leopard'. Lucinda opened one stall and led out Tiger. He was docile enough until he saw Victor Brewis. Baring his large teeth, he let out a whinny of disapproval.

'Hello, boy. I hope you're not thinking of trying it

on again with me today. I'm afraid I may have to show you who's master.'

'Mr Brewis,' Lucinda began tentatively, 'I'm honestly not sure that that's the right approach with Tiger. I think coaxing him probably works better. His mouth's still sore from the last time you—'

'Look, I'm paying you to look after my bloody horses, not give your opinions on how I should treat them. Tiger's my horse, and I know how to handle him.'

'Well, I'm not sure—'

'Come on. We're already behind because you didn't get my message. Tackle him up quickly.'

'Mr Brewis, "tackle him up" is not an expression that people in equestrian circles—'

'As I said, I don't want opinions from a bloody woman. Just get on with it.'

'Oh now, Victor,' said Yolanta coyly, 'you are being very rude. I also am a "bloody woman". Is it also my opinions you are not wanting?'

'No, my little angel.' The nickname could hardly have been less appropriate, as Victor Brewis looked the long way up to his wife's eyes. 'There are women and women, you know. I always value my little Yolanta's opinion.'

'I am glad to hear it. Otherwise I might stamp my little foot' – at least size 9 from where Jude was standing – 'and be horrid to my little Vixy. Might even make my little Vixy sleep in the spare room.'

'Oh, you wouldn't, Yolanta.'

'Not now my little Vixy has said he values his

125

Yolanta's opinion. Not this time. But you be careful, you naughty boy.'

Jude was glad Lucinda, saddling up Tiger, was not facing her while this trail of yuckiness trickled out. If they'd made eye contact, she'd never have managed to control her laughter.

'I think we should put the gentler bit on him today,' said Lucinda firmly to Victor Brewis.

'What?'

'We used the slotted Kimberwick last time. That was too hard on his mouth.'

'But the slotted Kimberwick gives me more control, doesn't it?'

'Yes, maybe, but—'

'Listen, I own the bloody animal. I'll do with it what I think is fit.'

'I'm just thinking of the horse. I don't want—'

'Mrs Fleet, will you please put on the slotted Kimberwick! That's the bit that gives me most control, and I like to be in control.'

Yolanta gigglingly complained about how masterful Vixy always was, while Lucinda pursed her lips and continued preparing Tiger for his master. Then she did the same for Snow Leopard. All the time the Brewises kept up their inane flirtation, stopping only occasionally to berate Lucinda for her slowness.

Their mounting was a sight to be seen. Snow Leopard was a much smaller horse – little more than a pony – and Yolanta had no difficulty getting one foot in the stirrup and swinging her other long leg over. From the way she moved, it looked like she had a personal trainer as well as a personal stylist.

But for Victor Brewis the task wasn't so easy. Not only did Tiger tower over him, the horse was in no mood to cooperate for someone he had reason to dislike. Lucinda held the bridle and tried to keep him calm; his owner kept getting one foot in the stirrup, while Tiger himself backed away. The three of them circled round the yard in some kind of grotesque square dance. Jude, who had long since given up any attempt to heal Chieftain's knee, watched, trying not to laugh too openly.

Eventually Victor was up, and with relief Lucinda opened the yard gate and let them out into the paddocks. Yolanta had clearly learnt about horses – perhaps in her Eastern European homeland – and she had quite a good seat. But her husband's sum of skill was less than zero. From the back, his rotund frame, bouncing on top of the huge horse, had all the elegance of a sack of potatoes.

'They are funny,' said Jude, as Lucinda crossed back towards her.

'Maybe.' The reply was accompanied by a rueful smile. 'But it's less funny when people are actually cruel to the horses.'

'And are they?'

Lucinda screwed up her face. 'Only by incompetence. I don't think Victor Brewis actually does anything that could be reported to the RSPCA. And I'm afraid I'm not in a position to report him, anyway.'

'How do you mean?'

'The way things are at the stables right now, I can't afford to lose two horses. The Brewises are right pains, but they do pay up on time, without fail – unlike some of my other owners.'

'Ah.'

'And they pay for a few little extras, as well. Like me getting the horses saddled up for them. I don't do that for anyone else, you know – well, except very small kids. Long Bamber's meant to be just DIY livery.' She sighed. 'No, I'm afraid I'm stuck with them.'

'But the way he talked to you . . .'

'That's how he gets his kicks, Jude. He doesn't realize it, but he gets charged extra for being rude to me. Victor Brewis, you see, suffers from small man syndrome – just loves throwing his weight around.'

'Born to rule, eh?'

'Far from it. People who're born to rule never act so autocratically. It's only people who're embarrassed about where they come from who behave like that.'

'You're right. And I'm sorry, I must ask you – slotted Kimberwick?'

'It's a horse's bit. Acts as brakes on the horse, actually. There are two slots for the reins, according to how much pressure you want to put on the horse's tongue. It's quite a tough bit for a horse with as soft a mouth as Tiger.'

'OK, I think I get it. More or less.'

Lucinda smiled a smile of small triumph. 'Mind you, I didn't put the slotted Kimberwick on Tiger.'

'But Victor Brewis thinks you did.'

'Yes!' Lucinda Fleet winked. 'Which shows exactly how much he knows about matters equestrian.'

Jude grinned and looked up at the tall horse beside her. 'I'm sorry, trying to do any healing on Chieftain was impossible with all that going on.'

'I'm not surprised. Do you want to have another go, now things have quietened down?'

'No. My concentration's shot to pieces. I won't be any good now.'

'OK.' Lucinda undid the rope from the rail, and led the horse away. 'Come on, Chieftain boy, you get back inside. Be nice and warm in there, and you can get back to your salt lick.'

Jude followed her, rather disconsolately. 'I don't know that I'm ever going to help him much. First time I've tried healing a horse, and it doesn't seem to be going too well.'

Lucinda didn't disagree or offer words of comfort. Instead she said, 'Maybe I should get Donal to take a look at the old boy.'

'Is Donal around? Have you seen him since his little session with the police.'

'No, but he'll be round the yard sometime soon,' said Lucinda as she bolted the door to Chieftain's stall. 'The original bad penny, that Donal.'

'I'd be interested to meet him.' Then, covering up, Jude added, 'I mean, to talk about horse healing, that kind of thing.'

'Well, as I say, he's bound to be round here before too long. Or, if you really want to find him . . .'

'Yes?'

'He always drinks up at the Cheshire Cheese – you know, up in Fedborough. It's near George Tufton's racing stables. All his lads drink in the Cheese. And, unless he's been banned again, that's where you'll find Donal.'

Well, thank you, Lucinda, thought Jude. You really have been most helpful.

Chapter Fifteen

There were a couple of hostelries in Fedborough that Carole and Jude had got to know quite well during a previous investigation. But not the Cheshire Cheese.

It was a dark low-ceilinged pub, which, unlike most in the town, had made no concessions to attracting the tourist trade. The others all claimed that the gleaming brasswork of their rustic interiors, their open fires and their hearty gastro-menus recreated how English pubs used to be. The Cheshire Cheese, however, was how English pubs really used to be – dingy, and quite possibly grubby beneath the gloom. The dark wood counter and tables looked as though they would be sticky to the touch. The smell of old beer and tobacco seemed to have permeated the very walls of the place.

Jude was subjected to another tradition of old English pubs as she entered – a cessation of the low-level chatter which had been going on and a circle of baleful eyes cast towards the unrecognized newcomer. Undeterred, but aware of the eyes following her, she strode boldly up to the bar. An anaemic girl looked up grudgingly from her copy of *Hello!* magazine, but didn't say anything.

'Could I have a glass of white wine, please? Do you have a Chardonnay?'

'We got white wine,' said the girl, and produced a half-full screw-top bottle from a cold shelf. In the murk, Jude couldn't assess the cleanliness of the wine glass, which was probably just as well. But she could assess that this was not a situation for subtlety of approach. 'I'm looking for a man called Donal. Expert on horses. I'm told he often drinks in here.'

Before the girl had a chance to say anything, there was a raucous shout from a table behind Jude. 'Got a new bit of stuff, have you, Donal?'

'Or is one of your wives after her maintenance?' suggested another voice.

Taking the money for the wine, the barmaid nodded towards the source of the catcalls. Jude turned to face a table of four rough-looking men dressed in grubby padded jackets, breeches and battered riding boots. Their size suggested they were all ex-jockeys, and the smell of horse that surrounded them suggested they all worked at George Tufton's racing stables. They seemed to fit the scale of the pub, as though its low ceilings had been designed to accommodate this pygmy species.

After the two shouts, the men fell silent, and there was no noise from any of the other tables. Jude was aware of her audience, and sensed that they looked forward to her making a fool of herself.

'So which one of you is Donal?'

All four men laughed, and seemed for a moment to

contemplate some trickery in their reply. But then three of them pointed to the one furthest away. His head was a scouring brush of short white bristles, his face deeply lined from a life spent in the open air, and, beneath a broken nose, his uneven greenish teeth hadn't come under the scrutiny of a dentist for a long, long time. Almost lost in the wrinkles around them, two blue eyes sparkled, calculating and devious. There was an air of danger about him. Even if Jude hadn't known of his reputation, she would have recognized a man with a combustibly short fuse.

'Donal, I wonder if I could talk to you?'

'You could talk to me. Whether I talk back or not is another matter.' The voice was Irish, but without the charm of leprechauns and blarney stones.

'Donal doesn't talk for free,' said one of his companions.

'Except to his mates in the police,' said another, prompting a round of discordant laughter.

'So what's the price of your talking?' asked Jude.

Donal grinned, baring more of the bombsite in his mouth, but let one of the others answer her question. 'Large Jameson's will usually get him started.'

Jude turned back to the counter. The barmaid, who like everyone else had been listening to the exchange, was already filling the glass. She rang up the price and took the proffered money. Clearly, speaking was something she avoided whenever possible.

Facing the four men again, Jude could see Donal stretching out his hand for the drink, but she held on to it. 'No, I want a quiet word. Come and sit with me at that table. It won't take long.'

This prompted rowdy suggestions from Donal's mates, on the lines of, 'You're on a promise there, you lucky sod,' and, 'When did you last have an offer like that?' But Donal, lured by the drink, did get up out of his seat and limp gracelessly across to the table Jude had indicated.

She raised her glass. 'Cheers.'

He said nothing till he had downed two-thirds of his Jameson's in a single swallow. 'So you want to know what the police asked me, do you?'

'What makes you assume that?'

'Recent experience. That's the only reason anyone wants to talk to me. God, you know the only product made in this entire area is gossip. And I assume you're just another local who's got some crackpot theory as to who killed Walter Fleet?'

He had come surprisingly near the truth, but Jude started off on another tack. 'In fact, it was about your expertise with horses I wanted to talk to you.'

'Oh?'

'I do some healing myself.'

He nodded, showing none of the derision those words sometimes prompted.

'. . . and someone asked me to try my skills on a horse that's lame. I'm afraid I haven't been successful, but I was told by Lucinda Fleet at Long Bamber that you might have more luck.'

'It wouldn't be luck,' he said.

'No, I'm sorry. I didn't mean that.'

'Where is the horse? Whose is it?'

'It's at Long Bamber.'

'Then I probably know it.'

'Called Chieftain.'

He smiled a crooked smile. 'Oh yes. Mrs Butter-wouldn't-melt-in-her-mouth Dalrymple. I'll bet I know why he's lame.'

'Well, I don't. Sonia didn't tell me.'

'No, she wouldn't.'

'Then why do you think he is lame?'

'I know. No reason why *you* should.'

The way he said this was not exactly rude, but it left her in no doubt she wasn't about to find out more.

'So would you have a look at him?'

'The Dalrymples have got plenty of money,' Donal ruminated. 'That stable complex of theirs must have set them back a bob or two.'

'Oh yes. I'm sure Sonia would pay for your services. She was going to pay me, but I couldn't ask for anything unless I got a result.'

'You're stupid,' he said, without vindictiveness. 'People should pay for the healing, not for the results.'

Donal downed the remainder of his Jameson's and grinned enigmatically. 'I'm like a slot machine. When your money runs out, I stop working.'

'You mean you'd like another of those?'

'If you want me to talk more, yes.'

Another silent transaction was conducted with the girl at the bar, and Jude placed the refilled glass back in front of her interviewee. 'As your friend said, the police

135

didn't keep you topped up with Jameson's when they asked you questions.'

'No.'

The monosyllable was spoken without intonation. Jude couldn't tell whether he'd follow the change of conversation or clam up on her. But she tried her luck.

'Presumably they didn't have anything on you? They just questioned you because you were quite often round Long Bamber Stables?'

'Oh, they had more reasons than that.' His eyes twinkled teasingly and he was silent, as if not going to give any more. Then he relented. 'They had the reason that I've a record for petty crime, a bit of thieving and that stuff. They had the reason that I drink, that I sometimes get violent in my cups. Then the reason that I'm Irish and . . . what? A vagrant? A diddicoy? A tinker? They had the reason that I don't live in a nice neat little house like everyone else in this *lovely part of England.*' The words were heavy with irony. 'Oh yes. So far as the police were concerned, I was the perfect identikit murderer. They were really gutted when they couldn't pin it on me. So they had to let me go in the end. They'd got nothing on me. Nothing that would stand up in court. And, more to the point, their time was up.' He pointed to his empty glass. 'As is yours.'

'But another refill will keep you talking?'

'For a very short time. I'm afraid a law of diminishing returns operates here, you see. I tend to drink faster as I go along.'

Another wordless transaction at the bar, and Jude was back at the table. Donal at least kept his side of the bargain and picked up the conversation exactly where he had left it. 'I think most of the detectives who questioned me have still got me down as the killer. But they don't have a shred of evidence.'

'So you think they're still keeping an eye on you?'

'That wouldn't surprise me at all.' He looked out through the clouded pub windows. 'Probably an unmarked car out there, waiting to pick up my trail when I get out of here.' He took a lengthy sip of the Jameson's. 'Which won't be for a long while yet.' He let out a cracked laugh. 'Yes, if I go down to Long Bamber to have a look at Chieftain, the police'll see that as further proof that I'm the villain.'

'How do you work that out?'

'Have you not heard the great cliché: The perpetrator always revisits the scene of the crime?'

'Ah, right. Does that mean you're not going to go there?'

'No, of course it doesn't.' He chuckled. 'It'll give me great pleasure to lead the police on a wild goose chase.'

'So you will try and heal Chieftain?'

'I'll be down at Long Bamber tomorrow morning,' he said, suddenly efficient. 'Round eleven.' He drained his drink. 'And that's me switched off again. Now I will return to my mates, to be perverse and argumentative, and talk a load of bollocks, and lead the conversation down a lot of whimsical cul-de-sacs, and then lose my temper and start threatening people.'

'Why?'

'Because, Jude –' he winked '– that is what is expected of a stage Irishman.'

She scribbled down her mobile number on a scrap of paper and gave it to him.

This prompted more ribaldry from George Tufton's stable lads, whose table Donal rejoined, stepping immediately back into his expected role.

Chapter Sixteen

Jude rang Sonia Dalrymple's number, but only got the answering machine. So she called Long Bamber Stables to check with Lucinda Fleet that it would be all right for Donal to work on Chieftain the following morning.

'Yes, that's fine. I'd been expecting him to turn up sometime soon. I'll hide the petty cash.'

'I have actually just met Donal.'

'Oh yes?'

'He lives up to his image, doesn't he?'

'A point of honour with him, I've always thought.'

'But as a healer?'

'Oh, he's good. Whatever power it is that's needed, Donal's got it. I always recommend him to all my owners.'

'Yes. Something's just struck me, Lucinda.'

'Uhuh? What's that?'

'If you recommend him to all your owners, then presumably you also recommended him to Sonia?'

'Yes.'

'And yet, when Chieftain got lame and the vet couldn't do anything about it, she turned to me rather than to Donal.'

If a shrug could be audible, then that's what Jude would have heard down the phone line. 'So? It's a free country. If she doesn't want to take my suggestion, then that's up to her.'

Again Jude was aware of the frostiness between the two women, the feeling she had got when she'd first heard Lucinda mention Sonia Dalrymple's name. 'Yes. Incidentally, Donal said something about Chieftain.'

'Mm?'

'He said he could guess how the horse got lame.'

'Did he?'

'Do you know what he meant by that?'

'No.' But something in Lucinda's voice betrayed her. She did know exactly what Donal had meant. But there was no way she was going to tell Jude.

'By the way, do you know whether Sonia has ever met Donal?'

'I don't know for certain, but I'd have thought she must have done at some point. They both keep coming down to the stables; they probably have seen each other.'

'But you don't know whether they've ever had any disagreement about anything?'

'Why should they have?'

'Only because Sonia didn't consult Donal about Chieftain . . .'

There was a level of exasperation in the sigh that came from the other end of the phone. 'Jude, I've no idea. And I've got to give a riding lesson in five minutes, so if you don't mind . . .'

'Sorry, sorry. You haven't heard from Sonia recently, have you?'

'She rang this morning. Said she wouldn't be able to come and sort out Chieftain for a couple of days.'

'Oh?'

'She's gone to a health farm. Yeomansdyke – do you know it?'

'Yeomansdyke as in the hotel?'

'Yes. Down towards Yapton.'

'I know it. In fact, someone gave me a free day voucher there as a Christmas present.'

'Then you've got some wealthy friends.'

'Oh, it never occurred to me that the place was that expensive.'

'Well, it is. Membership's about as much as I make in a good year here at the stables.'

'Not that that'd be a problem for Sonia.'

'Of course not. She often goes to Yeomansdyke to recuperate after Nicky's been home.'

'Lucinda, what on earth do you mean by—?'

'Must go. My lesson's arrived.'

Which was very frustrating and left Jude with more than one unanswered question.

'Hello, Mother, it's Stephen.'

He sounded more formal than ever. Round the time of the wedding, he had quite often relaxed into calling her 'Mum'. Such intimacy now seemed to have vanished like it had never existed.

'Oh, how nice to hear from you! How is everything?'

'Total chaos at work. Just don't seem to have a moment.'

'But it always seems to be like that, doing . . . what you do . . .' Whatever that might be. Carole reckoned she was destined never to understand her son's work.

'Well, let me tell you, now is absolutely worse than ever.'

'At least they pay you well.' Why Carole had said it, she didn't know. The words sounded crass, not at all what she had intended. She had an unfortunate knack of saying the wrong thing.

'I bloody earn it,' said Stephen, justifiably piqued. 'Anyway,' he went on brusquely, 'you rang. Was there something you wanted?'

This put her on the spot. She had rung because she was anxious about the state of her son's marriage, but it was not in her nature to raise the subject directly. She knew there were women who could boldly ask, 'What's going on with you and Gaby?', but she also knew she wasn't one of them. 'Erm . . .' she hazarded, sounding, to her distaste, just like David, 'it's just, I spoke to Gaby last week . . .'

'Yes, she said you'd rung.'

'. . . and I just wondered whether . . . erm . . .'

'What?' he asked shortly, sounding as grumpy with her as he had in his early teens.

'She sounded a bit down to me. I just really wondered whether she was all right?'

'She's fine,' he said in the same tone of voice.

'Oh, good. Because she's normally such a lively person, I was a bit worried to hear her so—'

'We're both fine, thank you, Mother. As you know, we both have very stressful jobs and—'

'Yes. Gaby was off work when I spoke to her. Is she better now?'

'There was nothing wrong with her. She just needed a break.'

'I thought she sounded—'

'There is nothing wrong with either of us, Mother, except that we don't get enough relaxed time together.'

'Well, if you need anything that I—'

'We don't need anything – except for a bit of space. Our relationship is fine, and it's our business, and the last thing we need is other people poking their noses into it.'

He rang off. Carole felt as though she had received a physical slap in the face. To her surprise, she felt tears prickling at her eyes . . . and it was a very long time since that had happened. By sheer willpower, she stemmed them. But she didn't feel good.

And, in spite of Stephen's assurances, her worries about the state of his marriage multiplied.

She felt in need of comfort, of moral support. But there was no one in at Woodside Cottage.

Yeomansdyke Hotel catered for the super-rich, of whom there were a surprising lot in the West Sussex area. Other clients came from London, and quite a few from the States. It was not a country house hotel, like the Hopwicke, where Carole and Jude had once become involved in the mysterious death of a young solicitor. There, the aim had been to reproduce the atmosphere of an Edwardian weekend party, whereas at Yeomansdyke the atmosphere aimed for was one of sheer luxury. It was not a place for people who needed to know how much anything cost.

Yeomansdyke had been built by a Victorian entrepreneur who had made a killing in the lawn-tennis boom of the late nineteenth century. Because of his sporting interests, he had designed the grounds to accommodate tennis courts, stables and an artificial lake for fishing and boating. The house itself was a huge structure in ornate red brick, whose spacious reception areas and plethora of guest bedrooms facilitated its conversion in the 1980s to a leisure complex for those who had cleaned up in the Thatcher financial bonanza.

As health faddishness developed during the 1990s, the hotel's small gym and pool area had been expanded into a large health spa, offering every kind of traditional and alternative therapy. There, the jaded wealthy could have their bodies balanced, their chakras realigned, their toes articulated, their force fields refocused, their skins scoured and scrubbed with a variety of unguents, their limbs wrapped in seaweed, or their colons irrigated.

Though Jude believed in the efficacy of many of these treatments, she was less than convinced by the way the health spa offered them, in a kind of pick 'n' mix assortment for the idle rich. Her own approach to alternative medicine was very different from the Yeomansdyke way.

But the fact remained that she did have a voucher for a free day at the place. It had been given her as a Christmas thank you by a grateful client who, though Jude hadn't thought about the fact before, was extremely well heeled and could afford such gestures.

Jude got the silver envelope out of the drawer where she had shoved it carelessly on Christmas Day. 'A full day's treatment in the understated luxury of Yeomansdyke's state-of-the-art health spa, with use of all the facilities. Just ring to book your day and one of our fitness professionals will advise you on the exciting range of health and beauty treatments available.'

So Jude rang to book her day. Or, since it was by then early afternoon, her less than half a day. But the fitness professional to whom she spoke said, yes, it would be fine for her to go straight there and wondered whether she would be requiring the services of a personal trainer to work out her gym routine. Jude, whose consistently good health derived from walking and yoga, declined the offer. She said she'd rather assess the therapies on offer when she got to Yeomansdyke, and the fitness professional was very happy with that. Without the words actually having been said, Jude got the distinct impression that business was pretty quiet that afternoon.

Carole, she was sure, would have given her a lift to the hotel, but Jude didn't want to impose. She ordered a cab and, aware of her neighbour's sensibilities to the slightest of imagined slights, fixed to be picked up at the seafront-end of the High Street.

Close to, the reality of Yeomansdyke was even huger than it had been in the brochure or glimpsed from the road. At the reception, a smartly suited young man of exquisite manners and a vestigial Swiss accent directed her to the spa entrance, where a female receptionist of equally exquisite manners welcomed her and proffered a silver menu of available treatments. Avoiding the most exotic, Jude plumped for a full-body massage. After that she planned to have a swim and then maybe make a further selection. The receptionist summoned a girl in clinical white, who – also exquisitely mannered – led Jude to the changing area, found her a locker and produced a swooningly soft bathing robe and pair of slippers. On hearing that her client had not brought a bathing costume, she offered a broad array from an adjacent cupboard. Jude, unself-conscious about her substantial figure, chose a black two-piece, too substantial to come under the definition of bikini. But she didn't put it on. Massage first.

Then the girl in white led her through to an elegantly tiled treatment room, and left her alone. A minute later, her masseur appeared. Tall, thin and very dark, his name was Ahmet and he wore a white uniform. And he was good. Jude knew more than a little about various forms of massage and the minute Ahmet started on her shoulders, she recognized she was under the hands of an expert. So she abandoned herself to the sensation. He said little, but – clearly it was part of the job description for anyone working at Yeomansdyke – he had exquisite manners.

The massage was thorough and took nearly an hour and a half. At the end, feeling deeply toned and relaxed, Jude showered off the oil on her body, donned her borrowed bathing costume and made her way to the swimming pool. It was set in a mini-Crystal Palace, a huge vaulted structure of cast iron and glass, whose previous role as a conservatory was hinted at by the huge potted palms and other tropical trees on the poolside area. The atmosphere was steamy and deliciously warm, in vivid contrast to the cold darkening February outside.

There were wicker loungers and tables around the pool. Abandoning her robe, slippers and towel, Jude eased herself down the steps into the water, whose temperature exactly matched that of the ambient air. She swam a brisk ten lengths, using the efficient crawl she had perfected during one long summer with a lover in the South of France. Then she bobbed about in the water for a few minutes, taking a covert look at the other spa users, searching for Sonia Dalrymple.

There was no sign of her in the poolside area. Four or five loungers were occupied, all by women, no men. And none of the bodies on display could ever have been mistaken for Sonia's. Perhaps it had taken a long time for these women – or, more likely, their husbands – to attain the kind of wealth that made the Yeomansdyke experience accessible, but none of them was in the first flush of youth, and indeed for most the first hot flush of the menopause was quite a distant memory. No, if Sonia Dalrymple was around, she was in some other part of the spa.

Jude got out of the water, towelled herself down, resumed her bathrobe and slippers, and ambled back to the spa reception.

'I was rather expecting to meet a friend of mine here today. Mrs Dalrymple – I don't know if she's been in.'

'Yes, Mrs Dalrymple has booked into the hotel for three nights. She's in one of the tanning suites at the moment,' said the girl with exquisite politeness. She consulted a printed sheet. 'Suite four.'

'Oh, well, I'll wait till she comes out.'

'You don't have to. If you're a friend, I'm sure she'd be delighted to see you. Just knock on the door. The tanning suites are down there.'

'Thank you very much.'

The suites' numbers were on brass plates worn smooth with much polishing. Jude tapped on the heavy oak door of number 4, but there was no response. She entered unbidden.

Sonia Dalrymple lay on a bed under the sunlamp, wearing only a wispy black bikini bottom. She was on her back, showing to full advantage the stunning figure which made Jude a little wistful for what she once had been. But, even at the height of her beauty, she had never been so precisely toned. Amazing to think that that firm flat stomach had given birth to twins. Sonia's body, like everything else about the Dalrymples, was absolutely perfect.

Rather than the dark goggles on the table, she wore

a designer eye-shade and, beneath it, a thin silk scarf was laid across her eyes. Either she was breathing very shallowly, or she was not breathing at all.

Jude felt a moment of anxiety. There was something wrong. She opened her mouth, but before she could speak, the mobile phone on the table beside Sonia rang. Instantly alive, she snatched at the phone as a man dying of thirst would snatch at a drink.

But at the same moment she recognized her visitor and stabbed at the phone to hold the call.

As she did so, the scarf slipped away from her face, to reveal the purplish bruising around both her eyes.

Jude wondered whether she now knew what Lucinda Fleet's words had meant. 'She often goes to Yeomansdyke to recuperate after Nicky's been home.'

Chapter Seventeen

Sonia Dalrymple snatched up the scarf to hide her eyes, then switched off the phone without answering it. 'Jude, what on earth are you doing here?'

Time for a little tactical finessing of the truth. 'Someone gave me a day's voucher here as a Christmas present' – that bit was true – 'and I saw your name on one of the receptionist's sheets. When I asked about you, she told me you were in here.'

'Ah.' Sonia realized she couldn't keep the scarf up for ever. Jude had seen the worst, anyway. She uncovered her face. 'I'm sorry I look such a sight. I . . . er . . . I had a fall from Chieftain.'

'Chieftain's lame,' said Jude gently.

'Yes, but he's on the mend. I thought I'd have a go this morning and then unfortunately—'

'Sonia, I was up at Long Bamber Stables this morning. With Chieftain. In another abortive attempt to heal his lameness.'

'Ah. Yes. Of course.'

Rather than beautiful, her nakedness now looked only vulnerable. Seeming to become aware of this,

150

Sonia reached for a Yeomansdyke robe and wrapped it around herself.

'Do you want to talk?'

'What, Jude? About what?'

'About your face. About the bruises.'

'No. There's nothing to say about them. I had an accident, that's all.'

'But not an accident falling from a horse?'

'No.'

Clearly further information on that subject was not going to be forthcoming. 'Actually, I'm glad to have bumped into you, Sonia.' Which was perhaps misleading about the amount of planning that had been involved. 'What I'm doing with Chieftain just doesn't seem to be working, so I've set up another healer to have a look at him.'

'Oh? Who's that?'

'Donal.'

Under her tan Sonia went instantly pale. 'Donal? No, I don't want to have anything to do with Donal. I don't want him ever to come near my stables again.'

'He's not coming to your stables. Chieftain's at Long Bamber.'

'Oh, yes. Of course.'

'Lucinda says he's very good with the horses.'

'So I've heard.'

'I thought it was worth trying. I've set him up to come to the stables at eleven tomorrow morning.'

'I suppose it's worth trying.'

'Do you want to be there when he—?'

'No!' The word, almost a shriek, came out far too quickly. 'No. I'm booked in here for three nights.'

'All right then. I can go in the morning, if you like. To the stables.'

'Yes, fine, but Donal'll be all right if Lucinda's there.'

'I think I might go, anyway.'

'Very well. See the bill's sent to me.'

There was a silence. Whatever ease had once existed between the women had dissipated.

'Sonia . . .'

'What?'

'Is the idea that you stay here till the bruises fade?'

'Maybe. After a few days I can cover anything up with make-up.'

'You make it sound like it's not the first time you've been here in these circumstances.'

'What if it isn't? I can't stay round Fethering. I keep meeting people in the streets.'

'This is not that far away.'

'No, but there's nobody I know up here, none of the members. Most of the members come on breaks from London, there are very few locals. And the staff are paid to be very discreet.'

'Right. Sonia, if there is anything you want to talk about, anything you want to say about—'

'No. Thank you, Jude. There isn't.'

For Carole Seddon lying was a big issue. She didn't have her neighbour's airy relationship with the truth, something that could be assumed or removed like an extra scarf. But Carole did need to lie. Well, no, to be accurate, she didn't *need* to lie, but if she wanted to get to the next stage of investigation, then she *had* to lie.

And she did want to get to the next stage of investigation. Thinking about Walter Fleet's murder was the only way she knew of allaying her anxieties about Stephen and Gaby's marriage.

But she was frankly feeling out of the loop on the case. Jude was the one with all the connections to Long Bamber Stables; she could move easily between individuals in an attempt to piece together how Walter Fleet died. But Carole had no one she could contact. Except Hilary Potton. And she couldn't make that contact without telling a lie.

Having decided she was going to tell one, Carole devoted considerable thought as to what that lie should be. Her former career hadn't trained her for this. In the Home Office the lying took place at a much higher level than she had ever attained. There, it was a reserved occupation for higher civil servants and cabinet ministers. Down at Carole Seddon's level, the most one was allowed to do was to finesse the truth.

But she was still quietly pleased with what she did eventually come up with. The lie had two qualities that all good ones should have: it couldn't be disproved by evidence, and it predisposed the person being lied to towards the liar. Having made her selection, Carole was quick to put it to the test. She looked up Potton in the local directory and dialled the number.

'Oh, Hilary, it's Carole Seddon here. You remember, we met at the Seaview Café yesterday.'

'Yes, of course.'

'It's just, after you'd gone, I noticed there was an Allinstore carrier bag with some shopping on the floor near your table, and I wondered if it might have been yours. I gave it to one of the women behind the counter, so she's going to keep it till it's picked up.'

Carole reckoned that was pretty safe. Since the carrier bag didn't exist, Hilary was extremely unlikely to go checking whether it had been handed in.

'Oh, Carole, that's so thoughtful of you. But no, in fact it wasn't mine. Certainly not if it was in an Allinstore carrier. I get quite enough of that place when I'm working – the last thing you're likely to catch me doing is shopping there on my day off.'

'Well, I did what I could. I'm sure the rightful owner will go and pick it up.'

'Yes.'

There was a lull in the conversation, and really no logical reason why it should be extended. Carole had done her good citizen act, but – unsurprisingly – the conjectural carrier bag had not belonged to Hilary Potton. Time for a final thank you and goodbye.

Before that could happen, Carole quickly interposed, 'You know we were talking yesterday about Walter Fleet's murder.'

'Yes. I don't think anyone in Fethering is talking about anything else. Now the police have released their first suspect it seems to be open season on unbridled speculation.'

'I know.' Carole giggled winsomely. 'Well, I'm afraid I'm also indulging in that unbridled speculation.'

'Don't apologize. We all are.'

'I was asking you yesterday what Imogen's view is – you know, because she knows the Long Bamber set-up so well? You said she was very upset about what happened.'

'Yes. When I came back from work, she was in a terrible state. Looked like she'd seen a ghost.'

'But she hadn't actually seen anything?'

'No. She was at school and then at home with me. She didn't go near the stables that day.'

'But has she given any indication of who she thinks might have done it?'

'Not really. She avoids talking about the whole business. But I get the impression . . .'

'Yes?' Carole prompted.

'. . . that Immy probably thinks Walter was killed by the Horse Ripper.'

'The one who's been attacking horses locally?'

'Yes. She's very devoted to the creatures, as you may have gathered. She thinks someone who'd be up to attacking them with a knife would be capable of any atrocity. In fact, she seemed less worried by Walter Fleet's death than she was by the threat the killer posed to Conker and the other horses.'

Rather the same reaction as his wife had, thought Carole.

'Mind you, that's not what *I* think happened,' Hilary Potton went on assertively.

'Oh?'

'Walter Fleet was a bit of a ladies' man, always chatting everyone up, the kind who always finds the opportunity to put an arm round your shoulder, hold your hand just that little bit longer than is strictly necessary – you know what I mean?'

Even though that kind of thing didn't happen to Carole as often as it did to Jude, she knew what Hilary meant.

'Well, I think Walter must've done something on those lines a little too blatantly and gone off with some woman, and his wife just couldn't take any more, and she snapped, and she stabbed him and stabbed him and stabbed him until the rotten bastard was dead!'

The raw emotion in the woman's voice was completely out of control. Carole wasn't a trained psychologist, but she could still work out that Hilary Potton was transferring feelings about her own marriage on to the Fleets'. Which made even scarier the kind of revenge that she might, given the opportunity, visit on her own unfortunate husband.

Chapter Eighteen

The following morning, the Friday, Jude went to High Tor for an early coffee. The two women pooled their individual progress on the investigation, and made arrangements for the rest of the day. Then Jude set off to meet Chieftain's latest healer.

The Donal who jumped out of the horsebox that had given him a lift to Long Bamber Stables was unrecognizable from the drunkard in the Cheshire Cheese. His clothes weren't different, nor was the stable-yard smell that surrounded him, nor the alcohol on his breath, but his manner transformed him. He was the professional horse expert, at ease in his chosen setting.

Lucinda Fleet was in the yard, overseeing a delivery of hay, and Imogen Potton, who was mucking out her beloved Conker's stable, emerged when she saw Donal was there.

He greeted Lucinda casually, and she seemed little concerned by his presence. He was part of the occasional furniture at Long Bamber Stables, and the fact that he had recently been questioned by the police about the murder of her husband did not trouble her. Or maybe they had already met since his release and discussed the matter. Jude could still remember Lucinda's disproportionate anxiety about Donal's having been taken in for questioning and her insistence that he was guiltless. That was something which, at some point, would need explanation.

Imogen grinned at the Irishman. She seemed as relaxed with him as she was with Conker. Here was an adult who didn't bring with him all the baggage of most of the other adults in her life. Donal knew about horses – that was all that mattered – and in his company Imogen's conversation need never stray from the subject of horses into more treacherous areas.

'I'm going to take Conker out for a long hack today,' she announced excitedly. 'She'll like that, won't she, Donal?'

'I would think it would be exactly what she wanted, young Immy. Conker's a pony that gets bored when she's not working.'

'You have cleared it with Sonia Dalrymple?' asked Lucinda. 'She's happy for you to take him out for a hack?'

'Yes, she said it's fine. So no problems.'

'Good.' But then a thought struck her. 'Just a minute, Immy. It's term time – shouldn't you be at school?'

'We've all got the morning off. It's an Ofsted day.'

Lucinda Fleet, having no children, had no idea what an Ofsted day was, so ceased to raise any objections, and Imogen returned to her mucking-out duties.

The morning was cold. Jude was glad she had managed to track down a fine pair of black leather gloves that a lover had once bought her in Florence. They were warm and fitted so well that her hands felt naked.

Donal led Chieftain out of his stall, breathing endearments or instructions at the horse's nose. The sight of the tethered Conker prompted a whinny of greeting, which was reciprocated. Donal stopped the horse in the centre of the yard, away from any tethering hooks, rings or rails.

'Aren't you going to tie him up?' asked Jude.

The Irishman shook his head. 'He'll be more relaxed if I don't.'

'And he won't try to get away?'

'He won't try to get away.'

'It's his front left knee.'

'I can tell that.'

But it wasn't the knee that Donal concentrated on first. He ran his gnarled hands over the horse's back, fingers hardly making contact with the dark hair. Then he concentrated on the neck, digging more deeply into the flesh beneath the black mane. And all the time, he kept up a murmuring commentary of comfort, in a language which was all breathing and no words.

Chieftain relaxed visibly under Donal's ministrations. Through his huge nostrils, his breath steamed evenly out into the February air. Apart from that, the great body was entirely still.

Only when that state had been achieved did Donal curve his body forward, and let his hands move down towards the injured knee. They didn't touch the animal, but seemed to close around a force-field, an invisible ring, some two inches away from the flesh. Donal tutted at what he felt there.

'I thought so. He's been ridden too hard.'

'But I'm sure Sonia would be very gentle with him.'

'It's not Sonia I'm talking about. It's that husband of hers. He's the bully.'

After what she'd seen at Yeomansdyke the day before, Jude could well believe that. Donal continued to read the information he was feeling from the horse's knee. 'He turned it, poor boy. Probably slipped. It was very wet underfoot a couple of weeks back, before everything froze up again. If the rider had jumped off as soon as he felt the slip, the horse wouldn't be in this state now. But no, Mr Nicky Dalrymple doesn't like weakness in an animal – or a human being.'

'Do you mean anything particular by that?'

He looked up from the horse's knee, the blue eyes either side of his broken nose glinting with mischief. 'And what might I mean, Jude?' Mocking, he teased out the vowel of her name.

'I was wondering if you were referring to Sonia – to Nicky not liking to see any weakness in her?'

'Well, I might have been meaning that – and I might not. There are certainly things I know about that marriage, but they're not things I would reveal.' He winked. 'At least not unless the price was right.'

'And would the price be charged in Jameson's?'

He chuckled. 'No, I think for information of this

kind I'd be looking for payment of a more foldable nature.'

'Ah. I don't believe in paying money for information.'

'And why would you want the information, anyway? From what I've seen of you, you're not one of the bitchy Fedborough gossips. Why do you care what's going on inside a couple's marriage?'

'I don't care at all.' She had to say it, though of course she was anxious to know everything she could about anyone involved with Long Bamber Stables. 'But do you think there are people who'd pay for the information you have?'

'I don't see why not. There are things I've seen which people might want to keep quiet, things they might not want an irresponsible drunken Paddy to spill out in his cups.'

As when he'd referred to himself the previous day as a 'stage Irishman', there was a knowingness about Donal's words. He was aware of the image that was expected of him and was quite prepared to live up to it. But again Jude got the feeling that he was a lot more intelligent than he allowed himself to appear.

'So who would you hope to get the money from?'

He grinned, still playing with her. 'If it's something discreditable about a marriage, I'd have thought the people most likely to pay for it being hushed up would be the people involved.'

'Yes, and in this case they could certainly afford it.'

'My thinking exactly, Jude.' A complacent smile cracked his wizened face, and he looked back down at Chieftain's leg. While they had been talking, he had kept his hands circling the invisible wrapping around the knee. Now he pointed his hands, swollen knuckles tight against each other, at the joint, and slowly, as if directing a hose, moved them up to the horse's shoulder. After a few moments of intense concentration, he took his hands away, and straightened up, wincing from the stiffness in his back.

'He'll be all right now.'

'You mean he's cured?'

'I mean he's ready now for nature to cure him. It'll take a couple of weeks. The muscle was torn. But it's on the mend now.' He reached up to take hold of Chieftain's head collar and lead him back to his stable. As he did so, Lucinda emerged from the tack room. 'Got him sorted, have you, Donal?'

'Yes. Can't be ridden for a couple of weeks, then he should be fine – until his owner does the same thing again.'

Lucinda looked rueful.

'Aren't you going to say anything to Mr High and Mighty Dalrymple then?' asked Donal.

'I can't risk them taking the horses away. I need the money.'

Just what she'd said about Victor and Yolanta Brewis. Her financial situation must be pretty serious for someone as devoted to horses as Lucinda to risk their being hurt by bullying owners. Jude wondered whether money pressures at Long Bamber Stables had anything to do with Walter Fleet's death.

Donal didn't seem surprised by her reaction, but led Chieftain into his stable. Conker, still tethered in the yard, whinnied, perhaps feeling it was about time he too was reinstalled. But the sound of a broom on cement flooring indicated that Imogen hadn't finished mucking-out.

Donal locked the bottom half of the door with practised ease, though he moved stiffly, his body still adjusting from the bent pose he had held so long. Lucinda stood waiting when he turned back from the stable. 'What?' he asked.

'I just wondered – I suppose as the widow of the victim I have a right to wonder – whether the police gave you any indication of what they thought might have happened to Walter?'

Ah, thought Jude, so Lucinda and Donal hadn't had an earlier conversation about the murder.

He grinned, without much humour. 'While they were questioning me, they gave the pretty firm impression they thought I'd topped him. Perhaps they still do. But they hadn't got a shred of evidence, so they had to let me go.'

'Didn't you have an alibi for the time of the murder?' Jude's words were out before she realized how unnaturally nosey they sounded.

Donal smiled, as if realising she'd jumped the gun. 'Whether I had an alibi or not, I didn't mention it to the police. I wasn't going to make their work too easy. I knew they couldn't pin anything on me, so I let them sweat.'

'I thought the police were meant to make their suspects sweat,' said Lucinda, 'not the other way round.'

'That is indeed the traditional way they like to do

things. But it's not the first time I've been questioned by the bastards – though probably the first time I've been questioned about something I didn't do. You get to know the form after a while. So I wasn't going to let them have an easy ride.'

'But they didn't give any indication of where their investigations were taking them?'

'No. Their investigations were taking them as far as me, and that was it. Whether they're now making some other poor sod's life a misery, I don't know.'

'There's been nothing on the news about anyone else being questioned,' said Jude.

'Oh. And do you not have a personal hotline to the police to find out how their investigations are proceeding?'

He was sending her up. She grinned ruefully. 'Sadly, no. I wish I had.'

'You're lying. I'll swear the police spend all their time coming round to consult you, like you were some kind of New Age Miss Marple.' But whatever game Donal was playing with Jude, he suddenly got bored with it, and turned back to Lucinda. 'Afraid I can't tell you anything about who else the police are talking to. You see, the police, having grabbed the obvious Paddy with form who's known to hang around stables and got nowhere with him, probably don't have the imagination to find another suspect.'

'And what about you, Donal? Do you have your own theory about who killed my husband?'

The blue eyes, embedded in their folds of wrinkles, twinkled sardonically. 'I could ask you the same question, Lucinda. Do you have your own theory on the subject?'

She shrugged. 'I really can't come up with much beyond the random intruder. A person or persons unknown. Walter wasn't a particularly popular man, he was irritating, but surely not enough for anyone to have killed him.'

'Well, there's no way it was suicide, so somebody did'.

'Yes.'

He let out a dry laugh. 'But if you really want my opinion – for what it's worth, and the opinion of a drunken Irishman, in the opinion of many people isn't worth very much – I'd say it was definitely a woman who killed Walter.'

'What makes you say that?'

'The nature of the attack. Men lose their tempers and lash out, but they don't go on doing it. They stop after a while. Once they know the blows have hit home. Also a man would never have used a bot knife for the attack.'

'It was the only weapon available.'

'A man still wouldn't have used it. Whoever attacked Walter was hysterical, and I don't need to tell you that means we're talking about a woman, from *hystera*, the Greek word for womb.'

Again Donal was letting his facade slip to reveal his true intelligence and education. As if aware of the lapse, he felt the need to follow it with something crass. 'And only a bloody woman would be as incompetent as to kill anyone that way.'

Lucinda Fleet's lips thinned. 'Well, thank you, Donal, for your most helpful assessment. I don't know why I bothered asking.'

'Because you're like every one else round here – a nosey cow.'

'Look, if you're going to insult me, I can—'

She was interrupted by the flustered arrival of Alec Potton. He came rushing through the gates of the yard, what remained of his hair sticking out at odd angles. He was once again wearing his corduroy suit, which seemed baggier than ever, and no overcoat.

'Good morning, Lucinda. And hello.' He knew he'd met Jude, but he couldn't place exactly where or how. And he was too rushed to work it out. 'Is Immy here?'

'Yes, Daddy.'

The girl came out of Conker's stable and stood leaning on a broom. There was an expression almost of insolence on her face, challenging her adoring father to be angry with her.

'I had a call from the school. They wanted to know where you are.'

'I'm here. As you see.'

'Immy, you can't bunk off lessons like that.'

'Why not?' She jutted out her lower lip and her right hip in the perfect posture of adolescent rebellion. 'They never teach us anything.'

'That's not the point. You're breaking the school rules. You're breaking the law, come to that.'

'Am I?'

Alec Potton wasn't sure enough of his legal ground to answer that. 'Never mind. Come on, you must come straight back to school with me. And you'd better think of something pretty good to tell your headmistress.'

'Why?'

'Because I say so, Imogen!'

This sudden outburst was the anger of a weak man, but it was so little expected by his daughter that she immediately burst into tears. Her mouth fell open, revealing the full ugliness of the brace on her teeth. Totally disarmed, and unable to maintain his pose of fury, her father moved instinctively forward and put his arms round the girl's shoulders.

'Come on, Immy, let's pick up something to eat on the way back to school.' And, with an embarrassed wave of goodbye to the two women, he led his daughter away from the stables.

Jude moved to the gate and saw that, as arranged earlier in the morning and punctual to the minute, Carole's Renault had arrived in the car park. 'Donal,' she said, 'can I buy you a drink by way of thank you?'

'What are you thanking me for? Chieftain's not your horse.'

'No. But I tried to heal him, and failed. So I owe you a thank you for getting it right.'

He nodded. 'That's fair enough. There's no pub very close to here, though.'

'No. My friend over there will drive us.'

'Ah. Where to?'

'Just down the road to Fethering.'

'All right.' The idea seemed to amuse him. 'Yes, I haven't been to Fethering for a while now. And it could be just the place that I need to settle back into.'

With which enigmatic comment, he started towards the Renault. Jude looked forward with some glee to the incongruous introduction to Carole that lay ahead.

She said goodbye to Lucinda, who was standing on exactly the spot in the stable yard where her husband had died. For the first time in their acquaintance, the sole owner of Long Bamber Stables looked slightly vulnerable, as if the enormity of what had happened had finally sunk in.

Chapter Nineteen

'My friend Carole. And Carole, this is Donal.'

Jude would treasure for always the expression on her friend's face, seen through the open passenger door, as Carole grimaced a smile and said, 'Very nice to see you, Donal.'

He didn't think this greeting worthy of more acknowledgment than a curt nod. Donal had changed now he was parted from Chieftain: he was jumpier, on edge. The element of danger which Jude had noticed in the Cheshire Cheese had returned.

'You sit in the front,' she said, only for the mischievous pleasure of seeing Carole's reaction. The thought of Donal's filthy clothes touching the Renault's pristine upholstery would be bad enough, but to have this creature in such immediate proximity to her – well, it would take Carole a long time to get over that.

Suppressing a grin, Jude got into the back of the car and said they were going to take Donal to Fethering.

'Erm . . .' said Carole, for all the world like her ex-husband, 'are you going to put on your seatbelt?'

'No,' said Donal.

Unwilling to take issue with him, she started the engine, and drove out of the Long Bamber Stables car park. They drove along the Fethering road in silence for a while.

'So tell me, Donal,' said Carole eventually, 'where do you live?'

'Nowhere.'

'Ah.'

'According to the police, I am "of no fixed abode".'

'Ah. Ah.' Carole was rather thrown for a genteel Fethering response to that. 'It must be nice not to have the responsibility of a house.'

Donal didn't think this worthy of comment. He was growing ever more fidgety. From her seat in the back, Jude could see the tensing of his neck muscles, and a slight gleam of sweat on his temple. She diagnosed that he was suffering from a hangover. He'd held himself together for healing the horse; now he was in desperate need of a drink.

'So,' Carole went on, still battling to maintain polite middle-class conversation, 'are you Irish, Donal?'

'No, I'm bloody Serbo-Croat! What do you think?'

Though clearly offended, Carole didn't rise to the rudeness. 'And I'm sorry, Donal, I didn't get your second name?'

'No, you didn't, because nobody's bloody mentioned it.' But, after that put-down, to Jude's surprise, he volunteered, 'Geraghty. Donal Geraghty. Is that enough of the central casting Irishman for you?'

Belatedly, Carole decided she had expended sufficient conversational effort on him. After a silence,

Jude volunteered, 'Donal cured Sonia Dalrymple's horse, where I failed. I'm going to buy him a drink to say thank you. You will join us, won't you?'

Carole was torn. The potential of actually getting some useful information about the case had to be weighed against the shame of being seen around Fethering in the company of this uncouth ragamuffin. Her detective instinct triumphed. 'Yes, that'd be very nice, thank you. I'd love to join you for a drink.'

'Talking of drink,' said Donal edgily, 'I'm dying for a drop. You wouldn't happen to have some with you, would you?'

'Alcohol?'

'Yes.'

'Alcohol in my Renault?'

Jude was sorry she couldn't at that moment see Carole's face full on. But what she could glimpse in the driving mirror was satisfying enough. She swallowed down an incipient giggle.

It was rather terrifying to see how quickly the first large Jameson's restored Donal Geraghty. One moment he was sweating, twitching and as jumpy as a kitten; a few sips later his body was still, and there was even a sardonic smile playing around the corners of his mouth, as he looked around the snug interior of the Crown and Anchor.

'Carole and I are going to have lunch here. Maybe you'd like to have something too?'

He laughed. 'I don't, as they say, "do lunch". I'm restricted to a liquid diet.'

'Is that on doctor's orders?' asked Carole, misunderstanding.

'The only order the doctor's ever given to me was to get the hell out of his surgery. His view was that he couldn't help me, unless I was prepared to make certain changes in my lifestyle.'

'Which you weren't,' said Jude.

'Take away the lifestyle, you take away the life. Take away the life, you take away the man.' He downed the remains of his glass, and looked at it rather wistfully.

Jude took the hint and went for a refill from the nose-pierced girl at the bar. Ted Crisp was either out in the kitchen or having a rare day off.

Left alone with Donal Geraghty, Carole's upbringing forced her to forget the earlier snubs and continue to prosecute her conversational campaign. 'I hope you don't mind my mentioning your recent encounter with the police—'

'Why should that bother me?' asked Donal, mellowed by the first drink. 'It's no secret they grilled me. The entire country knows, and no doubt when some other crime occurs locally, the police'll drag me in even quicker after this.'

'But you did know Walter Fleet, didn't you?' Carole persisted.

'Oh yes, I knew him.'

'And I believe had a disagreement with him?'

'It wasn't a disagreement, it was a fight I had with

him.' He looked up to see Jude approaching with his refill, took it without a word and downed a long swallow. 'And the fight happened in this very pub,' he added mischievously.

The two women exchanged horrified looks. Preoccupied by their opportunity to do a private grilling of the police's first suspect, they had both forgotten about Ted Crisp having banned the man from the Crown and Anchor. Thank God the landlord didn't appear to be about that day.

Donal Geraghty understood exactly what they were thinking. He had knowingly let them bring him into a pub where he was banned, and the fact that they had done so gave him great satisfaction. He giggled gleefully. 'Smart ladies like you should be a bit more careful about the company you keep.'

Jude grinned and raised her glass of Chilean Chardonnay to him. 'I've known worse.' That won a chuckle, so she pursued her advantage. 'Carole, Donal was telling me he thought the murderer of Walter Fleet was definitely a woman.'

'Oh, really?'

'Yes,' Donal confirmed. 'Using that knife – it's a woman's crime if ever I saw one.'

'So who would that make a suspect for the murder?' asked Carole.

He snickered. 'Well, Lucinda and Walter's wasn't the epitome of a happy marriage.'

Again his choice of words betrayed a much better education than was promised by his exterior blarney.

'So you think she might have done away with him?'

'Usual rule of police investigation: if the victim has a live-in partner, haul them in for questioning. That is, of course, after they've hauled *me* in for questioning. But if they can't pin it on me, then they go for the partner.'

Carole was thoughtful. 'Lucinda certainly doesn't seem to be making any pretence of being upset by having lost her husband.'

'Maybe she didn't do it herself,' Jude speculated. 'Paid someone else actually to do the deed, while she established an alibi for herself?'

'Oh, thank you,' said Donal in mock affront. 'So that'd bring the accusation back to me, would it? "Donal Geraghty's always helping Lucinda with odd jobs round the yard at Long Bamber. I'm sure he'd be only too glad to top the lady's husband for her." Is that what you're suggesting?'

'No, I'm not.'

'Well, be very careful. Don't forget you're dealing with a very dangerous paranoid Paddy who has a lot of form for acts of violence.' Yet again he demonstrated an ironical awareness of his image, the fact that he could choose when he wanted to live up to it.

'Putting Lucinda on one side,' said Carole, 'who else might be in the frame?'

'Ah.' Donal squinted at her. 'I didn't have you down as a racing woman, Carole.'

'What do you mean? I've never been to the races in my life. I'm certainly not a racing woman.'

'No, but you use racing talk.'

'I'm sorry?'

'"In the frame." Now isn't that a reference to horses in a photo finish?'

'I don't know. Is it?'

'Well, what else could it be?'

'I thought it had something to do with pictures, or photographs, that kind of frame.'

'No, no, I've done my research. The phrase definitely comes from the racing world.'

'It's funny, Donal,' said Jude. 'I wouldn't have had you down as an expert on semantics.'

'Which just shows how wrong you can be. Never judge a book by its cover.'

'No. Well, you are a dark horse.'

'Ah, you see now, Jude. You're a racing woman too.'

Jude chuckled. 'I have been racing, and I love it, but I wouldn't say I was a racing woman.'

'Well, I think you both are racing women.' Donal looked down at his empty glass. 'Mind you, you don't seem to be very fast-drinking women.'

Jude's eyes flashed a quick message to Carole, who stood up and said, 'Let me get this one. You still all right, Jude?'

'Nearly ready for another.' Her glass was half full, but she reckoned drinking with Donal might make him more relaxed and communicative.

With Carole at the bar, Jude plunged straight back into interrogation mode. 'We did hear something about the circumstances of your being banned from this pub, actually.'

'Oh yes?'

'Your having a fight with Walter Fleet.'

'Uhuh.' He didn't seem upset by her line of questioning, just waiting to see where she was really heading.

'Presumably the police knew about that?'

'Of course. Another reason for them to make me their first suspect.'

'We did also hear about something you said when you were arguing with Walter . . .'

'Well, you have been doing your research, haven't you?' he commented sardonically.

'Apparently you said, "You're not worthy of her! She's beautiful and you don't deserve her!"'

'What if I did?'

'To the casual listener, that could make it sound as if your argument with Walter was about a woman.'

'I suppose it could.'

'So was it about a woman?'

'You're a nosey cow, aren't you, Jude?' But it was said without malice; he was feeling the benefits of two large Jameson's with a third in prospect.

'Yes, I am a nosey cow, which is why I would quite like an answer.'

'And why should I give you one?'

'Why not?'

She had taken the right approach; he appeared tickled by her response. 'So you're reckoning maybe I was having a bit of the old illicit sex with Lucinda – is that where you're coming from?'

'It'd fit the known facts.'

'But it might fail rather badly to tie in with the unknown facts, mightn't it?' He smiled teasingly, as if weighing up what kind of answer to give her . . . and indeed whether to give her an answer at all. Eventually he said, 'Suppose I was talking about a horse?'

'The "she" who Walter was "not worthy of"?'

'Why not? It could have been a horse.'

'I think the odds are against it.'

Donal Geraghty chuckled. 'You're doing it again. You *are* a racing woman, you know.'

'Maybe,' Jude conceded with a smile. 'But is the horse answer the best I'm going to get?'

'It is so,' he replied, affecting an even heavier brogue. 'That's the best you'll have from me. And, as it happens, it's God's honest truth. The owner of the stables and the mad Irish tinker had words about a horse – that's all there was to it.'

'But surely—?'

'Here are the drinks,' said Carole.

Donal smiled at Jude, as if he'd engineered the end of their previous conversation. 'And that's all I'm going to tell you,' he said, reaching for his glass, without any thanks, and taking a long swallow.

'All you're going to tell me about that,' Jude countered. 'Maybe you'll tell me more about something else?'

Carole, recognizing that Jude might be getting some-where, sat down quietly with her drink.

'And what might that something else be?' asked Donal.

'Ooh . . .' Jude teased. 'What about blackmail?'

He chuckled. 'I don't think there's anything I could be blackmailed about by anyone in the world. You see, the one qualification you have to have for being blackmailed is to have something to lose, and' – he shrugged – 'that counts me out.'

'I wasn't meaning *you* being blackmailed. I was meaning you blackmailing someone else.'

'Oh yes?' He knew exactly what she was referring to, but played deliberately dumb.

'When we were at Long Bamber you spoke of your knowing something about a couple's marriage, and their being prepared to pay you money to keep you quiet.'

'Did I now?'

'Yes.'

'And you want me to tell you who I was talking about?'

'Yes.'

'Well, aren't you just the nosey one, Jude? I don't suppose you were thinking of offering me money for the information, were you?'

'No.'

'So let me get it straight what you're asking me. I have some information that is worth money to me – you want me to give you that information for free. It doesn't sound like much of a deal.'

'I'll buy you another drink.'

'Well, that's exceedingly generous, and yes, I'll take

you up on that offer.' He emptied what was left in his glass, and smiled impudently at Carole. 'Maybe you'd like to get me topped up, dear?'

Biting her lip to hold back an interesting variety of responses, she returned to the bar, where she had to take her place behind a queue of anoraked ramblers who had just entered the pub.

'But you could buy me a whole bottle of Jameson's, Jude,' Donal went on, 'a crate of the stuff – and I still don't see why I should tell you the secret that will hopefully provide me with a nice little meal ticket for the next few months – my only prospect of a meal ticket, as it happens. Why should I?'

Jude's charm had been known on occasions to work wonders. Oh, well, it was worth a try. 'Because I'm asking you to.'

Donal Geraghty shook his head. 'You know it's a long time since I've done something stupid for the sake of a pretty face. I think I could be said to have learnt my lesson there.'

She tried another approach. 'Then let me try a bit of guessing.'

'Guess away. It won't get you anywhere.'

'If you have a secret about a married couple, then it's probably not something they told you deliberately. It's more likely to be something you overheard.' He offered no encouragement, but Jude persevered. 'So the couple didn't know you were there and, given the kind of places where you spend most of your life, it was probably round some stables or other that you heard whatever it was – possibly some stables you were using at the time as your "no fixed abode". Not Long Bamber, because Lucinda wouldn't let you stay there, but somewhere else round here. You said at Long Bamber that you needed to come down to Fethering. So if it's, as you say, your *only* meal ticket, maybe your secret involves people who live round—'

'Will you shut up!' He was rattled now. It might be something she had said that had so suddenly changed his mood. Or it might be the return of his hangover. His hands twitched and once again there was a sheen of sweat on his brow. He was in desperate need of another infusion of alcohol. 'Will you hurry along with that drink, you silly cow!' he shouted.

Carole was prepared to put up with a lot in the cause of criminal investigation, but not to be called names in a public place in Fethering. Whatever would people think of her? She was unable to stop herself from shouting back, 'I'll thank you not to be so appallingly rude!'

The customers who hadn't been silenced by Donal's outburst certainly were by Carole's response. Raised voices were not common in Fethering. It was a very long time since anything so interesting had happened in the Crown and Anchor.

The shouting had another effect too. The door from the kitchen burst open, and framed in it stood the shaggy outline of Ted Crisp. 'All right, what's going on here?' he bellowed.

His eyes moved round the room, and very quickly fixed on the source of the disturbance. 'Why, you little swine!' he said, as he moved forward. 'Are you too Irish to understand plain English? You're banned from this pub! Get out!'

Donal rose to his – remarkably steady – feet. For a small man, he carried a lot of menace. 'And who's going to make me get out?'

'I am.' Ted Crisp's huge body loomed over his opponent. If there was going to be a fight, it looked like an unequal one.

But Donal was fast. Feinting with his right hand up towards the landlord's face, he flicked a hard left fist straight into the bulging midriff. As Ted folded in the middle, Donal's bunched right hand caught him full in the nose. Instantly, blood spattered.

But, in spite of his injuries, Ted Crisp was surprisingly speedy in his response. His huge arms swung forward and the hands caught on the shoulders of his retreating assailant. Quickly, they closed together around the stubbly neck.

Donal twisted and wriggled, raining blows into the unprotected stomach in front of him. Dripping blood from his opponent's nose flecked his face and clothes. But still Ted did not release his grip.

'All right, you asked for it, you stupid bastard!' the Irishman gasped through his constricted throat.

The movement was so fast that, afterwards, none of the appalled audience could describe what happened. Suddenly there was a small knife in Donal's right hand. The blade jerked upwards and disappeared into the folds of Ted Crisp's fleece.

That did make him release his grip. Tottering backwards, he fell against the support of his bar. His opponent, without even wiping it, slid the bloody knife back into its hiding place. He looked around at the silent onlookers with something approaching glee. Then, with a defiant laugh, he rushed out of the pub.

Chapter Twenty

The appalled silence continued. Then, to her surprise, Carole found herself rushing forward to Ted Crisp's side. A patch of red, almost black against the dark blue of his fleece was spreading over his chest. 'Are you all right? Ted – are you all right?'

His eyes looked wearily down at the spreading blood, then seemed to swim for a moment, unseeing. Oh God, Carole found herself thinking, don't let me lose him. She was surprised by the strength of her emotion. In the past she had had an incongruous relationship with Ted, and like most incongruous relationships it had been brief. And yet, now his life was threatened, she felt this surge of panicked desperation at the thought of his dying.

The moment passed. Refusing Carole's offered arm, Ted Crisp pushed himself against the counter back up to a standing position. 'God, that Donal's a stupid bastard.' Then, looking round at the hushed circle of Fethering pensioners, he said firmly, 'No one gets to hear about this – OK? I'm not going to mention it to the police, and I'll be bloody angry if I hear anyone else has done so. I don't want the Crown and Anchor getting a reputation for violence, just because of one lunatic Irishman. He's had a grudge against me for a long time, that's all. So I'll thank you to forget this ever happened – have you got that?'

Without waiting for a response – and rather magnificently – the landlord turned on his heel and walked round the counter into the pub kitchen. Even if she'd wanted to, Carole could not have stopped herself from following. And Jude went along too. Behind them they heard the shocked silence give way to twitterings of excited conversation.

The chef, who had been blithely heating up crumbly cod pies during the recent altercation, looked up in surprise at the invasion of his kitchen. His eyes widened as he saw the stain on Ted's chest.

'Don't worry about it. Only a flesh wound. Get back to your cooking.'

Unwillingly, the chef did as he was told. Ted subsided into a wooden chair.

'Do you have a first aid kit?' asked Jude practically.

'Over in that cupboard by the window.'

Carole moved towards him, reaching to unzip the perforated fleece. He brushed her hand away. 'I can do it.'

But he couldn't. After a couple of attempts, he let his arms flop to his sides and offered no resistance as Carole cautiously unzipped the garment and eased it off his shoulders. On the dirty grey of the sweatshirt beneath, the bloodstain was much bigger, seeping down towards the waistband of his jeans.

'I'm going to have to get that off too.'

He nodded, grimacing at the promise of pain. First Jude used a dampened teacloth to wipe away the blood from his nose. After that, she stood ready, the plastic first aid box open on a table beside her, while Carole first pulled the fabric away from the stickiness around the wound, then lifted the sweatshirt up from the bottom. His face set in a determination not to cry out, Ted raised his arms and let her slip it away from his body.

Jude moved in, towel at the ready. 'Stop me if it hurts.'

'Doesn't make much difference if it hurts or not,' said Ted, reasonably enough. 'Got to be done.'

There was a second's stillness while the two women looked at his torso. There was a lot of blood just below the left breast, still flowing through the matted hair of his paunch till it darkened the top of his jeans.

All Carole could think was how near the knife had gone to Ted's heart, how nearly he had been killed.

Jude moved the damp towel determinedly forward, and starting from the bottom, swept upward over his skin in gentle but firm strokes, mopping away the blood. For a moment the flow threatened to drench the flesh again, but then it slowed to a trickle. Jude wiped the gory towel around the area of the wound itself, finally revealing a one-inch open line of puncture in a fold of skin.

'See,' said Ted Crisp, who couldn't see it. 'Just a flesh wound. Thank God he'd only got a Stanley knife. The blade's too short to do any serious damage.'

Jude looked closely. 'Might benefit from a couple of stitches.'

'No. Just slap a dressing on. It'll be fine.'

Dubiously, Jude did as he suggested. A bit of gauze over the cut, a rectangular dressing of lint, held in place by strips of semi-transparent white tape.

'Well, you're patched up.'

'Sure,' said Ted. 'I'm fine. Pass me that T-shirt hanging on the back of the door.'

Carole did as instructed. The T-shirt had been printed for a lager promotion some several summers before and, from the smell of it, had hung on its peg ever since, absorbing the aromas of the kitchen.

Carole pulled the neckband wide to fit over Ted's shaggy head, guided his arms into the armholes and pulled the T-shirt down to cover him.

All three of them looked anxiously at the site of the wound to see if any tell-tale blood would seep through.

None did. Disguising the effort it cost him, Ted Crisp rose to his feet. 'Well, I don't know about you two, but I could use a large drink.'

Carole followed him through into the bar. She was still in shock, not from the violent confrontation she had just witnessed, but from the strength of her emotional reaction to Ted's jeopardy.

Until the other lunchtime customers had left, Ted Crisp was particularly loud and jovial in the bar, like a national leader determined to dispel press speculation about his health. But he drank a lot – Scotch, unlike his usual bitter – to counter the shock he had undoubtedly felt. And all the time, his two companions kept looking uneasily at his chest, to check that the flow of blood had really been staunched.

When there were just the three of them left, Carole asked, 'Are you really not going to tell the police, Ted?'

'What good would it do?'

'It might remove Donal from circulation.'

'And what use would that be? He's not really a threat to anyone.'

'*You* say that, with a fresh stab wound only inches from your heart?'

Ted could not prevent a small shudder at the image. 'Look, if I do shop him, the cops'll just have another go at stitching him up for the Long Bamber murder, which I'm sure he didn't do.'

'I think you're being very altruistic.'

'Altruistic nothing, Carole. I just don't see the point of someone being charged with a crime which they didn't commit.'

With her Home Office background, she could not help agreeing with him.

'It's a pity, though,' mused Jude, 'that we've lost touch with Donal. I think he does know something about what happened to Walter Fleet. He hinted as much.'

'Oh, I'm sorry.' Ted's voice was heavy with mock-apology. 'I'm sorry my inviting him to stab me has resulted in your losing your best source of information.'

'You know I didn't mean that.'

He grinned weakly. The skin above his unkempt beard was pale and strained. However much bravado he was showing, the fight had traumatized him.

'No, I know you didn't. Well, I can't imagine Donal's gone that far. He won't stray out of the area. Shouldn't be too hard to find him. He'll lay low for a few days in some unsuspecting owner's stables, then he'll be back round his usual haunts: the Cheshire Cheese, George Tufton's yard, Fontwell races. You'll track him down soon enough.'

'Mm . . .' Jude's brow wrinkled as she tried to get her thoughts in order. 'Donal accepted the offer of a lift to Fethering because he said it was "just the place I need to settle back into", which might suggest he's got a bolt-hole down here.'

'Could be,' Ted agreed. 'There are enough people with stables in the area.'

'Yes . . . But he also implied that he knew something about Sonia and Nicky Dalrymple's marriage which he might have overheard if he was dossing down at their stables.'

'I think that's rather a big leap of the imagination,' said Carole in her prim wet-blanket mode.

'Possibly not.' Jude's brown eyes sparkled as the logic came together. 'And now I come to think of it, Sonia did say something about not wanting Donal around her stables *again* – which implies that he had been there. And the Dalrymples travel so much that the stables are empty and unused a lot of the time. Yes, they'd be the perfect bolt-hole for him.'

Jude's enthusiasm was infectious and, though she tried to resist it, Carole found her spoilsport pose weakening. 'So, what are you suggesting – that we go and see Sonia Dalrymple and ask whether she has an unwelcome guest in her stables?'

'Something along those lines, yes. Except Sonia's not there at the moment. She's taking a few days' break at Yeomansdyke.'

'Oh.' And Carole could not completely disguise her disappointment as she said, 'Well, we'll have to wait till she comes back.'

Jude nodded, then turned to Ted. 'You're sure you're going to be all right?'

'Yes. Just have a kip upstairs, that'll sort me out.'

'Sure?' asked Carole anxiously.

'You betcha.' He grinned with manufactured bravado, and lapsed into the manner of the stand-up comedian he had once been. 'Take more than a little prick to put Ted Crisp out of commission – particularly when that little prick's only Donal Geraghty!'

'All right, but, as we've seen, he can be dangerous,' said Jude. 'You look after yourself.'

'Right you are, nurse. I'll do as I'm told.

'Well then, we'll say goodbye.' And she rose to her feet.

Carole looked up in puzzlement. 'Why, where are we going?'

'To the Dalrymples' house.'

'But you've said they're not there.'

'They're not.'

Carole's eyes widened in fascinated horror. 'Are you suggesting that we trespass – or even break and enter?'

'That's right,' said Jude.

Chapter Twenty-One

Some of the Dalrymples' fleet of cars may have been on the premises, but they were invisible behind closed garage doors. Jude persuaded a very uncertain Carole during their walk along the towpath that their best means of approach was through the front gate. She was known to Sonia and, if seen entering, felt confident she could invent some reason for doing so. Carole wasn't so sure, but she did have to concede that trespass was a lesser offence than breaking and entering. Though she was afraid they might have to move up the scale of criminality when they reached the stables.

Carole was also paranoid about the presence of burglar alarms and CCTV cameras, but as they walked across the gravel to the house, there was no sign of either. Nor, so far as they could tell, had there been any witnesses to their arrival.

When they reached the frontage, Carole's twitchiness increased. Walking up to the door and ringing the bell was a legitimate act. Jude could easily have been mistaken about how long Sonia Dalrymple was staying at Yeomansdyke. But the minute they started going round the side of the house, the two women had stepped over the barrier into wrongdoing.

Jude, unaffected by any such scruples and knowing the route, marched boldly ahead. Her companion, with scuttling gait and many furtive glances behind, gave a totally convincing impersonation of an intruder.

'We shouldn't be doing this,' she kept saying, 'it's illegal.'

'Not only illegal, but dangerous.'

'What do you mean?'

'If Donal *is* in the stables . . .'

She didn't need to finish the sentence. After the recent confrontation in the Crown and Anchor neither of them needed reminding they were dealing with a violent man.

'Maybe we should go back?'

'Do you really want to?'

There was a moment while Carole weighed up the demands of fear and curiosity. Then, firmly, she shook her head.

'Thought not.'

At least, when they got to the stables, no breaking and entering was required. The large outer gate of the block was not locked, nor had the padlocks been put through the rings of the individual stalls. Presumably, since, as Jude had witnessed, Sonia now kept all her tack inside the house, there was nothing worth stealing. The stables were only at risk from knife-wielding ex-jockeys who might choose to set up temporary homes there.

The two women moved through into the small

covered yard and looked around. Short of using one of the empty stalls, or bedding down on the neat stack of hay at the back of the central area, there was no suitable accommodation on the ground floor. But the rungs leading up the wall to the trapdoor in the wooden ceiling looked much more promising.

'Donal!' Jude called out, her voice suddenly loud after the silence of their approach. 'Donal, are you up there?'

There was no answering voice. Jude and Carole looked at each other, the latter's expression full of trepidation as she whispered, 'Suppose he's just waiting up there, with his knife?'

'I really don't think he represents any danger to us.'

'After what he did to Ted? Why not?'

'Don't know. Instinct.'

Carole's 'Huh!' fully expressed her views of the value of instinct in such circumstances.

But her friend just shrugged and started up the ladder. After a moment's hesitation, Carole followed suit. Through both of their minds went the same thought: Damn, we should have brought a torch.

They needn't have worried. As soon as she pushed up the trapdoor, Jude was aware of some light source above and, as she poked her head up through the aperture, she could see the Velux window set in the pitched roof. She pulled herself up into the loft space and looked around, waiting till Carole had joined her before saying anything.

'Well, it looks like we were right.'

The space was surprisingly tidy, and somehow gave

the impression that it had not been used since the place was converted. The Dalrymples appeared never to have taken advantage of the space for storage.

But someone had taken advantage of it as a bedroom. Long damp-speckled cushions from garden loungers had been laid down on the bare boards, and a grubby-looking sleeping bag had been placed on top. Beside the makeshift bed an old wine-box stood, candles and matches on its surface, tins, boxes and unidentified garments shoved inside it.

'I bet this is Donal's little hideaway.' It was strange. In spite of her recent shout, which would have alerted anyone who happened to be in the vicinity, up in the little loft Jude felt the need to whisper.

'But there's no sign of him, is there?'

'No.' Jude knelt down and scrutinized the sleeping bag. 'He hasn't been here for a while either. There's dust all over this.'

'Oh well . . .' Carole, anxious to leave, edged back towards the ladder. 'At least we know a place where he might come to.' All she wanted to do was to get back onto the road outside the Dalrymples' house. They'd been very lucky so far, nobody had seen them. But they shouldn't push their luck. Now it was time to go.

'Just a minute,' said Jude, and she moved back towards the window to get a better view of the bed. As she did so, she glanced down at the windowsill. 'Well, well, well.'

'What is it?'

Carefully, in her gloved hands, Jude lifted up an object covered in a thin layer of dust, not as much as on the sill where it lay. A Sabatier kitchen knife, discoloured with stains of rust or possibly blood. She ran the blade against the leather of her Florentine glove, leaving a distinct thin line. It was still sharp.

'A murder weapon?' she suggested.

'No,' said Carole with some exasperation. 'You may have forgotten, but the police already have a murder weapon – the bot knife that was found at the scene of the crime.'

'Oh yes. Yes, of course.' Jude returned the knife to its dusty haven, and redirected her attention to the makeshift bed on the floor. 'It's uneven.'

'What?'

'The bed. The foot end is higher than the pillow end.'

'Well, why not? It's not a proper bed, it's just been assembled from bits and pieces. Probably those disgusting things it's been put on are uneven.'

Jude said nothing, but moved forward and knelt down near the far end of the cushions. She reached under them, felt around, and then pulled out a bundle of something.

Uncurled, it was revealed to be a frayed and battered Barbour, wrapped around a pair of gloves.

Spattered all over both were the unmistakable rusty spots of dried blood.

Chapter Twenty-Two

'Good God,' said Carole, 'so it was Donal, after all.'

'We don't know that. It could have been someone else.'

'For heaven's sake, Jude! This is pretty incontrovertible evidence. The blood-stained garments which were worn when he killed Walter Fleet are found here in Donal's hideaway – what more do you want?' Carole was irritated to see her friend grinning at her. 'And what's that expression meant to mean?'

'Just that I thought you were meant to be the rational one, and what you just said did make quite a few major leaps of logic. For a start, we don't know that these were the clothes worn by the murderer of Walter Fleet and, on top of that, though there seems to be evidence that someone's been squatting in this loft, we have no proof that that person is Donal Geraghty.'

'Now you're just being picky.'

'Well, even if your theory's true – say it is Donal who's been camping in here – say these are the clothes worn by the murderer – what're we going to do about it?'

'Obviously we take the evidence to the police – or

no, we don't touch it. We call the police here and we—'

'Tell them that we just happened to be trespassing in the Dalrymples' stables, and we just happened by chance to come upon these bloodstained garments?'

'Ah. I see your point. No, what we do is, we get as far away from here as possible, and then we send the police an anonymous tip-off, recommending that they take a look in the Dalrymples' stables.'

'And how do we do that? Phone calls are traceable, so are text messages, faxes, emails . . .'

'We find a way to do it.' Carole was getting exasperated by Jude's uncharacteristic assumption of the wet-blanket role, and even more exasperated because she reckoned Jude was only doing it to tease her. 'That's not what's important. What *is* important is that we get away from here as quickly as possible.'

'Hm . . . Well, we're not leaving till I've had a little look at what we've found.'

'But you can't! You mustn't!' Carole's Home Office training once more asserted itself. 'If you touch anything, you'll probably get arrested for the murder yourself. You can't risk leaving any DNA.'

'I think I'll be all right,' said Jude, showing off her hands in the Florentine gloves. Carole watched, appalled, as her neighbour carefully inspected the bloodstained pair of gloves, almost turning them inside out to check for any marks of identification. But she was disappointed. Just cheap, ordinary woollen gloves that could be bought at any store or market in the country. And the one-size-fits-all expandable sort that gave no indication even of the wearer's gender.

'What about the jacket?' Jude picked the Barbour up and looked at it. Old, well-worn, average size. She held it up to the window. In better light, even more dull blood-spatters were visible on the old waxed fabric. If this was not the garment worn by Walter Fleet's killer, then there had been another recent bloody murder in the Fethering area.

Holding up the jacket by its collar, Jude checked the pockets. The inside ones only yielded a pencil stub and a crumpled tissue, the latter wonderfully revelatory to a police forensics team but entirely useless to the unqualified amateur.

Jude moved on to the outside pockets. Just a few bits of lint and shreds of paper. A wizened stump of carrot and a few fluffy Polo mints, presumably intended as treats for some lucky horse.

Punctiliously, she returned each item to where she'd found it. Only the small upright slit-pockets remained. Nothing in the left one. But in the right – her gloved hand closed round a scrap of slightly shiny paper.

She pulled it out. A scrumpled cardholder's copy of an American Express transaction. On which the name of the signatory could be clearly read.

Alec Potton.

Jude wrapped the gloves in the bloody Barbour, trying to reproduce exactly the previous creases and replaced the bundle in exactly the same place under the make-shift bed.

Then, with Carole still looking like a finalist in the Miss Paranoia Competition, they went back down the ladder and left the Dalrymples' stables.

They were well away from the house and on the tow-path back into Fethering when they heard the approaching sirens. But they were still close enough to see the pair of police cars hurtle up the road and turn into Nicky and Sonia Dalrymple's drive.

Chapter Twenty-Three

This was another of those many occasions which brought home to Carole and Jude the frustrations of being amateur investigators. The police had arrived at the Dalrymples' house only moments after they had made a discovery which could have enormous bearing on the search for Walter Fleet's killer. But the two women had no means of knowing if that was why the police had turned up. And, if they had come in search of that evidence, who had tipped them off as to where they would find it?

An even more troubling thought – particularly to Carole – was that someone had seen her and Jude breaking and entering and had tipped the police off. She lived in fear of a knock on the door of High Tor, leading to criminal charges.

But, not for the first time, all they could do was to wait for public announcements on news bulletins, and keep their ears close to the groundswell of Fethering gossip.

This last was certainly a flowing source, not to say a torrent. Something said in the Crown and Anchor would be quickly repeated (with embellishments) in

Allinstore, whence it would pass and grow in size through the media of bakery, off-licence and hairdresser. Within hours, everyone in the village seemed to know about the police going to the Dalrymples, and there were as many theories about their reasons for doing so as there were inhabitants to entertain them. The trouble was that none of these conjectures was based on any more information than Carole and Jude had, and a lot of them were frankly loony. When she first arrived in Fethering, Carole had quickly reached the conclusion that listening to village gossip was the way madness lay, and nothing that had happened since had done anything to change her opinion.

So the two women spent a restless and unsatisfactory few days until, on the Monday's *World at One*, it was announced that the police were questioning another man in connection with the death of Walter Fleet.

The jungle drums of Fethering beat loud for the next hour and, once the wilder rumours had been eliminated, there seemed to be a credible consensus that the man being questioned was Alec Potton.

'Jude?'

'Yes.'

'It's Sonia.'

'Ah, hello.' Jude just stopped herself from asking about the discovery in the hayloft; of course she didn't know about that. 'Are you still at Yeomansdyke?'

'No. I'm back home. I was summoned here by the police.'

'Oh, really?' Jude continued to feign ignorance.

'They had a tip-off about something found in our stables. Something to do with Walter Fleet's murder, apparently.'

'Good heavens. Maybe that also has something to do with Alec Potton being taken in for questioning.'

'Oh, is that what's happened? I hadn't heard.' Jude couldn't be certain, but she got the impression that Sonia was lying. Either that, or she hadn't spoken to a single person in Fethering over the whole weekend.

'You told me you knew Alec Potton. I wondered . . .'

'Well, I've met him. He's picked Imogen up from here the odd time. I wouldn't say I know him.' She seemed anxious to move on. 'Anyway, as you can imagine, Jude, this has all been very stressful.'

'I'm sure it has.'

'. . . and I was wondering if I could book a session with you . . . you know, balancing . . .? I mean, I'm sorry I had to cancel that one on Friday.'

'Don't worry. I'm free tomorrow morning. Would that suit you?'

'Oh, it'd be wonderful.'

'Say . . . what? Ten, eleven?'

'Ten'd be good.'

'OK, I'll see you then.'

'Oh, and, Jude . . .'

'Yes?'

'You know you got Donal to work on Chieftain.'

'Mm.'

'Do you know where I can find him? Donal. I need to talk to him.'

'No, I'm sorry, I don't. He seems to have gone to ground again.' No need to explain the reason why. Ted Crisp had been very insistent that the stabbing in the Crown and Anchor should be kept quiet.

'Oh. Oh, that's a pity.' But the way Sonia said the word, it sounded more like a tragedy.

Jude gave assurances that she'd put Donal in touch if she met him again, and their phone call ended. Puzzling, why Sonia was so desperate to make contact with the ex-jockey. For the second time. Increasingly, from her client's behaviour and from what Donal himself had said, Jude was becoming convinced that Sonia Dalrymple was the target for his blackmail demands. But what the dark secret he possessed was, she had no idea. It might be related to what Jude now felt sure was Nicky Dalrymple's violence against his wife, but she had a feeling there was more to it than that.

Still, one positive confirmation had come out of her conversation with Sonia. The evidence that had led the police to Alec Potton had been what they'd found in the Dalrymples' hayloft.

Fethering beach that Monday afternoon was resolutely monochrome. When the sun shone, the colours came to life like a child's magic painting splashed with water. Then, the blue in the sky drew out the blues and greens of the sea; the seaweed on the beach sparkled like a carpet of emeralds. Then the sand was – if not golden – at least a rich biscuity yellow.

But not on that dour late-February day. The idea

that a sun existed anywhere seemed an unlikely fabri-
cation. The sea was leaden, and the sky a darker lead.
The sand was the grey of damp cement. Even the coat
of Gulliver, scampering around like a host at a failed
party trying to inject some life into the proceedings,
was another shade of grey in the unremitting gloom.

'So we have to wait till tomorrow morning,' said
Carole moodily.

'Hm?'

'Till we can get any further with our investigation.
You said Sonia Dalrymple's coming to see you.'

'Yes, but she's coming to see me as a client. I can't
use our session as an excuse to pick her brains about
her being blackmailed.'

'Why not? Medical ethics?'

'Something like that, yes.'

Carole's snort expressed fully her attitude to the
concept of medical ethics being applied to the flaky,
spurious world of alternative medicine. 'Well, if you
don't want to find out who killed Walter Fleet . . .'

'I do, Carole, you know I do, and we do have other
lines of enquiry open to us.'

'Oh yes? Like what?

'Hilary Potton. You're sort of chums with her, aren't
you?'

'I wouldn't say "chums".'

'You've talked to her. You've phoned her before.
Why not give her another call?'

'Oh, I don't know. It'd would look pretty insensitive.
I mean, at a time like this. Her husband's being questioned as part of a murder enquiry – the last thing she's

going to want is inquisitive phone calls from people she hardly knows.'

'I'm not so sure. From what you said about the state of her marriage, her husband's not her favourite person.'

'There's a difference between not liking someone, and wanting to see them arrested for murder.'

'I wonder . . .' Jude scuffed her boot in the grey shingle as she thought about this. 'Of course, your approach needn't sound insensitive.'

'I don't see how.'

'It could sound caring.'

'Caring?' Carole echoed sceptically. 'Please explain.'

'Well, there are two possible approaches. Either you can pretend you've heard nothing about Alec's arrest—'

'That'd be clumsy, rather than caring.'

'Or you can say you have heard this rumour, and you can't believe it's true, and aren't people appalling the way they slander perfectly innocent citizens of this country, and can Hilary please reassure you that it's complete rubbish.'

'Hm.' Carole wasn't going to concede too quickly that this approach might work, but she was coming round to the idea.

'What time did you say her shift at Allinstore was?'

'Four to eight every weekday, except Wednesdays, late night Fridays.' Carole looked at the neat little watch on her wrist. While she could recognize the strength of Jude's argument, everything inside her protested at the idea of just ringing Hilary Potton out of the blue.

'Probably too late to catch her today. By the time I've got back home to the phone.'

'I've got my mobile with me.'

'Hello. Is that Hilary?'

'Yes.'

'This is Carole Seddon. You remember, we met in the Seaview Café.'

'Oh yes, of course.'

Carole felt very aware of Jude sitting with her in the rusty seafront shelter. She had never liked making phone calls with other people present. During her Home Office career, she had been hugely relieved when she became senior enough to have her own office with a door that closed. And she was glad she had left the civil service before open-plan office accommodation became universal. Even though she knew Jude to be the least judgmental person in the world, Carole still wished she was on her own.

'Look, I'm sorry to trouble you with a call right now, because I know you've got to be at Allinstore shortly.'

'Don't worry about it. I won't be going in to Allinstore this afternoon.'

'You're not ill, are you?'

'No. I'm afraid something rather dreadful's happened. Over the weekend my husband – my nearly ex-husband – was taken in for questioning by the police—'

'No!'

'In connection with the murder of Walter Fleet.'

So much for Carole's worries about how she was

going to initiate the conversation – or indeed invent a reason for her call. But that wasn't her primary thought right then. She was more struck by Hilary Potton's manner. Although the woman was relaying extremely bad news, there was no doubt that she was doing so with great relish. Whether this was just because Hilary enjoyed being at the centre of her drama, or because what had happened confirmed her worst suspicions about her husband's character, Carole had no means of knowing.

'Anyway, given that situation, Carole, I am absolutely determined to be at home when Imogen gets back from school. I mean, I hate to think what kind of whispering and innuendo she's had to put up with from the other kids. They can be so cruel. I didn't want her to go to school today, but she insisted. So I need to be here for her. As a result, I'm afraid this afternoon Allinstore will have to whistle for my services.'

'Yes. And of course it wouldn't be much fun for you, would it? Like poor Imogen at school. With everyone who came into the shop whispering and nudging about what had happened – you know, knowing that you were Alec's wife?'

'I suppose it would be rather horrid. I hadn't really thought about that aspect of it.' But she had. And she didn't sound appalled; in fact, the image was not without its attraction. Carole's inkling that Hilary Potton might be a bit of a drama queen was strengthened.

Having had the subject so painlessly broached for her, it was time for a bit of subterfuge. 'But it must be dreadful for you, Hilary, the police must've made a mistake, mustn't they? Surely they have no evidence to link Alec to the scene of the crime, do they?'

'I wish I could say that was true, Carole.' She didn't sound that unhappy about the situation, though. 'I'm afraid they did find something – obviously I can't tell you the details, but . . . It doesn't look too good for Alec, I'm afraid.'

'How on earth does that make you feel?'

'Ghastly, of course. And yet at the same time it does confirm some of my worst fears . . . you know, about Alec. I mean, when we first got married, I didn't realize how unstable he was. I came to see that over the years. I mean, there was the philandering – which I mentioned to you – and that's never a particularly encouraging indication of a man's character. But over the last months Alec has been getting increasingly unpredictable. Sudden mood-swings – you know what I mean? And his behaviour . . . I mean, he's been very – I don't know what the word is – *clingy* where Imogen's concerned.'

'Clingy?'

'Yes, sometimes he behaves more as if she were his lover than his daughter.'

'You're not suggesting . . .'

'Oh, good heavens, no. At least, I don't think he'd ever touch her in *that* way. Mind you, I don't really know what to think about Alec now. If he's capable of murdering someone, then I suppose there are other kinds of things he might . . !' Hilary Potton's words petered out, as though she were taking in the implications of what she'd said. A speech which had started off as a defence of her husband had ended up as a pretty thorough indictment.

'So you think he *is* capable of murder?'

'I don't know. He keeps getting these sudden rages and jealousies. He's certainly capable of having got it into his head that there was something between Walter Fleet and me.'

'But he didn't have any justification for that, did he?' asked Carole, phrasing her question with care.

'Good heavens, no. Nothing concrete. I mean, Walter did fancy me – there was no question about that. You know, we women can always tell when a man's interested, and Walter was certainly interested. Constantly putting his arm round me, holding my hand, when it wasn't quite necessary. I didn't mind. I even, probably, flirted with him a bit. Nothing serious, just fun. Being married to Alec, I found it quite a pleasant change to have a man saying nice things to me. But as I say, there was nothing there, just a bit of frivolity. But maybe Alec saw me and Walter together at some point when he was chatting me up and . . !' Carole could feel her shudder down the phone '. . . well, with what tragic consequences.'

'So you do actually think your husband killed Walter Fleet?'

'I'd love not to think that, Carole. I'd give anything not to think that, but I'm afraid the facts may be against me. Of course, I'll go on believing in his innocence as long as I can . . !' She trailed off without much optimism.

The next question was a tricky one. Carole had to

find a way of putting it which didn't reveal her private knowledge of what the police had presumably found in the stables at the Dalrymples'. 'Hilary, you don't know how the police found the evidence against your husband? I mean, where they found it, or whether someone tipped them off about where to look?'

'I'm sorry,' came the prim reply. 'I'm afraid I don't know anything about that. All I know—' She was interrupted. 'Oh, I'm sorry, Carole, that's Immy back from school. I must talk to her.'

'Of course.'

'But thanks so much for ringing. And, if you want to call again, please do.'

Thank you, thought Carole. I will.

Chapter Twenty-Four

That evening Jude's mind was full of images. Shapeless, ill-defined, blurred images, but they troubled her. She could not say precisely what they presaged, but her mind had been free of them before she heard the news about Alec Potton. Something felt wrong there. Something told her that he wasn't a murderer.

But she was not so arrogant as to assume that she was right in her reaction. Her instincts were as fallible as anyone else's. She could think of many occasions when she had been convinced of a certain truth, only to have it proved worthless by logic and evidence. But at that moment, she could not think of Alec Potton as a guilty man. Or at least not as a man guilty of murder.

Jude went through a routine she frequently followed when she was troubled. She did an hour of yoga. The familiar postures and movements, and the concentration required to achieve them, balanced her thoughts, put the unwelcome images into a better perspective.

Then she filled the bath and added a personal mix of herbs, lit fragrant candles around the room and, while her heavy body luxuriated in the steamy water, allowed her thoughts – not to dissipate, but to assume manageable proportions.

It was while she was towelling herself down and thinking what to cook for supper that her mobile rang.

'Hello?'

'Is that Jude?'

The voice was young, familiar, and yet at that moment so stretched with tension she could not immediately recognize it. Fortunately she did not have to wait long for identification.

'It's Imogen. Imogen Potton. You know, we met at—'

'Yes. Of course I know who you are. Is everything all right?'

'Fine,' asserted a voice whose tautness told a different story.

'Listen, Imogen. I heard about your father being taken in by the police. I'm sure it's just a mistake. Don't worry, they'll soon release him.'

There was no response from the other end. Jude felt this was not because Imogen had nothing to say, but because she didn't feel confident that she could keep her emotions in check if she did speak.

'Presumably it is about what happened to your father that you were ringing?'

'Yes,' the girl answered curtly. Brusqueness perhaps gave her a means of control. 'You remember that day you were at the stables?'

'What, at Sonia's? When I was healing?'

'No, the other time. Friday morning at Long Bamber.'

'Yes.'

'Well, I was mucking-out Conker's stable while you were talking to Lucinda and Donal, and I could hear everything you were saying.'

'I don't think we were saying anything particularly dreadful.'

'No, that's not the point.' Her voice now had a tone of teenage irritation at the inability of grown-ups ever to understand what was relevant. 'Donal said something about you having a hotline to the police.'

'I remember. I've no idea what he meant by that.'

'What, you mean you haven't got a hotline to the police?' Imogen almost wailed in disappointment.

'Well, I've been questioned by them, because I don't know if you know, but I actually found – I was the first person to arrive at the scene of the crime after Walter Fleet's death. But, apart from that, I don't know anything about how their enquiries are currently proceeding. I think Donal was just having a joke with me.'

'But you do have a name? The name of one of the detectives in charge of the investigation?'

'Well, I can tell you who the two I talked to were, yes.'

Imogen seemed desperate for the information, so Jude gave her the names.

'And do you know where they're based?'

'I'm not sure. It's somewhere in West Sussex. They just gave me mobile numbers if I needed to contact them again.'

'Could you let me have those numbers?'

Jude couldn't see any reason why not to. She had to go into her bedroom, towel wrapped around her, to find the scrap of paper where she'd written them down.

'What is this about, Imogen? Can you tell me?' There was no answer. 'I mean, do you have some information that you reckon can get your father off the hook?'

'Yes,' the girl replied. 'Yes, I do.' And she rang off.

Which was, in equal measure, intriguing and frustrating.

Carole Seddon was equally restless that Monday evening, and partly for the same reasons. Though she hadn't met him, she too was upset by the thought that Alec Potton was the police's prime suspect. Her unease derived, however, not from a conviction of his innocence, but from the recognition that he was quite possibly guilty.

If he was, the case was at an end. Carole would lose the mental displacement activity offered by picking apart its details and trying to construct chains of logic from them.

And she'd be left with nothing to occupy her brain but the *Times* crossword, and anxieties about the state of her son's marriage.

Then she remembered, rather guiltily, something else she should be worried about. Given the sudden access of emotion she had felt when she thought Ted Crisp's life was threatened, she had shown very little interest in his medical progress since the attack. She called his private number, the phone in his scruffy flat above the bar.

There was no reply. She let the phone ring and ring, in case he was in the bath or something, and then had a moment of panic. Maybe the wound had reopened – maybe he was lying in bed, drowning in blood, his voice too feeble to summon help.

She dialled the number of the pub itself. On the third ring her call was answered. 'Crown and Anchor,' said the unmistakable voice of Ted Crisp, over a hub-bub which, by Fethering's standards, was almost raucous.

'Ah. Er, Ted – it's me, Carole.'

'Right, and what can I do you for? Want to order tonight's special? It's a prawn curry, served with rice and poppadoms.' Following Jude's example, Carole had sometimes been known to order her meal before leaving home when she was going to eat at the Crown and Anchor.

'No, I'm not coming down to the pub tonight.'

'Oh, well, what is it? Sharpish, please, 'cause we're chocker in here tonight.'

'I just . . .'

'Mm?'

'I just rang to see how you are.'

'In what way?'

'I mean, after being stabbed on Friday. Whether you'd taken any time off or . . . seen the doctor or . . .?'

'Bloody hell, Carole, it was only a scratch. I'm feeling fine. And now look, I've got customers clamouring for pints, so sorry, got to ring off,' he said, and immediately did so.

Leaving Carole feeling very foolish indeed, and wishing she had even more control over her emotions.

'Is your name Jude?'

'Yes.' She had just subsided into one of the sitting room's shapeless sofas with a plate of one of her favourite Thai chicken and cashew recipes. 'Would you mind calling me back? I'm just eating my supper.'

'I don't care what you're doing!' The voice of the woman at the end of the line was extremely angry. 'I want to know what you've been saying to my daughter.'

'I don't know. I'm sorry, I don't know who you are. I don't know who your daughter is.'

'My name's Hilary Potton. My daughter's name's Imogen. Come on, don't deny that you know her.'

'I'm not denying that I know her. She rang me earlier this evening.'

'She rang you, did she? Are you sure you didn't ring her, to put vicious and hurtful ideas into her head?'

'I'm sorry, Mrs Potton, I have no idea what you're talking about.'

'I think you do, *Jude*.' She'd never heard her name invested with quite so much venom. 'You've been encouraging her in these stupid, harmful fantasies.'

'I'm still not with you.'

'Do you deny that you gave my daughter the names of the detectives involved in the investigation of Walter Fleet's murder?'

'No, I don't deny that. I did give her the names.'

'And do you deny that you encouraged her to ring them, and tell them a complete fabric of lies?'

'Yes, Mrs Potton, I deny that completely. I have no idea what Imogen told the police. All she told me was that she had some information which might help exonerate her father.'

'Oh.' For the first time, a bit of wind was taken from Hilary Potton's furious sails. 'But you have no idea what that information was.'

'Absolutely none. I'd be very interested to know, but I don't.'

'And you think I'm about to tell you?'

'No. I would say from your tone of voice and general manner that's extremely unlikely.'

'Well, you might be wrong there, *Jude*.' The loathing in the name had now been reduced to contempt.

'Oh?'

'And you're sure you didn't encourage Imogen to do what she's done?'

'Mrs Potton, I promise you I have no idea what she's done. And so far as I know, I've never encouraged your daughter to do anything. We've only met a couple of times. I hardly know her.'

'Well,' said a disgruntled Hilary Potton, 'if you didn't put her up to it, I'm sure someone else did.'

'Can you please tell me what it is she's done?'

'Hm . . .' The woman seemed to assess this request before answering. 'You know that my husband – my former husband – is being questioned by the police?'

'Yes, I do know that.'

'Of course you do. Everyone in bloody Fethering knows that! And whatever happens, I know I'll never hear the end of it. Anyway, what you don't probably know, if your acquaintance with my daughter is as minimal as you say it is –' the suspicion was still there in her words '– is that, in spite of the kind of man he is, Imogen is totally devoted to her father. Besotted. In her eyes he can do no wrong at all. So she just cannot cope with the idea that he might have committed murder.'

'It's a hard thing to think of anyone. I mean, don't you have difficulty in believing it?'

'I know Alec rather well.' Hilary Potton's words came out in a long hard line. 'And I keep finding out about more dreadful things he's done. I wouldn't be that surprised if murder turned out to be one of them.'

'Very well,' said Jude, making her response sound less shocked than she might have done. 'So, because Imogen's so devoted to her father, she's rung the police and given them some information she hopes will get him off the hook?'

'Fortunately, I have managed to stop her from contacting the police. No thanks to you,' she added savagely.

'But that was what Imogen intended to do – tell the police something that would exonerate her father?'

'Worse than that,' Hilary Potton almost shrieked. 'She was intending to give the police a confession. She was going to tell them that she stabbed Walter Fleet!'

Chapter Twenty-Five

The barrage which came from the other end of the line when Jude asked whether there could be any truth in Imogen's assertion made Hilary Potton's previous fury seems as mild as a summer breeze. For a start, it was logistically impossible that her daughter could have committed the crime, since she was with her mother at the relevant time. And the idea that anyone should think Imogen capable of such an appalling atrocity was . . . It took some time for Jude to get herself off the phone.

She rarely phoned Carole. Normally she just went round to High Tor and banged on the door. But it was late, so she rang the number.

Carole sounded slightly disappointed when she heard who it was. Jude sensed her neighbour had been hoping for some contact from Stephen. But Carole livened up when she heard about the latest development in the case.

'Imogen's devoted to her father, isn't she? And she's at the age for dramatic gestures. Taking his guilt on herself – it's like something out of *A Tale of Two Cities*.'

'Yes, but there's still something odd about the whole

business. I mean, Hilary was in such a state of fury. You don't know her that well, but have you ever heard her like that?'

'Not the way you describe it, no. She's certainly sounded off whenever she got on to the subject of Alec, but that was more vicious contempt than fury.'

'The kind of thing you hear from every divorcée about her ex—'

'Not *every* one,' said Carole frostily, making Jude feel guilty for her carelessness.

'No, of course not. It's odd, isn't it? Everyone else involved in this case seems to be keeping secrets, holding their cards very close to their chests, except for Hilary Potton, and she seems prepared to sound off to anyone about anything.'

'Not to *anyone*,' said Carole, offended. She was proud of the way she had nurtured her source of information, and didn't want to have her achievements belittled.

'No, sorry. You know what I meant.'

'Yes, I do,' said Carole, unmollified. 'Anyway, talking of sources of information . . .'

'Mm?'

'Don't forget you've got one of our most promising ones coming to see you tomorrow morning.'

'I hadn't forgotten.'

'And don't forget either that ethics is a comparative study. There are times when one ethical consideration – say the need to find out the truth – has to overrule another.'

'Like, say, the confidentiality between therapist and client?'

'Exactly, Jude.'

Anyone who had seen Sonia Dalrymple getting out of her Range Rover outside Woodside Cottage the next morning would have laughed at the idea that she had a care in the world. She looked supermodel-stunning in sleek black trousers, black silk top and perfectly cut black leather jacket. And if there still was any bruising around her eyes, it had been magicked away by expert make-up.

But as soon as Jude got her face down on the treatment bed and touched her back, the tensions within were immediately apparent. Jude parted the curtain of blonde hair to feel the knots of muscle where the neck met the skull, and ran her fingers down the taut length of Sonia's spine.

'You're holding a lot in, aren't you?'

The client grunted agreement.

'You always hold a lot in, but this is exceptional.'

'I know. If you can just get rid of the tension. It's really hurting. I can't get comfortable in bed, so I'm not sleeping.'

'I'm not surprised. You must be very careful, otherwise you'll do yourself permanent damage. Your balance is all over the place.'

Jude lit some candles, opened her pots of oil, and started a smooth gentle massage of Sonia Dalrymple's beautiful back. She didn't work into the flesh and joints

220

like a physiotherapist; she hardly touched, just let the warmth – both real and spiritual – irradiate the woman's body. After about ten minutes she moved her hands away.

'Is that better?'

'Mm.' Sonia's voice was deep, throaty and grateful.

'You know there's a limited amount I can do, don't you? Whatever it is that's troubling you, effectively poisoning you, you have to get rid of it yourself.'

'You mean by telling someone?'

'If it's something that can be told.'

'That's the whole point, Jude, it isn't. I can't tell anyone, which is why the pressure just builds and builds.'

'Are you sure there's no one you can talk to? I'm not offering myself as a listener,' Jude hastened to assure her.

'No, there isn't. I've got a wide range of acquaintances, but very few actual friends. And if I had any, I couldn't tell them anyway, because they know my domestic set-up and . . .' She trailed away.

'Listen, Sonia, I don't want to be nosey. It's not my place, that's not what I'm here for, but if there is anything you feel you can unload on to me – well, I'm not part of your family, you don't see me that often. It's up to you.'

'I'd like to talk about it, Jude, but it's so complicated. Everything's interlinked. Telling about one thing is automatically going to lead on to the next thing and . . .'

'Very well. Don't worry about it. Can you turn over?

I'd like to work on your shoulders and neck at the front.'

After a few minutes of this, Jude propped her client's head on to a special pillow and started the lightest of cranial massages. Again, she used her fingers not to manipulate or apply pressure, but as a conduit for energy.

'Sonia, let me talk. Not ask questions exactly, but make suggestions. If there are things you want to agree with, or to disagree with, fine. If you don't want to say anything, equally fine. And if you want me to shut up, just say.'

Having received a guarded assent, Jude continued, 'All right, you talked about your domestic set-up. Well, I know your marriage is not entirely happy. You've told me that on previous sessions and, now I've met Nicky, I can see where some of the problems may lie. He is a very controlling personality, who doesn't like people disagreeing with him.'

There was no sound from the woman whose skull she was continuing to massage, so Jude asked, 'You don't mind my saying this? Tell me when to stop.'

'No, it's fine,' Sonia murmured. 'As you say, I've already told you all this stuff.'

'So it might just be the continuing unhappiness in your marriage that's generating this tension in you . . . except that it's so much worse than when I last saw you, that I think there must be some new factor, something that's happened recently to upset you, some new secret you have to hide.'

Almost without words, Sonia agreed that there was.

'Now, I'm not asking you to tell me what that secret is. I don't think you can tell me, anyway – that's why the tension's building up so much. As you said, you can't tell anyone. But part of the trouble with your relationship with Nicky is that there are things you can't tell him, or things you've tried to tell him, but you know he won't listen to.'

There was the lightest of nods from the head beneath Jude's hands.

'And it's possible that only telling him these things can bring any kind of equality into your marriage, can give you perhaps an opportunity of saving it?'

Another quiver of assent.

'So, maybe, when Nicky's next home, you should try confronting him with some of these things you haven't said to him?' Jude had a momentary doubt about the wisdom of her advice. 'I don't want to make things worse between you.'

'You'd be hard put to do that.'

'I mean, I don't want to' – she phrased it as delicately as she could – 'put you at risk.'

'Nothing'll put me more at risk than I am at the moment, Jude. Go on.'

'When's Nicky next home?'

'The weekend.'

'Can't you try talking to him?'

'Oh, Jude,' said Sonia tearfully, 'you make it sound so easy. Just tell Nicky all the feelings I've been bottling up for all these years, not to mention what's happened recently. You don't know him. I've had ages to say those things to him, and I've never managed in the past. Why should this weekend be any different from any of his other fleeting visits to our so-called home?'

'I can't answer that. But you know that's the only chance you have of making the marriage workable.'

'I do know. I've known for years. And for years I've put it off.'

'Why? For fear such a confrontation might destroy the marriage?'

'Yes.'

'Well, is that such a terrible risk? Might that not be a solution? Is the marriage, as you currently have it, worth saving?'

There was a long silence. Jude continued the cranial massage with no particular expectation of a response. She felt no guilt. She had put no ideas into Sonia Dalrymple's mind, merely organized the information that Sonia had already given her. The thought processes that had been set in motion were not new ones; Sonia had spent much of her married life weighing up the pros and cons of these issues.

'But,' said Jude eventually, 'I get the feeling that it's not just Nicky who's troubling you at the moment. You're under pressure from some other source.'

'Yes,' Sonia agreed, almost eagerly, as if the confession took a weight off her mind.

'Donal Geraghty,' said Jude, and felt the body beneath her hands tremble at the name. 'Donal

Geraghty has implied to me that he's either blackmailing or planning to blackmail someone in this area.'

'Yes.'

'Is it you? Is Donal trying to blackmail you?'

'Yes,' said Sonia Dalrymple, and then burst into tears from sheer relief.

Chapter Twenty-Six

After their session had finished, Jude put away the treatment bed, re-covering it with an array of throws and drapes that made it indistinguishable from all the other furniture in her sitting room. Then she sat on what she knew to be a sofa, deep in thought.

Her worries followed on from her telephone conversation with Carole the night before, but it was not the first time they had troubled her. As a healer – or however people wanted to define what she did – Jude had a relationship of confidentiality to her clients. Like a priest taking confession, any medical – or quasi-medical – practitioner will from time to time hear things that he or she knows should not be spread abroad. And Sonia Dalrymple had told her things about her marriage which Jude would never dream of spreading abroad.

But when the information given might be relevant to a murder enquiry, the moral issues became more blurred. Though she hadn't directly questioned Sonia about any connections she might have to the Fleets, Jude felt she had been sailing dangerously close to that particular wind. Fortunately – well, in one sense fortunately – Sonia had not revealed the secret whose retention was so troubling her, so Jude's moral dilemma was, at least on that occasion, resolved.

But it was a problem that was almost bound to recur, and she just hoped she would have the moral courage to do the right thing when it did.

However, she couldn't sit there all morning agonizing about the ethics of her profession, or vocation, or whatever it was. There was one very positive, practical thing she had to do. Without revealing the secret knowledge Donal Geraghty held over her, Sonia Dalrymple had made it very clear that she was anxious to make contact with him. More than anxious – desperate. And since Jude seemed to have been one of the people who had seen Donal most recently, any help she could give Sonia in tracking him down would be most welcome.

Well, after the fight with Ted Crisp, the ex-jockey was probably lying low. But there might be ways of finding out where he was lying low.

Jude's first instinct was to go on the next stage of the quest alone. But the more she thought about it, the more she was amused by the idea of Carole coming with her. So that was what was arranged.

The Cheshire Cheese was no more welcoming than it had been the last time. Nor did the pub give the impression of having been cleaned since Jude's last visit. But, then again, it didn't give the impression of having been cleaned in the previous millennium. And then the cleaning smelled as though it had been done with a rag soaked in beer. She could sense Carole's nose wrinkling behind her.

Hopes for Chilean Chardonnay were so remote she didn't bother asking the same anaemic girl at the counter for anything more elaborate than, 'Two white wines.' These were silently produced.

As they picked up their sticky glasses, Carole hissed, 'I've looked round. He isn't here.'

'I wasn't expecting him to be here. Too soon after his run-in with Ted.' Carole took a sip from her wine and grimaced at the taste, as Jude went on, 'But there are people in here who might know where he is.'

'You mean you know people in here? Jude, I am constantly surprised by the range of your friends.'

'Hardly call them friends. Just people I've met before. Over there.'

Carole followed her friend's gesture with hardly disguised contempt. At the same table sat four short men, looking very similar to the four short men Jude had seen on her previous visit. All wore dirty weatherproof jackets, breeches and boots, one had a flat, discoloured tweed cap. Clearly they weren't all the same, because Donal wasn't there for one, and she couldn't be sure that she recognized the others.

One of them recognized her, however. 'Ah, look, it's Donal's bit of stuff, come to find him again. Did he not come home last night, dear?' he asked in a voice of mock concern.

'You don't think he could have been out *drinking*, do you?' asked another, ready to join in the game.

Jude smiled easily. 'I am actually looking for Donal. Do any of you know where he is?'

But none of the old stable lads was going to give a direct answer. There was a lot of heavily mimed head-shaking and oohing and aahing at her request, then the one who'd spoken first said, 'Now, if we did know where he was, should we tell you? We don't know what you're after him for, do we?'

'Might be maintenance, you see,' suggested one of them.

'Or a restraining order,' another proposed.

'Or,' offered the fourth, 'he might have got you into trouble.'

'Well, it would be a genuine miracle if he'd done that,' said Jude with a grin.

Carole recoiled inwardly. It was bad enough that Jude knew people like this; there was no need for her to sink to their conversational level.

'Come on, I need to find him,' Jude went on. 'Any suggestions?'

'Plenty of suggestions,' one of the wags replied, 'but not many of them printable.'

'Anyway,' said the first speaker, 'there's other reasons Donal might not want to see you. He's spent a fairly unpleasant few days with the police recently. How do we know it wasn't you who put them on to him?'

'I can assure you it wasn't. My only interest in him is because of his skills as a healer.'

'And, of course, his other skills,' roared one of the men. 'The old sexual healing, eh?'

They all found this extremely funny. Jude, smiling along and biding her time, was surprised to see Carole stepping past her and saying, in a frosty voice. 'Please! There is no need for this kind of smutty sexist vulgarity.'

Four male jaws dropped as one. Then the quickest of them to recover shouted, 'Bloody hell, Donal's got two of them after him now.'

'Always did fancy a threesome, old Donal.'

'Yes, he's a kinky old—'

'Will you please be quiet. It's extremely important we contact Donal Geraghty as soon as possible. If you have any idea where he is or how we can get in touch with him, will you please tell us.'

The men were totally confused by Carole's schoolmarm approach and fell silent. Then the leader said grudgingly, 'We don't know where he is. Gather he's had a bit of trouble recently, so don't know what gaff he's kipping down in. Somebody's stable or outhouse I expect, but I can't tell you whose. Mind you, if you really want to find him, I could tell you somewhere he's bound to be.'

'Then I think you'd better tell me.' Behind the rimless glasses Carole's blue eyes were steely.

'It's Fontwell Races day after tomorrow. No way Donal won't be at Fontwell. If you want to find him, that's going to be your best bet.'

'Thank you very much,' said Carole Seddon. Then she put down her hardly touched glass of wine on a nearby table and stalked, with considerable dignity, out of the Cheshire Cheese.

Jude, not wishing to spoil her friend's exit, put down her completely untouched glass, and hurried after her.

Chapter Twenty-Seven

'What's that in the back?' asked Jude, as Carole sedately drove the Renault the eleven miles from Fethering to Fontwell Park racecourse.

'Erm . . . well . . .'

Jude looked round at the purple-coloured straw creation she had last seen at Stephen and Gaby's wedding.

'It's a hat, isn't it?'

'Yes,' Carole conceded.

'Did you bring that for today?'

'Well, quite honestly I wasn't sure what the form was. I've never been racing before.'

'And the only racing you've seen has been when it's made it onto the national news?'

'Maybe.'

'In other words, Royal Ascot.' It was only then Jude noticed that, under her doughty Burberry, her neighbour was dressed in the full purple wedding outfit.

'Um . . . Carole . . . a Thursday Fontwell meeting in early March isn't quite like Ascot. It's quite low-key in terms of dress.'

'So I won't look *under*dressed?'

'Good heavens, no. Rather the reverse. I suggest you keep your raincoat firmly belted up.'

'And don't wear the hat?' asked Carole a little wistfully.

'*Definitely* don't wear the hat.'

'Oh.'

'I promise you, you'll be the only person there dressed anything like that. There'll be plenty of Burberries, and Barbours, and Drizabones and quite a few sheepskins, but no wedding outfits. We're not going to the Royal Enclosure. And it is only National Hunt.'

'Sorry? I thought it was racing, not hunting. And isn't hunting illegal these days?'

'Carole, you don't know anything about racing, do you?'

'Why should I? I spent my career in the civil service, not hanging round racecourses.'

'Well, listen, there are two sorts of racing in this country – National Hunt and the flat.'

'The flat?'

'Yes. And the flat, as the name might suggest, is run on the flat.'

'Not uphill, you mean?'

'No, there are hills on flat courses. Some are very hilly – like Epsom, for instance. But it's called flat racing because there are no jumps or hurdles.'

The tone of Carole's, 'Ah,' suggested Jude wasn't getting her message across. 'National Hunt races are run over jumps or hurdles. The horses not only have to run fast, they have to negotiate a series of obstacles. These might be fences in a steeplechase or, in a hurdle race, as the name suggests, they'd be hurdles. Then there are different sorts of races within those categories and . . .'

The expression on her neighbour's face for a moment dried up Jude's supply of words.

'Never mind,' she picked up again. 'The details aren't important. The main thing is that it's fun. The element of chance, having a flutter. There are very few things to beat that moment when your fancy is nearly winning and on the next few seconds depend your chances of making some huge multiple of your stake and . . .'

Carole's expression had the same dehydrating effect once again.

'Have you ever actually gambled, Carole?'

'Good heavens, no.'

Carole thought they were rather expensive, but Jude insisted they buy tickets for the premier enclosure. They didn't know whereabouts on the course Donal was going to be, and that way they'd have access to the whole area.

Walking across the mud from where they'd parked to the enclosures, Carole stepped fastidiously, wishing she hadn't put on the least sensible shoes she possessed, but looked around at the crowd with diminishing anxiety. She had been expecting to spend the afternoon surrounded by clones of the men in the Cheshire Cheese; to her relief, however, the crowds ambling cheerfully in the same direction seemed . . .

well, middle class. And from the occasional Sloaney squawk she heard, some of them were very definitely upper class. Camilla Parker-Bowles seemed to have been cloned many times over.

For all the crowd, what they were doing seemed completely natural. For them, going to the races was clearly a regular occurrence. They had the accoutrements – old-fashioned trench coats and Barbours to protect them against the weather, green wellingtons, soft dark olive-coloured trilbies (for women as well as men). Many carried battered binoculars, on whose straps hung the coloured strings of former day badges. From the lapels of the hardened race-goers dangled the metal badges of life members. Though Carole could not suppress the thought that not many of these people had any work to go to, she could not deny that they comprised one of the least threatening crowds she had ever encountered.

Inside the premier enclosure there was another expense to be dealt with. 'We've got to get racecards,' Jude insisted.

'But we're here to look for Donal, not waste the afternoon watching horses.'

'Carole, we're here at the races. It would be sacrilege for us not to have a bet.'

The look prompted by that suggested there were many things in life more sacrilegious, but the racecards were duly bought.

'Hm. First race is a two mile six and a half hurdle, so we'll watch from the grandstand.'

'I'm sorry? What do you mean?'

'Fontwell's got two courses. The hurdles go round in an oval, the steeplechase course is a figure of eight. On the chases, it's quite fun to go and watch from the middle. You can get very close to the jumps.'

Carole looked at Jude in bewilderment. 'How do you know all this stuff?'

'I have been racing before.'

'Yes, but not here.'

'Of course here.'

'Why?'

'Well, you move into an area, you look around for things. You want to see what the place has to offer, don't you?'

Carole didn't reply. When she'd first arrived in Fethering, she had looked around for a supermarket, a doctor, a dentist, and left it at that. The idea of checking out the local racecourse was completely alien to her.

'Anyway, let's go and look at the runners.'

'Why?'

'Because we want to know what they look like. Might get an idea of which one will win.'

'Do you actually know anything about racehorses, Jude?'

'I know as much as the average punter does.'

'Which is?'

'I know if I like the look of one, I know if I like its name, or the colours it's wearing, or its jockey's bottom.'

'And you actually bet according to that kind of whim?'

'Yes. That's what most people do. And you have as good a chance of winning as by any other method.'

'It doesn't sound very logical.'

'Carole, logic and gambling are two words that don't fit in the same sentence.'

All that got was a sniff.

'And another reason for going to the parade ring is that it's exactly the kind of place where we might see Donal.'

As Jude knew, Fontwell Park was a small race-course, with its parade ring to the left just inside the entrance. Behind it were the large stalls where the horses were saddled before being led round the brick oval, in the grassy centre of which their owners and 'connections' stood and speculated. All dreamed of winning, but a convention amongst them dictated that no one ever said anything more optimistic than, 'So long as the horse gets round all right – that's the only thing I'm worried about.'

Carole and Jude wriggled through the growing crowds around the parade ring to find a foothold on the paved viewing steps. For a while, Carole scanned the jovial sea of faces for the elusive Donal, but soon she found her eyes were drawn to the horses. Someone who had rarely been near to a real horse could not fail to be impressed by the sheer size and elegance of the creatures. In a few moments all but three of them would be condemned by the punters as useless donkeys, but now, clip-clopping beside their stable lads (mostly female), they did look truly beautiful.

And it was a nice, sharp day, whose thin sun

suggested spring wasn't that far away. The fact that they were now into March was comforting; it was so much more optimistic a month than February. Carole, as she had done so many times since she had moved to Fethering, thawed a little. Maybe going to the races wasn't such a pointless pastime, after all.

'Well, I'm Random Missile,' said Jude.

'I beg your pardon?'

'Random Missile. Number four. Going to walk it.'

'Do you know something? Do you have *inside information*?' asked Carole, like a character out of an early Le Carré.

'No, I told you. There's no science to it. I just like the look of the horse.'

'I'm sure there could be science applied to it. If you assessed all the variables . . . you know, the horse's fitness, where it had run before, who it had beaten, who it had lost to—'

'Don't go down that road. The world is full enough already of people who've worked out infallible systems for getting winners, and let me tell you – none of them work.'

'But if one *were* going to bet –' doing one's supermarket shopping on Mars sounded a likelier option '– wouldn't it be better to do it in an informed manner?'

'Depends on how you get your thrills. What I like about betting is that it's random. That's why I'm going to back Random Missile.'

'Just because of the name?'

'Yes, and the fact that I like the look of him, and the

fact that his stable girl has a nice-coloured scrunchy on her hair.'

'Sometimes I just don't believe you, Jude. You're really going to put money on it?'

'Of course I am. Come on, you just look at the horses. Tell me which one you think'll win.'

'Think'll win or like the look of?'

'Whichever. It comes to the same thing.'

Carole scrutinized all the circling horses with calculating care. Then she pointed to a tall grey. 'That one.'

'Number seven.' Jude consulted her racecard. 'Gerry's Tyke. Not a bad choice. Will probably start favourite.'

'You mean I've picked the winner?'

'You've picked the one most people think'll win . . .'

'Oh?'

'. . . which is a very different thing. Come on, let me show you where the bookies are.'

They dismounted from the viewing steps. As they moved away, the jockeys in their bright silks were starting to appear on the central green of the parade ring, chatting with eager politeness to their paymasters and eyeing up the opposition. As Carole and Jude walked up towards the stands, aromas of curry and onions and chips wafted from the high vans dispensing them. Large men with beer in plastic glasses milled around, but nothing threatened. The atmosphere remained benign, anticipatory, everyone having a good day out.

Jude led Carole through the milling bodies in a

passage between the stands that led to the trackside area. Here, two rows of bookies plied their trade, the more modern with the horses' names and odds red on electronic displays, but the majority still relying on whiteboards, a felt pen to write up the odds and a finger to wipe them away.

'You can bet on the Tote, but I much prefer doing it with the bookies. You can see the odds change from minute to minute.'

Carole nodded, as if she had a clue what she was being told. Jude pointed up at a bookie's board. 'See, Random Missile's at twenty-fives. Gerry's Tyke's eleven to eight favourite.'

'Ah.'

'Ooh.' Jude suddenly darted along the row. By the time Carole struggled her way through the crowd to catch up, she saw her friend holding up a ten-pound note to another bookie. 'Tenner on Random Missile.'

'Three hundred and thirty pound to ten, number four,' said the bookmaker, for the benefit of the recorder behind him, and waited till a ticket was printed out to hand to Jude.

'Why that bookmaker rather than the other one?' asked Carole.

'Because he was offering thirty-three to one. The other was only at twenty-fives.'

'Ah.'

'Which means I win three hundred and thirty quid.'

'If the horse wins.'

'He will win. I know it.'

'How do you know it?'

'I just do.'

'Hmph,' said Carole.

'Ooh, look! They're offering seven to four on yours over there.'

'What?'

'Seven to four on Gerry's Tyke. Go on, grab it, won't last long.'

'Are you suggesting that I should actually bet on the horse?'

'Yes. You think it's going to win, don't you?'

'That's hardly the point.'

'I'd have thought it was exactly the point.'

'Well, I'm not going to bet on it,' said Carole primly. 'I didn't spend all those years contributing to my pension so I could fritter it away on horses.'

'OK. Your decision.' Overhead the tannoy crackled welcomes to the visitors and announced that the horses were coming out on to the course for the first race. 'Come on, Carole, let's get a good vantage point in the stands.'

At the narrow gate from the bookmakers' area, a red-faced man in a blazer checked their day badges and let them through into the premier enclosure.

'There's the winning post, you see,' said Jude. 'If we get right up into the stands on a line with this, we'll get a perfect view of the finish.'

Though the crowds were starting to stream through from other parts of the course, Carole and Jude were ahead of the rush and managed to secure a good vantage point on the highest of the cement steps overlooking the winning post.

'They start over there for this one.' Jude pointed to the far side of the course, where a blur of moving colours could just be discerned.

'You can see why people bring binoculars,' Carole observed.

'Don't worry. There'll be a running commentary while the race is on. There are whole areas of the course that are out of sight. In terms of seeing everything, you do better watching racing on television, but of course it's more exciting when you're actually here.'

'Are you telling me, Jude, that you sometimes watch horse racing on television?'

'Yes, of course I do. When I'm bored. But I don't always have a bet.'

Deflated, Carole let the air puff out of her mouth, with the expression of a woman who had now heard everything.

The buzz of excitement around them grew as more and more people crammed into the stands. The grassy area below, near the winning post, was also filling up, and the level of decibels and excitement mounted as the start approached. Steam rose off the crowd in the March air and dissolved into the high roof of the stand.

Then, with their crackling pre-echoes, the loudspeakers announced the magic words, 'They're under starter's orders. They're off!'

As the commentary rumbled around the track, Carole found it difficult to pick out the individual words, but she kept hearing the name of Random Missile. From their vantage point, they could just about see the start, then the horses went almost out of sight down the bottom of the course, but became clearer as they entered the straight.

The commentary also seemed to become clearer at that point – or maybe Carole's ears were just getting used to the strange sound quality – and there was no doubt from what was being said that Random Missile was way out ahead. Ten lengths, twelve lengths. To her surprise, Carole found herself clutching Jude's arm. 'Goodness,' she said, 'yours is winning!'

'Yes, at the moment, but—'

'Ssh! He's coming up to the finish!'

Random Missile, by now some twenty lengths ahead of his nearest rival, flashed past the post. Carole, uncharacteristically, found herself jumping in the air. 'Jude!' she shrieked. 'Random Missile's won! You've won three hundred and thirty pounds!'

Perhaps it was the good-humoured laughter from the punters around them, or it could have been the fact that the horses all continued running that made Carole realize something was wrong. Crestfallen, she looked at her neighbour for an explanation.

'They've got two more circuits to go.' Jude was trying desperately hard not to sound patronizing. 'The one who wins will be the one who's ahead the third time they pass the post.'

'Oh,' said Carole.

By the next time the horses passed the stands, Random Missile's lead had been cut down to nothing, and as they climbed to the top of the course, he seemed to have found a reverse gear and was slipping back through the pack. Jude jutted out a rueful lower lip. 'He never was going to stay in this going.'

Carole didn't ask for a gloss on this; she got the gist.

The commentary continued, but on the final circuit the names had changed. The horses who had been leading for the first two went virtually unmentioned, though Random Missile did get a couple of name checks. They were: 'Random Missile's trailing the rest by a country mile' and 'Random Missile's pulled up'.

At this last, Jude pouted again, pulled her betting ticket out of her pocket and tore it in two.

'Why're you doing that?'

'He's pulled up. He's not going to finish.'

Meanwhile, at the head of affairs, the race was being fought out by the two second favourites who touched down together over the final fence. But only a couple of lengths behind them loomed the grey menace of Gerry's Tyke. He was fresher and holding something back. He overtook the two tiring horses and vindicated the form book by winning by four lengths and easing up.

Carole Seddon could not suppress a smile of satisfaction.

'I don't know why you're looking so pleased with yourself. You picked the winner and you hadn't got any money on it.'

'Oh, that's true. How much would I have won?'

'Well, say you'd put on a tenner . . .'

'I'd never have put on that much.'

'It makes the sums easier. And say you'd got that

seven to four, you would have won – seventeen pounds fifty.'

Carole looked disappointed. 'Doesn't compare very well to three hundred and thirty.'

'No, but the big difference is that Gerry's Tyke actually won, whereas Random Missile pulled up. It was always going to be much more likely that Gerry's Tyke won. That's why it was favourite, and why Random Missile was at thirty-three to one.'

'It still doesn't sound much of a return, though.'

'A hundred and seventy-five per cent? That's a lot better than a building society.'

'Yes. I suppose it is.' Carole looked thoughtful. 'Shall we go and look at the horses in the parade ring?'

Jude smiled inwardly at her friend's new-found enthusiasm. 'They won't be there yet, but we can wander round. Look at the unsaddling enclosure perhaps?'

'Why would we want to do that?'

'Well, it's the kind of place where Donal Geraghty might well hang about. And trying to find him,' Jude reminded her gently, 'was why we came here this afternoon.'

'Oh yes. Yes, of course,' said Carole.

But there was no sign of the missing Irishman around the unsaddling enclosure. Nor around the parade ring, where the two women again assessed the horseflesh on offer. Jude liked the look of a short chestnut horse with a white blaze on it forehead, called Missie Massie. In spite of the fact that the racecard said, 'Having fallen on her last three starts, makes little appeal here,' Jude was convinced she was worth an each-way gamble. Carole favoured the second favourite, a fastidiously high-stepping stallion called Becktrout, 'Likely to give a good account of himself,' according to the racecard.

At the bookies, as her form might suggest, Missie Massie ranged between forty and sixty-six to one, while the best they could see for Becktrout, seesawing for favouritism with another horse, was five to two.

'Is there any other way of betting?' asked Carole.

'Why do you need one?'

'What's to stop one of these bookmakers just running away while the race is on?'

'You've got a rather outdated image of bookies; maybe that occasionally used to happen. Now they're regulated like any other professional body. Anyway, if they run away today with a hundred quid from Fontwell, how're they going to turn up and continue to make their living tomorrow at Plumpton or Haydock or Uttoxeter or wherever it happens to be?'

'Mm. I see what you mean. But I still don't like the idea of all this money being handed over in the open air.'

'Well, there is another way of betting. You can do it on the Tote. One of those windows over there.'

'Oh, that looks a lot safer. More like a bank.'

So, as Jude rushed across to grab the sixty-six to one on Missie Massie while stocks lasted, Carole went sedately across and completed her transaction with the lady behind the Tote counter.

'It won't be that different from bookies' odds,' Jude

told her when they had once again secured their position overlooking the winning post. 'Sometimes the Tote's better, sometimes worse. Can be worth doing for a really long-priced outsider.'

'Like Missie Massie?'

'Maybe. I just get more of a buzz out of betting with the bookies.'

Missie Massie did better than Random Missile in that she actually completed the course. Sadly, eight other horses completed it ahead of her. Becktrout, on the other hand, led from start to finish and romped home by a distance.

Carole's smile this time was more than satisfied; it was smug.

'Well done!' Jude grinned as she tore up her second betting ticket of the afternoon.

'You don't seem to mind losing.'

'No, it's part of the fun. I mean, the excitement I got when Random Missile was leading in the last race – even though it all subsequently fell apart – well, I certainly got my ten quid's worth out of that.'

'Well. What did you get out of this race? Missie Massie was never better than seventh.'

'I got the excitement of possibility. The excitement of what might have happened.'

Though she didn't say it, Carole's face made clear that she was much more interested in the concrete – what had happened or what was definitely going to happen – than in the possible.

'Anyway, you're ahead. You've cleaned up. Becktrout had drifted to three to one by the off, so the

Tote won't be that different. How much did you put on him?'

'Two pounds.'

'Two pounds? Last of the big spenders. Well, never mind, now you're on a winning streak, you can build up your stakes on the next few races.'

'Oh, I'm not going to bet again,' said Carole.

'What?' asked Jude, thunderstruck.

'No. I've had a winner. If I stop now, I'll end up ahead on the afternoon. Well, except for paying the entrance money.'

'But you can't stop now, Carole. You're just coming into your own. You're on a lucky streak, I can tell. Go on, if you keep betting, you're in with a chance of covering your day badge too. You must have another bet.'

'I don't think so,' said Carole primly. 'That would be tempting Providence.'

'Oh, for heaven's sake!' But Jude didn't get a chance to continue explaining how Carole had failed to grasp the whole concept of gambling. Her eye was caught by something down by the track rail, over in the book-makers' area.

'Excuse me,' she said to the man next to her, 'could I borrow those for a moment?' Before he could acquiesce or refuse, Jude had grabbed his binoculars, still with their strap around the man's neck, and put them to her eyes.

The enlarged image showed three people down at the rail, all looking slightly furtive. A tall woman stood almost like a lookout, while a tubby man handed a large fistful of folded notes to another man.

'Who on earth are you looking at?' asked Carole testily.

'Victor and Yolanta Brewis.'

'Who?'

'And the man with them is Donal Geraghty!'

Chapter Twenty-Eight

'Thank you.' The binoculars were thrust back into the hands of their owner who, given the breadth of Jude's smile, could not fail to reciprocate with one of his own. But she didn't see it. Already, with a querulous Carole in tow, she was trying to weave a speedy way through the melee leaving the grandstand towards the rails.

When they got there, inevitably, Donal had filtered away into the crowd, but Victor and Yolanta Brewis were still at trackside. Though she knew who they were, Jude couldn't really claim acquaintance. It was extremely unlikely that they'd even noticed her on the occasion they'd all three been at Long Bamber Stables. So, with a cautionary gesture to Carole, Jude slowed to within earshot of the couple and became suddenly intrigued in the racecard details of the next set of runners.

The sight of Yolanta suggested that Carole's anxieties about being overdressed had been unwarranted. She loomed, icily beautiful, over her husband, and wore a long wide-skirted white sheepskin coat tied at the front with strings and bobbles. Thigh-length brown leather boots followed the shapely line of her legs down to unfeasibly sharp pointed toes, and on her magenta head was a brown leather hat with a two-foot radius. Her hands were encrusted with gemstone rings, like mussels round the edge of a rock pool.

Victor too had pushed the sartorial boat out. Over bright yellow corduroy trousers and stout brown shoes, he wore a long coat in a bold tweed of ginger and bog green. The hat he wore exactly matched his wife's, making his head look like an apoplectic ringed Saturn.

Jude had only seen them once, but she got the feeling the couple didn't possess any old clothes. Everything they wore seemed to have just come out of the cellophane, and gave the impression, like old music hall stars, of making 'one appearance only'.

Given the flamboyance of their exteriors, the snatch of conversation Jude and Carole overheard was self-effacing, almost furtive.

'Do you think that will be enough to keep him quiet?' asked Yolanta in her heavily accented English.

'For the time being,' Victor replied.

'But if he gets nasty?'

'I may have to get nasty too,' said her husband grimly. Then he smiled at his wife. 'If he makes trouble, at least we know where to find him. Couldn't be handier.'

She chuckled. Victor Brewis opened his racecard and spoke suddenly louder, all affability. 'Now the horse George Tufton recommended is in the next race. We want to take a close look at him.'

'You are going to buy him, my darling?'

'If he wins, yes. If not, forget it. Let's go and have a look at him in the parade ring.'

And they wandered off through the milling crowd, unaware of the sniggers that their appearance prompted.

'Who on earth are those people?'

Jude gave a quick resumé of the Brewises and their connection to Long Bamber Stables.

'So Donal's blackmailing them too, is he?'

Jude rubbed her chin thoughtfully. 'Maybe. A wealthy couple who have a connection to Long Bamber Stables. The Brewises fit that description just as well as the Dalrymples.'

'But isn't it a huge risk, handing over blackmail money in a public place like this?'

Jude chuckled. 'No, I would say it's about the safest place in the world. Nobody thinks twice at a racecourse when they see a large wodge of cash handed over. It happens all the time.'

'Yes, I suppose you're right. So what do we do next?'

'What we came to do. Find Donal. Now we definitely know he's here.'

'Where do we look?'

'Well, he could be round the stables or the horse-boxes, but knowing him, I'd have thought it's more likely he's in one of the bars.'

Jude knew that Fontwell Park racecourse boasted a lot of bars. She was familiar with the large one, the National Spirit Bar, on the ground floor under the Kerman Stand, the Comedy of Errors Bar nearby, and the Salmon Spray Bar next to the oncourse betting shop. But she had to explore to find the Premier Bar and the Garden Bar under the premier stand, and the exclusive Owners' and Trainers' Bar at the back of the Salmon Spray. Alcohol was also available in the hospitality suites, but Jude didn't think Donal Geraghty would be invited to any of those. He would have looked out of place among the suited executives and giggly wives enjoying their corporate freebie.

The National Spirit Bar was so full that Carole and Jude might easily have missed him, but they separated to do a dutiful trawl around the room, rejoining at the door to report their lack of success. They checked the Salmon Spray Bar, which was equally crammed with people downing paper plates full of food – and a surprising amount of champagne. Being so much smaller, this was easier to search, but there was still no sign of Donal. They were making for the Premier Bar when Jude noticed the horses were moving from the parade ring towards the course.

'Oh, quick! I haven't backed anything!'

'Surely finding Donal is more important than putting money on a horse?'

'Yes, but we haven't found him, and he's sure to be watching the race from somewhere, so we'd do better to continue looking after it's finished.'

'But you can give one race a miss, can't you, Jude?'

'No way.'

Jude's fancy in the third was a tall rangy bay called Tout Complet, which she managed to get from a track-side bookmaker at nine to one.

They were too late to take their accustomed place in the stand, and watched the race from the grassy area just by the entrance to the premier stand. The horses were so close they could see every fleck of sweat and spatter of mud.

Tout Complet did everything that was required of him, staying close up to the pace for most of the race in fourth or fifth position. Then, in the last five furlongs, he slowly accelerated, picking off the tiring horses in front of him, until he jumped the last just ahead of his nearest challenger. By this time Jude was bouncing up and down, shrieking deliriously. Carole, though less flamboyant in her excitement, also found herself shouting for the horse to win.

And it very nearly did. On the run-in, though, the odds-on favourite, which had been only fourth at the last jump, showed its flat-racing pedigree and sprinted to win by a short head.

'Oh well . . .' Jude looked glumly down at her ticket before tearing it neatly in two and dropping it into a nearby litter bin.

'You so nearly won ninety pounds,' Carole commiserated.

'A hundred and eighty.'

'What?' Maybe, Carole thought, there's some aspect of racecourse mathematics that I haven't grasped yet. 'How's that?'

'I put twenty on that one.'

'Twenty?' Carole's jaw dropped and, not for the first time, she wondered where Jude got her money from.

Her friend grinned. 'You have to speculate to accumulate.'

'Maybe. But you may have observed that, while you are doing very well on the speculation front, you haven't so far done much in the way of accumulating.'

'No. Early days, though. Three more races to come.'

'Surely you're not going to bet on—' But Carole didn't get the end of the sentence out. Instead she pointed towards the Salmon Spray Bar. Scuttling towards it was the unmistakable figure of Donal Geraghty.

'Come on, we'll get him!'

Though it hadn't given them as good a view of the course, their position by the entrance to the enclosure was now an advantage. They were well ahead of the post-race crowd and quickly into the bar. Donal, up at the counter trying to catch the barman's attention, saw them immediately. They'd been worried how he might react. Do a bunk? Turn violent? After all, the last time they'd met, he'd just plunged a knife into the ample form of Ted Crisp.

But the incident did not seem to weigh on Donal Geraghty. Instead of more extreme actions, he just gave them a crooked smile and said, 'Well, isn't that luck? Somebody to buy me a drink just at the moment I need one.'

'I'll do it,' said Carole, moving up to the bar and opening her handbag. 'White wine, Jude?'

'Please.'

'And is yours still the large Jameson's?' She tried to sound as though she spent all her life ordering drinks for knife-wielding ex-jockeys at racecourse bars.

'Could you make that a quadruple? Gets too crowded in here to do a second round.'

He backed away and leant against the shelf round the edge of the bar, designed for the eaters to balance their paper plates of food. 'So . . . Jude isn't it?'

'That's right.' She perched on one of the few tall stools.

'And what can I do for you? Is it a tip you're after?'

'Might be glad of a tip later. I've had a disastrous afternoon so far.'

'I can tell you what'll win the next. It'll cost you, though.'

'More than a quadruple Jameson's?'

'Maybe.'

Jude found it strange that he'd made no mention of their most recent encounter, given how dramatic it had been. Maybe he was ashamed of what had happened, but he didn't show any signs of embarrassment. He behaved instead as if he had forgotten about the incident, as if it had never taken place.

Carole joined them with the drinks. The white wine came in little bottles containing two modest glasses' worth. Her instinct would have been only to buy one for the two of them, but she wasn't sure such parsimony would be appropriate to Jude's expansive mood on the racecourse. Still, bearing in mind that they'd come in the Renault, Carole determined only to sip at hers.

Donal almost snatched his quadruple Jameson's and, as ever without thanks, took a long sip. Jude didn't beat about the bush. 'When we last spoke, you were talking about blackmail.'

'Was I now?'

'Yes,' said Carole incisively, 'and, in case you've forgotten, when we last spoke was in the Crown and Anchor, where you attacked the landlord with a knife.'

'So? Are you suggesting that gives you some kind of hold over me?'

'I'm suggesting that, if you don't want to have even more dealings with the police, you might be wise to cooperate with us.'

'Hm.' Donal assessed this for a minute, then turned, with the satirical look of a submissive lapdog, to Jude. 'So how can I help you?'

'You implied you knew something about a married couple, and you were prepared to demand money from them to secure your silence on the matter.'

'Demand's a strong word.' He grinned. 'I'd prefer ask.'

'Whatever. I want to know whether the married couple you're putting the squeeze on are Yolanta and Victor Brewis?'

The fact that she knew the names shocked him. Thrown for a moment, he took a long shuddering swallow of Jameson's. Seeming calmed, he smiled mischievously. 'No. There's all the answer I'm giving you. No.'

'So it's the Dalrymples?'

The flicker of Donal Geraghty's eyelids told Jude she'd hit a bull's eye, but of course he denied the assumption. 'I think you're narrowing down your suspects too much. There's going to be more than one couple having extra-marital flings in a place like Fethering – surely you know that?'

'I do. But, till you told me, I didn't know it was an extra-marital fling we were talking about.'

His face registered annoyance at his carelessness. 'Ah, well now, I didn't say . . .'

But backtracking was hopeless. Emboldened by the information she had procured, Jude pressed her advantage. 'And might this extra-marital fling have something to do with Walter Fleet's murder?'

He smiled enigmatically. 'I don't think the change of circumstances there is going to stop me from getting my little meal ticket.'

'What change of circumstances are you talking about?'

'You mean you don't know?' Teasing out his narrative, he took another long pull at his glass of Jameson's and smacked his lips elaborately before continuing, 'The case is over.'

'How do you mean?'

'The police know who killed Walter Fleet.'

'How?'

'Because they've had a confession.'

Jude looked appalled. 'Not that poor girl?'

'Poor girl? I don't know what you're talking about. It's a man who's confessed.'

'Who?' asked Carole.

'Alec Potton. Now, do you want this tip for the next race or don't you?'

He gave them a horse's name. Chateau Dego. Jude

put twenty pounds on it at sixteen to one. Carole desisted, not wishing to risk the precious three pounds fifty she had won on Becktrout. As a result, she missed out on the three hundred and twenty pounds that Jude won when Chateau Dego romped home by a mile.

But neither the winning punter nor the non-punter showed much emotion. They reacted numbly, as in a daze. Carole and Jude were both preoccupied by the news they had heard about Alec Potton.

Chapter Twenty-Nine

Carole Seddon was normally a very organized shopper. She planned ahead, making elaborate lists before her weekly forays to Sainsbury's. (There was also a Tesco's near Fethering, but, in spite of the huge rebranding and massive success of the company, Carole couldn't stop thinking of Tesco's as slightly common.) Surprise and shame were therefore her dominant emotions when, after her day's racing at Fontwell, she got back to High Tor to find she had run out of dog food. She had been somewhat preoccupied with Walter Fleet's murder and worries about Stephen and Gaby; she just hadn't noticed the dwindling stocks of Gulliver's favourite Pedigree Chum.

There was nothing else in the larder she could fob him off with. And there was no way she could endure an entire evening of reproachful looks from a hungry dog. So there was nothing for it, but to put her coat on again and take a brisk walk down to Allinstore.

Even though she avoided using the local super-market whenever possible, Carole still knew exactly where the pet-food section was and quickly filled her basket with enough tins – and no more – to see Gulliver through till her next scheduled Sainsbury's run. She wasn't planning to pay more Allinstore prices than she had to.

At that time of the evening, between the post-school-run rush and the returning commuters' flurry, the shop was fairly empty, and Carole couldn't have been more surprised to see, sitting behind one of the tills, Hilary Potton. If her ex-husband's arrest and the possible effect of that on Imogen had been enough to make her take time off work, why on earth wasn't she staying at home after the news of his confession? Maybe Carole was about to find out.

She took her purchases up to the counter and received a beam of recognition. For a moment this surprised her, but then she remembered that she had only had Hilary's shouting at Jude reported to her. She herself was in the clear. So far as Hilary Potton was concerned, she had nothing to do with the treacherous Jude.

'Glad to see you back,' she said uncontroversially. 'Are things a bit more settled at home?'

'Well, I suppose they are in the sense that I now know where I am.'

'Oh?' As usual in her encounters with Hilary, Carole reckoned only the smallest of prompts would be required.

Her surmise proved correct. 'Look, I may as well tell you this, Carole, because soon enough it'll be all over Fethering – not to mention the known world. The fact is that Alec, my ex-husband, has now been shown up as the monster he always was.'

'Well, I heard he'd been taken in for questioning by the police.'

'Things have moved on from there. It seems the police had very good reasons for questioning him. Alec has confessed.'

'What?'

'He's admitted that he stabbed Walter Fleet.'

'Good heavens! That must be terrible for you.'

'Well, yes, at one level, it is. I mean, I always knew Alec had a lot of personality defects, but it never occurred to me that he'd do anything on this scale. It's terrible and' – Hilary Potton shuddered – 'I also feel awful about the potential danger I've been in from him all these years – not to mention the threat he posed to Imogen.'

'But how has poor Imogen taken the news? She was upset enough, I seem to recall, about her father being taken in for questioning. This latest business must be appalling for her . . . you know, when her friends at school find out . . .'

'Yes, I thought of that. I've talked to the school, and they agree that it would be good for her to have a break till things settle down. I drove her up to stay with my mother in Northampton this morning.'

'That sounds very sensible.'

'Well, I thought it was for the best.'

'I don't know what to say, Hilary. I'm just so sorry you're being put through this dreadful trauma.'

'Yes, it's no fun, I can tell you. But at least, now I know the kind of man Alec really is – presumably always was – I no longer feel even the tiniest twinge of guilt about the fact that I'm divorcing him.'

The words were spoken with unmistakable satisfaction. Carole wondered whether something comparable would have helped her. If she had known David to be the perpetrator of some atrocious crime, would she have felt less of a failure for getting divorced? Would the public opprobrium have made her feel she was justified in getting rid of such a monster? She rather feared it wouldn't have made the slightest bit of difference. In her case, the guilt would still have been there.

One of the first commuter trains must have just arrived at the station, because Allinstore suddenly had an influx of customers, the first of whom was now approaching the checkout.

'Oh, I'd better take for these.' Hilary Potton ran the tins of Pedigree Chum past the barcode reader. 'For that lovely dog of yours I saw in the café – what was his name?'

'Gulliver.'

'That's right.'

Carole handed across the exact change. 'But listen, Hilary, if there's anything I can do to help out, do just give me a call, won't you?'

'That's so sweet of you, Carole. But I'll be strong – I'll have to be. I'll manage.'

This was said with considerable pluck – even nobility. And Carole realized that Hilary Potton was enjoying every minute of her new status. Not only was she getting rid of a hated husband, she was also being given the chance to play the central role in her favourite drama – the one about her own life.

'Jude, my back's just seized up completely.'

'How completely, Sonia? Can you move?'

'Not really. I'm stranded on the sofa in the sitting room. It's agony just trying to lie down, but even worse when I try to stand up.'

'I'll come round straight away. Will I be able to get in?'

'Yes, the front door's unlocked.'

Not even someone as naturally elegant as Sonia Dalrymple could look good immobilized with back pain. Under the skilful make-up her face was grey and the darkened circles round her eyes showed through. Her blonde hair was lank, and her eyes were red with weeping – though whether with tears caused by pain, frustration or something else Jude did not know.

She had brought an emergency kit of oils and microwaveable heat pads with her, but started first with just her hands. 'Where? Small of the back, is it? Just at the bottom of the spine?'

Nodding was too painful, but Sonia managed to confirm that that was indeed where the epicentre of her pain lay.

Jude concentrated and brought her hands down gently onto the affected area. Through Sonia's clothes, she could feel the rigid knots of tension that had tied up her movement. Jude focused and let the hot energy flow through her hands, melting the seized-up joints, easing the rigid muscles. Within about five minutes, her client had managed to sit up.

'Just relax. I'll give you a full massage in a moment. First, let that relaxation go all the way through your body. All right, how is that?'

'Better. Better,' Sonia murmured.

'There's something new, isn't there?'

'What do you mean?'

'Something new that's upsetting you. Since you came to see me at Woodside Cottage.'

Sonia Dalrymple's ravaged face turned to Jude, and the tears began again.

'Is Nicky coming home?'

A little nod. 'He rang this afternoon. He wasn't meant to be back till Sunday, but he's getting an early flight tomorrow. Which reminds me, I must ring the police.'

'What?'

'Oh, they said they wanted to talk to Nicky when he was next home. Presumably just to check if he knows anything about the stuff they found in the hayloft, which of course he doesn't.' Panic crossed Sonia Dalrymple's face. 'And he'll be back tomorrow.'

'It's not just that that's got you into this state, is it, Sonia? You're used to Nicky coming home unexpectedly.'

'Yes. Yes, I suppose I am. I never really get used to it, though.'

'It still frightens you?'

A little wordless nod. Sonia Dalrymple was too crippled, too abject to maintain her usual front of omnicompetence. She couldn't pretend to Jude about the state of her marriage.

'Do you think you'd be happier apart from him?' Jude asked gently.

The nod that greeted this was shamefaced. 'But he'd never accept that. Nicky would never accept anything that made him look stupid, that made him look in the wrong.'

'Yes, but if your health is suffering like this. There's got to come a point when you put your well-being before his.'

'There are the girls to think of too.'

'Teenage girls are remarkably resilient.'

'But then there's . . .' Sonia Dalrymple gestured hopelessly around her luxury home '. . . all this.'

'It would be possible to get out. It can be done. People have done it.'

'I know, I know. I can see all that stuff when I'm on my own here. I build myself up, psych myself up, work out all the bold sensible things I'm going to say but then, when Nicky comes home . . .'

'You're afraid of him?'

Sonia nodded. 'It's like he – his very presence – drains all the confidence out of me. All my will goes. I'm just . . . feeble.'

'Is it the violence that makes you so afraid?' Jude waited, fully expecting a denial of the charge. Sonia had never admitted before that Nicky sometimes hit her.

But no, the allegation was allowed to stand. Maybe it was her reduced state, or Jude's calming presence, but Sonia did not even attempt to defend her husband.

She almost smiled through her tears as she replied, 'No, it's not the violence, really. When he hits me, it's almost a relief. That I can cope with, that I understand. Painful, horrible, yes, but in a way straightforward. It's the way he undermines me verbally that really hurts. That's what melts away my personality to nothing.'

Jude had a sudden thought. She would be taking a risk saying what she was about to say, but she thought the risk was worth it. 'There's something I want to tell you.'

'Oh?'

'Perhaps tell isn't the right word. Confess might be nearer the mark.'

Sonia's brow wrinkled in puzzlement, which was a welcome sign. The more she thought about things other than her own predicament, the more her contorted body would relax.

'Right, Sonia. What I have to admit to is an act of trespass.'

'Really?'

'Here. Into your premises.'

'You broke in?'

'Effectively, yes.' She decided not to admit that her trespass had been accompanied. No need for Carole's name to be mentioned. 'A few days ago, while you were staying at Yeomansdyke. I didn't break into the house, just the stables. And that was hardly breaking in – everything was unlocked. But I went into the hayloft.'

'And you found the stuff up there? It was you who alerted the police to what they'd find?'

The idea angered Sonia, and Jude was glad to be

able to allay that suspicion. 'No. In fact we— I only missed the police by minutes. They arrived here just after I'd left. Someone must have tipped them off, but it certainly wasn't me.'

'But why did you come here? What made you think you'd find anything in the hayloft?'

'Donal.' Sonia trembled at the name. 'Some things Donal had told me made me suspect that he might have pitched camp in your stables.'

'What did he say?' she whispered.

'Nothing directly. I just pieced things together.'

'And you knew you were going to find the blood-stained clothes?' Sonia was almost weeping now. 'Alec's blood-stained clothes?'

'No. All I expected to find was evidence that Donal had set up base in the stables. The blood-stained clothes were a total surprise – well, shock's probably a better word.'

'But Donal didn't tell you anything else, did he?' Fear had reduced Sonia's voice to a thin whisper.

'He implied to me that he was preparing to black-mail somebody, a married couple, or one member of a married couple.'

'Oh God. He didn't tell you what it was about, did he?'

'No, he didn't.'

The answer seemed to remove a great strain from Sonia Dalrymple. Her body untwitched, like a baby going to sleep, as the tension flowed out of her. If there had been any doubt in Jude's mind as to who was the target of Donal's planned blackmail, it had now been dispelled.

But finding out what he wanted to blackmail Sonia about would have to wait. Jude had another question of greater priority. 'You know that, as well as the bloody clothes in the hayloft, the police also found a blood-stained knife.'

Sonia nodded. 'Presumably the murder weapon?'

Jude didn't disillusion her. 'Did you see it?'

'No. They described it to me. A Sabatier kitchen knife, I gather.'

'Do you have such a knife in your kitchen?'

'Well, yes, of course. Everyone does, don't they? The police checked through the stuff we'd got, but I don't suppose—' Sonia stopped short and looked at Jude curiously. 'You're not suggesting that the murderer stole the knife from our kitchen?'

Jude shrugged. No need to remind Sonia that the police had in their possession the knife that killed Walter Fleet. And that it had been a bot knife, not a kitchen knife. 'It's possible,' she replied.

She sat on the sofa beside her client. 'You were talking about Nicky coming home unexpectedly.'

'What?' Sonia looked confused by the sudden change of subject. 'Oh, yes.'

'So he's coming home tomorrow?'

'Mm.'

'And the last time he was home was, well, just before you went into Yeomansdyke?'

'Yes.'

'And the time before that?'

'He was home for a weekend at – No!' Sonia corrected herself as the memory came back to her. 'He did come home for – well, really just a few nights in the middle of February.'

'Would that stay have included the night Walter Fleet was murdered?'

'Well, it . . . I'm not sure. I . . .' A strange, new expression came into Sonia Dalrymple's face. 'Yes. Yes, it was late that afternoon that he came home.'

Chapter Thirty

'My name's Nicky Dalrymple. We met when you came to visit my wife.'

'That's right. And you gave me that very generous cheque for the NSPCC.'

'Yes,' he said shortly. 'I believe you also do some kind of therapy with Sonia.'

'I do.' When she heard that kind of scepticism in a voice, Jude never bothered with further explanations.

'I'm phoning because – I wondered if we could meet?'

Jude bit back the teasing instinct to ask if he too was in search of therapy. She didn't think Nicky Dalrymple was the kind of man who would understand the concept of a joke. 'Yes, of course.'

'It's in connection with that appalling business up at Long Bamber Stables. I've been giving the police some information they required, and I think there are a few points you might be able to help me with.'

'Really?'

'Well, I am right . . . you were the one who actually found Walter Fleet's body.'

'Yes, that was me.'

'I wonder, then, when would it be convenient for us to meet?'

'As soon as you like.'

'Shall I come to your place?'

Some instinct for caution stopped Jude from saying yes. 'No, everything's a terrible mess here. Could we meet at' – the unlikeliest of venues came into her mind – 'the Seaview Café?'

'Mother, I want to come down and see you.'

'What?'

'With Gaby, of course.'

'Oh?'

'There's something we need to tell you.'

'Something you can't tell me over the phone?'

'I – we would rather do it in person.'

'Very well.'

'Are you free tomorrow?'

Carole was thrown. 'Tomorrow? Sunday? Um, yes. Yes, I think so.'

'We'll come down to Fethering and take you out to lunch somewhere.'

'Come here. I'll cook Sunday lunch for you.'

'But—'

'No, Stephen, I insist.'

'All right. We'll aim for about twelve thirty. I must dash. All hell breaking loose here at work.'

When wasn't all hell breaking loose at Stephen's work, Carole wondered as she put the phone down. She felt bad. The small triumph she had achieved in persuading him to have lunch at High Tor was swamped in the dread of the confrontation ahead. Her son and Gaby were coming to announce the end of their marriage. Why hadn't she bitten the bullet and stayed with David? Why hadn't she been a better role model?

'There are, as I say, one or two things the detectives asked me which, though I answered them to the best of my ability . . . Well, I just wondered why they were asking them, and thought maybe you might be able to clarify that for me.'

Though his exterior urbanity remained intact, Jude could detect from Nicky Dalrymple's body language that he was far from at his ease. He looked huge, perched on the edge of one of the Seaview Café's plastic chairs. The place had only just opened, and the few other customers sipping their mournful teas were too far away to compromise the security of Jude and Nicky's conversation.

Deliberately, she tried to shut her mind to the fact that she was sitting opposite a man who used violence against his wife. Though she desperately sought the ending of that situation, Jude knew it would not be improved by her intervention. The impetus had to come from Sonia, and Jude was determined to help her find the strength for that impetus. In the meantime, she would forget the character of the handsome man in front of her, and concentrate on what he had to say about the night of Walter Fleet's murder.

'The detectives mentioned a couple of things that

made me curious and, as I said on the phone, since you found Walter Fleet's body . . .'

Jude's customary conversational manner encouraged people to speak, made them feel at ease to say anything they wanted. She didn't feel inclined, though, to make anything easy for Nicky Dalrymple.

'I was interested to know whether, when you found the body, you saw anyone else at the stables?'

She was intrigued by the question. Surely the police hadn't implied to Nicky that she had seen anyone else? Maybe they'd just mentioned to him that she'd heard the click of a wooden gate, that she'd just missed seeing someone. Either way, her instinct told her to ration very carefully the amount of information she gave him. That way, he might be forced to show his hand, to reveal what he knew.

'I was in no doubt that someone else *was* in the stables,' she replied. 'Or at least had been in the stables very recently.'

'Yes, but you didn't actually see anyone?'

She had a brainwave. 'I wasn't the only witness.'

'Oh?'

'What other people' – no harm in cloning Carole a few times – 'may have told the police they saw, I wouldn't know.'

'No. No. Of course not.' Nicky was in difficulties. Jude took indecent pleasure in seeing the over-confident bully squirm. There was something of which he needed to unburden himself, and her uncooperative response seemed to be the best way of making him do it.

'Look, the fact is, Jude – you don't mind my calling you Jude?' he asked, flashing one of his dazzling smiles.

But she was immune to his charms. She knew he was just prevaricating and said nothing.

'The reason I'm asking all this,' he struggled on, 'is that the police asked me whether I went to Long Bamber Stables that night.'

'That's an odd thing to ask.'

'My feelings exactly, but . . . er . . .'

'So you told them you didn't go there?'

'Of course.'

Suddenly she saw it all. Nicky Dalrymple *had* been at Long Bamber Stables the night Walter Fleet died. He'd denied it to the police detectives, but they'd left open the possibility that he might have been seen there. The reason that Nicky had sought her out was because he wanted to know whether Jude had seen him at the stables. Definitely time for a tactical lie.

'I didn't know it was you,' she said. 'I only saw the outline of a tall figure in the gateway as you left the yard.'

'Oh, well then, I—'

She saw too much relief in his eyes, too much hope of escape, and cut it off at source with another lie. 'But of course another witness saw where you'd parked the BMW.'

'I didn't park it in the car park. It was off the road, up a farm track.'

'Which is where the witness saw it,' said Jude, grateful for his unprompted generosity with information. 'So

275

I suppose the police,' she went on, 'putting two and two together, concluded that you must have been there and . . .'

For one of the very few times in her life, Jude got a charge of intense pleasure from her own cruelty. Nicky Dalrymple's handsome head dropped forward on to his hands.

'All right. I'll tell you what happened.'

'Have you told the police yet?'

'No, but I'll have to – now I know that you know.' All trace of bravado was gone from his voice. 'The fact is, I arrived home earlier than planned. I'd had some business in Rome, we got it sorted far quicker than expected, my secretary rescheduled my flight, and I got back to Unwins about five that afternoon.'

He paused to retrieve his precise memories or, Jude wondered cynically, to invent them. 'Well . . . I'm afraid Sonia and I had a row, and a lot of stupid, hurtful things were said – she's always been prone to hysterics.' Even when digging himself out of a hole, he couldn't resist a side-stab of disparagement at his wife. 'And she said something which implied she knew a man who would be kinder to her, more considerate than I ever was.

'I'm afraid that made me very jealous, and I insisted on her telling me who the man was.' Jude wondered how physical a form his 'insistence' had taken. 'Eventually, she told me it was Walter Fleet. I knew him for a smarmy bastard, always chatting up the ladies, but I hadn't realized he'd ever tried his smooth tricks on my wife. And I'm afraid what Sonia said made me absolutely furious – I have quite a short temper, you know.' I know, thought Jude. 'So I jumped into the car and drove straight to Long Bamber Stables.'

He stopped, aware of how carefully he must negotiate the next bit. Perhaps he was even rehearsing how he would present his embarrassing admission to the police. The silence was filled only with the clack of teacups on saucers, the complaints of distant seagulls and the regular sighing of the sea.

'To have it out with Walter Fleet?' Jude suggested.

'Yes. Yes, exactly that.'

'So what happened?' she asked gently. 'What time did you get there?'

'About – I don't know – quarter to six, maybe?'

All too vividly, Jude could picture the scene. The shock had diluted in the weeks since Walter's death, but Nicky's words made her confront it again.

'And there were no lights on?' she asked. 'The stables were dark?'

'Yes.'

'Exactly as they were when I got there about a quarter of an hour later.'

'Mm.'

'And there were no lights on in the Fleets' house either?'

'What?'

'Well, presumably you went to the house first? You'd have expected to find Walter there, rather than in the stables, particularly if there were no lights on in the stables.'

'Hm.' He seemed thrown for a minute, then went on, 'Yes, I suppose I should have gone to the house first, but I wasn't thinking very straight. I was so angry about this nasty smoothie coming on to Sonia that I – Anyway, the stable gates were unlocked.'

'Just as I found them.'

'Right. And I went in, I suppose you could say to have some kind of revenge on Walter.'

He was silent, and Jude felt a momentary pang of fear. Was Nicky about to confess to the murder? And if he did, what kind of danger would his confession put her in?

But no, Nicky Dalrymple was simply practising his narrative technique. This was exactly how he would retell his denouement when he did it for the benefit of the police. He slowed his voice down for the final line, and gulped uncomfortably at the recollection. 'But then I found the body lying in the middle of the yard, the blood on his face and chest glistening in the moonlight, and I knew that Alec Potton had already had a far more extreme revenge on Walter than any that I had planned.'

'How do you know Alec Potton killed Walter? Did you see Alec there?'

'No. But he did it. Maybe you haven't heard? Alec Potton has confessed to the police that he stabbed Walter Fleet.'

'Ah.' Jude made the monosyllable light and non-committal, neither confirming nor denying that she already knew about the confession. 'Well, good luck when you tell all that to the police. I don't think they're going to be terribly pleased about the fact that you lied to them.'

'No.' But he didn't sound too worried. In fact,

relieved by unburdening himself to Jude, some of Nicky Dalrymple's old confidence was returning. 'Probably get a rap over the knuckles for my little white lie. But at least I haven't done anything worse than lying. There's nothing else the police can get me for.'

Oh no? thought Jude. There are crimes other than murder, you know. And, in the view of some, no less serious. Like domestic violence, for one.

Chapter Thirty-One

'I don't know, Carole. I don't think Nicky was telling out-and-out lies. There was some truth in there. I mean, he'd got himself into a position where he had to admit that he was at Long Bamber Stables on the relevant evening.'

'Or you had got him into a position where he had to make that admission.'

'Whichever.'

'No, there's a big difference. From what you say, I think you played him very skilfully, Jude. Credit where credit's due.'

'Well, thank you. So yes, Nicky Dalrymple was at Long Bamber Stables, but I'm not entirely convinced about the reasons he gave me for his being there.'

'You're not suggesting he actually killed Walter?'

'I don't think so. His description of how he found the body was pretty accurate, and he did seem genuinely affected when he spoke about it. No, I don't think he's our murderer.'

'So Alec Potton is.'

'I'm not yet entirely convinced about that either. Mind you, there is one useful detail Nicky's given me.'

'What's that?'

'The timing of the murder. I've assumed – I don't know whether the police have too – that the person I heard leaving the yard was Walter Fleet's murderer. But now I know that person was Nicky Dalrymple . . . well, the stabbing could have happened at any time after the last owner left the yard, which I think was established to be about five o'clock. Maybe the police have already worked that out from the post-mortem.'

'I doubt it,' said Carole's Home Office experience. 'I don't think time of death can be established quite that accurately.'

'Hm. But it does open out the time frame a bit, doesn't it? Raise the possibility of other people being at Long Bamber Stables between five and six that evening.'

'Yes. What we really need to do is establish some alibis.'

'Which I'm sure the police have already done.' Jude ground her teeth in frustration at their lack of information. 'I wish I knew what Alec Potton was doing during the relevant hour that evening, and sadly the police are the only people who could tell us about that.'

Carole chuckled. 'Oh, come on, he's the one person we do know about, or at least in his case we know what the police think he was doing. If he's confessed, he must have told them that he was at Long Bamber Stables stabbing Walter Fleet.'

'Yes, I suppose so. Oh, if only the police would let us have access to their files.' Jude smiled lugubriously across at her neighbour. 'No fun being an amateur detective, is it, Carole?'

'Hello. Jude?'

'Yes?'

'It's Sonia. Listen, I've just had a rather worrying phone call from Imogen Potton.'

'Oh?'

'Apparently she's staying with her grandmother in Northampton, but she's very upset.'

'Hardly surprising, given her father's being charged with murder.'

'But that doesn't seem to be what's upsetting her. In fact, she didn't mention Alec at all. First, she asked if I was all right. Then she wanted to know if Nicky was home. And, finally, she got round to what was really upsetting her. She's worried about Conker.'

'There's nothing wrong with Conker, is there?'

'No, no, she's fine. I've checked with Lucinda. It's just, you know, Imogen feels very close to that pony.'

'Yes,' Jude agreed. 'She channels most of her emotions through her. Displacement anxiety. The pony's easier to deal with than her parents' divorce, and no doubt her father's murder charge.'

'But Imogen's terribly worried about her.'

'Anything specific?'

'She keeps going on about the Horse Ripper.'

'Why? There hasn't been another incident, has there?'

'Not so far as I know. But there were a lot around

this area. For some reason Imogen's got it into her head that Conker's going to be the next victim.'

'And she feels that, stuck up in Northampton, she can't do anything about it?'

'Exactly. Oh, I'm sure it's just an adolescent girl's over-active imagination at work, but she does sound in a bad state. I've tried to reassure her, but I don't think I'm much use to anyone at the moment.'

'Don't say that, Sonia. Do you have Imogen's grand-mother's number?'

'No, but Immy rang me on the mobile. I've got that.' She gave it to Jude. 'If you wouldn't mind ringing her . . .'

'I'll try, but she didn't have much time for me when we last met.'

'Please . . .'

'All right.'

'I'm sorry, Jude, I feel I should do something, but I just know if I suggested the idea, Nicky would forbid me from having anything to do with any of the Pottons.'

'By the way, did he tell you he came to see me?'

'Nicky?' At the other end of the phone, Sonia Dalrymple sounded thunderstruck. 'Why on earth would he come to see you?'

'He wanted to check some things that the police had said to him. Didn't he tell you?'

'No.'

Of course he wouldn't have. No way Nicky Dalrymple was going to spoil his image of infallibility for his wife, was there?

*

'Imogen?'

'Who is this?' The girl's voice on the phone was guarded. There was the sound of traffic around her; she was in the open air somewhere – presumably Saturday evening in Northampton.

'My name's Jude. Do you remember, we met at Sonia Dalrymple's.'

'Oh yes, you were trying to heal Chieftain. And failing,' said Imogen with some satisfaction.

'I just couldn't get through to him.'

'Huh!' It was one of those expressions of total contempt that only teenage girls can really do properly. 'But Donal could. He really understands about horses. Anything to do with horses, Donal's the person you want to talk to. I don't know why Mrs Dalrymple didn't ask him to do it in the first place.'

'Nor do I.' And the thought reminded Jude to check why Sonia had been so unwilling to have dealings with the Irishman. She had claimed to know nothing about his squatting in her hayloft, but there was some reason why she had wanted to keep away from him. Presumably the blackmail? Jude had asked Donal enough about that. Maybe the time had come to put a few more direct questions to Sonia on the subject.

'Anyway, what do you want?' asked Imogen gracelessly.

'I just had a call from Sonia – Mrs Dalrymple. She said she was worried about you.'

'So? What business is that of yours?'

That was actually a very good question. Imogen's emotional state was no business at all of Jude's, but she still replied, 'Mrs Dalrymple's very busy at the moment, so she can't help you. She thought I might be able to.'

'Why?' Imogen was proving to be rather good at relevant, but difficult questions.

'Well . . . Sonia doesn't like the thought of you being upset and . . .'

'I'm all right,' said the girl defiantly.

'And you're at your grandmother's?'

'Yes.'

'In Northampton?'

'Ooh, you've done your homework, haven't you?'

'But you're not in her house at the moment. I can hear traffic.'

'No, I'm nipping out to the corner shop to get some shopping for Granny. Is that all right? Am I allowed to do anything without reporting back to someone every ten minutes?'

'Yes, yes, of course you are, Imogen. Listen, I know you're worried about Conker.'

'You don't know what I'm worried about.' But suddenly the girl sounded very young, on the verge of tears.

'She's not in any danger. Conker's safe at Long Bamber Stables.'

'Thinking about what's happened there in the last few weeks,' said Imogen bitterly, 'it's the last place I'd call safe.'

'But Conker'll be all right there. Lucinda Fleet will look after her.'

'Huh!' But teenage toughness soon gave way to

tears as she went on. 'If anything happens to Conker – she's the only one who's really on my side. I'll kill anyone who tries to hurt Conker.'

'Imogen, tell me why you're worried about Conker? What is it that makes you think she's in danger? If you tell me, then—'

'Oh, shut up!' said the girl in a burst of savagery. 'All you grown-ups think you know what's going on in my mind. And none of you have got a bloody clue!'

The line went dead. Imogen Potton had ended the connection.

Chapter Thirty-Two

Jude was a heavy sleeper, but always woke up quickly as she did when the phone rang at five forty-five the following morning. Sonia. She'd just had a call from Lucinda Fleet, who always – even on Sundays – started work in the stables at five thirty.

Conker was missing. Her stall was empty. She'd been stolen.

While she threw on some clothes, it didn't take long for Jude to decide to ring Carole. Her neighbour's irritation at being woken early would be as nothing to her fury prompted by her exclusion from any part of the investigation. Besides, Jude'd get to Long Bamber Stables a lot quicker in the Renault.

Carole dressed quickly too. She rushed a very grumpy Gulliver out behind the house to do his business, ignored his complaints as she shut him in the kitchen, and hurried to get the car out. A few hundred yards down the road, she realized she should have got the joint out of the fridge for Stephen and Gaby's lunch, but she didn't go back.

*

It was still dark when they arrived, dark and cold. Sonia Dalrymple was there with Lucinda, both looking overwrought and hopeless. Sonia, normally so rigidly in control of her emotions, had burst into tears at the confirmation of Conker's disappearance. The door to the pony's stable was still open; there was something pathetic about the straw-lined empty space.

'Have you called the police?' asked Carole.

'There's no need to do that,' Sonia replied quickly. 'This isn't a police matter.'

'Surely, if something's been stolen—'

'I do *not* want the police involved,' Sonia snapped. 'I'm Conker's owner, so it's up to me.'

Jude was beginning to have her own ideas about why Sonia might want the police kept away, but support for the decision came from Lucinda.

'I agree. I've had quite enough flatfoots around this place to last me a lifetime.'

'But if a horse has been stolen—'

'Don't worry about it, Carole,' said Jude. 'If Sonia and Lucinda don't want to call the police, then we have to respect their decision.' The look she flashed at her friend carried the message's subtext: besides, if there are no police, we have a better chance of finding out what's really been going on.

'Yes, of course,' said Carole, getting the point.

'Apart from anything else,' said Lucinda, 'I want to keep this as quiet as possible. What happened to Walter hasn't exactly been good for business. I don't want the owners to start thinking their horses aren't safe here either.'

'No.' Carole became practical. 'So how did the thief
– or thieves – get in?'

'Through the front gates.'

'Which were locked?'

'Yes, but there are lots of keys around. All the
owners have keys – God knows how many people they
give copies to. It wouldn't be that difficult to find one.'

'So you think it's an inside job?' Carole felt a slight
thrill to be using such a professional criminal term.

'Could be,' Lucinda replied. 'That's the obvious
explanation of how easily they got in. But then again
logic's against it being one of the owners. By definition,
they've all already got horses, and where would any of
them stable Conker in secret if they had taken her? No,
it doesn't make sense.'

'Then what are the other possibilities?' asked Jude.

'Well, it could just be a common or garden horse
thief. They do still exist and –' Lucinda grimaced
piously '– though it doesn't do to say so in these politi-
cally correct times, most of them are gypsies. If they'd
taken her, they'd sell her on somewhere, possibly not
in this country, so it'd be virtually impossible to track
her down.'

'But she has got a freeze mark on her,' said Sonia.
'We had it done, so she could be identified. So whoever
she was offered to might be able to guess she'd been
stolen.'

'I don't think that'd bother them. The kind of
people Conker'd be offered to for sale would know full
well that she'd been stolen.'

'Oh,' said Sonia Dalrymple bleakly.

'What are the other possibilities?' asked Jude, trying to cheer things up. 'If she wasn't stolen by gypsies?'

'Well . . .' Lucinda Fleet sighed, but the sigh turned into a shudder. 'There's a chance – I hope I'm wrong, but there is a chance – that she might have been taken by the Horse Ripper.'

Sonia let out a little whimper.

'But why would he have taken her out?' asked Carole. 'If mutilating a horse was what he wanted to do, surely he could just as easily have done it in the stall?'

'Maybe, but that's not his way. All the other injured horses have been discovered out in the fields. In some cases that's where he found them, but other times he's led them out of the stables into the fields. Maybe it's just a security thing. Stables tend to be near houses. Out in the fields the injured creature's cries wouldn't be heard, they wouldn't disturb the other horses.'

'So how can we find out if that has happened?'

'Wait till it's light. Go and look through the paddocks. The Ripper never takes them far. No, if that's what's happened to Conker, we'll find her soon enough.'

Lucinda looked grim, and Sonia could not mask another involuntary sob.

'Have you checked whether anything else is missing,' asked Jude, 'apart from the pony?'

'No, I haven't, as it happens. If it's the Ripper, he's certainly not going to have taken anything else. He'd have brought his knife with him.'

'Yes, but if there are other things missing, then maybe you'll be able to eliminate the idea that it was the Ripper.'

'I see what you mean.' Lucinda Fleet moved across to the large tack room. 'The padlocks are still on the door, but then that doesn't mean much. Some of the owners have got keys to them too.'

'So they could have gone inside, taken stuff and then locked up again?' asked Jude.

'Yes.' Lucinda unlocked the door, looked inside the tack room and said immediately, 'Conker's saddle and bridle have gone. And her head collar.' Leaving the door open, she moved away. 'I'll just have a look in the barn where we keep the feed and stuff – see if anything's missing there.'

Jude grinned at Sonia Dalrymple. 'I'd say what we've just heard is pretty good news. It wasn't the Ripper. Whoever took Conker rode her away – or at least took her away with a view to riding her, and that's certainly not his style.'

'No.' The horse's owner still looked wretched. But then Jude remembered: of course, her husband was home. She took Sonia's arm, and led her out of the stables' front gates.

'Things all right,' she asked softly, aware how much Carole felt excluded by this intimacy, 'with Nicky?'

Sonia shook her head wearily. 'I don't know. We had another row last night. He didn't sleep at home.'

'Where did he go?'

She shrugged. 'Some hotel. He quite often does when we have words.' She allowed herself a half smile. 'Nicky thinks he's punishing me. Little does he know the relief I feel at his absence. Anyway,' she sighed, 'he's flying off to Chicago at lunchtime.'

'When Nicky leaves you for a night, Sonia, does he always go to the same hotel?'

Another shrug. She didn't know and she didn't care.

Carole cleared her throat, an aggrieved reminder that she was also present, and Jude led Sonia back into the yard.

'The logical thing to think,' said Carole, 'is that the pony was taken by Imogen Potton. You say the girl's obsessed with Conker. It makes sense that she should steal her away from the cruel world which fails to understand either of them.'

'It would make perfect sense,' Jude agreed, 'but for the fact that Imogen is staying with her grandmother in Northampton. She was there when I spoke to her yesterday evening at about seven thirty, out doing some shopping for her grandmother. So even if she left straight after speaking to me, there's no way she could have been here in time to take the horse. She doesn't drive, I can't imagine her being able to afford a cab to come all that way, so she'd have had to rely on the trains.'

Lucinda Fleet reappeared from the barn. 'There are some carrots and pony nuts missing.' She poked her head into the empty stable. 'And Conker's haynet. Whoever took her knew what the pony liked.'

'Imogen Potton,' Carole insisted.

'Yes, that would fit some of the facts,' Lucinda agreed, 'but why should she do that? Conker's here when she wants to see her; Sonia lets Imogen ride Conker more or less when she wants to.'

'Yes,' Sonia interposed excitedly, 'but Imogen told

me she thought Conker was in danger. So she probably took her away for her own protection.' A sob came into her voice as she said, 'Oh God, I hope nothing's happened to that poor pony.'

Carole was reminded of the night Walter Fleet had died, when both Lucinda and Sonia had seemed more worried by the idea of the Ripper having mutilated a horse than of any injury to a human being.

'The idea of Imogen having taken Conker fits most of the facts, I agree. Except . . .' And Jude reiterated the reasons why the girl could not chronologically or geographically have made it to Fedborough from Northampton in time.

'Oh, well . . .' Lucinda took a mobile phone out of the pocket of her body-warmer. 'I'd better ring her mum just to check Immy is where she's meant to be.' She recalled a number from the memory, but clearly getting an answering machine, left a message asking Hilary Potton to call her as soon as possible.

The four women stood around for a moment, looking at each other. Then Jude said, 'Sonia, I wonder if you have any idea why Conker should be targeted. Had she ever been . . .?'

But the pony's owner's plans didn't involve answering more questions. 'I'm sorry, I must get back. Lucinda, call me if you get any news of Conker, won't you?'

'Yes, of course. The minute I hear anything.'

The three were silent until they heard the sound of Sonia's Range Rover starting up.

'Not a lot we can do now,' said Lucinda. 'Just wait

till Hilary calls.' She looked around the stable yard with something approaching despair. 'There's any amount of stuff I should be doing here, but . . . Would either of you like a cup of coffee?'

'Yes, please,' Carole and Jude replied, with considerable alacrity.

The interior of Lucinda's house showed signs of neglect. That might have been expected in a home whose owner has been recently widowed, but the level of neglect suggested it predated Walter's murder. The Fleets seemed to have given up on domestic pride, in the same way that they seemed to have given up on their marriage.

The kitchen where the coffee was prepared might once have had a warm farmhouse feeling, but no longer. The large beige Aga onto which Lucinda put the kettle was dull and greasy. Surfaces were scattered with equestrian catalogues, invoices, unwashed-up plates, empty milk bottles and bits of tack. Carole and Jude were encouraged that Lucinda used a tea towel to wipe the mugs she detached from hooks on the dresser, but discouraged by the grubbiness of the tea towel she used. Half-eaten bowls of dog food stood on the floor, but the only sign of the animals themselves was a stale doggy smell. The calendar, given free by some horse-fodder wholesaler, was three years out of date. On the wall was a faded photograph of Walter Fleet in his heyday, being awarded some medal by Princess Anne. That, and a few brittle dusty rosettes, were the only ornamental elements in the kitchen. The impression was of a house which took second place to the stables, just somewhere to live in that was convenient for work.

Whether because she was unaware of the chaos or so used to it that she didn't notice, Lucinda made no apologies for the state of the place. She spooned instant coffee into the mugs. Her guests both chose to have it black, but into her own she poured milk from a bottle whose crustiness made Carole wince, along with four teaspoonsful of sugar.

'Have to keep up my energy. The old blood sugar.' Her sweet tooth was the only thing she was going to apologize for. She sat down at the paper-strewn kitchen table and sighed heavily.

'It probably will get out, about Conker having been taken. Hard to keep secrets round a place like this. Owners are a gossipy lot.'

'And would that be such bad news?' asked Carole.

'Just another piece in a sequence of cumulative bad news. Another reason for existing owners to think of taking their horses away, and for new owners to look for another stable. There are plenty around here. They'd be spoiled for choice.'

She spoke wearily, someone who had battled against the rising tide of adverse circumstances and now was close to giving up the struggle.

'Are things really that bad?' asked Jude.

Lucinda Fleet nodded glumly.

'But presumably,' suggested Carole, 'if you did have to give up, this place would fetch a pretty healthy price. You must have about ten acres.'

'Eight and a half.'

'In a very desirable part of West Sussex.'

'I agree. But if you knew the size of the mort-gage . . .'

'Ah.'

Lucinda ran both hands back through her hair, unwittingly revealing the grey at its roots. Like the house, her appearance had been neglected.

'But have things got more difficult since Walter died?' asked Jude. 'I mean, now you have to manage the place on your own?'

A short bark of laughter greeted that. 'Hasn't made a blind bit of difference. I've been managing this place on my own ever since we bought it. Walter always saw himself as front of house in the project. He was the one who chatted up the owners – particularly the female owners – and regaled them with stories of his glory days as an eventer. He wasn't very hands on – except again with the lady owners. I don't think Walter even knew what mucking out a stable meant – if he did, it certainly wasn't from personal experience. He was entirely useless, in almost every way.'

Carole, whose mind had been running recently on such matters, couldn't help asking, 'Then why did you stay with him?'

Lucinda shrugged and replied, as if the answer were self-evident, 'I was married to him.' She grimaced and let out another harsh little laugh. 'Quite honestly, it's easier running the place without him constantly under my feet.'

'So you're really thinking you may have to give it up?' asked Carole.

Another weary nod. 'Unless someone who reckons Long Bamber Stables has potential comes along with a huge injection of cash, and I don't think people like that exist outside fairy tales.'

'Lucinda,' Jude began carefully, 'you said that Walter was always coming on to the lady owners.'

'Yes. It's no secret. He had a reputation round the place as the local groper.'

'In spite of his injuries, he was still an attractive man?'

'Apparently.'

'And do you know if any of these lady owners . . .?'

Carole, who was getting tired of the softly-softly approach, butted in. 'What Jude's asking – in her roundabout way – is whether there were any women to whom your late husband was particularly close. I mean, for instance, Imogen's mother Hilary implied to me that he fancied her. I just wonder if that attraction might have gone further?'

'You're asking me if Walter had an affair with Hilary Potton?'

'Well, I . . . well, I . . . Yes, I am. Or indeed with anyone else.'

Lucinda Fleet found this almost funny. At least, she laughed at the suggestion. But there wasn't much humour in her laughter. Then she stopped, as if a tap had been turned off. 'The answer is no. I don't see why I shouldn't tell you. You two don't give the air of being gossips, and nothing I say can hurt Walter any more.

'The fact is that he could come on to women as much as he liked, he could chat them up – and did. Yes, the lady owners – though in many cases with them "lady" is not the appropriate word. And he'd also come on to the younger girls, which did worry me. I mean, there was no way he could do them any harm, but they didn't know that, and teenage girls . . . It's a difficult age, I think he frightened some of them. I tried to get him to stop that, but . . .' She shrugged at the hopelessness of the endeavour.

Jude picked up her words. 'You said Walter could not do the girls any harm?'

Lucinda Fleet stared intently ahead. 'Walter couldn't do any woman any harm. He couldn't even do me any harm. Not in that way . . .'

She read the same question in both women's eyes. 'He was impotent. Another effect of the accident which destroyed his life, and I suppose my life at the same time.'

'But the accident happened before you were married, didn't it?'

'Yes, but we were engaged. My father was an army man. I grew up in a household which believed that when you'd given your word about something, you stuck to it. I'd agreed to marry Walter, so I married him.'

'But it must have been . . .'

'Not much fun, no. I often used to wish I'd had a less rigid moral code. In retrospect, I sometimes think I was completely stupid, but . . .' her sigh seemed to encompass all of her wasted life '. . . that's the way I am.'

'I'm sorry,' murmured Jude.

Lucinda Fleet looked bleakly round the shabbiness of her kitchen. 'I suppose that's why there were a lot of things I just didn't care about. Perhaps, if I'd had children . . .' For the first time, emotions threatened, but she quickly stifled them. 'Anyway, I didn't, and it's probably a bit late to think about that now. If I met another man tomorrow' – she laughed bitterly at the unlikeliness – 'I think the old biological clock would be against me.'

She took a sip of coffee, after which she became brusque, as though embarrassed by her momentary lapse. 'So I concentrate on the horses. Horses are a lot easier to deal with than human beings, and a lot more rewarding. Certainly a lot more rewarding than Walter ever was.'

But she seemed immediately to regret this callousness and said, 'I don't know, though. The marriage was dreadful for me, but – poor Walter – he could never come to terms with what he had been . . . and what he had become. I think it was probably worse for him. For that reason, I'm relieved he's out of it.'

'But, Lucinda, surely—?'

Lucinda's mobile rang. Hilary Potton responding to her message. Lucinda told her about Conker's disappearance and asked if she could check with her mother that Imogen was still in Northampton.

Ten minutes later Hilary rang back. Imogen's grandmother had just checked the girl's bedroom. It hadn't been slept in. And Imogen had shut herself in there in a teenage strop about six the evening before.

She could have escaped any time after that. When Imogen had spoken to Jude on the phone, she had fairly definitely not been in Northampton but probably changing trains in London on her way down to Fethering.

All of which made Carole and Jude pretty certain that, wherever Conker was found, Imogen Potton would be there too.

Chapter Thirty-Three

They were both silent as they drove back to Fethering, Carole because she was grumpy after her early start, and Jude because she was deep in thought. There was something at the back of her mind, a connection between two pieces of information which, if found, would suddenly make sense of a lot of other free-floating details. It concerned Imogen and Donal and there was someone else . . . but that person remained elusive.

She tried to think back through the weeks since Walter Fleet's death, all the people she'd seen, all the people she'd spoken to. Someone, she felt sure, had said something that was relevant.

That line of thought didn't prove constructive, though, so she tried another approach. Tried to put herself in the shoes of Imogen Potton. Where would Imogen go with Conker? A pony is not an easy thing to hide, but the girl thought Conker was in danger so she definitely would try to hide her. But she had also gone to the trouble of taking pony nuts and carrots and the haynet. Imogen cared about Conker and would want to take her somewhere where she would be warm and comfortable. Which probably meant another stable, but a stable that was out of the way where no one would think of looking for a missing pony.

In fact, Jude thought with a sudden surge of excitement, exactly the sort of place a habitual user of unmonitored stables might know about. Donal Geraghty. Imogen thought the world of Donal. He knew about horses. 'Anything to do with horses,' the girl had said on the call that Jude thought came from Northampton, 'Donal's the person you want to talk to.' Presumably that would apply to stealing a horse, as well as anything else.

Increasingly, Jude felt certain that, in her confusion, Imogen would have gravitated towards Donal. An odd couple, the tortured adolescent and the embittered alcoholic, but in a way a logical one. Their relationship existed only through horses; both – like Lucinda Fleet – found horses easier to deal with than people. And though she had witnessed the ungovernable violence within Donal Geraghty when he had attacked Ted Crisp, Jude knew Imogen would never be in any danger from him.

So, the girl and Conker were with Donal, but where was he? Which of his various bolt-holes had he resorted to this time? Long Bamber was not a possibility and, given the police interest in the Dalrymples' stables, he'd never take the risk of going back there. So where? Jude had a nagging feeling that she almost knew, that she had the necessary information somewhere in her memory, if only she could access it . . .

'Victor and Yolanta Brewis!'

Her shout caused Carole to skew the Renault

halfway across the road into the path of an aggrieved Fethering pensioner in a Toyota Yaris who hooted his disapproval of all young hooligans in cars.

'What on earth do you mean?' demanded a very frosty Carole.

'I've suddenly remembered – When we were at Fontwell – what we overheard from Victor and Yolanta Brewis.'

'About Donal blackmailing them?'

'Yes. But it was what Victor Brewis said. He said if Donal Geraghty caused trouble, then at least they knew where to find him. And that wherever it was "couldn't be handier". Handy for them. We must go and see the Brewises.'

'But we don't know where they live,' Carole wailed.

'Lucinda does. I'll ring her.'

Characteristically, the Brewises didn't have a house, they had a mansion. Set in the village of Cordham, some couple of miles east of Fedborough, Cordham Manor *was* most of the village. A wooded lane went past a few other houses just visible behind tall laurel hedges, but everything around seemed to defer to the manor house.

A four-square Georgian building, over the years it had been allowed to fall into disrepair, but was now undergoing a very thorough refurbishment. It was an old property in need of new money, and of course new money was exactly what Victor Brewis had.

The frontage was heavily scaffolded, and the piles

of builders' materials – planks, pallets of bricks, pyramids of sand, cement mixers – bespoke large expense. Had it not been a Sunday, the site would have been swarming with labourers. The area immediately in front of the main door, which had once been – and no doubt would again be – an elegant garden, was a muddy mess. The chalk in the trampled soil meant that everything was covered with cement-coloured slime.

Carole and Jude, having parked the Renault, picked their way cautiously through the swamp towards the entrance. At some point the massive front door had been painted green, but the colour had faded and was fast disappearing under splashes of mud. The chain from the bell pull was broken and the lion's head knocker, once so impressive, was corroded and blurred with rust.

Still, there was no other way of attracting the occupants' attention. Jude reached up towards the ailing lion.

'Just a minute. Have you thought about what approach you're going to take?'

'Not really. I'm sure I'll think of something.'

Carole tutted at the amateurism of this approach. 'And why are we coming to see them so early on a Sunday morning?'

'To find out where Donal is.'

'And what is the basis of our introduction? How do we know these people?'

'I saw them up at Long Bamber Stables.'

'But, from what you told me, they didn't see you. And then, of course, we eavesdropped on them at

Fontwell. It's hardly a great basis for opening a conversation, is it?'

'I'll think of something.'

'No, Jude, we've got to plan this. Donal's blackmailing the Brewises about something they're prepared to pay a lot of money to keep quiet. If we stumble in with our hobnailed boots asking about it, they're going to clam up immediately.'

'Everything you say may well be true, but do you have another idea of how we can approach them?'

'As a matter of fact, I do.'

'May I ask how?'

'It's a case of using logic. What we're dealing with here is social-climbing blackmail victims – right?'

'Well, yes, I suppose so.'

'So what we need is an approach that appeals to them in both roles.'

'Both as social climbers and as blackmail victims?'

'Exactly.' And Carole reached forward fastidiously to lift the heavy lion knocker and let its impact reverberate through the mansion.

Some time elapsed before there was any response. In fact, Carole and Jude were on the verge of leaving, when the large door opened.

Yolanta Brewis stood there, but she was unlike the Yolanta Brewis Jude had encountered on two previous occasions. A rather grubby silk peignoir was hitched around her finely tuned body. The magenta hair was unbrushed, shapeless, stiff from too much dyeing. And Yolanta's lack of make-up showed a skin pitted with old acne scars and a couple of new spots starting. A cigarette, trailing a long cylinder of ash, hung from the corner of her mouth.

'What you want?' she asked, her accent heavier than ever.

'We're from the local equestrian society, Mrs Brewis,' said Carole smoothly, 'and we hear that you and your husband are riders.'

'Yes, we are.'

'Well, we make it our business to welcome new riders to the area – providing, of course, they're the sort of new riders we want in the area. Which' – she looked appreciatively up at the scaffolded splendour of Cordham Manor – 'you clearly are.'

'Oh.' Yolanta Brewis was gratified to be included in this exclusive circle and, now she realized who her guests were, felt she should excuse her appearance. 'I am so sorry, I am not dressed. I have been having the flu.'

'There's a lot of it about,' said Jude wisely.

'Yes. But, please, you will come in?' She backed away into the hall. 'I'm sorry, we have not engaged servants yet. The house is such a mess, there is no point in having staff to tidy things up until the building work inside has been finished.'

'So you are actually living here, Mrs Brewis?' asked Jude.

'Yes. We – what do you say – camp out? Our bedroom with the en-suite bathroom – that is more or less done.'

'Oh, well, if you've got a bedroom, a bathroom and a kitchen, you'll be fine.'

'The kitchen is not yet done, but it does not matter.' Yolanta laughed, grinding out her cigarette against a builder's plank in the hall. 'We eat out.'

'All the time?'

'All the time. And of course we do have the one good room downstairs.'

With this, she flung wide the double doors which opened from the building site of a hall onto a room of amazing opulence. And exactly the kind of taste that could have been predicted by anyone who had ever met the Brewises.

The decor wasn't complete, that was the only comfort to be taken. No doubt when the room was finished, there would be even more pink flounces on the tartan curtains. Maybe more huge ceramic poodles would cluster round the fireplace, more turquoise teddy bears would sit on the silver leather sofas, more droopy stuffed clowns would dangle down from the light fittings. Perhaps another wall would be taken up by a huge plasma screen, and there might even be a second wrought-iron onyx-topped bar in another corner.

All this seemed possible. Yolanta, as she proudly told them, had designed the room herself, and Yolanta's design style favoured excess. If you had one object you liked in a room, how much better to have two. Or three. Or four.

And her approach to decor had its own consistency. Having taken the controversial decision not to attempt recapturing the house's original Georgian period style, she eschewed all other period styles too. The room was a one-off. It could never be reproduced anywhere else. So, thought Carole and Jude, there was a God after all.

As they looked around, the phrase 'tart's boudoir' sprang to Jude's mind.

Yolanta ushered them in to sit between turquoise teddy bears on the silver leather. 'I would offer you hot drinks, but' – she shrugged – 'as I say, the kitchen . . .'

'Don't worry.'

'I have alcohol.' She gestured to a wrought-iron and onyx drinks trolley, which – quite an achievement in the narrow field of wrought-iron and onyx furniture – managed to clash with the wrought-iron and onyx bar.

'No, really, thank you.'

'A bit early in the day for me.'

'Yes.' Yolanta looked rather wistfully at a vodka bottle, but seemed to decide, now she had moved into the area, she'd better conform to the customs of other members of the local equestrian society.

'Is your husband not here?' asked Carole.

'No. He is away all this week. In Nigeria. Victor has to work.' Yolanta made a wide gesture, encompassing the whole room. 'To pay for all this.' She laughed, in a way that was not entirely kind.

There was a silence. Jude was tempted to break it, but that would have shown a lack of trust in Carole's agenda. The first part of the plan had certainly worked. Yolanta Brewis had fallen for the social-climbing bait. Would Carole be able to move with equal success onto the subject of blackmail? No doubt she had some subtle approach up her sleeve.

But 'subtle' was probably not the best word to

describe what Carole said next. 'We're really here to talk about blackmail.'

'Blackmail?' Yolanta Brewis was totally thrown. 'You are here to blackmail me?'

'Good heavens, no! I'm sure there'd never be any reason for someone like *you* to be blackmailed. But there is someone connected with the local equestrian community who is going around blackmailing people.'

'You are suggesting I am a blackmailer?'

Dear oh dear, Yolanta did seem very touchy on the subject of blackmail. Perhaps with reason, thought Carole, as she went smoothly on, 'Of course not, Mrs Brewis – what an idea! No, we are trying to find the person who is perpetrating this blackmail, so we are speaking to anyone in the area who rides, particularly people who have some kind of connection with Long Bamber Stables. I gather from my friend Jude here that you and your husband have horses there.'

'We do. Tiger and Snow Leopard,' came the automatic reply.

'There's a man who hangs around the stables at Long Bamber, an Irishman called Donal Geraghty – I don't know if you know him?'

'Perhaps,' she replied cautiously. 'Round the stables there are always so many people. Perhaps I recognize this man, but do not know his name.'

'Well, we're desperate to find him. This is why we are going round asking everyone who has any connection with Long Bamber if they know where he might be. We need to find Donal Geraghty very urgently.'

'But why is this so urgent for you?'

It would be hard to say whether Yolanta Brewis or Jude was more surprised by what Carole said next. 'Because he's blackmailing me. I need to find him to hand over a payment or . . .' She really was getting carried away with her performance; there was a genuine sob in her throat as she said, '. . . or he'll reveal everything.'

'Ah.' Yolanta was thoughtful. She also seemed a little amused by this middle-aged, middle-class woman, this apparent icon of Fethering rectitude, admitting to being blackmailed. What criminality or deviancy, she was clearly thinking, could this paragon have committed to make her valuable to Donal Geraghty?

She made her decision. 'I can tell you where Donal is.'

'Oh?'

'He is very close. Here on the estate there are stables. Not the stable block behind the house, the one we are going to turn into a swimming pool. But on the estate there is a small farm – *was* a small farm I should say. Now it is – what is the word? Delerict?'

'Derelict.'

'Ah. Yes. It is over . . .' She pointed out of the window. 'Over there, beyond the trees, you see?'

'Yes.'

'That is where Donal is at the moment – living. I don't know – hiding, perhaps? He has been giving us some advice on buying racehorses. We say thank you by letting him stay in the stables for a while. Tit for tat – is that the expression?'

It didn't seem worth saying that that wasn't exactly the expression, no.

'It is very convenient for him to be here, I think. Just for a little while.'

Also very convenient for you. You can keep an eye on him. And if his blackmail demands become too pressing . . . Neither Carole nor Jude could forget the implicit threat they had overheard from Victor Brewis at Fontwell.

'Do you mind if we go and see if Donal is there now?' asked Jude.

Yolanta opened her hands wide in a gesture of permission. Very much Lady Bountiful. Yes, she would enjoy the condescension that went with her position as Lady of the Manor. Whether the Great and the Good of West Sussex would welcome her and Victor with open arms . . . well, that remained to be seen.

'Can we drive there?' asked Carole.

'No, is not possible. I think once there was a track went from the house across there. Not any more. Then there is an old gate from the farm out onto the road, but you have to drive right round the walls of the estate – five miles perhaps. You are quicker to walk.'

They took their leave of their hostess, both complimenting her on her lovely house, and Jude even mischievously saying, 'I'm sure you can't wait till you get the rest of the place up to the standard of this room.'

As they walked across the damp grass towards the old farm, Jude made a mock obeisance to her neighbour. 'Well, what a performance. I didn't know you had that kind of deviousness in you.'

'Oh, it just seemed the most sensible approach to take,' said Carole, outwardly casual, but inwardly delighted.

Chapter Thirty-Four

The grass was wet underfoot but fortunately both of them were wearing sensible shoes (Carole scarcely possessed any others). As they approached the wooded area, they could see the outlines of what had once been the estate's home farm, but which was now in a worse state of dilapidation than the manor itself. Many years must have elapsed since the premises were last inhabited, and many before that since any maintenance work had been done on the property. The farmhouse appeared to have suffered from a fire at some point. Its roof was a cage of blackened rafters, and the barns around sagged, broken-backed. Presumably, in an area of barn-conversion mania like West Sussex, only the fact that the buildings belonged to Cordham Manor had prevented their being developed.

'I bet the Brewises have got planning applications in for this lot,' murmured Carole. 'Didn't you say he made his money in property development?'

'Yes. I wonder what Yolanta would like to convert *this* into?'

Carole's shudder was as evocative an answer as any number of words would have been.

They stopped for a moment to assess their next move. There was an element of potential danger in what they were doing. Donal Geraghty was presumably lying low because he didn't want to be found and, though they didn't really represent any threat to him, Carole and Jude knew his propensity for violence. Caution was advisable.

They had identified the stable block, a long low structure at the far side of the house. Though its tiled roof was full of holes and its ridge as uneven as a sea serpent's back, the building was in a better state of repair than those that surrounded it. The stout brick walls and leaky roof would provide a reasonable kind of shelter against the early March cold.

'I think we just call out as we approach,' said Carole. 'Donal's more likely to do something rash if we catch him by surprise.'

'You're right,' Jude agreed. She was impressed by her friend's dominance since they had arrived at Cordham Manor, particularly by the duplicitous way she had handled Yolanta Brewis. And, of course, being Jude, she felt pleased rather than threatened by the shift in their customary roles.

So they moved towards the derelict stables, gently identifying themselves and calling out Donal's name. But there was no response.

The main gates of the stable yard had long since rotted away, leaving only the drooping remnants of rusty hinges hanging from their pulpy uprights. The yard into which they stepped showed a few patches of bricked surface, but was mostly covered with the detritus of many years' leaves and rubbish. The square had three stalls either side, and the far wall was open where another pair of gates had rotted away. Passages either side led presumably to storage areas, a hay barn perhaps on one side and housing for wagons on the other.

'Donal,' Jude called out softly. 'Donal!'

Still nothing. Though Cordham Manor was only a few miles from the busy A27, some acoustic trick of the South Downs cut off the traffic noise. All they could hear was the susurration of wind in the nearby trees. And yet neither woman had the feeling they were alone. Both felt, if they stayed silent long enough, they would hear some sound, some giveaway of another human presence.

But it wasn't a human who gave away the secret, it was an animal. They heard the unmistakable scrape of a horse's hoof on a brick floor.

It came from the furthest stall to their right. Both moved forward, and were unsurprised to find themselves, over what remained of the stable gate, facing a defiant Imogen Potton, standing in front of a very relaxed-looking Conker. Imogen looked terrified and exhausted. She'd got some shreds of food trapped in the brace on her teeth. The ginger streak of hair hung down like a rat's tail over her forehead.

Conker had been made very comfortable in her new home. Her saddle and tack had been hung on old rusted hooks and she was tethered by a rope from her head collar to a corroded metal ring. Unaware of the sensation she had caused, the pony was placidly tugging mouthfuls of stalks out of her haynet and munching them with noisy relish.

'Oh, it's you,' said Imogen gracelessly, recognizing Jude.

'Yes. And this is my friend Carole Seddon.'

'We met with your mother in the Seaview Café.'

Whether or not she remembered the occasion, this information did not appear to interest the girl. She maintained her defensive posture in front of the pony.

'So you're not in Northampton.'

'Oh, well done.' The words were ladled over with sarcasm.

'Your mother's been very worried about you,' said Carole. Though now she came to think of it, the phone call Lucinda Fleet had taken in her kitchen had not suggested that Hilary Potton was in a state of panic.

Imogen didn't seem too worried about her mother's anxiety either. 'She doesn't care. She's never cared about me.'

'We'll have to ring her to tell her you're OK,' said Jude. 'And where you are.'

'I'm not moving. I'm not going to leave Conker. I'm not going to let anyone get at Conker.'

'She'll be safe back at Long Bamber.' Jude's voice was infinitely soothing. 'Or if you felt she was safer at Unwins, Sonia could take her back and look after her there.'

'No!' There was panic in the girl's eyes. 'No, I'm not going to let Conker out of my sight. She certainly wouldn't be safe with Mrs Dalrymple.'

'I think you underestimate how much Mrs

Dalrymple cares for that pony. She was terribly upset, in floods of tears this morning when she thought Conker had been stolen.'

'I don't care. I'm going to protect Conker, and nobody's going to stop me,' said the girl doggedly.

'Is Donal around? Maybe he can make you see sense?'

'No,' Imogen replied slowly. 'Donal's gone. Once he'd showed me where to put Conker, he went away.'

'Well,' said Jude, extracting her mobile from a pocket, 'the first thing I'm going to do is let Sonia know the pony's safe. You've no idea how relieved she'll be.'

She moved a little way away to make the call, leaving Carole the unrewarding task of trying to make conversation with Imogen. Sonia answered the phone immediately, and sobbed with relief when she heard that Conker was safe. She agreed with Jude that the best thing would be to get Imogen reunited with her mother as soon as possible. Then Sonia could make arrangements to pick up Conker later in the day. Maybe drive over with Lucinda and hack the pony back to Long Bamber Stables. That would probably be the solution.

Sonia apologized that she couldn't do anything earlier, but Nicky was there and needed her help getting stuff together for his trip to Chicago. He'd be driving up to Heathrow to get a lunchtime flight. Once he'd gone, everything would be simpler for her. In many ways, thought Jude.

She finished the call and returned to the silent stand-off between Carole and Imogen. She thought again how tired and tense the girl looked. Presumably she'd had no sleep the night before, sneaking out of her bedroom in Northampton, catching a train to London, another to Fedborough, then staging her horse-stealing raid on Long Bamber Stables. No wonder Imogen looked exhausted.

She also looked very fragile. Her anxiety about Conker's safety was a final screwing-up of the tension that had been building throughout her parents' estrangement. Jude got the feeling it would take very little to make the girl crack up completely.

She reported back what Sonia had said. Imogen immediately vetoed the idea of leaving Conker.

'Well, look, maybe you can stay with her till Sonia and Lucinda arrive. But that probably won't be till this afternoon. Sonia's got to sort things out for her husband before he goes off to get a flight to Chicago.'

'He's going off today?' asked Imogen.

'Yes. Lunchtime. Anyway, are you going to speak to your mother, Imogen?'

A very determined shake of the head.

'All right. One of us will. It'd better be you, actually, Carole. The last time we spoke, Hilary Potton wasn't exactly my number-one fan.'

Jude handed the mobile across and looked at Imogen. 'I don't know your home number.'

The girl's mouth set in a firm line. Jude certainly wasn't going to get it from that source.

But Carole's photographic memory for phone numbers came to their aid. She got through straight away.

'Hilary, it's Carole Seddon ringing.'

'Oh, how nice to hear you.' The tone didn't suggest a mother sick with worry about the disappearance of her teenage daughter.

'Look, for reasons that are too complicated to explain at the moment, I am actually with Imogen.'

'Good heavens. Where?'

'She's at Cordham Manor. Do you know it? Just outside Fedborough.'

'I've driven past the turning. But what on earth is Immy doing there?'

'She's got Conker with her. She took the pony from Long Bamber Stables last night. She's apparently worried about her safety. I don't really understand why. I'm sure Imogen herself can explain better than I can.'

'Can I talk to her?'

'I'm afraid she says she doesn't want to talk to you.' Carole looked across, and was surprised to see the girl's eyes were welling with tears. The rigidity had gone out of her body and her shoulders slumped. She had held herself together for as long as she could, but something – possibly the knowledge that her mother was now actually on the phone – had made Imogen realize she could not maintain the tension any longer. She looked about seven, as she reached out for the mobile.

The part of the conversation Carole and Jude heard was too tearful to be very coherent, but they got the message that Imogen had agreed to return to Fethering. Then the mobile was handed back to Carole to make the arrangements.

'Can you come and pick her up, Hilary?'

'I wish I could. No car.'

'But surely, with Alec being . . . er . . .' Carole didn't know the graceful way to put this. 'Well, he's not using your car at the moment, is he?'

'No. But the police have got it.'

'Ah.'

'Running all kinds of forensic tests, would you believe? Looking for Walter Fleet's DNA on the upholstery, I suppose, building up the prosecution case. Let me tell you, it is extremely inconvenient being married to a murderer.'

Not for the first time, Carole was struck by the oddness of Hilary Potton's response to her situation. This flippancy seemed to be another facet of her self-dramatization. What was happening to her husband was infinitely less important than the effect it was having on her. Maybe that was also the explanation for her lack of panic about Imogen's disappearance. In Hilary Potton's egocentric world, it was just another cross that the martyr had to bear.

Carole arranged that she would drive Imogen home in the Renault. She expected resistance, but all fight seemed to have gone out of the girl. She looked feeble, a broken rag doll.

Only as they were leaving did Imogen suddenly look back in panic at Conker.

'I can't leave her. I must ride her back.'

'No, Imogen, you can't,' said Carole firmly. 'It's a long way, and you'd have to ride on the main roads.'

'Conker's fine on the roads.'

'No. I'm sorry. I'm not going to be responsible for you riding that pony back to Fethering.'

'But suppose something happens to her?'

Jude came to the rescue. 'Nothing's going to happen to her. I'll stay here till Sonia arrives.'

And even Imogen couldn't find any objection to that arrangement.

Chapter Thirty-Five

Jude was hungry. All very well to agree to look after
Conker, but she'd not had time for any breakfast when
she was summoned to Long Bamber early that morning
and was beginning to feel the effects.

She inspected the pony's temporary stable. Not
being a hay-eater, she wasn't going to challenge Conker
for the contents of her net. Nor did the pony nuts look
very appealing. But a carrot . . .

There were still some in a bucket, which Imogen
had shrewdly placed out of Conker's range. They
looked unlike the kind of carrots that might appear
in a supermarket. In fact, they were carrots which
would have been disqualified from appearing in supermarkets. The mandatory image in the world of
supermarkets demands that a carrot be a perfect
tapered cylinder built on the lines of a space rocket.
Whereas, in nature, carrots come in a variety of knob-
bly shapes and sizes. The perfect ones go to the
customers of Sainsbury's and Tesco, the imperfect ones
are fed to horses.

As well as being misshapen, the carrots in the
bucket were a bit old and muddy, but Jude was very

hungry. To ease her conscience, she also gave one to the pony, and the two of them chomped in contented unison. The carrots were pretty woody, but better than nothing.

She decided to stay in the stall, not principally to keep an eye on Conker, but because the air was very cold outside its shelter. She put the remaining carrots in with the pony nuts, and sat on the upturned empty bucket.

Her enforced wait was in many ways inconvenient, but did at least give her a chance to think through the case and the various anomalies that it presented. Having met Alec Potton, she had great difficulty in casting him in the role of murderer. If half of what his wife said about his philandering were true, his behaviour was hardly admirable. Jude didn't think a lot of men who kept their wives short while spending the family money on girlfriends. But Alec Potton still seemed to her too weak a personality to make an attack like the one Walter Fleet had suffered.

On the other hand, the blood-spattered Barbour found in the Dalrymples' hayloft undoubtedly belonged to Alec Potton, and the police had had no hesitation about taking him in for questioning. Maybe, as ever, they knew a lot more than Carole and Jude would ever know.

What about motivation, though? Hilary Potton's suggestion, relayed by Carole, that Alec was jealous of Walter's attention to her seemed pretty flimsy. Given the state of their marriage, would he have cared that much about anyone coming on to his soon to be ex wife?

But then again, he had confessed to the murder. Alec Potton had actually told the police he had killed Walter Fleet. That was quite a difficult fact to get round.

Jude's only explanation was that Alec had reacted instantly to the news from Imogen that she was planning to confess to the murder. Whatever his other character deficiencies, there was no questioning his love for his daughter. He would do anything to protect Imogen.

In fact, Jude reckoned, daughter and father had behaved instinctively in exactly the same way. Very soon after hearing that Alec had been taken in for questioning, Imogen had planned to get him off the hook by confessing to the murder herself, an intention which her mother had only just managed to thwart.

And, as soon as Alec had heard what his daughter was proposing to do, he had immediately hoped to get her off the hook by confessing himself. By the time the details came out – that Imogen couldn't have been at Long Bamber Stables at the relevant time because she was with her mother – the deed was done. A confession of murder had been made by the man whose clothes had been found stained with the victim's blood. The police weren't going to throw away a gift like that in a hurry.

The other niggling questions that would not go away concerned Donal Geraghty: who exactly he was blackmailing, and whether his blackmailing efforts had anything to do with Walter Fleet's death.

Well, from what they'd overheard at Fontwell – and indeed from Yolanta's behaviour that morning – there seemed little doubt that Donal was putting the squeeze on the Brewises. Why he was putting the squeeze on them was a question Jude couldn't at that moment answer, nor was it the highest in her order of priority. More significant was whether Donal was blackmailing anyone else. The Dalrymples kept coming back into Jude's mind, and the more she had found out about the state of their marriage, the more reasons she could find why they might be open to blackmail.

She was sure that Sonia was holding out on her. From working professionally with the woman, Jude knew the level of tension she was suffering, and Sonia had virtually admitted that its cause was information she dared not divulge. Her husband's violence was a constant pressure in her life, but Jude got the feeling there was something else torturing Sonia Dalrymple. If only she could find out what the secrets were that seemed to be corroding the woman from the inside out. An early visit to Sonia was called for, one when a few more cards should be placed on the table.

And then again there was Donal. Donal the disappearing Irishman. Vanished once again. Yolanta had thought he was in the stables where Jude was sitting, Imogen had implied he'd been there until recently. Where had he disappeared to this time?

Suddenly Jude recalled the little hesitation in Imogen's voice when she'd been asked where Donal was. Had she been lying? Was Donal Geraghty actually still present in the derelict stables?

Jude pulled herself up with difficulty from her crouched position on the bucket. Her limbs had almost locked in the cold, and she shook her legs to restore the circulation.

Conker got the reward of another carrot in anticipation of good behaviour, and a cheery, 'See you,' as Jude set out to explore the rest of the buildings.

She gave the other five stables a cursory look. If there had been anyone holed up in them, she and Carole would, she felt sure, have seen or heard something. And so it proved. No human agency had stirred the mess in the stables for decades.

Jude went through the narrow passage to the left of the main entrance and found herself in a barn-like structure full of decaying farm carts and rusted machinery. Sagging doors and missing tiles gave her enough daylight to inspect the whole area and confirm that it was uninhabited.

She moved back to the central courtyard and continued in a straight line through the passage to the right of the main gates. The space she entered seemed as large as the one she had just left, but its roof was in better repair, so it took a moment for her eyes to accommodate to the darkness.

As she stood there, trying to make out the shapes that loomed around her, Jude heard a strange sound.

A whimper, like that of an animal in pain.

Except that it definitely came from a human being.

Chapter Thirty-Six

Jude moved towards the source of the sound. The space smelled of old grain, so damp as almost to be fermented. The floor was littered with ancient sacks, long pre-dating plastic, shredded perhaps by the rats who had years ago made away with their contents. Everything underfoot felt slimy.

In the far corner lay what looked like just another pile of torn sacking, and it was from there that the human whimpering came. The darkness was intense. Prudent Carole, of course, would have her torch in the Renault, but Carole and the Renault were now far away. Jude looked around for a light source and saw an old window over which a whole sack appeared to have been nailed. But that had been a long time ago, and when she touched it the fabric tore away like tissue paper. The extant panes of the window were obscured by green slime, but enough were broken to let in the daylight.

Jude looked back to the corner and saw Donal Geraghty.

He lay on a pile of filthy sacks and looked as filthy himself. His face was discoloured with dried blood, which had also sprayed down over his clothes. The way he hugged himself suggested his injuries might include broken ribs. One blue eye was closed by bruising, but the other looked up trying to identify the intruder.

'It's Jude.'

'Oh God, that's all a man needs when he's in a state like this – a visit from the Fethering Miss Marple.'

The old insouciance was still in his voice, but the words were blurred, as though some of his teeth as well as his ribs had been broken.

'Donal, what happened to you?'

He did the nearest to a shrug his broken body could achieve. 'I got into a fight,' he said with mock-pathos. 'Again.'

'Who with?'

'I don't remember his name. I don't know if I even knew it. He was just someone in the Cheshire Cheese last night. All I do know is that he was a lot younger and fitter than me.'

'How did you get here?'

'I suppose I must have walked.'

'Do you really not remember?'

'No, I really don't remember. When I get into a fight, it's like . . . you know the expression "red mist"? Well, I guess that's not a bad description for what happens. I don't see anything else, I don't think anything else. All I know is I have to lash out, and I do . . . and sometimes when I come back to myself, I'm all right, though I haven't a clue what's happened to the other guy . . . and sometimes when I come back to

myself – well, it's like today. One thing I know for sure
– I lost.'

What he said did provide some explanation for the
way he'd suddenly turned on Ted Crisp. And indeed,
why he hadn't mentioned the incident when he next
saw Carole and Jude. Maybe his mind had just blanked
it out.

'But what are you going to do now, Donal? Don't
you think you should be in a hospital?'

'Nah. What good would a hospital do for me?
There's nothing broken, nothing that needs setting.
And fractures, well, they just heal in their own time.'

'I imagine you've had a few over the years.'

He tried to laugh. 'Few? That's what might be
termed an understatement. If you're a jump jockey, the
falls and the broken bones, they come with the job
description. My collarbones have been broken more
times than a politician's promise. First thing you learn
in my business is to heal quick. Otherwise you're out of
a job.'

'But then, when you get older, with all those broken
bones, the arthritis sets in.'

He looked at her bleakly, recognizing the accuracy
of her diagnosis.

'Which is why you drink so much. To deal with the
pain.'

'So?' He looked at her with some of the old cocki-
ness in his one open eye. 'To my mind, Jameson's has
got a much better taste than bloody paracetamol.'

'But would paracetamol get you into so many
fights?'

He attempted another shrug. 'I lead my life the way I want to lead it.'

Looking at him, abject, in terrible pain, lying on filthy sacks, Jude found that hard to believe, but she didn't take issue. Instead, she asked, 'Is there anything I can do for you? You say you won't go to hospital, but—'

'You don't have any Jameson's with you, do you?'

'No. Not normally something I carry about my person.'

'Ah, that's a shame. I'm feeling shitty all over, but the most painful bit is the hangover. So, if you could fetch me some, you'd be doing a Christian act.'

'I think a more Christian act might be to get you off the stuff.'

'You don't know what you're talking about.'

'You know, Donal, there are other ways of controlling pain apart from alcohol and drugs.'

'Oh yes? What are they – topping yourself?'

'No. Massage can help.'

He spat contempt at the idea. 'I had a lot of massages when I was riding. Then they helped. I'm past that now.'

'And healing.'

He was silent.

'You know about healing, Donal. I saw you heal Sonia Dalrymple's horse. Well, I do a bit of that. And – before you say anything – my results are better with humans than they are with animals.'

'Bloody have to be, I'd have thought, by the law of averages.'

'Well, if you ever want to come to me and try a session, just to get the basics of pain management . . .'

'Does the process involve Jameson's?'

'No, it doesn't. But it's a good offer.'

'A very good offer, for which I am appropriately grateful. But' – he put on a teasing voice again – 'I'm a bit wary of these alternative medicines. You hear these terrible stories of people who take up with some quack and give up drinking the Jameson's altogether. Now that's not something I would want happening to me. I think it could seriously undermine my health.'

The argument was not worth pursuing. Jude moved on to another topic. 'Presumably Imogen rang you last night?'

'Yes. Thank the Lord she got me while I was still sober.'

'She told you what she was planning to do?'

'She was worried about that little Conker. Got it into her head that the Horse Ripper was after her. I didn't know, maybe she was right, maybe she did know something. So I told her how to find this place.'

'But she couldn't have stayed here for ever.'

'Who's talking about for ever? Kid wanted to find somewhere to hide the horse, I told her about this place. Nothing more to it. Gave her a chance to get away from that dreadful mother. She's a good kid. I've got a lot of time for her. She understands horses.'

Jude, who'd been standing since she arrived in the barn, moved to prop herself up against the remains of an old workbench. Thin ribbons of sunlight, even more diluted than they were outside, made their way down through holes in the tiles to the slimy floor.

'And Imogen's father,' she said thoughtfully, 'is about to be charged with murder.'

'Yes,' Donal agreed. 'Not that he did it, mind.'

'I don't think he did either. But,' Jude asked eagerly, 'do you have any reason for saying that, apart from gut instinct?'

'Oh, I have a reason, yes. I know he didn't do it.'

'Can you tell me why?'

A pained chuckle came from the corner of the room. 'You don't give up, do you, Jude?'

'No, I don't. The reason you won't tell me . . . you know, why you know Alec Potton didn't kill Walter – is it something to do with your blackmailing activities?'

'Now why would you think that?'

'Because I can't see any other reason why you'd keep quiet about it, unless the information was of some financial value to you.'

'Well now, that might be a very shrewd observation.'

'I can take that as a "yes" then, can I?'

'You're welcome to do so. But I'm still not going to tell you why I know Alec Potton didn't do it.'

'Is it something to do with the Dalrymples?'

'And why should it be?'

'Because Sonia's very tense about something, which could be a threat of blackmail. And if you knew details about her marriage which she didn't want made public, or even details she didn't want her husband to find out about . . . ?'

She let the ideas trail hopefully in the air, but Donal

only let out another painful chuckle and said, 'I'm enjoying listening to how your mind works, Jude, but you're still not going to get anything out of me.'

She tried yet another tack. 'I know about other people you're blackmailing.'

'Is that so?'

'Yes. Very generous of the Brewises to let you camp out here, isn't it?'

This time the idea seemed genuinely to amuse him. Jude pressed home her advantage. 'Are you going to tell me what you're blackmailing them about?'

'Well, I'm a fair man, and I don't see why I shouldn't because the secret in that case is not one I can imagine you spreading around.'

'So what is the secret?'

'Would you be surprised, Jude, if I told you that Mrs Brewis had a past?'

'Nothing would surprise me less.'

'Right. Well, I got this from a Russian horse-dealer I do the occasional bit of business with. He was down at Long Bamber with me one day when the Brewises were riding out, and he told me he recognized her.'

'Oh?'

'Whore who used to work the Moscow international hotels. Expensive one but still a whore.'

So Jude's thought, a tart's boudoir hadn't been so far off the mark after all.

'Well, thank you, Donal, that's most generous. You're right, though. It's not information I would use.'

'I know, but I think it could be a nice little earner for me for quite a while.'

'Be careful, though. If you get too pressing, I think Victor Brewis could turn nasty.'

'I'm damned sure he could. Don't worry, I'll watch my back.'

'So, though you're so generous with the Brewises' secrets, are you still not going to share the Dalrymples' with me?'

'No, I'm not,' he said firmly. Then came a 'Damn' when he realized he'd fallen into her trap.

'Thank you very much, Donal. At least you've confirmed that you are blackmailing the Dalrymples.'

'Ah, but I haven't given you anything else. I may be Irish, but I'm not entirely stupid, you know.'

'You're very far from stupid.'

'That's true. Do you know, out of school I got a scholarship to Trinity College, Dublin. To read history.'

'But—'

'I never took it up, though. Far more interested in horses. Always was.'

This was a fascinating insight into Donal Geraghty's past, and at any other time Jude would have followed up on it. But not right then.

'Donal, listen . . . You know that Nicky Dalrymple is a violent man?'

'I'd got that impression, yes.'

'He might not take very kindly to being blackmailed either.'

'I'll watch my back with that one too.'

'But it's Sonia I'm concerned about. Do you have to blackmail her?'

'A man has to make a living, and that couple are

almost indecently well heeled. They're not going to miss a few thousand' – he smiled wryly – 'given to such a worthy cause as the Injured Jockeys Fund. And I can't pretend I didn't see what I saw from the hayloft, so . . .'

'Donal, all I'm asking is for you to show a little pity. Sonia's in a terrible state and—'

They seemed to hear the sound at the same time. Both raised hands to silence the other. Footsteps were approaching the stable block from the side away from the manor house.

Jude moved softly to the broken window.

Walking past, almost close enough for her to touch, with his eyes set determinedly ahead of him, was Nicky Dalrymple.

In his hand was a large kitchen knife.

Chapter Thirty-Seven

Except for giving directions, Imogen Potton said nothing to Carole on the way home in the Renault. All the fight seemed to have gone out of her. She shrank into her seat, sniffling occasionally, looking younger by the minute.

Once at home, all she seemed to want was for her mother to baby her, and her mother, rather to Carole's surprise, obliged. Having set her guest up with a cup of coffee in the sitting room, Hilary Potton vanished upstairs with her daughter. She was some time getting Imogen in and out of a bath, and didn't come down till the girl was tucked up in bed with a hot-water bottle and on the verge of sleep.

'Sorry about that,' she said, entering the sitting room with a cafetière. 'Can I top you up?'

'Thank you.'

Hilary settled down in a frayed armchair with her own cup and, as usual, there was no problem in getting her to start talking. 'Poor Immy. She's taken about as much as she can. You know, I often wish I'd never met Alec.'

'You think all her problems are down to him, do you?'

'What else is there to think? His constantly going off with other women is what broke up our marriage, which meant Immy had to grow up in an atmosphere of constant rowing and arguments. And now he's proved to be a murderer too.'

'That hasn't actually been proved yet,' said Carole cautiously.

'As good as. Just needs the court proceedings to dot the "i"s and cross the "t"s. And what's that going to do for Immy – having a father in prison for life? No, as soon as this is all over, we'll move away from Fethering.'

'Any idea where?'

'I don't know. A long way. Australia? New Zealand, maybe.'

'But if you did that, neither of you would be able to visit your husband in prison.'

Hilary Potton's look turned venomous. 'Do you think either of us will *want* to visit my husband in prison?'

'I can understand why *you* might not, but Imogen still seems to be devoted to her father.'

'All the more reason to get her as far away from him as possible,' Hilary snapped. 'Cauterize the wound, get rid of all the poison that man has brought into our lives. Immy and I need a completely new start.' She looked defiantly at her guest. 'And I'm going to ensure that we get it.'

*

Jude thought quickly. There was only one explanation for Nicky Dalrymple's presence at the old stables. He had been at home when Sonia had taken the call revealing where Imogen and Conker had been found. Nicky knew that the girl spent a lot of time with Donal Geraghty at Long Bamber Stables, and must have deduced that the ex-jockey had suggested the pony's hiding place. Donal was blackmailing the Dalrymples. Nicky had arrived to silence the Irishman for good.

'Don't make a sound,' she whispered, as she hurried out to the main yard. She didn't know yet how she was going to do it, but she was determined to prevent any harm from coming to Donal.

In his search of the premises, Nicky Dalrymple had reached the stall where Conker had been hidden. He stood in the doorway, his back to Jude, the knife still in his hand.

'What are you doing here, Nicky?'

He turned as if he had been stung, and the face he revealed was a terrifying one. Congested with unreasoning fury, his expression had erased all trace of his good looks. There was something savage, even bestial, about him.

'I could ask you the same,' he hissed. 'I can't remember what your name is . . .'

'Jude.'

'Well, Jude.' He raised his knife hand as he approached her. Jude backed away towards the main gates, but she knew escape was hopeless. If she ran, a man as big and fit as Nicky Dalrymple would overtake her within seconds. No, argument was going to be a better defence than flight. Still not much of a defence, though.

The knife blade showed a dull gleam in the pale sunlight. Nicky's contorted face almost smiled. 'Have you ever heard the expression "being in the wrong place at the wrong time"? Because I would say you, at this moment, are the perfect example of that.'

'What – you're planning to kill me?'

'I don't think you've left me much alternative. You're not the kind of person to keep quiet about something like this. Or the other cases.'

He was closing in on her, with his back to the hay-barn entrance. Jude backed away till she came up hard against one of the stables' rotting gateposts, and tried desperately to think of reasons for him to spare her life.

'Look, Nicky, nothing's happened yet. You're quite safe at the moment. So long as you don't attack either me or Donal, you'll be all right.'

He looked bewildered. 'Donal? You mean that tinker and thief who—?'

But that was as far as he got. Suddenly a small demented fury was on his back, reaching strong hands to grip at his throat.

Donal. Who had somehow found the strength to drag himself up out of the barn and come to Jude's rescue.

It was an unequal contest. Nicky Dalrymple was twice the size of his assailant and at the peak of fitness. Donal was suffering from cracked ribs and all the other pains of his previous night's beating. With almost contemptuous ease, Nicky swung the Irishman round off his shoulders and sent him crashing to the ground next to Jude. At the impact, Donal let out a shriek of agony.

'So I've got two of you to dispose of now, have I?' Nicky Dalrymple felt the weight of the kitchen knife in his hand. 'Two who know rather more than they should about my activities.'

'I'd be open to negotiation,' said Donal, with some of his old bravado. 'I'm sure we could reach a mutually agreeable sum of money that would pay for my silence.'

'I'm afraid we're beyond that. This has got very serious now. I've got far too much to lose to allow either of you ever to speak to another human being.'

As he moved towards them, Nicky Dalrymple became calmer. The natural colour returned to his face. He was once again the successful man, the practical man. He was facing a problem, but he had worked out a way of dealing with that problem, and he was about to put it into practice.

'Now, do you feel strongly about which of you goes first?' He smiled graciously. 'Etiquette, of course, demands that it should be the lady.'

He moved towards Jude, the kitchen knife raised.

'So, Hilary, are you going to go on working at Allinstore?'

'For the time being, yes.'

'What, still the same shift? Four to eight every week-day except Wednesday?'

'That's it. I haven't any alternative, Carole. I'm

afraid Alec's earning capacity is rather diminished by being in police custody. But, of course, when Imogen and I move I won't work.'

'What will you live on then?'

'Property prices are a lot cheaper in New Zealand.' Australia was apparently no longer part of the equation. Carole got the feeling Hilary had been planning her escape for quite a while. Probably long before her husband's arrest had made it a real possibility.

'And then,' she went on, 'I'm set to make quite a lot of money from the newspapers.'

'Really? What, you mean writing about the murder case?'

'Yes. Obviously nothing can appear in print until Alec's convicted, but I've already had exploratory approaches from the *News of the World*, the *Mail* and the *Express*. I've been in touch with a very high-profile publicist, who's going to handle all that for me.'

There was no mistaking the glee with which Hilary Potton announced this. Not only was she planning to take extreme revenge on her ex-husband, she was also going to attain the kind of media celebrity of which she had always dreamed.

Nicky Dalrymple slowly brought the knife to touch Jude's cheek, running it along the smooth skin, almost like a lover's caress.

Then he raised it to stab, his eyes narrowing to focus on the top of her cleavage.

Jude felt calm, satisfied with the life that she had had and closed her eyes to await the blow.

Then she was aware of a sudden movement from below, and just managed to see Donal's hand dart upwards, as he plunged a Stanley knife into Nicky Dalrymple's stomach.

The banker looked down in horror, to see the blood spreading over his perfectly laundered Turnbull & Asser shirt. Off-guard, he hardly resisted when Donal Geraghty snatched the kitchen knife from his hand.

Nicky Dalrymple was in shock. He gave a bewildered look at what had been his two prospective victims, then turned and staggered back towards the road, whimpering like a child.

Chapter Thirty-Eight

Jude called the Fethering taxi firm she always used, and they said, 'because it was her', they'd have someone there in twenty minutes. She asked for the car to come to the entrance to the old farm, where Nicky Dalrymple must have parked his BMW. No need to involve Yolanta Brewis in further questions and explanations.

She also insisted that Donal should come with her, and he was too exhausted by his recent exertions to put up much of an argument. 'But no hospitals,' he said.

'No hospitals. I'll put you to bed in my house.'

'When did I last have an offer like that?' he asked with a weary wink.

Of course, what she was doing meant Jude was not fulfilling her promise to Imogen, that she would stay with Conker until Sonia arrived. But, as with charities, when it came to the crunch, Jude always put human beings above animals.

She checked that the pony was happy – which she was, extremely. And Conker was even happier when the bucket of carrots and pony nuts was moved to within her range. Jude left her chomping merrily.

Under other circumstances, she would have stayed

to run a bath for Donal and see him settled into bed at Woodside Cottage, but she was in a rush, so she just showed him where everything was. The cab was still waiting outside, ready to move on to her next destination.

'Right,' she said as she was about to leave. 'Have you got everything you want?'

Donal grimaced ruefully. 'Well, now, you wouldn't happen to have a bottle of Jameson's in the house, would you?'

Jude apologized that she hadn't got any Jameson's, only Famous Grouse. Donal agreed that he'd make an exception.

'Can I get you a glass?'

'No, the bottle'll do just fine.'

She ran upstairs to fetch a notebook from a bedside drawer, said goodbye to an already imbibing Donal, and left.

Before getting back into the cab, Jude knocked on the door of High Tor. She wanted to have Carole with her for the next encounter. But there was no reply.

She told the driver where she wanted to go.

On the short drive to Unwins, Jude tried to separate the conflicting strands of information she had received in the last dramatic hour.

Of Nicky Dalrymple's violence – whose existence she had never much doubted – she now had first-hand experience.

Another nugget of information rose to the surface

of her confusion. Donal had actually given more details of how he was blackmailing the Dalrymples. He had talked about something he'd seen from the hayloft. Jude would have pursued the hint at the time, but that was just when Nicky had arrived with the knife and in the ensuing drama it had been forgotten.

Damn. She should have asked Donal before leaving him at Woodside Cottage, but the idea had gone completely out of her mind.

There was something else, though, some scrap of information, some oddity, something that didn't quite strike the right chord . . .

Something to do with Nicky Dalrymple. Painful though it was to remember, Jude tried to reconstruct everything that had happened, everything that had been said during their recent confrontation at Cordham Manor stables.

The most striking detail was Nicky's response when she had first mentioned Donal's name. He had seemed surprised. His reaction had certainly not been that of a vengeful man whose quarry has just been named.

In other words, contrary to Jude's assumption, Nicky had not arrived at the Cordham Manor stables in search of Donal Geraghty.

He had come for another reason.

She shuddered as she took in the implications of this.

*

'Why don't you stay for lunch?'

'Oh no, really. I'd better be getting back to High Tor. There's rather an aggrieved dog there who hasn't been out since about half past five this morning.'

'Having waited this long, another hour's not going to kill him. Besides, if you started at that time, you must be starving by now. Did you have any breakfast?'

Carole admitted that she hadn't had any.

'Then, no question, you must stay. My little thank you for bringing Immy safely home.'

The invitation was an appealing one. Carole certainly felt extremely hungry. And, even though Alec Potton's confession seemed to have sewn up the case, she would get the chance to ask more questions about the murder of Walter Fleet.

Besides, Hilary Potton had led her through to the kitchen and was already opening a bottle of white wine.

Jude asked the driver to stop on the road outside Unwins. She didn't want the noise of tyres on the gravel to alert the residents to her arrival. If the front door was locked, she would have to ring the bell for admission in the traditional way. But if it wasn't . . .

The door was locked, and when Sonia Dalrymple opened it, Jude felt embarrassed about the dramatic scenarios she had been spinning in her mind. Everything at the house seemed so ordinary, so peaceful. Sonia looked once again beautiful and soignée, the dark cloud of Nicky's presence once again removed from her horizon.

'Jude! What on earth are you doing here? I was just about to ring Lucinda and sort out picking up Conker. Thinking it's probably safer if she drives one of the horseboxes over, rather than riding Conker back on the roads.'

'Yes.' She had been steeling herself for this confrontation but now she was actually at Unwins, she was having difficulty working out the best approach. To say straight away that Sonia's husband had just tried to stab her to death might be dramatic, but might not help her towards the information she needed. So she contented herself with asking a question which was already answered by Sonia's demeanour and the absence of a large BMW in the drive. 'Has Nicky gone?'

'Yes, about an hour ago. He was driving straight up to Heathrow.'

No, he wasn't. He was making a detour via Cordham Manor.

'Do come in, Jude. Would you like a cup of tea?'

She would certainly like something. The woody carrot lay uneasily on her stomach. They went through to the kitchen, where Sonia made tea. When she offered a packet of shortbread biscuits, Jude fell on them.

She still hadn't quite worked out what she was going to say next. But, as she frequently did, she opted for a direct approach. 'Sonia, I saw Donal again recently.'

'Oh.' The very name was enough to set her clattering tea cups.

'And I know he's blackmailing you over something he saw from the hayloft.'

Sonia said nothing, but sank into a kitchen chair, as though all strength had been drained out of her. But, at the same time, she showed signs of relief. Maybe at last the cancer of the secret she had been holding inside for so long could be removed.

'I knew it would have to come out eventually.' Her voice was weak, but calm. 'Probably as well it's come out now, when Nicky's just gone away. Gives me a few days to prepare myself for his reaction.' Her face looked grim. 'He's not going to like it. This will be the row to end all rows.'

'Literally? This might be the one that makes you leave him?'

Sonia looked across at Jude with yearning hopelessness in her eyes. 'If only . . .'

The phone on the table rang. 'Probably Nicky, saying he's safely at Heathrow and checking whether I packed something. He usually manages to find something I've forgotten, something that puts me in the wrong.' She reached for the phone.

'If he asks whether you've seen me, say no,' Jude hissed.

With a look of surprise, Sonia answered the call. As predicted, it was her husband. As predicted, he asked if she'd remembered to pack the charger for his shaver. When she said she hadn't, a predictable earful ensued.

Then, after a few more yes and no answers, the call ended.

Sonia looked across the table in bewilderment. 'He did ask if you were here.'

'And you said no?'

'Yes. Jude, what's going on?'

'It's something rather nasty.'

'About Nicky?' Sonia asked, knowing what the answer would be.

'Yes, about Nicky. You said there are some nights he doesn't stay at home?'

'He spends most of his life travelling the globe.'

'I know that. But you said sometimes he stays in a hotel round here.'

'Oh yes. After we've had a particularly major row.'

'Like you did last night?'

'Yes.'

'And when you have those major rows, does he hit you?'

Sonia gave her answer as if it was the first time she'd thought about the question. 'No, he doesn't. That's odd, actually. He hits me over small things. The big rows, he— no, he just leaves me, goes out.'

'But when he does that, he's not in a calm state?'

'Good God, no. He's absolutely furious, red in the face, bottling everything up.'

'And when you next see him, has he calmed down again?'

'Yes. I hadn't really thought about it before, but I suppose he has. No,' she said thoughtfully, 'I'm not afraid of Nicky when he comes back after one of those nights away.'

'Hm.' Jude tapped her fingers lightly on the table as she considered how to phrase the next bit. 'Sonia, would you be able to give me dates for the nights when Nicky stayed out – say, for the last six months?'

'Well, yes, I could, actually.' She crossed to the kitchen units and opened the cutlery drawer. There was a purpose-built segmented tray inside. Sonia lifted this out to reveal a thin hard-backed manuscript book underneath.

'My diary. He'd never look in there.'

'Is it just for this year?'

'No, it's not marked up as a diary. I just go on until I run out of space and then start another one.'

Sonia flicked through and found the relevant dates. Jude checked them against notes in the little book she had picked up at Woodside Cottage.

One of the dates seemed particularly to trouble Sonia. 'That was just after Christmas, I remember. The twins were still here, still on holiday.'

'And you had a big row? Quite common in families at Christmas, I believe.'

'Yes, but . . .' Sonia choked back a sob. 'This one was worse. The reason we had the row was . . . worse.'

Jude bided her time. She had an instinct that the revelation would not stop there.

'The girls had gone to bed, and Nicky had gone up to say goodnight to them, and then I remembered some dirty clothes I had to pick up from Alice's room and

I . . . I found Nicky on Alice's bed. He was – touching her.'

'And that prompted the row?'

'Huge row. Worst row ever. Nicky stormed out of the house.'

'And came back the next morning calmed?'

Sonia nodded tearfully. 'That's why I insisted the girls go to boarding school. At least during term-time Nicky can't – can't get at them.'

Jude took a folded newspaper cutting out of her notebook and spread it out on the table. 'This was printed a couple of days later. The events it refers to happened the night Nicky stormed out of here.'

Sonia Dalrymple could only have had time to read the headline 'HORSE RIPPER STRIKES AGAIN', before she burst into uncontrollable tears.

To Jude it all made sense now. What Sonia had said about her husband interfering with his daughter served only to confirm her thesis. The theory of a connection between horse molestation and paedophilia was gaining credibility in academic circles. And Jude had a feeling Sonia might have suspected what Nicky had been up to.

'Is it a possibility you'd thought about before? Something you were afraid might be true?'

The shattered woman managed to nod assent.

'This morning,' said Jude grimly, 'only about an hour ago, I saw your husband at the old stables at Cordham Manor. He had a knife with him.'

'Oh, no,' Sonia moaned. 'Conker.'

'Yes. I think he was out to harm Conker.'

It seemed impossible that Sonia's crying could become more intense, but it did. Jude reached out and placed a hand on her arm. 'Don't worry. Conker's all right. And, as you see, I'm all right. I have Donal to thank for that.'

'Donal?' Sonia repeated in bewilderment.

'Yes. He saved my life by stabbing Nicky.'

'Stabbing?'

'Only a flesh wound. I'm sure your husband has patched himself up at Heathrow, bought a new shirt and will be fine for his business meetings in Chicago.'

'Yes.' There was a long silence. 'Oh, Jude, what do we do?'

'I think we have to tell the police.'

Sonia nodded in the face of the inevitable.

'But will there be any evidence?'

'Donal and I can testify to the attack he made on us this morning. With regard to the horses – well, the dates offer quite a strong pointer. I would imagine the police could get some DNA evidence, maybe from the kitchen knife found in the hayloft. I think there will probably be enough to convict him.'

'Yes. Yes.' Sonia had stopped crying. She now seemed confused, as she tried to work out the ramifications of what she had just heard.

But she didn't seem surprised. The news that her husband was the Horse Ripper confirmed something she had been thinking for a long time. And maybe, finally, it offered her a justification for leaving him.

'A lot to take in, Jude,' she said slowly. 'It's a lot to take in.'

'Yes. And then, of course, there's something else, isn't there?'

'Hm?'

'What Donal saw from the hayloft . . .'

'Ah. Ah, yes.'

'And was prepared to blackmail you about.'

'Mm.'

'Can you tell me about it? I know you couldn't before, and from seeing what keeping the secret was doing to your body, I know how much it meant, but now?'

'Now it seems a lot less important. I was terrified how Nicky would react if Donal told him – that's why I was prepared to pay Donal so much money.'

'When did he first make his demands?'

'I can't remember. Month or so back maybe.'

'Before Walter Fleet's death?'

'Oh yes.'

'So you don't know exactly when he saw you?'

'No, and it was only later I worked out that the hayloft must have been his vantage point. Anyway, it all seems rather less significant now. I mean, given the new circumstances. I can't see that Nicky and I are ever going to get back into a normal married situation again.'

'I'd doubt it.'

'So the fact that I was having an affair with another man suddenly becomes infinitely less important.'

'Donal saw you together? From the hayloft?'

Sonia Dalrymple nodded, suddenly more confident. 'Yes. Of course, at the time I had no idea he was up there. I had no idea he was even using our stables as a temporary home until the police raided the place.'

'But why were you and your lover out there?'

'I don't know. I was afraid in the house. This place is so dominated by Nicky's presence, even when he's not here. I suppose I was a bit worried about leaving evidence that Nicky might find, but it wasn't really that. I just couldn't relax in the house.'

'Whereas in the stables . . .?'

'Yes. And there was something rather exciting about the whole set-up. Adolescent thrills, like having a snog in the cycle sheds.'

Jude chuckled softly. 'You don't have to tell me who the man is – unless you want to—'

'Oh, why not? You know everything else. Alec Potton.'

'God.' That really did knock Jude sideways.

But it also gave her another idea. 'And when was the last time you and Alec were together in the stables?'

Sonia Dalrymple dropped her head into her hands for a moment of complete silence before saying, 'That's what's so dreadful. It was late afternoon on the day that Walter Fleet was murdered. That's why I was late meeting you at Long Bamber Stables. I'd been with Alec for the last two hours. And then Nicky came home early from a business trip, and so nearly found Alec and me together, and I went into the house to see Nicky and Alec stayed hidden in the stables and it was so ghastly—'

Jude let her get no further. Brown eyes sparkling,

she exclaimed, 'But, Sonia, if Alec Potton was with you for all that time, then there's no way that he could have killed Walter Fleet.'

'I know, I know.'

And Jude finally understood the magnitude of the secret that had been torturing Sonia Dalrymple.

Chapter Thirty-Nine

Hilary Potton's kitchen was surprisingly old-fashioned for someone whose husband worked in the fitted-kitchen business. Maybe it was just another reflection of the state of their marriage, of Alec's priorities lying increasingly outside the domestic nest. But Hilary put together an excellent lunch, pasta with tuna and broccoli in a creamy sauce. She had good domestic skills. Maybe they would be put to good use one day in another marriage. Because, from the way Hilary talked about the future, meeting a nice caring New Zealander was included in her plans.

Carole kept trying to get the conversation back to Alec, and indeed to Walter Fleet's murder, but without marked success. The marriage, along with everything else that had happened in Fethering, would soon be in the past, and Hilary didn't want to talk about it all. A few necessarily uncomfortable months lay ahead of her, until her husband was finally behind bars for a good long stretch, and then her new life would begin to blossom.

'What's Imogen's reaction to the idea of New

Zealand?' asked Carole when she could get a word in edgeways.

'Oh, I haven't talked to her about it in great detail yet. I don't want to worry her. She's got enough on her plate at the moment.'

Yes, thought Carole, she certainly has. And she wasn't sure that playing a supporting role in her mother's new life in New Zealand would be the best outcome for Imogen.

Carole found it strange how her attitude to Hilary Potton had changed. When they first met, she had thought her a potential kindred spirit. But the more time Carole spent with her, the more she became aware of the woman's deep selfishness and taste for self-dramatization. She knew it was never possible to look inside another marriage and find the real truth, but she was beginning to feel a little sympathy for Alec Potton.

Hilary's clearing-up the pasta bowls and fetching fruit and cheese gave Carole an opportunity to redirect the conversation. 'Going back to that awful night when Walter Fleet was stabbed—'

'Do we have to go back to it?' Hilary laid out the second course on the table. 'You can imagine what it's like for me, particularly in the new circumstances – with Alec, and the thought that I'll have to go through it all over again when the trial starts, have the media spotlight on me, all those endless television interviews – it doesn't bear thinking of.'

But the mock shudder with which she uttered these words suggested she already was thinking of it quite a lot. And with considerable enthusiasm.

'Well, I was just working something out . . .'

'Yes?'

'That night was a Tuesday, wasn't it?'

'Was it? I can't remember.'

'Take my word for it, it was.'

'All right.' Hilary Potton shrugged. 'I don't really see that it's important.'

'It may not be. But please, just indulge me for a moment while I try to work this thing out.'

Another shrug, this time of uninterested acquiescence.

'And obviously you weren't anywhere near Long Bamber Stables at the relevant time.'

'No.'

'Because you were here at home with Imogen.'

'That's what I said, yes.'

'And yet, every weekday except Wednesday, you do a four to eight shift at Allinstore.'

'Oh yes. Yes, I do, but that evening there was a delay. Imogen got held up at school, so I had to call Allinstore to say I'd be late, and then,' she concluded lamely, 'I somehow didn't make it.'

'And is that what you told the police when they questioned you?'

'Yes, of course. Or I would have done, if the police had asked me about it in detail. But, in fact, Alec had told them that Imogen and I were here, and I was just asked to confirm what he'd said.'

'But how could Alec have known you were both here at the relevant time?'

'Sorry?'

'If he was at that very moment at Long Bamber Stables stabbing Walter Fleet to death?'

Hilary Potton looked straight at Carole, and there was a new hardness in her eyes. Their conversation had definitely reached another level. Whether that level would have incorporated denial or outrage or negotiation was impossible to say.

And nor was Carole about to find out, because at that moment the front doorbell rang, and Hilary Potton went out to the hall, to return with a jubilant Jude. 'Don't you understand – it's all all right,' she was crowing, as she followed Hilary in, leaving the door open behind her.

'No, I'm sorry. I don't understand.'

'Oh, hello, Carole.' Only a glancing acknowledgement to her friend as Jude bubbled on, 'Your husband could not have killed Walter Fleet. He has an alibi for the time when the murder took place.'

There was no disguising the effect this news had on Hilary. Disappointment burned in her eyes. Images on the screen of her mind of nice caring New Zealanders were instantly switched off.

'What was his alibi? Where was he?'

Given the facts, Jude thought it more diplomatic not to answer at that particular moment. 'The person who can vouch for him is contacting the police direct. I don't think anyone else should be told at this point.'

'I'm Alec's wife. I have a right to know.'

'I'm sure you will hear the details from the police very soon.'

'Well, I . . .' Hilary Potton was momentarily lost for

words. Then exasperation returned, exasperation with its usual target. 'Isn't that typical of bloody Alec? Presumably, if someone else had an alibi for him, he knew about it too. He could have stopped all this nonsense about going in for days of questioning and confessing to the murder.'

'Then why do you think he didn't?' asked Carole softly.

'Hm?'

'Why did he confess to a murder he didn't commit? When there was someone who could give him an alibi all the time?'

'Well, presumably – I don't know. God only knows what goes on inside that man's head.'

'Suppose,' suggested Jude, 'that the revelation of who he was with might have injured that person?'

'I don't see how it could.'

'If that person were a married woman?'

'Oh God. Alec wasn't with one of his floozies, was he?'

'I'm just saying that might be a possible explanation for his behaviour.'

'That he was saving a lady's honour?' asked Hilary cynically. 'What a chivalrous gesture. Pity he never gave a thought to saving my bloody honour.'

Carole picked up the conversation, or had it now become an interrogation? 'As Jude says, that's just one possibility. Another possibility is that Alec confessed to protect someone else.'

'What do you mean?'

'I mean he knew who had committed the murder, and he was prepared to take the rap for him, or her.'

'But why the hell would he do that?' Hilary Potton was blustering now.

'Love? Duty? Who can say? Who can say what goes on inside a marriage?'

'Carole, are you suggesting that I killed Walter?'

'No, I'm not saying that. I'm just saying that your alibi for the relevant time looks pretty shaky. Of course, it would be possible to check at Allinstore about your calling in to say you were delayed that afternoon and—'

'No! No, don't do that.'

'So, are you telling us you weren't here between five and six that Tuesday evening?'

There was a long silence. Then another voice behind them said, 'You might as well tell the truth, Mummy. You weren't here, were you?'

Chapter Forty

Imogen Potton stood in the doorway, wearing fleecy pyjamas with a design of rabbits on them. Her teeth had been cleaned and her brace was a line of unforgiving metal. From one hand dangled a teddy bear whose fur had almost all been loved away. The small breasts that pushed against her pyjama tops looked out of place on one so young.

'I don't know where you were at that time,' she continued. 'I hadn't seen you for the previous forty-eight hours. And I didn't see you again until about quarter past eight that evening, when I assumed you had just come in from Allinstore. Go on, that's true, isn't it, Mummy?'

Hilary nodded wordlessly, as her daughter went on, 'I had been worried about Conker. I kept hearing these stories about someone going round and attacking mares – always mares – and I couldn't have borne it if Conker . . . Conker was the only creature in the world I cared about.' She fixed her mother with a venomous eye. 'I had long since stopped caring about you. I don't think I ever cared about you. I think I've always hated you because of the way you treated Daddy and . . .

'I care about Daddy, but it was difficult to care about him because he was always changing his mind, and always saying he'd be somewhere at a certain time and then not turning up. So I cared about Daddy, but I couldn't rely on him . . . But Conker, Conker understood me. I couldn't bear the idea of someone hurting Conker. If she'd died, I would have died.'

Imogen was silent, but the spell she exerted over the three women was so potent none of them spoke until she again picked up her narrative. 'I was worried about Conker – particularly night-times. Lucinda or someone else was there all the day, but at night . . . And there was someone I'd seen looking at Conker in a certain way. I didn't like the way he looked at her, as if he was planning how to hurt her.'

'Who was this person?' asked Jude, almost in a whisper.

'Someone who knows Conker well, but he doesn't love her. He hates her.'

'Nicky Dalrymple?'

At this Hilary Potton burst out, 'Don't be ridiculous. Nicky Dalrymple is an international banker. He's a pillar of the Fethering community – when he's here, which granted is not all the time. Immy, you can't go round making false accusations against people.'

The girl focused her eyes on her mother's. 'No, I should leave that to you, should I, Mummy? Like you did with Daddy?'

'I didn't make false accusations against your father.'

'No, but you let him take the rap without raising a finger. There were things you could have told the police that would have got him off, but you didn't say any of them.'

'Why should I go out of my way to help someone who'd made my life a total misery?'

The look of contempt Imogen cast on her mother was more eloquent than any words could have been.

'So,' Jude prompted, 'you started to stay at Long Bamber overnight, to look after Conker?'

'Yes. Only when I knew there was danger.'

'When you knew that Mr Dalrymple was at home?'

The girl nodded.

'Did you know about this, Hilary?' asked Carole.

'Yes. Immy was perfectly safe at the stables. I knew it was just a stupid adolescent fantasy but if she wanted to live it out, I wasn't about to stop her. And, quite honestly, the way she'd been behaving since Alec and I split up, it was a relief not to have her round the house.'

'It was a relief not to *be* around the house!' When it came to vitriol, Imogen could easily match her mother's output.

'So,' said Jude easily, 'you used to sleep in the sleeping bag on the top level of Lucinda's tack room?'

'That's right. And I'd go there for the evenings if – you know, if I knew he was about and Lucinda wasn't.'

'Mm.' A thought came to Jude. 'I've suddenly realized why you were happy to come back here this morning.'

The girl looked bewildered.

'You'd come from Northampton to Fethering because you knew Nicky Dalrymple was at home and you were worried about Conker. But, as soon as you heard he was on his way to Heathrow to fly to America, you relaxed. You realized the danger to Conker was over.'

Jude didn't think it was the time to add how far from over the danger to Conker had been.

Imogen gave a quick nod of agreement to what she had said.

'So,' said Carole, 'you were there that Tuesday night, weren't you? The night Walter Fleet died?'

'Yes, I was there.'

'What happened?'

'This is ridiculous!' Hilary Potton objected. 'I won't have you bullying my daughter. She's in shock. She's had quite enough of this badgering. She needs to get back to bed.'

'No, Mummy.' Imogen moved slowly forward, and sat on the vacant chair at the table. 'I want to tell them what happened.'

'You'll regret it,' her mother hissed.

'I don't think I will.' The girl took a long breath, as if to gather her thoughts, and then launched into her account. 'I was there in the tack room, kind of snuggling down in the sleeping bag. It was a cold night, maybe I was dozing off a bit. I hadn't slept much the night before. It's never quiet round the stables, and that night I kept hearing noises I thought might be . . .' her voice faltered '. . . might be him coming.

'So the next evening I probably was half asleep. I'd gone to the stables straight from school and tried to do a bit of homework, but the light was bad, and I was too tired. So I just sort of snuggled down.

'And then a noise woke me: the front gate opening. Someone had come into the stables. There's a little window up near where I put my sleeping bag, and I could look out on to the yard. I saw . . . I saw . . .' She struggled to get the words out. 'I saw Mr Dalrymple. He was – he was carrying a knife.'

The three listening women waited while the girl recovered herself sufficiently to continue.

'I rushed downstairs. I wanted to stop him. But when I got to the tack room door, there was nobody in sight. I could see Conker's stall across the yard, and she was fine. I think she knew I was there, and she had her head over the door, hoping I'd give her a bit of carrot or a Polo.

'But I knew I'd seen Mr Dalrymple – there was no doubt about that. He was still around there somewhere – with – with his knife. So I hid behind the tack-room door, and I just waited.

'I don't know how long it was, but I was just about thinking he'd gone away, and I could get back into my sleeping bag when I heard the front gate bang again. I waited, expecting to hear footsteps going towards Conker's stable, but they didn't. They came straight towards the tack room, straight towards me.

'I'm not quite sure what happened then. I was just furious, furious at the idea that anyone could treat horses like that. I grabbed the nearest thing on the bench – I didn't even know it was a bot knife until afterwards – and when the man came into the tack room I leapt on him.' Her voice had now gone uncannily calm. 'And I slashed at him and slashed at him, and went on slashing as he backed away from me. I went on – I went on and on – until he fell over backwards in the yard.

'It was only then that I looked down at him, and realized it was Mr Fleet.'

Hilary, who had let out a little gasp earlier in her daughter's narrative, was now sobbing softly, hopelessly.

'So what did you do?' asked Carole.

'I panicked. Of course I panicked. I threw the bot knife on the ground. Then I looked down at myself. I was covered with blood. Daddy's old Barbour, his gloves that I was wearing – they were all covered with blood.'

The recollection was too vivid for her. She swayed on her seat, as if she were about to faint. Jude went quickly to the sink and fetched a glass of water.

After a long sip, Imogen was ready to continue. 'I left the stables and ran. I didn't really know what was happening, what I was doing, but some instinct told me to go by the river, follow the Fether down to Fethering. I didn't know what I was going to do when I got there. Mummy was at Allinstore . . .'

Carole directed a piercing look to Hilary Potton, who turned away.

'. . . and when I could manage to think, I knew it was Daddy I wanted, Daddy I wanted to talk to, Daddy who might be able to help me. So I rang him on his mobile, and he said he was at the stables at Unwins, you know, the Dalrymples' house. And I couldn't think why he was there, but it didn't worry me at the time. I just went there and found him. When I got there, I felt dreadful, because he said Mr and Mrs Dalrymple were in the house . . . just there. The man who wanted to hurt Conker was right there, so close to us.

'And Daddy kept asking me what had happened and I tried to tell him, and I told him I'd killed Mr Fleet, and he said I must get out of those clothes, and he bundled up the Barbour and the gloves and he hid them up in the hayloft – he said no one ever went up there.

'Then he took me home and he took off my other clothes and . . . I think he said he was going to burn them. I don't know what happened. But he made me have a bath, made me scrub everywhere very thoroughly, and then he spent ages washing the bath afterwards. Then I got dressed in jeans and a jumper, and Daddy went, and I watched television until Mummy got back from Allinstore.'

The girl looked up towards the window, her eyes unfocused. 'It was as if it had never happened. I'd wake up in the mornings often, thinking it hadn't happened, thinking I'd dreamt it. Then I'd slowly remember, but it still didn't feel real. When I heard that Donal had been taken in for questioning, I almost managed to convince myself that he had done it. I mean, I like Donal, but it seemed to make more sense that he had killed Mr Fleet than that I had. Daft, I know, but that was how my mind was working.

'Then they let Donal free, and suddenly they were questioning Daddy, and I knew what was real and what wasn't. And for a few days I just didn't know what to do. Then all at once it became very clear to me: I wanted to confess – I wanted to say everything that I've just said to you – but Mummy wouldn't let me.'

Hilary Potton looked defensively at the other two women. 'I didn't know, did I? I just thought she was being self-dramatizing again.' Rich, coming from you, thought Carole. 'I thought her idea of confessing was just to get her precious father off the hook.'

'And you didn't want him to come off the hook, did you? Ever?'

'Shut up, Carole! Stop making me feel like I've done something wrong in all this!'

'I think you have done a few things wrong,' said Jude. 'You've lied about your alibi—'

'That was only to protect Immy.'

'There's something else, though, isn't there?'

'What?'

'You told the police where to find the bloodstained clothes.'

Hilary Potton's face took on an expression of injured innocence. 'That was my duty as a citizen. Once Alec had told me they were there, I had to do it.'

'Did Alec tell you everything? That Imogen had killed Walter Fleet?'

Now Hilary looked confused. 'He garbled on about something. He said it involved Immy, but I didn't take it seriously. I thought he was just trying to exonerate himself. The only information I retained was that Alec's blood-stained Barbour was hidden in the hayloft at the Dalrymples' stables.'

'And suddenly you saw the perfect way to get

revenge on him for all the real and imagined slights he had inflicted on you during your marriage.'

'You make it sound so calculating.'

'I think,' said Jude, 'it was pretty calculating.'

'I genuinely believed that Alec was the murderer!'

But Hilary Potton's bluster was not convincing. She couldn't meet the three implacable pairs of eyes that were fixed on her, least of all Imogen's.

'For heaven's sake, I'm not the villain of the piece.' She pointed at her daughter. 'There's the villain of the piece.'

But neither Carole nor Jude thought that was completely true.

Chapter Forty-One

The hope had fluttered briefly in Jude's mind that they might be able to do nothing, that the police need never know the details of Imogen Potton's crime, but Carole soon put her right about that. Apart from the moral issue – her Home Office training had ensured that Carole had a great respect for the processes of British justice – there were practical considerations. Alec Potton was still in custody. The only thing that would make him – albeit unwillingly – retract his confession was the knowledge that his daughter's guilt for the crime had been unarguably proved.

But Carole was optimistic about the outcome for Imogen. The processes of British justice did not exclude compassion, and there where many extenuating circumstances connected with the girls' offence, particularly once the details of Nicky Dalrymple's crimes had been established. Imogen's motive had been the protection of a beloved pony from appalling molestation. That the man she had stabbed was not the perpetrator of those crimes was simply an issue of mistaken identity. These facts, taken in consideration with the girl's age and the pressure of her parents' divorce made Carole pretty certain she would escape a custodial sentence, and be given a few years of judicial monitoring.

So, in fact, it proved. By the age of eighteen, Imogen Potton no longer had even to see her probation officer, and was happily enrolled at Brinsbury Agricultural College on a course in horse management.

But that lay a long way ahead.

While the case of Walter Fleet's murder was satisfactorily resolved, the case against Nicky Dalrymple sadly never came to court. His money enabled him to buy lawyers whose infinite expertise in the law's delays put off any charges until he persuaded his bank to find him a permanent – and very highly paid – job in Hong Kong. He could never return to his native land, but at least he escaped the ignominy of having his name and reputation dragged through the courts and tabloids.

In the circumstances, however, he could not make any objections to his wife's demand for a divorce. From the moment she knew she would never have to see Nicky again, Sonia Dalrymple opened up like a Japanese flower in water, and the granting of the divorce crowned her feeling of emancipation.

Her affair with Alec Potton continued for a while, but soon sputtered out. Even such a biddable and beautiful woman as Sonia Dalrymple could not completely fix his roving eye and, after the first couple of infidelities, she, with some relief, drew the plugs on the relationship.

She kept in touch with Imogen, however, and, after Alice and Laura had shown absolutely no interest in Conker over their next holidays, transferred ownership to her. Imogen was ecstatic, and the exemplary care she gave Conker was one of the most valuable elements in her process of healing and growing up.

Her feckless father, whom she saw intermittently, did at least pay the livery and fodder bills at Long Bamber Stables.

Meanwhile, Conker got plenty of love, and attention, and riding – and carrots – which was all she had ever wanted from life.

Chieftain, as Donal had predicted, recovered completely from his lameness and, no longer fearful of Nicky Dalrymple's bullying, provided Sonia with many years of happy riding and companionship.

After sticky teenage years with Alice and Laura, their mother was delighted when they both married early to rich young men, one emigrating to Florida and the other to South Africa. She kept in touch, paying dutiful visits to a spreading horde of grandchildren, who promised to grow up just as spoilt as their parents. So far as she knew, neither Alice nor Laura maintained any contact with their father.

Then, in her early fifties, Sonia Dalrymple was destined, while walking the Inca trail, to meet the love of her life, and live happily ever after.

But that too lay a long way ahead.

*

Men like Donal Geraghty don't change, but, as the arthritis crippled him more and more, he did take up Jude's offer of trying to ease his pain. Her ministrations helped and, though he was never going to give up the Jameson's completely, he did moderate his intake, at least to the point where he could remember getting into fights. And the fact that he could remember them meant he got into less. After some years, Ted Crisp grudgingly lifted the ban on him at the Crown and Anchor.

The traumas they had both experienced did not serve to bring Hilary Potton and her daughter closer together. They continued to share the house in Fethering, in a state of silence interrupted by rows, until Imogen started college. Then Hilary, with enough money saved from the divorce settlement and her share of the house sale – though sadly without the largesse of the tabloid newspapers – fulfilled her dream of upping sticks and moving alone to New Zealand. Where it was to be hoped that no nice caring New Zealander was so unfortunate as to get caught in her tentacles.

But that lay in the future too.

Victor Brewis made one property speculation too many and lost all his money. The renovations at Cordham Manor came to a sudden halt and it was put on the market, which at least saved the lovely old house from undergoing a total makeover by Yolanta.

She, finding that all of her husband's attractions went away when the money went away, divorced him and married an eighty-year-old shipping magnate, whose last years she determined to make happy – and few.

Lucinda Fleet, meanwhile, continued to run Long Bamber Stables, single-handed. She never re-married or even had a boyfriend, finding, as had many people before her, that horses are much more rewarding companions than human beings.

And the finances of the stables juddered from crisis to crisis until, eventually, Lucinda was forced to sell them.

But that, as well, lay far in the future.

What lay closer to the present was the ring on the bell of High Tor, just after Carole had returned from Imogen Potton's dramatic revelations and released an extremely disgruntled Gulliver from the kitchen. She moved to the front door with some bewilderment. Jude had just been dropped at Woodside Cottage, so it couldn't be her, and it wasn't the general habit of Fethering residents to arrive unannounced.

Carole was astonished and ashamed to open her door to Stephen and Gaby. In all the excitements of the morning, she had completely forgotten their arrangement. Oh God, this was to be the dreadful meeting, when they told her they were splitting up.

Even worse, she remembered that she had promised to cook lunch for them. And she hadn't done a thing. The joint and everything else were still in the fridge. There was nothing Carole Seddon hated more than inefficiency. Particularly when the inefficiency was her own.

Full of embarrassed apology, she announced they'd have to eat at the Crown and Anchor. Desperately hoping he wouldn't be full, she rang Ted Crisp to ask him to hold a table for them. He immediately went into a worrying routine about everyone wanting to be squeezed in and how people were having to book weeks ahead because of the Crown and Anchor's mounting gastronomic reputation. Then he relented, stopped fooling about, and said it was fine.

So it proved when they got there. Only three tables were occupied.

Carole, insisting that this must be her treat, went to get the drinks. Both Stephen and Gaby ordered fizzy water, which was worrying and suggested their mission was going to be an austere one. She ordered herself a large Chilean Chardonnay; she felt she was going to need it.

They sat down and raised their glasses in a wordless toast. Then Stephen said, with that heavy formality of which Carole hoped Gaby had cured him, 'Mother, there's something we have to tell you.'

'Oh yes?' Her voice came out very small.

'It is, not to put too fine a point on it, erm . . . erm . . .'

Oh no, he was getting just like his father. And at

that moment Carole felt as alienated from Stephen as she was from David. Get on with it, she prayed, tell me the worst.

'Well, the fact is, Mother . . . you're going to become a grandmother.'

This was so far from the news she had been expecting that at first Carole thought she must have misheard. But then, in the chaos of conversation that followed, details slowly emerged.

Stephen and Gaby had wanted to start a family as soon as they were married, but for months nothing was happening and they were both getting very tense about it. The day Gaby had sounded so listless on the phone she had just found out she wasn't pregnant – again.

But then suddenly it had happened. She was only about eight weeks gone. It was really too early to tell anyone, but they so wanted her to know.

'Does your father know yet?'

'No, we wanted to tell you first.'

Nothing Stephen could have said could have given Carole a deeper glow.

'Current estimated arrival date is the twenty-eighth of October,' said Gaby excitedly.

'Isn't it wonderful news?' Stephen crowed.

'Yes, wonderful,' Carole agreed.

Her knee-jerk reaction was, Oh dear, another relationship to get wrong. She wouldn't have been Carole Seddon if she hadn't thought that. But the anxiety lasted only a second before it was overwhelmed by a warm flood of excitement. Now she really had got something to look forward to.

DEATH UNDER THE DRYER

When Carole goes for a hair trim at 'Connie's Clip Joint', she doesn't expect to find herself at the scene of a murder. But in the backroom, strangled by the lead of a hairdryer, sits Connie's young assistant, Kyra.

Whilst Carole and her sleuthing friend Jude enjoy some tactical snooping, Fethering fingers are pointing at Kyra's boyfriend, Nathan, who has disappeared. But Nathan's family are also acting rather oddly.

Meanwhile Connie's ex-husband Martin, owner of competing hairdressing chain 'Martin & Martina', appears to have been quite the ladies' man with his young assistants, including Kyra herself. Could he have silenced her before she divulged his sordid secret?

As our lady detectives decide there are only so many haircuts they can have, so too do they realize this is no cut and dry case. And some people will do anything to keep their private lives concealed . . .

Death Under the Dryer, the delightful new novel by
Simon Brett, is out now in Macmillan hardback.

The opening scenes follow here.

Chapter One

If her hairdresser had not been killed, Carole Seddon would never have become involved in the murder at Connie's Clip Joint. Though she knew the salon well – and indeed had to walk past it every time she went along the High Street to the inadequate local super-market Allinstore – Carole had never before crossed its threshold. There was something too public about actually having her hair done in Fethering. Since she had moved permanently to West Sussex some ten years previously, her reclusive instincts had favoured an anonymous salon in Worthing, where every six weeks her straight grey hair would be trimmed to helmet-like neatness by a taciturn man called Graham. The arrangement had suited her. She and Graham were polite, but showed no curiosity about each other, and their haircuts were blissfully silent.

The first time Carole knew anything about his life outside the salon was when she heard that Graham had been killed in a motor-cycle accident. This had happened when she rang to make her latest regular appointment. The emotion in the voice of the girl who relayed the sad news decided Carole that she needed to find another salon. She didn't want the perfect detachment of her relationship with Graham to be spoiled by the maudlin reminiscences of other hairdressers after his death.

So the question then was where should she go. She checked the *Yellow Pages*, but was paralysed into indecision by the sheer number of options available. Carole hated the hidebound nature that made her react like that. About everything. Why did she have to make an issue of things? She ought to have grown out of that kind of introspection by now. She was well into her fifties – about to become a grandmother, for God's sake – and yet, contrary to the appearance she gave the outside world, still vacillated about decisions like a young teenager.

Eventually, as part of her knew she would end up doing, she consulted Jude. Her next-door neighbour's bird's-nest style was probably not the best of advertisements for the art of hairdressing, but she must get it cut somewhere.

Predictably, Jude turned out to be not that bothered where she went. Her haircuts weren't conducted according to a rigid timetable. She would just wake up one morning feeling that her blonde locks were getting a bit shaggy, or be passing a salon and go in on a whim. She did, however, say that Connie, of Connie's Clip Joint on the High Street, was 'absolutely fine'. Also, Fethering rumour had it, the salon wasn't doing that well, and so booking in there would be supporting local industry.

These arguments – together with the unruly state

of her hair – were enough to sway Carole. She seized the phone that very day, a Wednesday, and had a telling lack of difficulty in booking the first, nine o'clock, appointment at Connie's Clip Joint for the following morning.

As she stood waiting outside on the pavement at ten past nine, she regretted her decision. Local people, lightly dressed for the soft September day, were walking past. She knew who they were; they knew who she was; some of them were even people she spoke to. And now they all knew that she was waiting to get her hair cut at Connie's Clip Joint. From when she was a child, Carole Seddon had always wanted to keep an air of secrecy about what she did; she hated having her intentions known.

She tried to look nonchalant, as if she had just stopped outside the salon to check its window display. But the beautifully coiffed women and men whose photographs gazed artfully from behind rubber plants were not objects to retain the interest for long. In spite of her pretences, Carole Seddon looked exactly what she was: a middle-aged woman locked out of the hairdressers'.

Discreetly she drew up the sleeve of her Burberry and looked down at her wristwatch. Although the only other person in sight along Fethering High Street at that moment was a pensioner deep in his own thoughts and a duffel coat, Carole moved as if she was under the scrutiny of a prison camp watchtower.

Twelve minutes past nine. Surely she hadn't got the time wrong . . . ? Surely the girl who answered the phone hadn't said the first appointment was nine-thirty . . . ? Such doubts were quickly banished. No, she had definitely said 'nine o'clock', and Carole had planned her whole morning around that time. She had taken her Labrador Gulliver out for his walk along Fethering Beach, and after she'd had her hair cut, she was going to do her weekly food shop at Sainsbury's.

Oh, this was stupid, just standing about. Trying to give the oblivious pensioner the impression that moving away from Connie's Clip Joint after precisely seventeen minutes (being Carole, she had of course arrived early) was a long-planned intention, she set off firmly back towards her house, High Tor.

As she took the first step, a silver hatchback screeched to a halt outside the salon, and a small, harassed-looking woman in her forties jumped out. She looked as if she had dressed in a hurry and clutched to her bosom an overflowing leather bag. Her brown eyes were tight with anxiety. No make-up . . . and her red-streaked hair, untidily swept back into a scrunchy, was not a good advertisement for the business she ran.

Because of course Carole recognized her instantly. Connie Rutherford, after whom Connie's Clip Joint was named. Fethering gossip ensured that almost everyone in the village knew who everyone else was, but village protocol demanded that you still didn't speak to them until you had been introduced. So Carole continued her stately progress towards High Tor.

The hairdresser, however, showed no such inhibitions. 'Mrs Seddon!' she called out.

Which, Carole supposed, was better than using her first name. She turned graciously. 'Yes?'

'I'm sorry, you're the nine o'clock, aren't you?'

'Well, I thought I was,' came the frosty response.

'Look, I'm so sorry. That idiot girl was meant to be here to open up at quarter to nine.' The woman fumbled in her bag for keys. 'I wonder what on earth's happened to her.' Still getting no reaction from her client, she said, 'I'm Connie. Connie Rutherford. I run the place.'

'Oh.' Carole received the information as though surprised by the identification. 'I'm Carole Seddon.'

'Yes, I know. You live next door to Jude.'

Carole was slightly miffed to think that this was her claim to fame in Fethering. No one knew about her past, her career in the Home Office. Here she was just Jude's neighbour. And Jude hadn't lived in Woodside Cottage nearly as long as Carole had been in High Tor. She shouldn't have been surprised, though. Jude was outgoing. Jude was easy with people. Everyone knew Jude.

Having opened the salon door, Connie Rutherford ushered her client in and went across to switch on the lights, chattering the while. 'This is really bad. Kids these days, they have no sense of time-keeping. You give them a job – and are they grateful? They don't even understand the basics of turning up when they say they will. God, if I ever have any children, I won't let them behave the way most of the youngsters do these days.'

Judging from Connie's age, Carole decided that, if she was going to have any children, she'd better be quick about it.

But the hairdresser was off into another apology. 'I'm so sorry, Kyra should have opened up and been ready to greet you at nine. I gave her the spare set of keys – I've only got the one – I thought I could trust her. Then she was meant to wash your hair, so that it'd be ready for me to cut when I came in. Oh well, don't worry, I'll wash it. May I take your coat, Mrs Seddon? Now, I can call you "Carole", can't I?'

'Yes,' her client conceded.

'Well, you just take a seat here, and I'll put on some music. You'd like some music, wouldn't you?'

'No, I'm quite happy not to—'

But Connie was already away, fiddling with a CD player. 'I think Abba, don't you?'

'Erm, no, I—'

'Nothing like Abba for clearing away the cobwebs in the morning, is there?' As she spoke, the sounds of 'Dancing Queen' filled the room. 'Now would you like . . . ?' Connie stopped, apparently thinking better of the suggestion.

'Would I like what?'

'Nothing.'

'What I would like, if you don't mind, is for you to do my hair . . . since I already am a bit behind schedule.' Carole hoped that made it sound as if she had a more impressive destination later in the morning than the pasta aisle in Sainsbury's.

'Very well.' Connie turned on a tap above the sink. 'Just give the water a moment to heat up. It's cold first thing in the morning. And let's get this robe on.'

While the water warmed, Carole took a look around the salon. The pine boarding on the walls and the large cheese plants in the windows gave it a slightly dated feel, which was not dispelled by the Greek holiday posters and photos of models with exotic hairstyles. The basic decor probably hadn't changed for a good ten years, and endorsed Jude's suggestion that Connie's Clip Joint was not doing great business.

The stylist flicked her hand under the pouring water. 'Nearly warm enough.' Then she caught an unwelcome glimpse of herself in the mirror. 'Haven't had time to put a face on yet. Oh dear, if Kyra had been here when she was supposed to . . .'

But she decided that going on about the short-comings of her staff was probably not the best way of recommending her salon to a new client. Instead, she stood behind the chair, rather closer than Carole might have wished, so that their two faces stood one on top of the other in the mirror. Connie ran her hands gently over her client's hair.

'So . . . how would you like it, Carole?'

She got the same reply all hairdressers had got for the past fifteen years – a gruff 'Same shape, but shorter'.

'You haven't thought of giving it a bit of colour?' suggested Connie.

'I have thought of it, but decided against the idea.'

'Not even highlights?'

'No, thank you.'

Connie Rutherford was far too practised in her profession to argue with a new client. 'I think you're right, Carole. This style really suits a strong face like yours.' Another test of the water, and a towel was fixed neatly in place around the neck. 'Now may I take your glasses off?'

'I'll do it,' replied Carole, aware of how graceless she sounded. She removed the rectangular rimless spectacles and placed them next to the sink. Her pale blue eyes looked naked, even threatened.

Expertly Connie swivelled the chair round and lowered the back, so that her client's neck slotted neatly into the groove at the front of the basin. Every time she underwent this manoeuvre, Carole could not quite erase the mental image of a guillotine. Even through the protective towel, she could feel the coldness of her ceramic yoke.

By now the temperature of the water was just right and Connie, though long since graduated beyond such menial tasks, had not forgotten the skills of hairwashing. Her strong fingers probed down into the scalp, working in a way that was both sensual and invigorating. Carole began to relax.

And the flow of Connie's talk matched the flow of the water, soothing, rippling away the tensions of her client. She had quickly caught on to Carole's private nature and knew better than to ask for personal information. Instead she kept up a light prattle about the concerns of Fethering: the fact that there had been more visitors than expected that summer; the possibility that English seaside holidays were coming back into fashion; the difficulty of parking in the High Street.

Only at one point was a detail of Carole's personal history mentioned. Connie, who wore no ring on her wedding finger, mentioned in passing that she was divorced, and added, 'Just like you.'

Immediately realizing that she had to cover this lapse, she explained, 'Jude mentioned that when she was in here once.'

Oh yes? And how much else, Carole wondered, has my neighbour been telling all and sundry about me? But she couldn't really make herself cross about it. Jude was by nature discreet, and in a hotbed of gossip like Fethering everyone's marital status was fair game.

'So is Seddon your married name?'

'Yes.' Though Carole wasn't sure what business of the hairdresser that was.

'Yes, I got stuck with mine too. By the time I thought about reverting to my maiden name, the other one was on so many legal documents and what-have-you . . . Of course, the divorce was particularly difficult for me, because Martin was involved in the business too. Yes, we started Connie's Clip Joint together. We'd met when we were both working in a salon in Worthing and . . .' she shrugged ruefully as she looked around, 'I suppose this was our dream. Like most dreams, it fell apart when it came up against reality.'

Recognizing that this was too downbeat a note for

her performance as your friendly local hairdresser, she picked herself out of the potential trough. 'Anyway, let me tell you, any divorce is a nightmare, but one where you're also trying to divide up business assets . . . well, I hope yours didn't involve that . . .'

The cue was there to volunteer information about the end of her marriage, had Carole wished to pick it up. Unsurprisingly, she didn't. Connie moved quickly on. 'Still, mustn't grumble. Got a very nice little business here. Having a High Street position . . . well, of course that helps. As they always say, "Location, location, location". All going very well.'

Remembering Jude's words about the precarious state of Connie's Clip Joint, Carole took this assertion with a pinch of salt, and ventured a question of her own. 'And your ex-husband . . . is he still involved in the hairdressing business?'

Connie Rutherford's lips tightened. 'You could say that. Yes, he runs one of the biggest chains of salons along the South Coast.'

There was clearly a lot more information available and Carole felt she had only to issue the smallest prompt to release an avalanche of resentment. She refrained from doing so and fortunately, before Connie could self-start into her diatribe, the salon door opened to admit a slender man in black leather jacket and trousers. A gold chain showed against tanned flesh in the open neck of his shirt. His neat tobacco-coloured hair was highlighted in blonde and his teeth were veneered to a perfect smile. Over brown eyes as dark as coffee beans, he wore tinted glasses with small gold stars at the corners. From a distance he might have passed for twenty-five; close to, he was well into his forties.

'Morning, Theo.'

'Morning, Connie love.' His voice was light, self-consciously camp.

'This is my nine o'clock. Carole Seddon. First time she's been here.'

'Really? I'm Theo.' He gave a little wave; she couldn't have shaken his hand from under the robe, anyway. 'But you do look awfully familiar, Carole.'

'I live right here in Fethering. Just along the High Street.'

'Oh, then I must have seen you around.' A hand flew up to his mouth in mock-amazement. 'With a dog! Yes, I've seen you with a dog. Lovely big Labby.'

'He's called Gulliver.'

'Ooh, I'm such a dog person. I've got a little Westie called Priscilla.'

'Ah.'

'Connie's into cats, aren't you, love. I can never see the point of cats. Nasty, self-obsessed, spiteful little beasts.'

'Takes one to know one,' riposted Connie.

'Ooh, you bitch!'

Their badinage was a well-practised routine, insults batted back and forth without a vestige of malice. Carole Seddon got the feeling that for regulars it was as much a part of the Connie's Clip Joint ambience as the Abba soundtrack.

Theo looked around the salon. 'Where's the human pincushion?'

'Late. She'd got the spare set of keys and was meant to open up at eight forty-five. No sign of her.'

'Probably stayed in bed for naughties with that young boyfriend of hers. And actually . . .' he raised an eyebrow towards his boss's mirror image '. . . you look as if you might have been doing something similar.'

His insinuation prompted a rather sharper response. 'Don't be ridiculous!' Embarrassed by her own outburst, Connie looked at her watch. 'I don't know what she's doing, but when she does finally deign to arrive, I may have a thing or two to say to Miss Kyra Bartos.'

Theo slapped his hands to his face in a parody of Munch's *Scream*. 'Oh no! I'll have to wash my nine-thirty's hair myself!'

'Just as I've had to do with my nine o'clock.'

'Yes.' Theo grinned in the mirror at Carole. 'I hope you're appreciative of the quality of service you're getting.' And he flounced off to hang up his leather jacket.

Carole caught Connie's eye and mouthed, 'What did he mean about "the human pincushion"?'

'Ah. Young Kyra's taste for body piercing. It seems to be her ambition to get more perforations than a tea bag.' Another peeved look at her watch. 'Where is the bloody girl? I'll ring her when I've finished with you. Now do you want the cut slightly layered?'

'No,' Carole countered doggedly. 'I want it the same shape, but shorter.'

'Right.' Whatever reservations Connie might have

had to this conservative approach, she kept them to herself, and started cutting.

At that moment Theo's nine-thirty skulked into the salon. In spite of the mild September day, she wore a raincoat with the collar turned up, a headscarf and dark glasses.

'Sheeeeeena!' Theo emoted. 'Sheena, my love, how gorgeous to see you.'

'Not gorgeous at all, Theo darling,' his client drawled. 'That's why I'm here. Morning, Connie,' she said as Theo removed her coat.

'Morning, Sheena. This is Carole.'

'Hi. I tell you, Theo, I just need the most total makeover since records began. When I looked at myself in the mirror this morning . . . well, it took great strength of will not to top myself on the spot.'

'Oh, come on,' Theo wheedled, 'we'll soon have you looking your beautiful self again. Now let's take off that scarf and those glasses.'

'No, no. I'm just not fit to be seen!'

'You're amongst friends here, Sheena darling. Nobody'll breathe a word about what you looked like *before* . . . Will you, Carole?'

Though rather unwilling to pander to the woman's vanity, Carole agreed that she wouldn't.

'And when we get to *after*, Sheena . . . *after* I've worked my magic . . . you'll look so gorgeous, men in the street will be falling over each other to get at you.'

'Oh, Theo, you're so full of nonsense.' But it was clearly nonsense his client liked.

After further dramatic delays, Sheena was finally

settled into the chair, and there followed the great ceremony of removing her scarf and glasses. Carole, squinting at an angle into the adjacent mirror, wondered what horrors were about to be unveiled. What optical disfigurement lay behind the glasses? What trichological disaster beneath the scarf?

After the build-up, the revelation was a bit of a disappointment. Sheena was a perfectly attractive woman in her late forties – and, what's more, one whose blonded hair appeared to have been cut quite recently.

But she had set up her scenario, and was not going to be deterred from playing it out. 'There, Theo. Now that's going to be a challenge, even for you, isn't it?'

Her stylist, who must have been through the same scene many times before, knew his lines. 'Don't worry, darling. Remember, Theo is a miracle worker. So what are we going to do?'

'We are going to make me so attractive, Theo, that I become a positive man-magnet.'

'Too easy. You're a man-magnet already.'

'I wish. I don't understand.' Sheena let out a long sigh. 'There just don't seem to be any men in Fethering.'

'Ooh, I wouldn't say that,' he said coyly.

'Are you saying you've taken them all, Theo? I bet you never have any problem finding men.'

The stylist let out an enigmatic, silvery laugh.

Throughout Carole's haircut, this archness continued. Connie, who had tried commendably hard to keep conversation going with her client, eventually gave up and joined in the false brightness of Sheena and Theo. Carole found it quite wearing. A little too lively for her taste. She wasn't sure whether Connie's Clip Joint was going to be a long-term replacement for Graham and the anonymous salon in Worthing.

On the other hand, Connie did cut hair very well. Though keeping within Carole's minimal guidelines, she had somehow managed to give a freshness to her client's traditional style. With glasses restored, Carole couldn't help admiring the result she saw in the mirror.

'Excuse me for a moment,' said Connie, 'I must just ring Kyra and find out what on earth's happened to her. Now, I've got her mobile number somewhere.' She crossed to the cash register table and started shuffling through papers.

Carole felt awkward about the business of paying. When booking the appointment, she hadn't asked how much it would cost and now she was worried it might have been very expensive. Prices varied so much. And then there was the big challenge of tipping. Should she tip and, if so, how much? She'd never tipped Graham – that had been an accepted feature of their austere relationship – but she was in a new salon now and she wasn't sure of the protocol.

Connie listened impatiently to the phone. 'Well, she's not answering.'

She was poised to end the call, when suddenly they were all aware of a new noise, cutting through the harmonies of Abba. The insistent jangle of a phone ringing.

Carole and Connie exchanged looks. The hairdresser

huffed in exasperation, 'Oh, don't say the bloody girl's left her mobile here.'

As Connie moved towards the source of the sound, Carole, curiosity overcoming her natural reticence, found herself following.

A door led through to the back area, storeroom, kitchenette and lavatory. As Connie opened it, there was a smell of stale alcohol and cigarette smoke. Beer cans and a vodka bottle on its side lay on a low table. On the work surface beside the sink stood a vase containing twelve red roses.

But it wasn't those that prompted the involuntary scream from Connie's lips. It was what she could see – and Carole could see over her shoulder – slumped in a chair over which loomed the dome of a spare dryer.

The girl's clothes were torn. There were scratches on her metal-studded face.

And, tight as a garrotte, around the neck of her slumped body was the lead from the unplugged dryer.

Chapter Two

'Drink this.' Jude placed a large glass of Chilean Chardonnay on the table in front of her neighbour. 'You look as though you need it.'

The extent of Carole's trauma could be judged from the fact that she didn't look at her watch and ask, 'Isn't it a bit early in the day . . . ?' It was in fact only two-thirty in the afternoon, but a lifetime seemed to have elapsed since she had entered Connie's Clip Joint that morning. She hadn't felt it proper to leave until the police had arrived and, once they were there, she couldn't leave until she had submitted to some polite, though persistent, questioning. Her training in the Home Office told her that they were only doing their job, and she knew that they were starting from an empty knowledge base, but she did feel frustrated by the depth of information they seemed to require. Though she kept reiterating that it was the first time she had ever entered the salon, the police still wanted her to fill in far more of her personal background than she thought entirely necessary. What business of theirs was it that she was divorced? Surely, rather than following up such fruitless blind alleys, they ought to have been out there finding the murderer. Again she reminded herself of the huge mosaic of facts from which a successful conviction was built up, and managed to endure the questioning with the appearance of co-operation. But she hadn't enjoyed the experience.

And it had all been made considerably worse by the presence of Sheena. Theo's client had taken the discovery of the girl's body as a cue for a full operatic mix of posturing and hysterics. 'Something like this was bound to happen!' she had wailed. 'I knew when I got up, this was an inauspicious day. I shouldn't have left the house. I should have stayed in bed. It's horrible! Though the poor girl may have deserved something, she didn't deserve this!' But through the woman's tears and screams, Carole could detect a real relish for the drama of the situation. Kyra's murder was the most exciting thing that had happened in Sheena's life for a long time.

Eventually Carole had managed to escape. While the Scene of Crime Officers embarked on their painstaking scrutiny of the premises, the detectives told her they were from the Major Crime Branch, and would be working from the Major Crime Unit in Littlehampton police station. They gave her a list of contact numbers, and urged her to get in touch if she thought of or heard anything which might have relevance to the investigation.

'I've done a bacon and avocado salad,' said Jude, and went off to the kitchen to fetch it. That was quick, thought Carole. But then perhaps more time had elapsed from the moment when she had knocked on her neighbour's door at the end of the interrogation and the moment she had come back to Woodside Cottage. Her recollection was a bit hazy. She had gone to High Tor and taken Gulliver out to do his business on the rough ground behind the house. And she had stood for a moment of abstraction, from which his barking had roused her. Maybe it had been a longer moment than she thought. Maybe that too was a measure of the shock she had suffered.

'So . . .' said Jude, finally nestled into one of the shapeless armchairs in her untidy front room, 'tell me exactly what happened.'

And Carole did. Unaware of the speed at which she was sinking the Chilean Chardonnay, or the readiness with which Jude was replenishing her glass, she told everything. Dealing with unpleasant subject matter during her Home Office days had taught her the value of drily marshalling facts and investing a report with the objective anonymity that made its horror containable.

At the end of the narrative Jude let out a long sigh and sat for a moment with her round face cupped in her chubby hands. As ever, she was swathed in many layers of floaty fabric, which blurred the substantial outlines of her welcoming body. Her blonde hair, which had been innocent of the attentions of a hairdresser for some time, was twisted up into an unlikely topknot, held in place by what looked like a pair of knitting needles.

'So you didn't get any insight into who might have killed the girl?'

'For heaven's sake, Jude. This morning was the first time I've even stepped inside that place. I don't know anything about any of the people involved.'

'I wasn't meaning that. I thought perhaps the police might've let something slip about the direction in which their suspicions are moving.'

'So far as I could tell, they're clueless. When they arrived, they had as little information as I had. Besides, you may recall from past experience that even when the police do start having theories about the identity of a murderer, people like us are the last they're going to share them with.'

Jude nodded ruefully. 'True.'

'In fact, you're probably a more useful source than I am.'

'How do you mean?'

'Well, you actually know all the people involved. You're a regular at Connie's Clip Joint.'

'Hardly a regular, but I suppose you're right.'

'And,' Carole went on, unable to keep out of her voice the note of envy that such thoughts usually prompted, 'people always confide in you, so probably you actually know a great deal about Connie Rutherford and her set-up.'

'A certain amount, yes.'

'She isn't one of your *patients*, is she?' This word too had a special recurrent intonation for Carole. Jude worked as a healer, which to Carole still meant that she operated in the world of mumbo-jumbo. And the people who believed that such ministrations could do them any good were, to Carole's mind, gullible neurotics.

'You know I prefer to use the word "client",' Jude responded calmly. It wasn't in her nature to take issue about such matters. She knew that healing worked. Some people shared her opinion; some were violently opposed to it. Jude was prepared to have her case made by successful results rather than verbal argument. And she knew that depriving Carole of her scepticism about healing would take away one of the pillars of bluster that supported her prickly, fragile personality. 'But no,' she went on, 'I haven't treated Connie. I just know her from chatting while I've been having my hair done.'

'Well, she volunteered to me that she was divorced – and that the divorce hadn't taken place under the happiest of circumstances . . .'

'What divorce does?'

Carole did not pick up on this. Though some ten years old, her own divorce from David was still an area as sensitive as an infected tooth. And lurking at the back of her mind was a new anxiety. Her son Stephen's wife Gaby was soon to give birth. Grandparenthood might mean that Carole was forced into even more contact with David. Resolutely dispelling such ugly thoughts from her mind, she went on, 'And I gather that she and . . . what was her husband's name? . . . Martin, that's right . . . used to own Connie's Clip Joint together, but now he's got a rather more successful set-up . . .'

'That's an understatement. He owns Martin & Martina. You must have seen their salons.'

'Oh, yes, I have. I'd never particularly paid attention

to them, but they've got that big swirly silver logo, haven't they? There's one in Worthing.'

'Worthing, Brighton, Chichester, Horsham, Midhurst, Newhaven, Eastbourne, Hastings. Martin Rutherford seems to have the whole of the South Coast sewn up.'

'So every time Connie sees one of his salons, it must rather rub salt in the wound of the divorce.'

'Yes, Carole. Particularly since the name of the woman he left her for was Martina.'

'Ah. Not so much rubbing salt as rubbing her nose in it.' Carole tapped her chin reflectively. She was relaxing. The Chardonnay and Jude's calming presence were distancing her from the horrors of the morning. 'And has Connie found her equivalent of Martina? Has she got someone else?'

'No one permanent, as far as I know. I think she has had a few tentative encounters, but from what she said, most of them had a lot in common with car crashes. I don't think Connie's a great picker when it comes to men.'

'Pity. Because she seems to have a pleasant personality . . . You know, under the professional hairdresser banter . . .'

'Yes, she's a lovely girl. And very pretty. Always beautifully groomed.'

'Well, she wasn't this morning. No make-up, hair scrunched up any-old-how.'

'Really?' Jude looked thoughtful. 'That's most unlike her. I wonder why . . .'

'No idea. She implied she would have done her

make-up in the salon . . . you know if Kyra hadn't been late . . .'

'Unfortunate choice of words in the circumstances, isn't it?'

'Yes, I suppose it is.' The thought brought Carole up short. The screen of her mind was once again filled by the contorted, immobile face, and she felt the reality of what had happened. Someone had deliberately cut short a young girl's life.

'Did you know her? Kyra?'

'She washed my hair last time I was in the salon. Didn't say much. Rather shy, I thought. Or maybe she was concentrating on learning the basics of practical hairdressing before she moved on to the refinements of inane client chatter. So, no, I can't really say I knew her.'

'Theo mentioned there was a boyfriend. Did Kyra say anything about anyone special in her life?'

Jude shook her head. 'Poor boy. I should think the police would be getting very heavy with him.'

'Yes. He'd be the obvious first port of call. And from the look of the back room of the salon, Kyra had been entertaining someone there. Empty bottles, beer cans, you know . . .'

'Adolescent passions are very confusing . . . they can so easily get out of hand,' said Jude, with sympathy.

'Yes,' Carole agreed, without any.

'Hm.' Jude refilled their glasses. Still Carole made no demur. 'So we're back in our usual position when faced with a murder . . . total lack of information.'

'And not much likelihood of getting any,' Carole agreed gloomily.

'Oh, there may be ways . . .'

'Like . . . ?'

'Well, obviously Connie's Clip Joint is going to be closed for a few days. It is a Scene of Crime, after all. But, assuming it does reopen . . . I think I should have a haircut.' Jude shook her precarious topknot; it threatened to unravel, but the knitting needles just managed to keep it in place. 'I could certainly do with one.'

Visit **www.panmacmillan.com** to read more about all our books and to buy them. You will also find features, author interviews and news of any author events, and you can sign up for e-newsletters so that you're always first to hear about our new releases.

www.panmacmillan.com

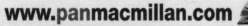

Coming Soon...

Reading Groups

Competitions
Feeling Lucky?

Extracts
Sneak Previews

Interviews

Events
Meet Our Stars

Reviews
What The Critics Say

News & Awards

Editor's Choice
What We're Reading